Hilda Wade by Grant Allen

A WOMAN WITH TENACITY OF PURPOSE

Charles Grant Blairfindie Allen was born on February 24th, 1848 at Alwington, near Kingston, Canada West (now part of Ontario).

Home schooled until 13 when his family moved to England, Grant was to become a highly regarded science writer who branched out to a fiction career and became enormously popular.

His work helped propel several genres of fiction and whilst his career was short it was enormously productive.

Grant's scientific background enabled him to root much of his work in a plausibility that was denied to others. He had little fear in challenging a society that treated women as second class citizens and creating best sellers from such works.

On October 25th 1899 Grant Allen died at his home in Hindhead, Haslemere, Surrey, England. He died just before finishing this book; Hilda Wade. The novel's final episode, which he dictated to his friend, doctor and neighbour Sir Arthur Conan Doyle from his bed appeared under the appropriate title, The Episode of the Dead Man Who Spoke in 1900.

PUBLISHERS' NOTE

In putting before the public the last work by Mr. Grant Allen, the publishers desire to express their deep regret at the author's unexpected and lamented death, a regret in which they are sure to be joined by the many thousand readers whom he did so much to entertain. A man of curiously varied and comprehensive knowledge, and with the most charming personality; a writer who, treating of a wide variety of subjects, touched nothing which he did not make distinctive, he filled a place which no man living can exactly occupy. The last chapter of this volume had been roughly sketched by Mr. Allen before his final illness, and his anxiety, when debarred from work, to see it finished, was relieved by the considerate kindness of his friend and neighbour, Dr. Conan Doyle, who, hearing of his trouble, talked it over with him, gathered his ideas, and finally wrote it out for him in the form in which it now appears, a beautiful and pathetic act of friendship which it is a pleasure to record.

Index of Contents
CHAPTER I - THE EPISODE OF THE PATIENT WHO DISAPPOINTED HER DOCTOR
CHAPTER II - THE EPISODE OF THE GENTLEMAN WHO HAD FAILED FOR EVERYTHING
CHAPTER III - THE EPISODE OF THE WIFE WHO DID HER DUTY
CHAPTER IV - THE EPISODE OF THE MAN WHO WOULD NOT COMMIT SUICIDE
CHAPTER V - THE EPISODE OF THE NEEDLE THAT DID NOT MATCH
CHAPTER VI - THE EPISODE OF THE LETTER WITH THE BASINGSTOKE POSTMARK
CHAPTER VII - THE EPISODE OF THE STONE THAT LOOKED ABOUT IT
CHAPTER VIII - THE EPISODE OF THE EUROPEAN WITH THE KAFFIR HEART

CHAPTER IX - THE EPISODE OF THE LADY WHO WAS VERY EXCLUSIVE
CHAPTER X - THE EPISODE OF THE GUIDE WHO KNEW THE COUNTRY
CHAPTER XI - THE EPISODE OF THE OFFICER WHO UNDERSTOOD PERFECTLY
CHAPTER XII - THE EPISODE OF THE DEAD MAN WHO SPOKE
GRANT ALLEN – A SHORT BIOGRAPHY
GREANT ALLEN – A CONCISE BIBLIOGRAPHY

CHAPTER I

THE EPISODE OF THE PATIENT WHO DISAPPOINTED HER DOCTOR

Hilda Wade's gift was so unique, so extraordinary, that I must illustrate it, I think, before I attempt to describe it. But first let me say a word of explanation about the Master.

I have never met anyone who impressed me so much with a sense of GREATNESS as Professor Sebastian. And this was not due to his scientific eminence alone: the man's strength and keenness struck me quite as forcibly as his vast attainments. When he first came to St. Nathaniel's Hospital, an eager, fiery-eyed physiologist, well past the prime of life, and began to preach with all the electric force of his vivid personality that the one thing on earth worth a young man's doing was to work in his laboratory, attend his lectures, study disease, and be a scientific doctor, dozens of us were infected by his contagious enthusiasm. He proclaimed the gospel of germs; and the germ of his own zeal flew abroad in the hospital: it ran through the wards as if it were typhoid fever. Within a few months, half the students were converted from lukewarm observers of medical routine into flaming apostles of the new methods.

The greatest authority in Europe on comparative anatomy, now that Huxley was taken from us, he had devoted his later days to the pursuit of medicine proper, to which he brought a mind stored with luminous analogies from the lower animals. His very appearance held one. Tall, thin, erect, with an ascetic profile not unlike Cardinal Manning's, he represented that abstract form of asceticism which consists in absolute self-sacrifice to a mental ideas, not that which consists in religious abnegation. Three years of travel in Africa had tanned his skin for life. His long white hair, straight and silvery as it fell, just curled in one wave-like inward sweep where it turned and rested on the stooping shoulders. His pale face was clean-shaven, save for a thin and wiry grizzled moustache, which cast into stronger relief the deep-set, hawk-like eyes and the acute, intense, intellectual features. In some respects, his countenance reminded me often of Dr. Martineau's: in others it recalled the knife-like edge, unturnable, of his great predecessor, Professor Owen. Wherever he went, men turned to stare at him. In Paris, they took him for the head of the English Socialists; in Russia, they declared he was a Nihilist emissary. And they were not far wrong—in essence; for Sebastian's stern, sharp face was above all things the face of a man absorbed and engrossed by one overpowering pursuit in life, the sacred thirst of knowledge, which had swallowed up his entire nature.

He WAS what he looked, the most single-minded person I have ever come across. And when I say single-minded, I mean just that, and no more. He had an End to attain, the advancement of science, and he went straight towards the End, looking neither to the right nor to the left for anyone. An American millionaire once remarked to him of some ingenious appliance he was describing: "Why, if you were to perfect that apparatus, Professor, and take out a patent for it, I reckon you'd make as much money as I have made." Sebastian withered him with a glance. "I have no time to waste," he replied, "on making money!"

So, when Hilda Wade told me, on the first day I met her, that she wished to become a nurse at Nathaniel's, "to be near Sebastian," I was not at all astonished. I took her at her word. Everybody who meant business in any branch of the medical art, however humble, desired to be close to our rare teacher, to drink in his large thought, to profit by his clear insight, his wide experience. The man of Nathaniel's was revolutionising practice; and those who wished to feel themselves abreast of the modern movement were naturally anxious to cast in their lot with him. I did not wonder, therefore, that Hilda Wade, who herself possessed in so large a measure the deepest feminine gift, intuition, should seek a place under the famous professor who represented the other side of the same endowment in its masculine embodiment, instinct of diagnosis.

Hilda Wade herself I will not formally introduce to you: you will learn to know her as I proceed with my story.

I was Sebastian's assistant, and my recommendation soon procured Hilda Wade the post she so strangely coveted. Before she had been long at Nathaniel's, however, it began to dawn upon me that her reasons for desiring to attend upon our revered Master were not wholly and solely scientific. Sebastian, it is true, recognised her value as a nurse from the first; he not only allowed that she was a good assistant, but he also admitted that her subtle knowledge of temperament sometimes enabled her closely to approach his own reasoned scientific analysis of a case and its probable development. "Most women," he said to me once, "are quick at reading THE PASSING EMOTION. They can judge with astounding correctness from a shadow on one's face, a catch in one's breath, a movement of one's hands, how their words or deeds are affecting us. We cannot conceal our feelings from them. But underlying character they do not judge so well as fleeting expression. Not what Mrs. Jones IS in herself, but what Mrs. Jones is now thinking and feeling, there lies their great success as psychologists. Most men, on the contrary, guide their life by definite FACTS, by signs, by symptoms, by observed data. Medicine itself is built upon a collection of such reasoned facts. But this woman, Nurse Wade, to a certain extent, stands intermediate mentally between the two sexes. She recognises TEMPERAMENT, the fixed form of character, and what it is likely to do, in a degree which I have never seen equalled elsewhere. To that extent, and within proper limits of supervision, I acknowledge her faculty as a valuable adjunct to a scientific practitioner."

Still, though Sebastian started with a predisposition in favour of Hilda Wade, a pretty girl appeals to most of us, I could see from the beginning that Hilda Wade was by no means enthusiastic for Sebastian, like the rest of the hospital:

"He is extraordinarily able," she would say, when I gushed to her about our Master; but that was the most I could ever extort from her in the way of praise. Though she admitted intellectually Sebastian's gigantic mind, she would never commit herself to anything that sounded like personal admiration. To call him "the prince of physiologists" did not satisfy me on that head. I wanted her to exclaim, "I adore him! I worship him! He is glorious, wonderful!"

I was also aware from an early date that, in an unobtrusive way, Hilda Wade was watching Sebastian, watching him quietly, with those wistful, earnest eyes, as a cat watches a mouse-hole; watching him with mute inquiry, as if she expected each moment to see him do something different from what the rest of us expected of him. Slowly I gathered that Hilda Wade, in the most literal sense, had come to Nathaniel's, as she herself expressed it, "to be near Sebastian."

Gentle and lovable as she was in every other aspect, towards Sebastian she seemed like a lynx-eyed detective. She had some object in view, I thought, almost as abstract as his own, some object to which, as I judged, she was devoting her life quite as single-mindedly as Sebastian himself had devoted his to the advancement of science.

"Why did she become a nurse at all?" I asked once of her friend, Mrs. Mallet. "She has plenty of money, and seems well enough off to live without working."

"Oh, dear, yes," Mrs. Mallet answered. "She is independent, quite; has a tidy little income of her own, six or seven hundred a year, and she could choose her own society. But she went in for this mission fad early; she didn't intend to marry, she said; so she would like to have some work to do in life. Girls suffer like that, nowadays. In her case, the malady took the form of nursing."

"As a rule," I ventured to interpose, "when a pretty girl says she doesn't intend to marry, her remark is premature. It only means—"

"Oh, yes, I know. Every girl says it; 'tis a stock property in the popular masque of Maiden Modesty. But with Hilda it is different. And the difference is—that Hilda means it!"

"You are right," I answered. "I believe she means it. Yet I know one man at least—" for I admired her immensely.

Mrs. Mallet shook her head and smiled. "It is no use, Dr. Cumberledge," she answered. "Hilda will never marry. Never, that is to say, till she has attained some mysterious object she seems to have in view, about which she never speaks to anyone—not even to me. But I have somehow guessed it!"

"And it is?"

"Oh, I have not guessed what it IS: I am no Oedipus. I have merely guessed that it exists. But whatever it may be, Hilda's life is bounded by it. She became a nurse to carry it out, I feel confident. From the very beginning, I gather, a part of her scheme was to go to St. Nathaniel's. She was always bothering us to give her introductions to Dr. Sebastian; and when she met you at my brother Hugo's, it was a preconcerted arrangement; she asked to sit next you, and meant to induce you to use your influence on her behalf with the Professor. She was dying to get there."

"It is very odd," I mused. "But there!—women are inexplicable!"

"And Hilda is in that matter the very quintessence of woman. Even I, who have known her for years, don't pretend to understand her."

A few months later, Sebastian began his great researches on his new anaesthetic. It was a wonderful set of researches. It promised so well. All Nat's (as we familiarly and affectionately styled St. Nathaniel's) was in a fever of excitement over the drug for a twelvemonth.

The Professor obtained his first hint of the new body by a mere accident. His friend, the Deputy Prosector of the Zoological Society, had mixed a draught for a sick raccoon at the Gardens, and, by some mistake in a bottle, had mixed it wrongly. (I purposely refrain from mentioning the ingredients, as they are drugs which can be easily obtained in isolation at any chemist's, though when compounded they form one of the most dangerous and difficult to detect of organic poisons. I do not desire to play into the hands of would-be criminals.) The compound on which the Deputy Prosector had thus accidentally lighted sent the raccoon to sleep in the most extraordinary manner.

Indeed, the raccoon slept for thirty-six hours on end, all attempts to awake him, by pulling his tail or tweaking his hair being quite unavailing. This was a novelty in narcotics; so Sebastian was asked to come and look at the slumbering brute. He suggested the attempt to perform an operation on the somnolent raccoon by removing, under the influence of the drug, an internal growth, which was considered the probable cause of his illness. A surgeon was called in, the growth was found and removed, and the raccoon, to everybody's surprise, continued to slumber peacefully on his straw for five hours afterwards. At the end of that time he awoke, and stretched himself as if nothing had happened; and though he was, of course, very weak from loss of blood, he immediately displayed a most royal hunger. He ate up all the maize that was offered him for breakfast, and proceeded to manifest a desire for more by most unequivocal symptoms.

Sebastian was overjoyed. He now felt sure he had discovered a drug which would supersede chloroform—a drug more lasting in its immediate effects, and yet far less harmful in its ultimate results on the balance of the system. A name being wanted for it, he christened it "lethodyne." It was the best pain-luller yet invented.

For the next few weeks, at Nat's, we heard of nothing but lethodyne. Patients recovered and patients died; but their deaths or recoveries were as dross to lethodyne, an anaesthetic that might revolutionise surgery, and even medicine! A royal road through disease, with no trouble to the doctor and no pain to the patient! Lethodyne held the field. We were all of us, for the moment, intoxicated with lethodyne.

Sebastian's observations on the new agent occupied several months. He had begun with the raccoon; he went on, of course, with those poor scapegoats of physiology, domestic rabbits. Not that in this particular case any painful experiments were in contemplation. The Professor tried the drug on a dozen or more quite healthy young animals, with the strange result that they dozed off quietly, and never woke up again. This nonplussed Sebastian. He experimented once more on another raccoon, with a smaller dose; the raccoon fell asleep, and slept like a top for fifteen hours, at the end of which time he woke up as if nothing out of the common had happened. Sebastian fell back upon rabbits again, with smaller and smaller doses. It was no good; the rabbits all died with great unanimity, until the dose was so diminished that it did not send them off to sleep at all. There was no middle course, apparently, to the rabbit kind, lethodyne was either fatal or else inoperative. So it proved to sheep. The new drug killed, or did nothing.

I will not trouble you with all the details of Sebastian's further researches; the curious will find them discussed at length in Volume 237 of the Philosophical Transactions. (See also Comptes Rendus de l'Academie de Medecine: tome 49, pp. 72 and sequel.) I will restrict myself here to that part of the inquiry which immediately refers to Hilda Wade's history.

"If I were you," she said to the Professor one morning, when he was most astonished at his contradictory results, "I would test it on a hawk. If I dare venture on a suggestion, I believe you will find that hawks recover."

"The deuce they do!" Sebastian cried. However, he had such confidence in Nurse Wade's judgment that he bought a couple of hawks and tried the treatment on them. Both birds took considerable doses, and, after a period of insensibility extending to several hours, woke up in the end quite bright and lively.

"I see your principle," the Professor broke out. "It depends upon diet. Carnivores and birds of prey can take lethodyne with impunity; herbivores and fruit-eaters cannot recover, and die of it. Man, therefore, being partly carnivorous, will doubtless be able more or less to stand it."

Hilda Wade smiled her sphinx-like smile. "Not quite that, I fancy," she answered. "It will kill cats, I feel sure; at least, most domesticated ones. But it will NOT kill weasels. Yet both are carnivores."

"That young woman knows too much!" Sebastian muttered to me, looking after her as she glided noiselessly with her gentle tread down the long white corridor. "We shall have to suppress her, Cumberledge.... But I'll wager my life she's right, for all that. I wonder, now, how the dickens she guessed it!"

"Intuition," I answered.

He pouted his under lip above the upper one, with a dubious acquiescence. "Inference, I call it," he retorted. "All woman's so-called intuition is, in fact, just rapid and half-unconscious inference."

He was so full of the subject, however, and so utterly carried away by his scientific ardour, that I regret to say he gave a strong dose of lethodyne at once to each of the matron's petted and pampered Persian cats, which lounged about her room and were the delight of the convalescents. They were two peculiarly lazy sultanas of cats, mere jewels of the harem, Oriental beauties that loved to bask in the sun or curl themselves up on the rug before the fire and dawdle away their lives in congenial idleness. Strange to say, Hilda's prophecy came true. Zuleika settled herself down comfortably in the Professor's easy chair and fell into a sound sleep from which there was no awaking; while Roxana met fate on the tiger-skin she loved, coiled up in a circle, and passed from this life of dreams, without knowing it, into one where dreaming is not. Sebastian noted the facts with a quiet gleam of satisfaction in his watchful eye, and explained afterwards, with curt glibness to the angry matron, that her favourites had been "canonised in the roll of science, as painless martyrs to the advancement of physiology."

The weasels, on the other hand, with an equal dose, woke up after six hours as lively as crickets. It was clear that carnivorous tastes were not the whole solution, for Roxana was famed as a notable mouser.

"Your principle?" Sebastian asked our sibyl, in his brief, quick way.

Hilda's cheek wore a glow of pardonable triumph. The great teacher had deigned to ask her assistance. "I judged by the analogy of Indian hemp," she answered. "This is clearly a similar, but much stronger, narcotic. Now, whenever I have given Indian hemp by your direction to people of sluggish, or even of merely bustling temperament, I have noticed that small doses produce serious effects, and that the after-results are most undesirable. But when you have prescribed the hemp for nervous, overstrung, imaginative people, I have observed that they can stand large amounts of the tincture without evil results, and that the after-effects pass off rapidly. I who am mercurial in temperament, for example, can take any amount of Indian hemp without being made ill by it; while ten drops will send some slow and torpid rustics mad drunk with excitement, drive them into homicidal mania."

Sebastian nodded his head. He needed no more explanation. "You have hit it," he said. "I see it at a glance. The old antithesis! All men and all animals fall, roughly speaking, into two great divisions of type: the impassioned and the unimpassioned; the vivid and the phlegmatic. I catch your drift now. Lethodyne is poison to phlegmatic patients, who have not active power enough to wake up from it unhurt; it is relatively harmless to the vivid and impassioned, who can be put asleep by it, indeed, for a few hours more or less, but are alive enough to live on through the coma and reassert their vitality after it."

I recognised as he spoke that this explanation was correct. The dull rabbits, the sleepy Persian cats, and the silly sheep had died outright of lethodyne; the cunning, inquisitive raccoon, the quick hawk, and the active, intense-natured weasels, all most eager, wary, and alert animals, full of keenness and passion, had recovered quickly.

"Dare we try it on a human subject?" I asked, tentatively.

Hilda Wade answered at once, with that unerring rapidity of hers: "Yes, certainly; on a few, the right persons. I, for one, am not afraid to try it."

"You?" I cried, feeling suddenly aware how much I thought of her. "Oh, not YOU, please, Nurse Wade. Some other life, less valuable!"

Sebastian stared at me coldly. "Nurse Wade volunteers," he said. "It is in the cause of science. Who dares dissuade her? That tooth of yours? Ah, yes. Quite sufficient excuse. You wanted it out, Nurse Wade. Wells-Dinton shall operate."

Without a moment's hesitation, Hilda Wade sat down in an easy chair and took a measured dose of the new anaesthetic, proportioned to the average difference in weight between raccoons and humanity. My face displayed my anxiety, I suppose, for she turned to me, smiling with quiet confidence. "I know my own constitution," she said, with a reassuring glance that went straight to my heart. "I do not in the least fear."

As for Sebastian, he administered the drug to her as unconcernedly as if she were a rabbit. Sebastian's scientific coolness and calmness have long been the admiration of younger practitioners.

Wells-Dinton gave one wrench. The tooth came out as though the patient were a block of marble. There was not a cry or a movement, such as one notes when nitrous oxide is administered. Hilda Wade was to all appearance a mass of lifeless flesh. We stood round and watched. I was trembling with terror. Even on Sebastian's pale face, usually so unmoved, save by the watchful eagerness of scientific curiosity, I saw signs of anxiety.

After four hours of profound slumber, breath hovering, as it seemed, between life and death, she began to come to again. In half an hour more she was wide awake; she opened her eyes and asked for a glass of hock, with beef essence or oysters.

That evening, by six o'clock, she was quite well and able to go about her duties as usual.

"Sebastian is a wonderful man," I said to her, as I entered her ward on my rounds at night. "His coolness astonishes me. Do you know, he watched you all the time you were lying asleep there as if nothing were the matter."

"Coolness?" she inquired, in a quiet voice. "Or cruelty?"

"Cruelty?" I echoed, aghast. "Sebastian cruel! Oh, Nurse Wade, what an idea! Why, he has spent his whole life in striving against all odds to alleviate pain. He is the apostle of philanthropy!"

"Of philanthropy, or of science? To alleviate pain, or to learn the whole truth about the human body?"

"Come, come, now," I cried. "You analyse too far. I will not let even YOU put me out of conceit with Sebastian." (Her face flushed at that "even you"; I almost fancied she began to like me.) "He is the enthusiasm of my life; just consider how much he has done for humanity!"

She looked me through searchingly. "I will not destroy your illusion," she answered, after a pause. "It is a noble and generous one. But is it not largely based on an ascetic face, long white hair, and a moustache that hides the cruel corners of the mouth? For the corners ARE cruel. Some day, I will show you them. Cut off the long hair, shave the grizzled moustache, and what then will remain?" She drew a profile hastily. "Just that," and she showed it me. 'Twas a face like Robespierre's, grown harder and older and lined with observation. I recognised that it was in fact the essence of Sebastian.

Next day, as it turned out, the Professor himself insisted upon testing lethodyne in his own person. All Nat's strove to dissuade him. "Your life is so precious, sir, the advancement of science!" But the Professor was adamantine.

"Science can only be advanced if men of science will take their lives in their hands," he answered, sternly. "Besides, Nurse Wade has tried. Am I to lag behind a woman in my devotion to the cause of physiological knowledge?"

"Let him try," Hilda Wade murmured to me. "He is quite right. It will not hurt him. I have told him already he has just the proper temperament to stand the drug. Such people are rare: HE is one of them."

We administered the dose, trembling. Sebastian took it like a man, and dropped off instantly, for lethodyne is at least as instantaneous in its operation as nitrous oxide.

He lay long asleep. Hilda and I watched him.

After he had lain for some minutes senseless, like a log, on the couch where we had placed him, Hilda stooped over him quietly and lifted up the ends of the grizzled moustache. Then she pointed one accusing finger at his lips. "I told you so," she murmured, with a note of demonstration.

"There is certainly something rather stern, or even ruthless, about the set of the face and the firm ending of the lips," I admitted, reluctantly.

"That is why God gave men moustaches," she mused, in a low voice; "to hide the cruel corners of their mouths."

"Not ALWAYS cruel," I cried.

"Sometimes cruel, sometimes cunning, sometimes sensuous; but nine times out of ten best masked by moustaches."

"You have a bad opinion of our sex!" I exclaimed.

"Providence knew best," she answered. "IT gave you moustaches. That was in order that we women might be spared from always seeing you as you are. Besides, I said 'Nine times out of ten.' There are exceptions—SUCH exceptions!"

On second thought, I did not feel sure that I could quarrel with her estimate.

The experiment was that time once more successful. Sebastian woke up from the comatose state after eight hours, not quite as fresh as Hilda Wade, perhaps, but still tolerably alive; less alert, however, and complaining of dull headache. He was not hungry. Hilda Wade shook her head at that. "It will be of use only in a very few cases," she said to me, regretfully; "and those few will need to be carefully picked by an acute observer. I see resistance to the coma is, even more than I thought, a matter of temperament. Why, so impassioned a man as the Professor himself cannot entirely recover. With more sluggish temperaments, we shall have deeper difficulty."

"Would you call him impassioned?" I asked. "Most people think him so cold and stern."

She shook her head. "He is a snow-capped volcano!" she answered. "The fires of his life burn bright below. The exterior alone is cold and placid."

However, starting from that time, Sebastian began a course of experiments on patients, giving infinitesimal doses at first, and venturing slowly on somewhat larger quantities. But only in his own case and Hilda's could the result be called quite satisfactory. One dull and heavy, drink-sodden navvy, to whom he administered no more than one-tenth of a grain, was drowsy for a week, and listless long after; while a fat washerwoman from West Ham, who took only two-tenths, fell so fast asleep, and snored so stertorously, that we feared she was going to doze off into eternity, after the fashion of the rabbits. Mothers of large families, we noted, stood the drug very ill; on pale young girls of the consumptive tendency its effect was not marked; but only a patient here and there, of exceptionally imaginative and vivid temperament, seemed able to endure it. Sebastian was discouraged. He saw the anaesthetic was not destined to fulfil his first enthusiastic humanitarian expectations. One day, while the investigation was just at this stage, a case was admitted into the observation-cots in which Hilda Wade took a particular interest. The patient was a young girl named Isabel Huntley, tall, dark, and slender, a markedly quick and imaginative type, with large black eyes which clearly bespoke a passionate nature. Though distinctly hysterical, she was pretty and pleasing. Her rich dark hair was as copious as it was beautiful. She held herself erect and had a finely poised head. From the first moment she arrived, I could see nurse Wade was strongly drawn towards her. Their souls sympathised. Number Fourteen, that is our impersonal way of describing CASES, was constantly on Hilda's lips. "I like the girl," she said once. "She is a lady in fibre."

"And a tobacco-trimmer by trade," Sebastian added, sarcastically.

As usual, Hilda's was the truer description. It went deeper.

Number Fourteen's ailment was a rare and peculiar one, into which I need not enter here with professional precision. (I have described the case fully for my brother practitioners in my paper in the fourth volume of Sebastian's Medical Miscellanies.) It will be enough for my present purpose to say, in brief, that the lesion consisted of an internal growth which is always dangerous and most often fatal, but which nevertheless is of such a character that, if it be once happily eradicated by supremely good surgery, it never tends to recur, and leaves the patient as strong and well as ever. Sebastian was, of course, delighted with the splendid opportunity thus afforded him. "It is a beautiful case!" he cried, with professional enthusiasm. "Beautiful! Beautiful! I never saw one so deadly or so malignant before. We are indeed in luck's way. Only a miracle can save her life. Cumberledge, we must proceed to perform the miracle."

Sebastian loved such cases. They formed his ideal. He did not greatly admire the artificial prolongation of diseased and unwholesome lives, which could never be of much use to their owners or anyone else; but when a chance occurred for restoring to perfect health a valuable existence which might otherwise be extinguished before its time, he positively revelled in his beneficent calling. "What nobler object can a man propose to himself," he used to say, "than to raise good men and true from the dead, as it were, and return them whole and sound to the family that depends upon them? Why, I had fifty times rather cure an honest coal-heaver of a wound in his leg than give ten years more lease of life to a gouty lord, diseased from top to toe, who expects to find a month of Carlsbad or Homburg once every year make up for eleven months of over-eating, over-drinking, vulgar debauchery, and under-thinking." He had no sympathy with men who lived the lives of swine: his heart was with the workers.

Of course, Hilda Wade soon suggested that, as an operation was absolutely necessary, Number Fourteen would be a splendid subject on whom to test once more the effects of lethodyne. Sebastian, with his head on one side, surveying the patient, promptly coincided. "Nervous diathesis," he observed. "Very vivid fancy. Twitches her hands the right way. Quick pulse, rapid perceptions, no meaningless unrest, but deep vitality. I don't doubt she'll stand it."

We explained to Number Fourteen the gravity of the case, and also the tentative character of the operation under lethodyne. At first, she shrank from taking it. "No, no!" she said; "let me die quietly." But Hilda, like the Angel of Mercy that she was, whispered in the girl's ear: "IF it succeeds, you will get quite well, and, you can marry Arthur."

The patient's dark face flushed crimson.

"Ah! Arthur," she cried. "Dear Arthur! I can bear anything you choose to do to me—for Arthur!"

"How soon you find these things out!" I cried to Hilda, a few minutes later. "A mere man would never have thought of that. And who is Arthur?"

"A sailor—on a ship that trades with the South Seas. I hope he is worthy of her. Fretting over Arthur's absence has aggravated the case. He is homeward-bound now. She is worrying herself to death for fear she should not live to say good-bye to him."

"She WILL live to marry him," I answered, with confidence like her own, "if YOU say she can stand it."

"The lethodyne, oh, yes; THAT'S all right. But the operation itself is so extremely dangerous; though Dr. Sebastian says he has called in the best surgeon in London for all such cases. They are rare, he tells me, and Nielsen has performed on six, three of them successfully."

We gave the girl the drug. She took it, trembling, and went off at once, holding Hilda's hand, with a pale smile on her face, which persisted there somewhat weirdly all through the operation. The work of removing the growth was long and ghastly, even for us who were well seasoned to such sights; but at the end Nielsen expressed himself as perfectly satisfied. "A very neat piece of work!" Sebastian exclaimed, looking on. "I congratulate you, Nielsen. I never saw anything done cleaner or better."

"A successful operation, certainly!" the great surgeon admitted, with just pride in the Master's commendation.

"AND the patient?" Hilda asked, wavering.

"Oh, the patient? The patient will die," Nielsen replied, in an unconcerned voice, wiping his spotless instruments.

"That is not MY idea of the medical art," I cried, shocked at his callousness. "An operation is only successful if—"

He regarded me with lofty scorn. "A certain percentage of losses," he interrupted, calmly, "is inevitable, of course, in all surgical operations. We are obliged to average it. How could I preserve my precision and accuracy of hand if I were always bothered by sentimental considerations of the patient's safety?"

Hilda Wade looked up at me with a sympathetic glance. "We will pull her through yet," she murmured, in her soft voice, "if care and skill can do it, MY care and YOUR skill. This is now OUR patient, Dr. Cumberledge."

It needed care and skill. We watched her for hours, and she showed no sign or gleam of recovery. Her sleep was deeper than either Sebastian's or Hilda's had been. She had taken a big dose, so as to secure immobility. The question now was, would she recover at all from it? Hour after hour we waited and watched; and not a sign of movement! Only the same deep, slow, hampered breathing, the same feeble, jerky pulse, the same deathly pallor on the dark cheeks, the same corpse-like rigidity of limb and muscle.

At last our patient stirred faintly, as in a dream; her breath faltered. We bent over her. Was it death, or was she beginning to recover?

Very slowly, a faint trace of colour came back to her cheeks. Her heavy eyes half opened. They stared first with a white stare. Her arms dropped by her side. Her mouth relaxed its ghastly smile.... We held our breath.... She was coming to again!

But her coming to was slow, very, very slow. Her pulse was still weak. Her heart pumped feebly. We feared she might sink from inanition at any moment. Hilda Wade knelt on the floor by the girl's side and held a spoonful of beef essence coaxingly to her lips. Number Fourteen gasped, drew a long, slow breath, then gulped and swallowed it. After that she lay back with her mouth open, looking like a corpse. Hilda pressed another spoonful of the soft jelly upon her; but the girl waved it away with one trembling hand. "Let me die," she cried. "Let me die! I feel dead already."

Hilda held her face close. "Isabel," she whispered, and I recognised in her tone the vast moral difference between "Isabel" and "Number Fourteen,"—"Is-a-bel, you must take it. For Arthur's sake, I say, you MUST take it."

The girl's hand quivered as it lay on the white coverlet. "For Arthur's sake!" she murmured, lifting her eyelids dreamily. "For Arthur's sake! Yes, nurse, dear!"

"Call me Hilda, please! Hilda!"

The girl's face lighted up again. "Yes, Hilda, dear," she answered, in an unearthly voice, like one raised from the dead. "I will call you what you will. Angel of light, you have been so good to me."

She opened her lips with an effort and slowly swallowed another spoonful. Then she fell back, exhausted. But her pulse improved within twenty minutes. I mentioned the matter, with enthusiasm, to Sebastian later. "It is very nice in its way," he answered; "but... it is not nursing."

I thought to myself that that was just what it WAS; but I did not say so. Sebastian was a man who thought meanly of women. "A doctor, like a priest," he used to declare, "should keep himself unmarried. His bride is medicine." And he disliked to see what he called PHILANDERING going on in his hospital. It may have been on that account that I avoided speaking much of Hilda Wade thenceforth before him.

He looked in casually next day to see the patient. "She will die," he said, with perfect assurance, as we passed down the ward together. "Operation has taken too much out of her."

"Still, she has great recuperative powers," Hilda answered. "They all have in her family, Professor. You may, perhaps, remember Joseph Huntley, who occupied Number Sixty-seven in the Accident Ward, some nine months since, compound fracture of the arm, a dark, nervous engineer's assistant, very hard to restrain, well, HE was her brother; he caught typhoid fever in the hospital, and you commented at the time on his strange vitality. Then there was her cousin, again, Ellen Stubbs. We had HER for stubborn chronic laryngitis, a very bad case, anyone else would have died, yielded at once to your treatment; and made, I recollect, a splendid convalescence."

"What a memory you have!" Sebastian cried, admiring against his will. "It is simply marvellous! I never saw anyone like you in my life... except once. HE was a man, a doctor, a colleague of mine, dead long ago.... Why—" he mused, and gazed hard at her. Hilda shrank before his gaze. "This is curious," he went on slowly, at last; "very curious. You—why, you resemble him!"

"Do I?" Hilda replied, with forced calm, raising her eyes to his. Their glances met. That moment, I saw each had recognised something; and from that day forth I was instinctively aware that a duel was being waged between Sebastian and Hilda, a duel between the two ablest and most singular personalities I had ever met; a duel of life and death, though I did not fully understand its purport till much, much later.

Every day after that, the poor, wasted girl in Number Fourteen grew feebler and fainter. Her temperature rose; her heart throbbed weakly. She seemed to be fading away. Sebastian shook his head. "Lethodyne is a failure," he said, with a mournful regret. "One cannot trust it. The case might have recovered from the operation, or recovered from the drug; but she could not recover from both together. Yet the operation would have been impossible without the drug, and the drug is useless except for the operation."

It was a great disappointment to him. He hid himself in his room, as was his wont when disappointed, and went on with his old work at his beloved microbes.

"I have one hope still," Hilda murmured to me by the bedside, when our patient was at her worst. "If one contingency occurs, I believe we may save her."

"What is that?" I asked.

She shook her head waywardly. "You must wait and see," she answered. "If it comes off, I will tell you. If not, let it swell the limbo of lost inspirations."

Next morning early, however, she came up to me with a radiant face, holding a newspaper in her hand. "Well, it HAS happened!" she cried, rejoicing. "We shall save poor Isabel Number Fourteen, I mean; our way is clear, Dr. Cumberledge."

I followed her blindly to the bedside, little guessing what she could mean. She knelt down at the head of the cot. The girl's eyes were closed. I touched her cheek; she was in a high fever. "Temperature?" I asked.

"A hundred and three."

I shook my head. Every symptom of fatal relapse. I could not imagine what card Hilda held in reserve. But I stood there, waiting.

She whispered in the girl's ear: "Arthur's ship is sighted off the Lizard."

The patient opened her eyes slowly, and rolled them for a moment as if she did not understand.

"Too late!" I cried. "Too late! She is delirious, insensible!"

Hilda repeated the words slowly, but very distinctly. "Do you hear, dear? Arthur's ship... it is sighted.... Arthur's ship... at the Lizard."

The girl's lips moved. "Arthur! Arthur!... Arthur's ship!" A deep sigh. She clenched her hands. "He is coming?" Hilda nodded and smiled, holding her breath with suspense.

"Up the Channel now. He will be at Southampton tonight. Arthur... at Southampton. It is here, in the papers; I have telegraphed to him to hurry on at once to see you."

She struggled up for a second. A smile flitted across the worn face. Then she fell back wearily.

I thought all was over. Her eyes stared white. But ten minutes later she opened her lids again. "Arthur is coming," she murmured. "Arthur... coming."

"Yes, dear. Now sleep. He is coming."

All through that day and the next night she was restless and agitated; but still her pulse improved a little. Next morning she was again a trifle better. Temperature falling, a hundred and one, point three. At ten o'clock Hilda came in to her, radiant.

"Well, Isabel, dear," she cried, bending down and touching her cheek (kissing is forbidden by the rules of the house), "Arthur has come. He is here... down below... I have seen him."

"Seen him!" the girl gasped.

"Yes, seen him. Talked with him. Such a nice, manly fellow; and such an honest, good face! He is longing for you to get well. He says he has come home this time to marry you."

The wan lips quivered. "He will NEVER marry me!"

"Yes, yes, he WILL, if you will take this jelly. Look here, he wrote these words to you before my very eyes: 'Dear love to my Isa!'... If you are good, and will sleep, he may see you, to-morrow."

The girl opened her lips and ate the jelly greedily. She ate as much as she was desired. In three minutes more her head had fallen like a child's upon her pillow and she was sleeping peacefully.

I went up to Sebastian's room, quite excited with the news. He was busy among his bacilli. They were his hobby, his pets. "Well, what do you think, Professor?" I cried. "That patient of Nurse Wade's—"

He gazed up at me abstractedly, his brow contracting. "Yes, yes; I know," he interrupted. "The girl in Fourteen. I have discounted her case long ago. She has ceased to interest me.... Dead, of course! Nothing else was possible."

I laughed a quick little laugh of triumph. "No, sir; NOT dead. Recovering! She has fallen just now into a normal sleep; her breathing is natural."

He wheeled his revolving chair away from the germs and fixed me with his keen eyes. "Recovering?" he echoed. "Impossible! Rallying, you mean. A mere flicker. I know my trade. She MUST die this evening."

"Forgive my persistence," I replied; "but—her temperature has gone down to ninety-nine and a trifle."

He pushed away the bacilli in the nearest watch-glass quite angrily. "To ninety-nine!" he exclaimed, knitting his brows. "Cumberledge, this is disgraceful! A most disappointing case! A most provoking patient!"

"But surely, sir—" I cried.

"Don't talk to ME, boy! Don't attempt to apologise for her. Such conduct is unpardonable. She OUGHT to have died. It was her clear duty. I SAID she would die, and she should have known better than to fly in the face of the faculty. Her recovery is an insult to medical science. What is the staff about? Nurse Wade should have prevented it."

"Still, sir," I exclaimed, trying to touch him on a tender spot, "the anaesthetic, you know! Such a triumph for lethodyne! This case shows clearly that on certain constitutions it may be used with advantage under certain conditions."

He snapped his fingers. "Lethodyne! pooh! I have lost interest in it. Impracticable! It is not fitted for the human species."

"Why so? Number Fourteen proves—"

He interrupted me with an impatient wave of his hand; then he rose and paced up and down the room testily. After a pause, he spoke again. "The weak point of lethodyne is this: nobody can be trusted to say WHEN it may be used—except Nurse Wade, which is NOT science."

For the first time in my life, I had a glimmering idea that I distrusted Sebastian. Hilda Wade was right, the man was cruel. But I had never observed his cruelty before, because his devotion to science had blinded me to it.

CHAPTER II

THE EPISODE OF THE GENTLEMAN WHO HAD FAILED FOR EVERYTHING

One day, about those times, I went round to call on my aunt, Lady Tepping. And lest you accuse me of the vulgar desire to flaunt my fine relations in your face, I hasten to add that my poor dear old aunt is a very ordinary specimen of the common Army widow. Her husband, Sir Malcolm, a crusty old gentleman of the ancient school, was knighted in Burma, or thereabouts, for a successful raid upon naked natives, on something that is called the Shan frontier. When he had grown grey in the service of his Queen and country, besides earning himself incidentally a very decent pension, he acquired gout and went to his long rest in Kensal Green Cemetery. He left his wife with one daughter, and the only pretence to a title in our otherwise blameless family.

My cousin Daphne is a very pretty girl, with those quiet, sedate manners which often develop later in life into genuine self-respect and real depth of character. Fools do not admire her; they accuse her of being "heavy." But she can do without fools; she has a fine, strongly built figure, an upright carriage, a large and broad forehead, a firm chin, and features which, though well-marked and well-moulded, are yet delicate in outline and sensitive in expression. Very young men seldom take to Daphne: she lacks the desired inanity. But she has mind, repose, and womanly tenderness. Indeed, if she had not been my cousin, I almost think I might once have been tempted to fall in love with her.

When I reached Gloucester Terrace, on this particular afternoon, I found Hilda Wade there before me. She had lunched at my aunt's, in fact. It was her "day out" at St. Nathaniel's, and she had come round to spend it with Daphne Tepping. I had introduced her to the house some time before, and she and my cousin had struck up a close acquaintance immediately. Their temperaments were sympathetic; Daphne admired Hilda's depth and reserve, while Hilda admired Daphne's grave grace and self-control, her perfect freedom from current affectations. She neither giggled nor aped Ibsenism.

A third person stood back in the room when I entered, a tall and somewhat jerry-built young man, with a rather long and solemn face, like an early stage in the evolution of a Don Quixote. I took a good look at him. There was something about his air that impressed me as both lugubrious and humorous; and in this I was right, for I learned later that he was one of those rare people who can sing a comic song with immense success while preserving a sour countenance, like a Puritan preacher's. His eyes were a little sunken, his fingers long and nervous; but I fancied he looked a good fellow at heart, for all that, though foolishly impulsive. He was a punctilious gentleman, I felt sure; his face and manner grew upon one rapidly.

Daphne rose as I entered, and waved the stranger forward with an imperious little wave. I imagined, indeed, that I detected in the gesture a faint touch of half-unconscious proprietorship. "Good-morning, Hubert," she said, taking my hand, but turning towards the tall young man. "I don't think you know Mr. Cecil Holsworthy."

"I have heard you speak of him," I answered, drinking him in with my glance. I added internally, "Not half good enough for you."

Hilda's eyes met mine and read my thought. They flashed back word, in the language of eyes, "I do not agree with you."

Daphne, meanwhile, was watching me closely. I could see she was anxious to discover what impression her friend Mr. Holsworthy was making on me. Till then, I had no idea she was fond of anyone in particular; but the way her glance wandered from him to me and from me to Hilda showed clearly that she thought much of this gawky visitor.

We sat and talked together, we four, for some time. I found the young man with the lugubrious countenance improved immensely on closer acquaintance. His talk was clever. He turned out to be the son of a politician high in office in the Canadian Government, and he had been educated at Oxford. The father, I gathered, was rich, but he himself was making an income of nothing a year just then as a briefless barrister, and he was hesitating whether to accept a post of secretary that had been offered him in the colony, or to continue his negative career at the Inner Temple, for the honour and glory of it.

"Now, which would YOU advise me, Miss Tepping?" he inquired, after we had discussed the matter some minutes.

Daphne's face flushed up. "It is so hard to decide," she answered. "To decide to YOUR best advantage, I mean, of course. For naturally all your English friends would wish to keep you as long as possible in England."

"No, do you think so?" the gawky young man jerked out with evident pleasure. "Now, that's awfully kind of you. Do you know, if YOU tell me I ought to stay in England, I've half a mind... I'll cable over this very day and refuse the appointment."

Daphne flushed once more. "Oh, please don't!" she exclaimed, looking frightened. "I shall be quite distressed if a stray word of mine should debar you from accepting a good offer of a secretaryship."

"Why, your least wish—" the young man began—then checked himself hastily—"must be always important," he went on, in a different voice, "to everyone of your acquaintance."

Daphne rose hurriedly. "Look here, Hilda," she said, a little tremulously, biting her lip, "I have to go out into Westbourne Grove to get those gloves for to-night, and a spray for my hair; will you excuse me for half an hour?"

Holsworthy rose too. "Mayn't I go with you?" he asked, eagerly.

"Oh, if you like. How very kind of you!" Daphne answered, her cheek a blush rose. "Hubert, will you come too? and you, Hilda?"

It was one of those invitations which are given to be refused. I did not need Hilda's warning glance to tell me that my company would be quite superfluous. I felt those two were best left together.

"It's no use, though, Dr. Cumberledge!" Hilda put in, as soon as they were gone. "He WON'T propose, though he has had every encouragement. I don't know what's the matter; but I've been watching them both for weeks, and somehow things seem never to get any forwarder."

"You think he's in love with her?" I asked.

"In love with her! Well, you have eyes in your head, I know; where could they have been looking? He's madly in love, a very good kind of love, too. He genuinely admires and respects and appreciates all Daphne's sweet and charming qualities."

"Then what do you suppose is the matter?"

"I have an inkling of the truth: I imagine Mr. Cecil must have let himself in for a prior attachment."

"If so, why does he hang about Daphne?"

"Because—he can't help himself. He's a good fellow and a chivalrous fellow. He admires your cousin; but he must have got himself into some foolish entanglement elsewhere which he is too honourable to break off; while at the same time he's far too much impressed by Daphne's fine qualities to be able to keep away from her. It's the ordinary case of love versus duty."

"Is he well off? Could he afford to marry Daphne?"

"Oh, his father's very rich: he has plenty of money; a Canadian millionaire, they say. That makes it all the likelier that some undesirable young woman somewhere may have managed to get hold of him. Just the sort of romantic, impressionable hobbledehoy such women angle for."

I drummed my fingers on the table. Presently Hilda spoke again. "Why don't you try to get to know him, and find out precisely what's the matter?"

"I KNOW what's the matter—now you've told me," I answered. "It's as clear as day. Daphne is very much smitten with him, too. I'm sorry for Daphne! Well, I'll take your advice; I'll try to have some talk with him."

"Do, please; I feel sure I have hit upon it. He has got himself engaged in a hurry to some girl he doesn't really care about, and he is far too much of a gentleman to break it off, though he's in love quite another way with Daphne."

Just at that moment the door opened and my aunt entered.

"Why, where's Daphne?" she cried, looking about her and arranging her black lace shawl.

"She has just run out into Westbourne Grove to get some gloves and a flower for the fete this evening," Hilda answered. Then she added, significantly, "Mr. Holsworthy has gone with her."

"What? That boy's been here again?"

"Yes, Lady Tepping. He called to see Daphne."

My aunt turned to me with an aggrieved tone. It is a peculiarity of my aunt's, I have met it elsewhere, that if she is angry with Jones, and Jones is not present, she assumes a tone of injured asperity on his account towards Brown or Smith, or any other innocent person whom she happens to be addressing. "Now, this is really too bad, Hubert," she burst out, as if I were the culprit. "Disgraceful! Abominable! I'm sure I can't make out what the young fellow means by it. Here he comes dangling after Daphne every day and all day long, and never once says whether he means anything by it or not. In MY young days, such conduct as that would not have been considered respectable."

I nodded and beamed benignly.

"Well, why don't you answer me?" my aunt went on, warming up. "DO you mean to tell me you think his behaviour respectful to a nice girl in Daphne's position?"

"My dear aunt," I answered, "you confound the persons. I am not Mr. Holsworthy. I decline responsibility for him. I meet him here, in YOUR house, for the first time this morning."

"Then that shows how often you come to see your relations, Hubert!" my aunt burst out, obliquely. "The man's been here, to my certain knowledge, every day this six weeks."

"Really, Aunt Fanny," I said; "you must recollect that a professional man—"

"Oh, yes. THAT'S the way! Lay it all down to your profession, do, Hubert! Though I KNOW you were at the Thorntons' on Saturday, saw it in the papers, the Morning Post—'among the guests were Sir Edward and Lady Burnes, Professor Sebastian, Dr. Hubert Cumberledge,' and so forth, and so forth. YOU think you can conceal these things; but you can't. I get to know them!"

"Conceal them! My dearest aunt! Why, I danced twice with Daphne."

"Daphne! Yes, Daphne. They all run after Daphne," my aunt exclaimed, altering the venue once more. "But there's no respect for age left. I expect to be neglected. However, that's neither here nor there. The point is this: you're the one man now living in the family. You ought to behave like a brother to Daphne. Why don't you board this Holsworthy person and ask him his intentions?"

"Goodness gracious!" I cried; "most excellent of aunts, that epoch has gone past. The late lamented Queen Anne is now dead. It's no use asking the young man of to-day to explain his intentions. He will refer you to the works of the Scandinavian dramatists."

My aunt was speechless. She could only gurgle out the words: "Well, I can safely say that of all the monstrous behaviour—" then language failed her and she relapsed into silence.

However, when Daphne and young Holsworthy returned, I had as much talk with him as I could, and when he left the house I left also.

"Which way are you walking?" I asked, as we turned out into the street.

"Towards my rooms in the Temple."

"Oh! I'm going back to St. Nathaniel's," I continued. "If you'll allow me, I'll walk part way with you."

"How very kind of you!"

We strode side by side a little distance in silence. Then a thought seemed to strike the lugubrious young man. "What a charming girl your cousin is!" he exclaimed, abruptly.

"You seem to think so," I answered, smiling.

He flushed a little; the lantern jaw grew longer. "I admire her, of course," he answered. "Who doesn't? She is so extraordinarily handsome."

"Well, not exactly handsome," I replied, with more critical and kinsman-like deliberation. "Pretty, if you will; and decidedly pleasing and attractive in manner."

He looked me up and down, as if he found me a person singularly deficient in taste and appreciation. "Ah, but then, you are her cousin," he said at last, with a compassionate tone. "That makes a difference."

"I quite see all Daphne's strong points," I answered, still smiling, for I could perceive he was very far gone. "She is good-looking, and she is clever."

"Clever!" he echoed. "Profound! She has a most unusual intellect. She stands alone."

"Like her mother's silk dresses," I murmured, half under my breath.

He took no notice of my flippant remark, but went on with his rhapsody. "Such depth; such penetration! And then, how sympathetic! Why, even to a mere casual acquaintance like myself, she is so kind, so discerning!"

"ARE you such a casual acquaintance?" I inquired, with a smile. (It might have shocked Aunt Fanny to hear me; but THAT is the way we ask a young man his intentions nowadays.)

He stopped short and hesitated. "Oh, quite casual," he replied, almost stammering. "Most casual, I assure you.... I have never ventured to do myself the honour of supposing that... that Miss Tepping could possibly care for me."

"There is such a thing as being TOO modest and unassuming," I answered. "It sometimes leads to unintentional cruelty."

"No, do you think so?" he cried, his face falling all at once. "I should blame myself bitterly if that were so. Dr. Cumberledge, you are her cousin. DO you gather that I have acted in such a way as to—to lead Miss Tepping to suppose I felt any affection for her?"

I laughed in his face. "My dear boy," I answered, laying one hand on his shoulder, "may I say the plain truth? A blind bat could see you are madly in love with her."

His mouth twitched. "That's very serious!" he answered, gravely; "very serious."

"It is," I responded, with my best paternal manner, gazing blankly in front of me.

He stopped short again. "Look here," he said, facing me. "Are you busy? No? Then come back with me to my rooms; and—I'll make a clean breast of it."

"By all means," I assented. "When one is young, and foolish, I have often noticed, as a medical man, that a drachm of clean breast is a magnificent prescription."

He walked back by my side, talking all the way of Daphne's many adorable qualities. He exhausted the dictionary for laudatory adjectives. By the time I reached his door it was not HIS fault if I had not learned that the angelic hierarchy were not in the running with my pretty cousin for graces and virtues. I felt that Faith, Hope, and Charity ought to resign at once in favour of Miss Daphne Tepping, promoted.

He took me into his comfortably furnished rooms, the luxurious rooms of a rich young bachelor, with taste as well as money, and offered me a partaga. Now, I have long observed, in the course of my practice, that a choice cigar assists a man in taking a philosophic outlook on the question under discussion; so I accepted the partaga. He sat down opposite me and pointed to a photograph in the centre of his mantlepiece. "I am engaged to that lady," he put in, shortly.

"So I anticipated," I answered, lighting up.

He started and looked surprised. "Why, what made you guess it?" he inquired.

I smiled the calm smile of superior age, I was some eight years or so his senior. "My dear fellow," I murmured, "what else could prevent you from proposing to Daphne, when you are so undeniably in love with her?"

"A great deal," he answered. "For example, the sense of my own utter unworthiness."

"One's own unworthiness," I replied, "though doubtless real—p'f, p'f—is a barrier that most of us can readily get over when our admiration for a particular lady waxes strong enough. So THIS is the prior attachment!" I took the portrait down and scanned it.

"Unfortunately, yes. What do you think of her?"

I scrutinised the features. "Seems a nice enough little thing," I answered. It was an innocent face, I admit; very frank and girlish.

He leaned forward eagerly. "That's just it. A nice enough little thing! Nothing in the world to be said against her. While Daphne—Miss Tepping, I mean—" His silence was ecstatic.

I examined the photograph still more closely. It displayed a lady of twenty or thereabouts, with a weak face, small, vacant features, a feeble chin, a good-humoured, simple mouth, and a wealth of golden hair that seemed to strike a keynote.

"In the theatrical profession?" I inquired at last, looking up.

He hesitated. "Well, not exactly," he answered.

I pursed my lips and blew a ring. "Music-hall stage?" I went on, dubiously.

He nodded. "But a girl is not necessarily any the less a lady because she sings at a music-hall," he added, with warmth, displaying an evident desire to be just to his betrothed, however much he admired Daphne.

"Certainly not," I admitted. "A lady is a lady; no occupation can in itself unladify her.... But on the music-hall stage, the odds, one must admit, are on the whole against her."

"Now, THERE you show prejudice!"

"One may be quite unprejudiced," I answered, "and yet allow that connection with the music-halls does not, as such, afford clear proof that a girl is a compound of all the virtues."

"I think she's a good girl," he retorted, slowly.

"Then why do you want to throw her over?" I inquired.

"I don't. That's just it. On the contrary, I mean to keep my word and marry her."

"IN ORDER to keep your word?" I suggested.

He nodded. "Precisely. It is a point of honour."

"That's a poor ground of marriage," I went on. "Mind, I don't want for a moment to influence you, as Daphne's cousin. I want to get at the truth of the situation. I don't even know what Daphne thinks of you. But you promised me a clean breast. Be a man and bare it."

He bared it instantly. "I thought I was in love with this girl, you see," he went on, "till I saw Miss Tepping."

"That makes a difference," I admitted.

"And I couldn't bear to break her heart."

"Heaven forbid!" I cried. "It is the one unpardonable sin. Better anything than that." Then I grew practical. "Father's consent?"

"MY father's? IS it likely? He expects me to marry into some distinguished English family."

I hummed a moment. "Well, out with it!" I exclaimed, pointing my cigar at him.

He leaned back in his chair and told me the whole story. A pretty girl; golden hair; introduced to her by a friend; nice, simple little thing; mind and heart above the irregular stage on to which she had been driven by poverty alone; father dead; mother in reduced circumstances. "To keep the home together, poor Sissie decided—"

"Precisely so," I murmured, knocking off my ash. "The usual self-sacrifice! Case quite normal! Everything en regle!"

"You don't mean to say you doubt it?" he cried, flushing up, and evidently regarding me as a hopeless cynic. "I do assure you, Dr. Cumberledge, the poor child, though miles, of course, below Miss Tepping's level—is as innocent, and as good—"

"As a flower in May. Oh, yes; I don't doubt it. How did you come to propose to her, though?"

He reddened a little. "Well, it was almost accidental," he said, sheepishly. "I called there one evening, and her mother had a headache and went up to bed. And when we two were left alone, Sissie talked a great deal about her future and how hard her life was. And after a while she broke down and began to cry. And then—"

I cut him short with a wave of my hand. "You need say no more," I put in, with a sympathetic face. "We have all been there."

We paused a moment, while I puffed smoke at the photograph again. "Well," I said at last, "her face looks to me really simple and nice. It is a good face. Do you see her often?"

"Oh, no; she's on tour."

"In the provinces?"

"M'yes; just at present, at Scarborough."

"But she writes to you?"

"Every day."

"Would you think it an unpardonable impertinence if I made bold to ask whether it would be possible for you to show me a specimen of her letters?"

He unlocked a drawer and took out three or four. Then he read one through, carefully. "I don't think," he said, in a deliberative voice, "it would be a serious breach of confidence in me to let you look through this one. There's really nothing in it, you know—just the ordinary average every-day love-letter."

I glanced through the little note. He was right. The conventional hearts and darts epistle. It sounded nice enough: "Longing to see you again; so lonely in this place; your dear sweet letter; looking forward to the time; your ever-devoted Sissie."

"That seems straight," I answered. "However, I am not quite sure. Will you allow me to take it away, with the photograph? I know I am asking much. I want to show it to a lady in whose tact and discrimination I have the greatest confidence."

"What, Daphne?"

I smiled. "No, not Daphne," I answered. "Our friend, Miss Wade. She has extraordinary insight."

"I could trust anything to Miss Wade. She is true as steel."

"You are right," I answered. "That shows that you, too, are a judge of character."

He hesitated. "I feel a brute," he cried, "to go on writing every day to Sissie Montague—and yet calling every day to see Miss Tepping. But still—I do it."

I grasped his hand. "My dear fellow," I said, "nearly ninety per cent. of men, after all—are human!"

I took both letter and photograph back with me to Nathaniel's. When I had gone my rounds that night, I carried them into Hilda Wade's room and told her the story. Her face grew grave. "We must be just," she said at last. "Daphne is deeply in love with him; but even for Daphne's sake, we must not take anything for granted against the other lady."

I produced the photograph. "What do you make of that?" I asked. "I think it an honest face, myself, I may tell you."

She scrutinised it long and closely with a magnifier. Then she put her head on one side and mused very deliberately. "Madeline Shaw gave me her photograph the other day, and said to me, as she gave it, 'I do so like these modern portraits; they show one WHAT MIGHT HAVE BEEN.'"

"You mean they are so much touched up!"

"Exactly. That, as it stands, is a sweet, innocent face, an honest girl's face, almost babyish in its transparency but... the innocence has all been put into it by the photographer."

"You think so?"

"I know it. Look here at those lines just visible on the cheek. They disappear, nowhere, at impossible angles. AND the corners of that mouth. They couldn't go so, with that nose and those puckers. The thing is not real. It has been atrociously edited. Part is nature's; part, the photographer's; part, even possibly paint and powder."

"But the underlying face?"

"Is a minx's."

I handed her the letter. "This next?" I asked, fixing my eyes on her as she looked.

She read it through. For a minute or two she examined it. "The letter is right enough," she answered, after a second reading, "though its guileless simplicity is, perhaps, under the circumstances, just a leetle overdone; but the handwriting, the handwriting is duplicity itself: a cunning, serpentine hand, no openness or honesty in it. Depend upon it, that girl is playing a double game."

"You believe, then, there is character in handwriting?"

"Undoubtedly; when we know the character, we can see it in the writing. The difficulty is, to see it and read it BEFORE we know it; and I have practised a little at that. There is character in all we do, of course, our walk, our cough, the very wave of our hands; the only secret is, not all of us have always skill to see it. Here, however, I feel pretty sure. The curls of the g's and the tails of the y's, how full they are of wile, of low, underhand trickery!"

I looked at them as she pointed. "That is true!" I exclaimed. "I see it when you show it. Lines meant for effect. No straightness or directness in them!"

Hilda reflected a moment. "Poor Daphne!" she murmured. "I would do anything to help her.... I'll tell what might be a good plan." Her face brightened. "My holiday comes next week. I'll run down to Scarborough, it's as nice a place for a holiday as any, and I'll observe this young lady. It can do no harm, and good may come of it."

"How kind of you!" I cried. "But you are always all kindness."

Hilda went to Scarborough, and came back again for a week before going on to Bruges, where she proposed to spend the greater part of her holidays. She stopped a night or two in town to report progress, and, finding another nurse ill, promised to fill her place till a substitute was forthcoming.

"Well, Dr. Cumberledge," she said, when she saw me alone, "I was right! I have found out a fact or two about Daphne's rival!"

"You have seen her?" I asked.

"Seen her? I have stopped for a week in the same house. A very nice lodging-house on the Spa front, too. The girl's well enough off. The poverty plea fails. She goes about in good rooms and carries a mother with her."

"That's well," I answered. "That looks all right."

"Oh, yes, she's quite presentable: has the manners of a lady whenever she chooses. But the chief point is this: she laid her letters every day on the table in the passage outside her door for post, laid them all in a row, so that when one claimed one's own one couldn't help seeing them."

"Well, that was open and aboveboard," I continued, beginning to fear we had hastily misjudged Miss Sissie Montague.

"Very open, too much so, in fact; for I was obliged to note the fact that she wrote two letters regularly every day of her life—'to my two mashes,' she explained one afternoon to a young man who was with her as she laid them on the table. One of them was always addressed to Cecil Holsworthy, Esq."

"And the other?"

"Wasn't."

"Did you note the name?" I asked, interested.

"Yes; here it is." She handed me a slip of paper.

I read it: "Reginald Nettlecraft, Esq., 427, Staples Inn, London."

"What, Reggie Nettlecraft!" I cried, amused. "Why, he was a very little boy at Charterhouse when I was a big one; he afterwards went to Oxford, and got sent down from Christ Church for the part he took in burning a Greek bust in Tom Quad, an antique Greek bust, after a bump supper."

"Just the sort of man I should have expected," Hilda answered, with a suppressed smile. "I have a sort of inkling that Miss Montague likes HIM best; he is nearer her type; but she thinks Cecil Holsworthy the better match. Has Mr. Nettlecraft money?"

"Not a penny, I should say. An allowance from his father, perhaps, who is a Lincolnshire parson; but otherwise, nothing."

"Then, in my opinion, the young lady is playing for Mr. Holsworthy's money; failing which, she will decline upon Mr. Nettlecraft's heart."

We talked it all over. In the end I said abruptly: "Nurse Wade, you have seen Miss Montague, or whatever she calls herself. I have not. I won't condemn her unheard. I have half a mind to run down one day next week to Scarborough and have a look at her."

"Do. That will suffice. You can judge then for yourself whether or not I am mistaken."

I went; and what is more, I heard Miss Sissie sing at her hall, a pretty domestic song, most childish and charming. She impressed me not unfavourably, in spite of what Hilda said. Her peach-blossom cheek might have been art, but looked like nature. She had an open face, a baby smile and there was a frank girlishness about her dress and manner that took my fancy. "After all," I thought to myself, "even Hilda Wade is fallible."

So that evening, when her "turn" was over, I made up my mind to go round and call upon her. I had told Cecil Holsworthy my intentions beforehand, and it rather shocked him. He was too much of a gentleman to wish to spy upon the girl he had promised to marry. However, in my case, there need be no such scruples. I found the house and asked for Miss Montague. As I mounted the stairs to the drawing-room floor, I heard a sound of voices, the murmur of laughter; idiotic guffaws, suppressed giggles, the masculine and feminine varieties of tomfoolery.

"YOU'D make a splendid woman of business, YOU would!" a young man was saying. I gathered from his drawl that he belonged to that sub-species of the human race which is known as the Chappie.

"Wouldn't I just?" a girl's voice answered, tittering. I recognised it as Sissie's. "You ought to see me at it! Why, my brother set up a place once for mending bicycles; and I used to stand about at the door, as if I had just returned from a ride; and when fellows came in, with a nut loose or something, I'd begin talking with them while Bertie tightened it. Then, when THEY weren't looking, I'd dab the business end of a darning-needle, so, just plump into their tires; and of course, as soon as they went off, they were back again in a minute to get a puncture mended! I call THAT business."

A roar of laughter greeted the recital of this brilliant incident in a commercial career. As it subsided, I entered. There were two men in the room, besides Miss Montague and her mother, and a second young lady.

"Excuse this late call," I said, quietly, bowing. "But I have only one night in Scarborough, Miss Montague, and I wanted to see you. I'm a friend of Mr. Holsworthy's. I told him I'd look you up, and this is my sole opportunity."

I FELT rather than saw that Miss Montague darted a quick glance of hidden meaning at her friends the chappies; their faces, in response, ceased to snigger and grew instantly sober.

She took my card; then, in her alternative manner as the perfect lady, she presented me to her mother. "Dr. Cumberledge, mamma," she said, in a faintly warning voice. "A friend of Mr. Holsworthy's."

The old lady half rose. "Let me see," she said, staring at me. "WHICH is Mr. Holsworthy, Siss?—is it Cecil or Reggie?"

One of the chappies burst into a fatuous laugh once more at this remark. "Now, you're giving away the whole show, Mrs. Montague!" he exclaimed, with a chuckle. A look from Miss Sissie immediately checked him.

I am bound to admit, however, that after these untoward incidents of the first minute, Miss Montague and her friends behaved throughout with distinguished propriety. Her manners were perfect, I may even say demure. She asked about "Cecil" with charming naivete. She was frank and girlish. Lots of innocent fun in her, no doubt, she sang us a comic song in excellent taste, which is a severe test, but not a suspicion of double-dealing. If I had not overheard those few words as I came up the stairs, I think I should have gone away believing the poor girl an injured child of nature.

As it was, I went back to London the very next day, determined to renew my slight acquaintance with Reggie Nettlecraft.

Fortunately, I had a good excuse for going to visit him. I had been asked to collect among old Carthusians for one of those endless "testimonials" which pursue one through life, and are, perhaps, the worst Nemesis which follows the crime of having wasted one's youth at a public school: a testimonial for a retiring master, or professional cricketer, or washerwoman, or something; and in the course of my duties as collector it was quite natural that I should call upon all my fellow-victims. So I went to his rooms in Staples Inn and reintroduced myself.

Reggie Nettlecraft had grown up into an unwholesome, spotty, indeterminate young man, with a speckled necktie, and cuffs of which he was inordinately proud, and which he insisted on "flashing" every second minute. He was also evidently self-satisfied; which was odd, for I have seldom seen anyone who afforded less cause for rational satisfaction. "Hullo," he said, when I told him my name. "So it's you, is it, Cumberledge?" He glanced at my card. "St. Nathaniel's Hospital! What rot! Why, blow me tight if you haven't turned sawbones!"

"That is my profession," I answered, unashamed. "And you?"

"Oh, I don't have any luck, you know, old man. They turned me out of Oxford because I had too much sense of humour for the authorities there, beastly set of old fogeys! Objected to my 'chucking' oyster shells at the tutors' windows, good old English custom, fast becoming obsolete. Then I crammed for the Army. But, bless your heart, a GENTLEMAN has no chance for the Army nowadays; a pack of blooming cads, with what they call 'intellect,' read up for the exams, and don't give US a look-in; I call it sheer piffle. Then the Guv'nor set me on electrical engineering, electrical engineering's played out. I put no stock in it; besides, it's such beastly fag; and then, you get your hands dirty. So now I'm reading for the Bar; and if only my coach can put me up to tips enough to dodge the examiners, I expect to be called some time next summer."

"And when you have failed for everything?" I inquired, just to test his sense of humour.

He swallowed it like a roach. "Oh, when I've failed for everything, I shall stick up to the Guv'nor. Hang it all, a GENTLEMAN can't be expected to earn his own livelihood. England's going to the dogs, that's where it is; no snug little sinecures left for chaps like you and me; all this beastly competition. And no respect for the feelings of gentlemen, either! Why, would you believe it, Cumberground, we used to call you Cumberground at Charterhouse, I remember, or was it Fig Tree?—I happened to get a bit lively in the Haymarket last week, after a rattling good supper, and the chap at the police court, old cove with a squint, positively proposed to send me to prison, WITHOUT THE OPTION OF A FINE!—I'll trouble you for that, send ME to prison just—for knocking down a common brute of a bobby. There's no mistake about it; England's NOT a country now for a gentleman to live in."

"Then why not mark your sense of the fact by leaving it?" I inquired, with a smile.

He shook his head. "What? Emigrate? No, thank you! I'm not taking any. None of your colonies for ME, IF you please. I shall stick to the old ship. I'm too much attached to the Empire."

"And yet imperialists," I said, "generally gush over the colonies, the Empire on which the sun never sets."

"The Empire in Leicester Squire!" he responded, gazing at me with unspoken contempt. "Have a whisky-and-soda, old chap? What, no? 'Never drink between meals?' Well, you DO surprise me! I suppose that comes of being a sawbones, don't it?"

"Possibly," I answered. "We respect our livers." Then I went on to the ostensible reason of my visit, the Charterhouse testimonial. He slapped his thighs metaphorically, by way of suggesting the depleted condition of his pockets. "Stony broke, Cumberledge," he murmured; "stony broke! Honour bright! Unless Bluebird pulls off the Prince of Wales's Stakes, I really don't know how I'm to pay the Benchers."

"It's quite unimportant," I answered. "I was asked to ask you, and I HAVE asked you."

"So I twig, my dear fellow. Sorry to have to say NO. But I'll tell you what I can do for you; I can put you upon a straight thing—"

I glanced at the mantelpiece. "I see you have a photograph of Miss Sissie Montague," I broke in casually, taking it down and examining it. "WITH an autograph, too. 'Reggie, from Sissie.' You are a friend of hers?"

"A friend of hers? I'll trouble you. She IS a clinker, Sissie is! You should see that girl smoke. I give you my word of honour, Cumberledge, she can consume cigarettes against any fellow I know in London. Hang it all, a girl like that, you know, well, one can't help admiring her! Ever seen her?"

"Oh, yes; I know her. I called on her, in fact, night before last, at Scarborough."

He whistled a moment, then broke into an imbecile laugh. "My gum," he cried; "this IS a start, this is! You don't mean to tell me YOU are the other Johnnie."

"What other Johnnie?" I asked, feeling we were getting near it.

He leaned back and laughed again. "Well, you know that girl Sissie, she's a clever one, she is," he went on after a minute, staring at me. "She's a regular clinker! Got two strings to her bow; that's where the trouble comes in. Me and another fellow. She likes me for love and the other fellow for money. Now, don't you come and tell me that YOU are the other fellow."

"I have certainly never aspired to the young lady's hand," I answered, cautiously. "But don't you know your rival's name, then?"

"That's Sissie's blooming cleverness. She's a caulker, Sissie is; you don't take a rise out of Sissie in a hurry. She knows that if I knew who the other bloke was, I'd blow upon her little game to him and put him off her. And I WOULD, s'ep me taters; for I'm nuts on that girl. I tell you, Cumberledge, she IS a clinker!"

"You seem to me admirably adapted for one another," I answered, truthfully. I had not the slightest compunction in handing Reggie Nettlecraft over to Sissie, nor in handing Sissie over to Reggie Nettlecraft.

"Adapted for one another? That's just it. There, you hit the right nail plump on the cocoanut, Cumberground! But Sissie's an artful one, she is. She's playing for the other Johnnie. He's got the dibs, you know; and Sissie wants the dibs even more than she wants yours truly."

"Got what?" I inquired, not quite catching the phrase.

"The dibs, old man; the chink; the oof; the ready rhino. He rolls in it, she says. I can't find out the chap's name, but I know his Guv'nor's something or other in the millionaire trade somewhere across in America."

"She writes to you, I think?"

"That's so; every blooming day; but how the dummy did you come to know it?"

"She lays letters addressed to you on the hall table at her lodgings in Scarborough."

"The dickens she does! Careless little beggar! Yes, she writes to me—pages. She's awfully gone on me, really. She'd marry me if it wasn't for the Johnnie with the dibs. She doesn't care for HIM: she wants his money. He dresses badly, don't you see; and, after all, the clothes make the man! I'D like to get at him. I'D spoil his pretty face for him." And he assumed a playfully pugilistic attitude.

"You really want to get rid of this other fellow?" I asked, seeing my chance.

"Get rid of him? Why, of course! Chuck him into the river some nice dark night if I could once get a look at him!"

"As a preliminary step, would you mind letting me see one of Miss Montague's letters?" I inquired.

He drew a long breath. "They're a bit affectionate, you know," he murmured, stroking his beardless chin in hesitation. "She's a hot 'un, Sissie is. She pitches it pretty warm on the affection-stop, I can tell you. But if you really think you can give the other Johnnie a cut on the head with her letters, well, in the interests of true love, which never DOES run smooth, I don't mind letting you have a squint, as my friend, at one of her charming billy-doos."

He took a bundle from a drawer, ran his eye over one or two with a maudlin air, and then selected a specimen not wholly unsuitable for publication. "THERE'S one in the eye for C.," he said, chuckling. "What would C. say to that, I wonder? She always calls him C., you know; it's so jolly non-committing. She says, 'I only wish that beastly old bore C. were at Halifax, which is where he comes from and then I would fly at once to my own dear Reggie! But, hang it all, Reggie boy, what's the good of true love if you haven't got the dibs? I MUST have my comforts. Love in a cottage is all very well in its way; but who's to pay for the fizz, Reggie?' That's her refinement, don't you see? Sissie's awfully refined. She was brought up with the tastes and habits of a lady."

"Clearly so," I answered. "Both her literary style and her liking for champagne abundantly demonstrate it!" His acute sense of humour did not enable him to detect the irony of my observation. I doubt if it extended much beyond oyster shells. He handed me the letter. I read it through with equal amusement and gratification. If Miss Sissie had written it on purpose in order to open Cecil Holsworthy's eyes, she couldn't have managed the matter better or more effectually. It breathed ardent love, tempered by a determination to sell her charms in the best and highest matrimonial market.

"Now, I know this man, C.," I said when I had finished. "And I want to ask whether you will let me show him Miss Montague's letter. It would set him against the girl, who, as a matter of fact, is wholly unwor—I mean totally unfitted for him."

"Let you show it to him? Like a bird! Why, Sissie promised me herself that if she couldn't bring 'that solemn ass, C.,' up to the scratch by Christmas, she'd chuck him and marry me. It's here, in writing." And he handed me another gem of epistolary literature.

"You have no compunctions?" I asked again, after reading it.

"Not a blessed compunction to my name."

"Then neither have I," I answered.

I felt they both deserved it. Sissie was a minx, as Hilda rightly judged; while as for Nettlecraft, well, if a public school and an English university leave a man a cad, a cad he will be, and there is nothing more to be said about it.

I went straight off with the letters to Cecil Holsworthy. He read them through, half incredulously at first; he was too honest-natured himself to believe in the possibility of such double-dealing, that one could have innocent eyes and golden hair and yet be a trickster. He read them twice; then he compared them word for word with the simple affection and childlike tone of his own last letter received from the same lady. Her versatility of style would have done honour to a practised literary craftsman. At last he handed them back to me. "Do you think," he said, "on the evidence of these, I should be doing wrong in breaking with her?"

"Wrong in breaking with her!" I exclaimed. "You would be doing wrong if you didn't, wrong to yourself; wrong to your family; wrong, if I may venture to say so, to Daphne; wrong even in the long run to the girl herself; for she is not fitted for you, and she IS fitted for Reggie Nettlecraft. Now, do as I bid you. Sit down at once and write her a letter from my dictation."

He sat down and wrote, much relieved that I took the responsibility off his shoulders.

"DEAR MISS MONTAGUE," I began, "the inclosed letters have come into my hands without my seeking it. After reading them, I feel that I have absolutely no right to stand between you and the man of your real choice. It would not be kind or wise of me to do so. I release you at once, and consider myself released. You may therefore regard our engagement as irrevocably cancelled.

"Faithfully yours,

"CECIL HOLSWORTHY."

"Nothing more than that?" he asked, looking up and biting his pen. "Not a word of regret or apology?"

"Not a word," I answered. "You are really too lenient."

I made him take it out and post it before he could invent conscientious scruples. Then he turned to me irresolutely. "What shall I do next?" he asked, with a comical air of doubt.

I smiled. "My dear fellow, that is a matter for your own consideration."

"But—do you think she will laugh at me?"

"Miss Montague?"

"No! Daphne."

"I am not in not in Daphne's confidence," I answered. "I don't know how she feels. But, on the face of it, I think I can venture to assure you that at least she won't laugh at you."

He grasped my hand hard. "You don't mean to say so!" he cried. "Well, that's really very, kind of her! A girl of Daphne's high type! And I, who feel myself so utterly unworthy of her!"

"We are all unworthy of a good woman's love," I answered. "But, thank Heaven, the good women don't seem to realise it."

That evening, about ten, my new friend came back in a hurry to my rooms at St. Nathaniel's. Nurse Wade was standing there, giving her report for the night when he entered. His face looked some inches shorter and broader than usual. His eyes beamed. His mouth was radiant.

"Well, you won't believe it, Dr. Cumberledge," he began; "but—"

"Yes, I DO believe it," I answered. "I know it. I have read it already."

"Read it!" he cried. "Where?"

I waved my hand towards his face. "In a special edition of the evening papers," I answered, smiling. "Daphne has accepted you!"

He sank into an easy chair, beside himself with rapture. "Yes, yes; that angel! Thanks to YOU, she has accepted me!"

"Thanks to Miss Wade," I said, correcting him. "It is really all HER doing. If SHE had not seen through the photograph to the face, and through the face to the woman and the base little heart of her, we might never have found her out."

He turned to Hilda with eyes all gratitude. "You have given me the dearest and best girl on earth," he cried, seizing both her hands.

"And I have given Daphne a husband who will love and appreciate her," Hilda answered, flushing.

"You see," I said, maliciously; "I told you they never find us out, Holsworthy!"

As for Reggie Nettlecraft and his wife, I should like to add that they are getting on quite as well as could be expected. Reggie has joined his Sissie on the music-hall stage; and all those who have witnessed his immensely popular performance of the Drunken Gentleman before the Bow Street Police Court acknowledge without reserve that, after "failing for everything," he has dropped at last into his true vocation. His impersonation of the part is said to be "nature itself." I see no reason to doubt it.

CHAPTER III

THE EPISODE OF THE WIFE WHO DID HER DUTY

To make you understand my next yarn, I must go back to the date of my introduction to Hilda.

"It is witchcraft!" I said the first time I saw her, at Le Geyt's luncheon-party.

She smiled a smile which was bewitching, indeed, but by no means witch-like, a frank, open smile with just a touch of natural feminine triumph in it. "No, not witchcraft," she answered, helping herself with her dainty fingers to a burnt almond from the Venetian glass dish, "not witchcraft, memory; aided, perhaps, by some native quickness of perception. Though I say it myself, I never met anyone, I think, whose memory goes quite as far as mine does."

"You don't mean quite as far BACK," I cried, jesting; for she looked about twenty-four, and had cheeks like a ripe nectarine, just as pink and just as softly downy.

She smiled again, showing a row of semi-transparent teeth, with a gleam in the depths of them. She was certainly most attractive. She had that indefinable, incommunicable, unanalysable personal quality which we know as CHARM. "No, not as far BACK," she repeated. "Though, indeed, I often seem to remember things that happened before I was born (like Queen Elizabeth's visit to Kenilworth): I recollect so vividly all that I have heard or read about them. But as far IN EXTENT, I mean. I never let anything drop out of my memory. As this case shows you, I can recall even quite unimportant and casual bits of knowledge when any chance clue happens to bring them back to me."

She had certainly astonished me. The occasion for my astonishment was the fact that when I handed her my card, "Dr. Hubert Ford Cumberledge, St. Nathaniel's Hospital," she had glanced at it for a second and exclaimed, without sensible pause or break, "Oh, then, of course, you're half Welsh, as I am."

The instantaneous and apparent inconsecutiveness of her inference took me aback. "Well, m'yes: I AM half Welsh," I replied. "My mother came from Carnarvonshire. But, why THEN, and OF COURSE? I fail to perceive your train of reasoning."

She laughed a sunny little laugh, like one well accustomed to receive such inquiries. "Fancy asking A WOMAN to give you 'the train of reasoning' for her intuitions!" she cried, merrily. "That shows, Dr. Cumberledge, that you are a mere man, a man of science, perhaps, but NOT a psychologist. It also suggests that you are a confirmed bachelor. A married man accepts intuitions, without expecting them to be based on reasoning.... Well, just this once, I will stretch a point to enlighten you. If I recollect right, your mother died about three years ago?"

"You are quite correct. Then you knew my mother?"

"Oh, dear me, no! I never even met her. Why THEN?"

Her look was mischievous. "But, unless I mistake, I think she came from Hendre Coed, near Bangor."

"Wales is a village!" I exclaimed, catching my breath. "Every Welsh person seems to know all about every other."

My new acquaintance smiled again. When she smiled she was irresistible: a laughing face protruding from a cloud of diaphanous drapery. "Now, shall I tell you how I came to know that?" she asked, poising a glace cherry on her dessert fork in front of her. "Shall I explain my trick, like the conjurers?"

"Conjurers never explain anything," I answered. "They say: 'So, you see, THAT'S how it's done!'—with a swift whisk of the hand—and leave you as much in the dark as ever. Don't explain like the conjurers, but tell me how you guessed it."

She shut her eyes and seemed to turn her glance inward.

"About three years ago," she began slowly, like one who reconstructs with an effort a half-forgotten scene, "I saw a notice in the Times, Births, Deaths, and Marriages, 'On the 27th of October'—was it the 27th?" The keen brown eyes opened again for a second and flashed inquiry into mine.

"Quite right," I answered, nodding.

"I thought so. 'On the 27th of October, at Brynmor, Bournemouth, Emily Olwen Josephine, widow of the late Thomas Cumberledge, sometime colonel of the 7th Bengal Regiment of Foot, and daughter of Iolo Gwyn Ford, Esq., J.P., of Hendre Coed, near Bangor. Am I correct?" She lifted her dark eyelashes once more and flooded me.

"You are quite correct," I answered, surprised. "And that is really all that you knew of my mother?"

"Absolutely all. The moment I saw your card, I thought to myself, in a breath: 'Ford, Cumberledge; what do I know of those two names? I have some link between them. Ah, yes; found Mrs. Cumberledge, wife of Colonel Thomas Cumberledge, of the 7th Bengals, was a Miss Ford, daughter of a Mr. Ford, of Bangor.' That came to me like a lightning-gleam. Then I said to myself again, 'Dr. Hubert Ford Cumberledge must be their son.' So there you have 'the train of reasoning.' Women CAN reason—sometimes. I had to think twice, though, before I could recall the exact words of the Times notice."

"And can you do the same with everyone?"

"Everyone! Oh, come, now: that is expecting too much! I have not read, marked, learned, and inwardly digested everyone's family announcements. I don't pretend to be the Peerage, the Clergy List, and the London Directory rolled into one. I remembered YOUR family all the more vividly, no doubt, because of the pretty and unusual old Welsh names, 'Olwen' and 'Iolo Gwyn Ford,' which fixed themselves on my memory by their mere beauty. Everything about Wales always attracts me; my Welsh side is uppermost. But I have hundreds, oh, thousands, of such facts stored and pigeon-holed in my memory. If anybody else cares to try me," she glanced round the table, "perhaps we may be able to test my power that way."

Two or three of the company accepted her challenge, giving the full names of their sisters or brothers; and, in three cases out of five, my witch was able to supply either the notice of their marriage or some other like published circumstance. In the instance of Charlie Vere, it is true, she went wrong, just at first, though only in a single small particular; it was not Charlie himself who was gazetted to a sub-lieutenancy in the Warwickshire Regiment, but his brother Walter. However, the moment she was told of this slip, she corrected herself at once, and added, like lightning, "Ah, yes: how stupid of me! I have mixed up the names. Charles Cassilis Vere got an appointment on the same day in the Rhodesian Mounted Police, didn't he?" Which was in point of fact quite accurate.

But I am forgetting that all this time I have not even now introduced my witch to you.

Hilda Wade, when I first saw her, was one of the prettiest, cheeriest, and most graceful girls I have ever met, a dusky blonde, brown-eyed, brown-haired, with a creamy, waxen whiteness of skin that was yet warm and peach-downy. And I wish to insist from the outset upon the plain fact that there was nothing uncanny about her. In spite of her singular faculty of insight, which sometimes seemed to illogical people almost weird or eerie, she was in the main a bright, well-educated, sensible, winsome, lawn-tennis-playing English girl. Her vivacious spirits rose superior to her surroundings, which were often sad enough. But she was above all things wholesome, unaffected, and sparkling, a gleam of sunshine. She laid no claim to supernatural powers; she held no dealings with familiar spirits; she was simply a girl of strong personal charm, endowed with an astounding memory and a rare measure of feminine intuition. Her memory, she told me, she shared with her father and all her father's family; they were famous for their prodigious faculty in that respect. Her impulsive temperament and quick instincts, on the other hand, descended to her, she thought, from her mother and her Welsh ancestry.

Externally, she seemed thus at first sight little more than the ordinary pretty, light-hearted English girl, with a taste for field sports (especially riding), and a native love of the country. But at times one caught in the brightened colour of her lustrous brown eyes certain curious undercurrents of depth, of reserve, and of a questioning wistfulness which made you suspect the presence of profounder elements in her nature. From the earliest moment of our acquaintance, indeed, I can say with truth that Hilda Wade interested me immensely. I felt drawn. Her face had that strange quality of compelling attention for which we have as yet no English name, but which everybody recognises. You could not ignore her. She stood out. She was the sort of girl one was constrained to notice.

It was Le Geyts first luncheon-party since his second marriage. Big-bearded, genial, he beamed round on us jubilant. He was proud of his wife and proud of his recent Q.C.-ship. The new Mrs. Le Geyt sat at the head of the table, handsome, capable, self-possessed; a vivid, vigorous woman and a model hostess. Though still quite young, she was large and commanding. Everybody was impressed by her. "Such a good mother to those poor motherless children!" all the ladies declared in a chorus of applause. And, indeed, she had the face of a splendid manager.

I said as much in an undertone over the ices to Miss Wade, who sat beside me, though I ought not to have discussed them at their own table. "Hugo Le Geyt seems to have made an excellent choice," I murmured. "Maisie and Ettie will be lucky, indeed, to be taken care of by such a competent stepmother. Don't you think so?"

My witch glanced up at her hostess with a piercing dart of the keen brown eyes, held her wine-glass half raised, and then electrified me by uttering, in the same low voice, audible to me alone, but quite clearly and unhesitatingly, these astounding words:

"I think, before twelve mouths are out, MR. LE GEYT WILL HAVE MURDERED HER!"

For a minute I could not answer, so startling was the effect of this confident prediction. One does not expect to be told such things at lunch, over the port and peaches, about one's dearest friends, beside their own mahogany. And the assured air of unfaltering conviction with which Hilda Wade said it to a complete stranger took my breath away. WHY did she think so at all? And IF she thought so why choose ME as the recipient of her singular confidences?

I gasped and wondered.

"What makes you fancy anything so unlikely?" I asked aside at last, behind the babel of voices. "You quite alarm me."

She rolled a mouthful of apricot ice reflectively on her tongue, and then murmured, in a similar aside, "Don't ask me now. Some other time will do. But I mean what I say. Believe me; I do not speak at random."

She was quite right, of course. To continue would have been equally rude and foolish. I had perforce to bottle up my curiosity for the moment and wait till my sibyl was in the mood for interpreting.

After lunch we adjourned to the drawing-room. Almost at once, Hilda Wade flitted up with her brisk step to the corner where I was sitting. "Oh, Dr. Cumberledge," she began, as if nothing odd had occurred before, "I WAS so glad to meet you and have a chance of talking to you, because I DO so want to get a nurse's place at St. Nathaniel's."

"A nurse's place!" I exclaimed, a little surprised, surveying her dress of palest and softest Indian muslin; for she looked to me far too much of a butterfly for such serious work. "Do you really mean it; or are you one of the ten thousand modern young ladies who are in quest of a Mission, without understanding that Missions are unpleasant? Nursing, I can tell you, is not all crimped cap and becoming uniform."

"I know that," she answered, growing grave. "I ought to know it. I am a nurse already at St. George's Hospital."

"You are a nurse! And at St. George's! Yet you want to change to Nathaniel's? Why? St. George's is in a much nicer part of London, and the patients there come on an average from a much better class than ours in Smithfield."

"I know that too; but... Sebastian is at St. Nathaniel's, and I want to be near Sebastian."

"Professor Sebastian!" I cried, my face lighting up with a gleam of enthusiasm at our great teacher's name. "Ah, if it is to be under Sebastian that you desire, I can see you mean business. I know now you are in earnest."

"In earnest?" she echoed, that strange deeper shade coming over her face as she spoke, while her tone altered. "Yes, I think I am in earnest! It is my object in life to be near Sebastian, to watch him and observe him. I mean to succeed.... But I have given you my confidence, perhaps too hastily, and I must implore you not to mention my wish to him."

"You may trust me implicitly," I answered.

"Oh, yes; I saw that," she put in, with a quick gesture. "Of course, I saw by your face you were a man of honour, a man one could trust or I would not have spoken to you. But, you promise me?"

"I promise you," I replied, naturally flattered. She was delicately pretty, and her quaint, oracular air, so incongruous with the dainty face and the fluffy brown hair, piqued me not a little. That special mysterious commodity of CHARM seemed to pervade all she did and said. So I added: "And I will mention to Sebastian that you wish for a nurse's place at Nathaniel's. As you have had experience, and can be recommended, I suppose, by Le Geyt's sister," with whom she had come, "no doubt you can secure an early vacancy."

"Thanks so much," she answered, with that delicious smile. It had an infantile simplicity about it which contrasted most piquantly with her prophetic manner.

"Only," I went on, assuming a confidential tone, "you really MUST tell me why you said that just now about Hugo Le Geyt. Recollect, your Delphian utterances have gravely astonished and disquieted me. Hugo is one of my oldest and dearest friends; and I want to know why you have formed this sudden bad opinion of him."

"Not of HIM, but of HER," she answered, to my surprise, taking a small Norwegian dagger from the what-not and playing with it to distract attention.

"Come, come, now," I cried, drawing back. "You are trying to mystify me. This is deliberate seer-mongery. You are presuming on your powers. But I am not the sort of man to be caught by horoscopes. I decline to believe it."

She turned on me with a meaning glance. Those truthful eyes fixed me. "I am going from here straight to my hospital," she murmured, with a quiet air of knowledge—talking, I mean to say, like one who really knows. "This room is not the place to discuss this matter, is it? If you will walk back to St. George's with me, I think I can make you see and feel that I am speaking, not at haphazard, but from observation and experience."

Her confidence roused my most vivid curiosity. When she left I left with her. The Le Geyts lived in one of those new streets of large houses on Campden Hill, so that our way eastward lay naturally through Kensington Gardens.

It was a sunny June day, when light pierced even through the smoke of London, and the shrubberies breathed the breath of white lilacs. "Now, what did you mean by that enigmatical saying?" I asked my new Cassandra, as we strolled down the scent-laden path. "Woman's intuition is all very well in its way; but a mere man may be excused if he asks for evidence."

She stopped short as I spoke, and gazed full into my eyes. Her hand fingered her parasol handle. "I meant what I said," she answered, with emphasis. "Within one year, Mr. Le Geyt will have murdered his wife. You may take my word, for it."

"Le Geyt!" I cried. "Never! I know the man so well! A big, good-natured, kindly schoolboy! He is the gentlest and best of mortals. Le Geyt a murderer! Im—possible!"

Her eyes were far away. "Has it never occurred to you," she asked, slowly, with her pythoness air, "that there are murders and murders?—murders which depend in the main upon the murderer... and also murders which depend in the main upon the victim?"

"The victim? What do you mean?"

"Well, there are brutal men who commit murder out of sheer brutality, the ruffians of the slums; and there are sordid men who commit murder for sordid money, the insurers who want to forestall their policies, the poisoners who want to inherit property; but have you ever realised that there are also murderers who become so by accident, through their victims' idiosyncrasy? I thought all the time while I was watching Mrs. Le Geyt, 'That woman is of the sort predestined to be murdered.'... And when you asked me, I told you so. I may have been imprudent; still, I saw it, and I said it."

"But this is second sight!" I cried, drawing away. "Do you pretend to prevision?"

"No, not second sight; nothing uncanny, nothing supernatural. But prevision, yes; prevision based, not on omens or auguries, but on solid fact, on what I have seen and noticed."

"Explain yourself, oh, prophetess!"

She let the point of her parasol make a curved trail on the gravel, and followed its serpentine wavings with her eyes. "You know our house surgeon?" she asked at last, looking up of a sudden.

"What, Travers? Oh, intimately."

"Then come to my ward and see. After you have seen, you will perhaps believe me."

Nothing that I could say would get any further explanation out of her just then. "You would laugh at me if I told you," she persisted; "you won't laugh when you have seen it."

We walked on in silence as far as Hyde Park Corner. There my Sphinx tripped lightly up the steps of St. George's Hospital. "Get Mr. Travers's leave," she said, with a nod, and a bright smile, "to visit Nurse Wade's ward. Then come up to me there in five minutes."

I explained to my friend the house surgeon that I wished to see certain cases in the accident ward of which I had heard; he smiled a restrained smile—"Nurse Wade, no doubt!" but, of course, gave me permission to go up and look at them. "Stop a minute," he added, "and I'll come with you." When we got there, my witch had already changed her dress, and was waiting for us demurely in the neat dove-coloured gown and smooth white apron of the hospital nurses. She looked even prettier and more meaningful so than in her ethereal outside summer-cloud muslin.

"Come over to this bed," she said at once to Travers and myself, without the least air of mystery. "I will show you what I mean by it."

"Nurse Wade has remarkable insight," Travers whispered to me as we went.

"I can believe it," I answered.

"Look at this woman," she went on, aside, in a low voice—"no, NOT the first bed; the one beyond it; Number 60. I don't want the patient to know you are watching her. Do you observe anything odd about her appearance?"

"She is somewhat the same type," I began, "as Mrs.—"

Before I could get out the words "Le Geyt," her warning eye and puckering forehead had stopped me. "As the lady we were discussing," she interposed, with a quiet wave of one hand. "Yes, in some points very much so. You notice in particular her scanty hair, so thin and poor, though she is young and good-looking?"

"It is certainly rather a feeble crop for a woman of her age," I admitted. "And pale at that, and washy."

"Precisely. It's done up behind about as big as a nutmeg.... Now, observe the contour of her back as she sits up there; it is curiously curved, isn't it?"

"Very," I replied. "Not exactly a stoop, nor yet quite a hunch, but certainly an odd spinal configuration."

"Like our friend's, once more?"

"Like our friend's, exactly!"

Hilda Wade looked away, lest she should attract the patient's attention. "Well, that woman was brought in here, half-dead, assaulted by her husband," she went on, with a note of unobtrusive demonstration.

"We get a great many such cases," Travers put in, with true medical unconcern, "very interesting cases; and Nurse Wade has pointed out to me the singular fact that in almost all instances the patients resemble one another physically."

"Incredible!" I cried. "I can understand that there might well be a type of men who assault their wives, but not, surely, a type of women who get assaulted."

"That is because you know less about it than Nurse Wade," Travers answered, with an annoying smile of superior knowledge.

Our instructress moved on to another bed, laying one gentle hand as she passed on a patient's forehead. The patient glanced gratitude. "That one again," she said once more, half indicating a cot at a little distance: "Number 74. She has much the same thin hair, sparse, weak, and colourless. She has much the same curved back, and much the same aggressive, self-assertive features. Looks capable, doesn't she? A born housewife!... Well, she, too, was knocked down and kicked half-dead the other night by her husband."

"It is certainly odd," I answered, "how very much they both recall—"

"Our friend at lunch! Yes, extraordinary. See here"; she pulled out a pencil and drew the quick outline of a face in her note-book. "THAT is what is central and essential to the type. They have THIS sort of profile. Women with faces like that ALWAYS get assaulted."

Travers glanced over her shoulder. "Quite true," he assented, with his bourgeois nod. "Nurse Wade in her time has shown me dozens of them. Round dozens: bakers' dozens! They all belong to that species. In fact, when a woman of this type is brought in to us wounded now, I ask at once, 'Husband?' and the invariable answer comes pat: 'Well, yes, sir; we had some words together.' The effect of words, my dear fellow, is something truly surprising."

"They can pierce like a dagger," I mused.

"And leave an open wound behind that requires dressing," Travers added, unsuspecting. Practical man, Travers!

"But WHY do they get assaulted, the women of this type?" I asked, still bewildered.

"Number 87 has her mother just come to see her," my sorceress interposed. "SHE'S an assault case; brought in last night; badly kicked and bruised about the head and shoulders. Speak to the mother. She'll explain it all to you."

Travers and I moved over to the cot her hand scarcely indicated. "Well, your daughter looks pretty comfortable this afternoon, in spite of the little fuss," Travers began, tentatively.

"Yus, she's a bit tidy, thanky," the mother answered, smoothing her soiled black gown, grown green with long service. "She'll git on naow, please Gord. But Joe most did for 'er."

"How did it all happen?" Travers asked, in a jaunty tone, to draw her out.

"Well, it was like this, sir, yer see. My daughter, she's a lidy as keeps 'erself TO 'erself, as the sayin' is, an' 'olds 'er 'ead up. She keeps up a proper pride, an' minds 'er 'ouse an' 'er little uns. She ain't no gadabaht. But she 'AVE a tongue, she 'ave"; the mother lowered her voice cautiously, lest the "lidy" should hear. "I don't deny it that she 'AVE a tongue, at times, through myself 'avin' suffered from it. And when she DO go on, Lord bless you, why, there ain't no stoppin' of 'er."

"Oh, she has a tongue, has she?" Travers replied, surveying the "case" critically. "Well, you know, she looks like it."

"So she do, sir; so she do. An' Joe, 'e's a man as wouldn't 'urt a biby, not when 'e's sober, Joe wouldn't. But 'e'd bin aht; that's where it is; an' 'e cum 'ome lite, a bit fresh, through 'avin' bin at the friendly lead; an' my daughter, yer see, she up an' give it to 'im. My word, she DID give it to 'im! An' Joe, 'e's a peaceable man when 'e ain't a bit fresh; 'e's more like a friend to 'er than an 'usband, Joe is; but 'e lost 'is temper that time, as yer may say, by reason o' bein' fresh, an' 'e knocked 'er abaht a little, an' knocked 'er teeth aht. So we brought 'er to the orspital."

The injured woman raised herself up in bed with a vindictive scowl, displaying as she did so the same whale-like curved back as in the other "cases." "But we've sent 'im to the lockup," she continued, the scowl giving way fast to a radiant joy of victory as she contemplated her triumph "an' wot's more, I 'ad the last word of 'im. 'An 'e'll git six month for this, the neighbours says; an' when he comes aht again, my Gord, won't 'e ketch it!"

"You look capable of punishing him for it," I answered, and as I spoke, I shuddered; for I saw her expression was precisely the expression Mrs. Le Geyt's face had worn for a passing second when her husband accidentally trod on her dress as we left the dining-room.

My witch moved away. We followed. "Well, what do you say to it now?" she asked, gliding among the beds with noiseless feet and ministering fingers.

"Say to it?" I answered. "That it is wonderful, wonderful. You have quite convinced me."

"You would think so," Travers put in, "if you had been in this ward as often as I have, and observed their faces. It's a dead certainty. Sooner or later, that type of woman is cock-sure to be assaulted."

"In a certain rank of life, perhaps," I answered, still loth to believe it; "but not surely in ours. Gentlemen do not knock down their wives and kick their teeth out."

My Sibyl smiled. "No; there class tells," she admitted. "They take longer about it, and suffer more provocation. They curb their tempers. But in the end, one day, they are goaded beyond endurance; and then, a convenient knife, a rusty old sword, a pair of scissors, anything that comes handy, like that dagger this morning. One wild blow—half unpremeditated—and... the thing is done! Twelve good men and true will find it wilful murder."

I felt really perturbed. "But can we do nothing," I cried, "to warn poor Hugo?"

"Nothing, I fear," she answered. "After all, character must work itself out in its interactions with character. He has married that woman, and he must take the consequences. Does not each of us in life suffer perforce the Nemesis of his own temperament?"

"Then is there not also a type of men who assault their wives?"

"That is the odd part of it—no. All kinds, good and bad, quick and slow, can be driven to it at last. The quick-tempered stab or kick; the slow devise some deliberate means of ridding themselves of their burden."

"But surely we might caution Le Geyt of his danger!"

"It is useless. He would not believe us. We cannot be at his elbow to hold back his hand when the bad moment comes. Nobody will be there, as a matter of fact; for women of this temperament, born naggers, in short, since that's what it comes to, when they are also ladies, graceful and gracious as she is; never nag at all before outsiders. To the world, they are bland; everybody says, 'What charming talkers!' They are 'angels abroad, devils at home,' as the proverb puts it. Some night she will provoke him when they are alone, till she has reached his utmost limit of endurance—and then," she drew one hand across her dove-like throat, "it will be all finished."

"You think so?"

"I am sure of it. We human beings go straight like sheep to our natural destiny."

"But—that is fatalism."

"No, not fatalism: insight into temperament. Fatalists believe that your life is arranged for you beforehand from without; willy-nilly, you MUST act so. I only believe that in this jostling world your life is mostly determined by your own character, in its interaction with the characters of those who surround you. Temperament works itself out. It is your own acts and deeds that make up Fate for you."

For some months after this meeting neither Hilda Wade nor I saw anything more of the Le Geyts. They left town for Scotland at the end of the season; and when all the grouse had been duly slaughtered and all the salmon duly hooked, they went on to Leicestershire for the opening of fox-hunting; so it was not till after Christmas that they returned to Campden Hill. Meanwhile, I had spoken to Dr. Sebastian about Miss Wade, and on my recommendation he had found her a vacancy at our hospital. "A most intelligent girl, Cumberledge," he remarked to me with a rare burst of approval, for the Professor was always critical, after she had been at work for some weeks at St. Nathaniel's. "I am glad you introduced her here. A nurse with brains is such a valuable accessory, unless, of course, she takes to THINKING. But Nurse Wade never THINKS; she is a useful instrument, does what she's told, and carries out one's orders implicitly."

"She knows enough to know when she doesn't know," I answered, "which is really the rarest kind of knowledge."

"Unrecorded among young doctors!" the Professor retorted, with his sardonic smile. "They think they understand the human body from top to toe, when, in reality, well, they might do the measles!"

Early in January, I was invited again to lunch with the Le Geyts. Hilda Wade was invited, too. The moment we entered the house, we were both of us aware that some grim change had come over it. Le Geyt met us in the hall, in his old genial style, it is true; but still with a certain reserve, a curious veiled timidity which we had not known in him. Big and good-humoured as he was, with kindly eyes beneath the shaggy eyebrows, he seemed strangely subdued now; the boyish buoyancy had gone out of him. He spoke rather lower than was his natural key, and welcomed us warmly, though less effusively than of old. An irreproachable housemaid, in a spotless cap, ushered us into the transfigured drawing-room. Mrs. Le Geyt, in a pretty cloth dress, neatly tailor-made, rose to meet us, beaming the vapid smile of the perfect hostess, that impartial smile which falls, like the rain from Heaven, on good and bad indifferently. "SO charmed to see you again, Dr. Cumberledge!" she bubbled out, with a cheerful air, she was always cheerful, mechanically cheerful, from a sense of duty. "It IS such a pleasure to meet dear Hugo's old friends! AND Miss Wade, too; how delightful! You look so well, Miss Wade! Oh, you're both at St. Nathaniel's now, aren't you? So you can come together. What a privilege for you, Dr. Cumberledge, to have such a clever assistant, or, rather, fellow-worker. It must be a great life, yours, Miss Wade; such a sphere of usefulness! If we can only feel we are DOING GOOD, that is the main matter. For my own part, I like to be mixed up with every good work that's going on in my neighbourhood. I'm the soup-kitchen, you know, and I'm visitor at the workhouse; and I'm the Dorcas Society, and the Mutual Improvement Class; and the Prevention of Cruelty to Animals and to Children, and I'm sure I don't know how much else; so that, what with all that, and what with dear Hugo and the darling children"—she glanced affectionately at Maisie and Ettie, who sat bolt upright, very mute and still, in their best and stiffest frocks, on two stools in the corner—"I can hardly find time for my social duties."

"Oh, dear Mrs. Le Geyt," one of her visitors said with effusion, from beneath a nodding bonnet, she was the wife of a rural dean from Staffordshire—"EVERYBODY is agreed that YOUR social duties are performed to a marvel. They are the envy of Kensington. We all of us wonder, indeed, how one woman can find time for all of it!"

Our hostess looked pleased. "Well, yes," she answered, gazing down at her fawn-coloured dress with a half-suppressed smile of self-satisfaction, "I flatter myself I CAN get through about as much work in a day as anybody!" Her eye wandered round her rooms with a modest air of placid self-approval which was almost comic. Everything in them was as well-kept and as well-polished as good servants, thoroughly drilled, could make it. Not a stain or a speck anywhere. A miracle of neatness. Indeed, when I carelessly drew the Norwegian dagger from its scabbard, as we waited for lunch, and found that it stuck in the sheath, I almost started to discover that rust could intrude into that orderly household.

I recollected then how Hilda Wade had pointed out to me during those six months at St. Nathaniel's that the women whose husbands assaulted them were almost always "notable housewives," as they say in America, good souls who prided themselves not a little on their skill in management. They were capable, practical mothers of families, with a boundless belief in themselves, a sincere desire to do their duty, as far as they understood it, and a habit of impressing their virtues upon others which was quite beyond all human endurance. Placidity was their note; provoking placidity. I felt sure it must have been of a woman of this type that the famous phrase was coined—"Elle a toutes les vertus, et elle est insupportable."

"Clara, dear," the husband said, "shall we go in to lunch?"

"You dear, stupid boy! Are we not all waiting for YOU to give your arm to Lady Maitland?"

The lunch was perfect, and it was perfectly served. The silver glowed; the linen was marked with H. C. Le G. in a most artistic monogram. I noticed that the table decorations were extremely pretty. Somebody complimented our hostess upon them. Mrs. Le Geyt nodded and smiled, "I arranged them. Dear Hugo, in his blundering way, the big darling, forgot to get me the orchids I had ordered. So I had to make shift with what few things our own wee conservatory afforded. Still, with a little taste and a little ingenuity—" She surveyed her handiwork with just pride, and left the rest to our imaginations.

"Only you ought to explain, Clara—" Le Geyt began, in a deprecatory tone.

"Now, you darling old bear, we won't harp on that twice-told tale again," Clara interrupted, with a knowing smile. "Point da rechauffes! Let us leave one another's misdeeds and one another's explanations for their proper sphere—the family circle. The orchids did NOT turn up, that is the point; and I managed to make shift with the plumbago and the geraniums. Maisie, my sweet, NOT that pudding, IF you please; too rich for you, darling. I know your digestive capacities better than you do. I have told you fifty times it doesn't agree with you. A small slice of the other one!"

"Yes, mamma," Maisie answered, with a cowed and cowering air. I felt sure she would have murmured, "Yes, mamma," in the selfsame tone if the second Mrs. Le Geyt had ordered her to hang herself.

"I saw you out in the park, yesterday, on your bicycle, Ettie," Le Geyt's sister, Mrs. Mallet, put in. "But do you know, dear, I didn't think your jacket was half warm enough."

"Mamma doesn't like me to wear a warmer one," the child answered, with a visible shudder of recollection, "though I should love to, Aunt Lina."

"My precious Ettie, what nonsense, for a violent exercise like bicycling! Where one gets so hot! So unbecomingly hot! You'd be simply stifled, darling." I caught a darted glance which accompanied the words and which made Ettie recoil into the recesses of her pudding.

"But yesterday was so cold, Clara," Mrs. Mallet went on, actually venturing to oppose the infallible authority. "A nipping morning. And such a flimsy coat! Might not the dear child be allowed to judge for herself in a matter purely of her own feelings?"

Mrs. Le Geyt, with just the shadow of a shrug, was all sweet reasonableness. She smiled more suavely than ever. "Surely, Lina," she remonstrated, in her frankest and most convincing tone, "I must know best what is good for dear Ettie, when I have been watching her daily for more than six months past, and taking the greatest pains to understand both her constitution and her disposition. She needs hardening, Ettie does. Hardening. Don't you agree with me, Hugo?"

Le Geyt shuffled uneasily in his chair. Big man as he was, with his great black beard and manly bearing, I could see he was afraid to differ from her overtly. "Well, m—perhaps, Clara," he began, peering from under the shaggy eyebrows, "it would be best for a delicate child like Ettie—"

Mrs. Le Geyt smiled a compassionate smile. "Ah, I forgot," she cooed, sweetly. "Dear Hugo never CAN understand the upbringing of children. It is a sense denied him. We women know"—with a sage nod. "They were wild little savages when I took them in hand first—weren't you, Maisie? Do you remember, dear, how you broke the looking-glass in the boudoir, like an untamed young monkey? Talking of monkeys, Mr. Cotswould, HAVE you seen those delightful, clever, amusing French pictures at that place in Suffolk Street? There's a man there, a Parisian, I forget his honoured name, Leblanc, or Lenoir, or Lebrun, or something, but he's a most humorous artist, and he paints monkeys and storks and all sorts of queer beasties ALMOST as quaintly and expressively as you do. Mind, I say ALMOST, for I never will allow that any Frenchman could do anything QUITE so good, quite so funnily mock-human, as your marabouts and professors."

"What a charming hostess Mrs. Le Geyt makes," the painter observed to me, after lunch. "Such tact! Such discrimination!... AND, what a devoted stepmother!"

"She is one of the local secretaries of the Society for the Prevention of Cruelty to Children," I said, drily.

"And charity begins at home," Hilda Wade added, in a significant aside.

We walked home together as far as Stanhope Gate. Our sense of doom oppressed us. "And yet," I said, turning to her, as we left the doorstep, "I don't doubt Mrs. Le Geyt really believes she IS a model stepmother!"

"Of course she believes it," my witch answered. "She has no more doubt about that than about anything else. Doubts are not in her line. She does everything exactly as it ought to be done, who should know, if not she?—and therefore she is never afraid of criticism. Hardening, indeed! that poor slender, tender, shrinking little Ettie! A frail exotic. She would harden her into a skeleton if she had her way. Nothing's much harder than a skeleton, I suppose, except Mrs. Le Geyt's manner of training one."

"I should be sorry to think," I broke in, "that that sweet little floating thistle-down of a child I once knew was to be done to death by her."

"Oh, as for that, she will NOT be done to death," Hilda answered, in her confident way. "Mrs. Le Geyt won't live long enough."

I started. "You think not?"

"I don't think, I am sure of it. We are at the fifth act now. I watched Mr. Le Geyt closely all through lunch, and I'm more confident than ever that the end is coming. He is temporarily crushed; but he is like steam in a boiler, seething, seething, seething. One day she will sit on the safety-valve, and the explosion will come. When it comes"—she raised aloft one quick hand in the air as if striking a dagger home—"good-bye to her!"

For the next few months I saw much of Le Geyt; and the more I saw of him, the more I saw that my witch's prognosis was essentially correct. They never quarrelled; but Mrs. Le Geyt, in her unobtrusive way, held a quiet hand over her husband which became increasingly apparent. In the midst of her fancy-work (those busy fingers were never idle) she kept her eyes well fixed on him. Now and again I saw him glance at his motherless girls with what looked like a tender, protecting regret; especially when "Clara" had been most openly drilling them; but he dared not interfere. She was crushing their spirit, as she was crushing their father's—and all, bear in mind, for the best of motives! She had their interest at heart; she wanted to do what was right for them. Her manner to him and to them was always honey-sweet, in all externals; yet one could somehow feel it was the velvet glove that masked the iron hand; not cruel, not harsh even, but severely, irresistibly, unflinchingly crushing. "Ettie, my dear, get your brown hat at once. What's that? Going to rain? I did not ask you, my child, for YOUR opinion on the weather. My own suffices. A headache? Oh, nonsense! Headaches are caused by want of exercise. Nothing so good for a touch of headache as a nice brisk walk in Kensington Gardens. Maisie, don't hold your sister's hand like that; it is imitation sympathy! You are aiding and abetting her in setting my wishes at naught. Now, no long faces! What I require is CHEERFUL obedience."

A bland, autocratic martinet: smiling, inexorable! Poor, pale Ettie grew thinner and wanner under her law daily, while Maisie's temper, naturally docile, was being spoiled before one's eyes by persistent, needless thwarting.

As spring came on, however, I began to hope that things were really mending. Le Geyt looked brighter; some of his own careless, happy-go-lucky self came back again at intervals. He told me once, with a wistful sigh, that he thought of sending the children to school in the country, it would be better for them, he said, and would take a little work off dear Clara's shoulders; for never even to me was he disloyal to Clara. I encouraged him in the idea. He went on to say that the great difficulty in the way was... Clara. She was SO conscientious; she thought it her duty to look after the children herself, and couldn't bear to delegate any part of that duty to others. Besides, she had such an excellent opinion of the Kensington High School!

When I told Hilda Wade of this, she set her teeth together and answered at once: "That settles it! The end is very near. HE will insist upon their going, to save them from that woman's ruthless kindness; and SHE will refuse to give up any part of what she calls her duty. HE will reason with her; he will plead for his children; SHE will be adamant. Not angry, it is never the way of that temperament to get angry, just calmly, sedately, and insupportably provoking. When she goes too far, he will flare up at last; some taunt will rouse him; the explosion will come; and... the children will go to their Aunt Lina, whom they dote upon. When all is said and done, it is the poor man I pity!"

"You said within twelve months."

"That was a bow drawn at a venture. It may be a little sooner; it may be a little later. But, next week or next month, it is coming: it is coming!"

June smiled upon us once more; and on the afternoon of the 13th, the anniversary of our first lunch together at the Le Geyts, I was up at my work in the accident ward at St. Nathaniel's. "Well, the ides of June have come, Sister Wade!" I said, when I met her, parodying Caesar.

"But not yet gone," she answered; and a profound sense of foreboding spread over her speaking face as she uttered the words.

Her oracle disquieted me. "Why, I dined there last night," I cried; "and all seemed exceptionally well."

"The calm before the storm, perhaps," she murmured.

Just at that moment I heard a boy crying in the street: "Pall mall Gazette; 'ere y'are; speshul edishun! Shocking tragedy at the West-end! Orful murder! 'Ere y'are! Spechul Globe! Pall Mall, extry speshul!"

A weird tremor broke over me. I walked down into the street and bought a paper. There it stared me in the face on the middle page: "Tragedy at Campden Hill: Well-known Barrister Murders his Wife. Sensational Details."

I looked closer and read. It was as I feared. The Le Geyts! After I left their house, the night before, husband and wife must have quarrelled, no doubt over the question of the children's schooling; and at some provoking word, as it seemed, Hugo must have snatched up a knife—"a little ornamental Norwegian dagger," the report said, "which happened to lie close by on the cabinet in the drawing-room," and plunged it into his wife's heart. "The unhappy lady died instantaneously, by all appearances, and the dastardly crime was not discovered by the servants till eight o'clock this morning. Mr. Le Geyt is missing."

I rushed up with the news to Nurse Wade, who was at work in the accident ward. She turned pale, but bent over her patient and said nothing.

"It is fearful to think!" I groaned out at last; "for us who know all—that poor Le Geyt will be hanged for it! Hanged for attempting to protect his children!"

"He will NOT be hanged," my witch answered, with the same unquestioning confidence as ever.

"Why not?" I asked, astonished once more at this bold prediction.

She went on bandaging the arm of the patient whom she was attending. "Because... he will commit suicide," she replied, without moving a muscle.

"How do you know that?"

She stuck a steel safety-pin with deft fingers into the roll of lint. "When I have finished my day's work," she answered slowly, still continuing the bandage, "I may perhaps find time to tell you."

CHAPTER IV

THE EPISODE OF THE MAN WHO WOULD NOT COMMIT SUICIDE

After my poor friend Le Geyt had murdered his wife, in a sudden access of uncontrollable anger, under the deepest provocation, the police naturally began to inquire for him. It is a way they have; the police are no respecters of persons; neither do they pry into the question of motives. They are but poor casuists. A murder is for them a murder, and a murderer a murderer; it is not their habit to divide and distinguish between case and case with Hilda Wade's analytical accuracy.

As soon as my duties at St. Nathaniel's permitted me, on the evening of the discovery, I rushed round to Mrs. Mallet's, Le Geyt's sister. I had been detained at the hospital for some hours, however, watching a critical case; and by the time I reached Great Stanhope Street I found Hilda Wade, in her nurse's dress, there before me. Sebastian, it seemed, had given her leave out for the evening. She was a supernumerary nurse, attached to his own observation-cots as special attendant for scientific purposes, and she could generally get an hour or so whenever she required it.

Mrs. Mallet had been in the breakfast-room with Hilda before I arrived; but as I reached the house she rushed upstairs to wash her red eyes and compose herself a little before the strain of meeting me; so I had the opportunity for a few words alone first with my prophetic companion.

"You said just now at Nathaniel's," I burst out, "that Le Geyt would not be hanged: he would commit suicide. What did you mean by that? What reason had you for thinking so?"

Hilda sank into a chair by the open window, pulled a flower abstractedly from the vase at her side, and began picking it to pieces, floret after floret, with twitching fingers. She was deeply moved. "Well, consider his family history," she burst out at last, looking up at me with her large brown eyes as she reached the last petal. "Heredity counts.... And after such a disaster!"

She said "disaster," not "crime"; I noted mentally the reservation implied in the word.

"Heredity counts," I answered. "Oh, yes. It counts much. But what about Le Geyt's family history?" I could not recall any instance of suicide among his forbears.

"Well, his mother's father was General Faskally, you know," she replied, after a pause, in her strange, oblique manner. "Mr. Le Geyt is General Faskally's eldest grandson."

"Exactly," I broke in, with a man's desire for solid fact in place of vague intuition. "But I fail to see quite what that has to do with it."

"The General was killed in India during the Mutiny."

"I remember, of course, killed, bravely fighting."

"Yes; but it was on a forlorn hope, for which he volunteered, and in the course of which he is said to have walked straight into an almost obvious ambuscade of the enemy's."

"Now, my dear Miss Wade"—I always dropped the title of "Nurse," by request, when once we were well clear of Nathaniel's, "I have every confidence, you are aware, in your memory and your insight; but I do confess I fail to see what bearing this incident can have on poor Hugo's chances of being hanged or committing suicide."

She picked a second flower, and once more pulled out petal after petal. As she reached the last again, she answered, slowly: "You must have forgotten the circumstances. It was no mere accident. General Faskally had made a serious strategical blunder at Jhansi. He had sacrificed the lives of his subordinates needlessly. He could not bear to face the survivors. In the course of the retreat, he volunteered to go on this forlorn hope, which might equally well have been led by an officer of lower rank; and he was permitted to do so by Sir Colin in command, as a means of retrieving his lost military character. He carried his point, but he carried it recklessly, taking care to be shot through the heart himself in the first onslaught. That was virtual suicide, honourable suicide to avoid disgrace, at a moment of supreme remorse and horror."

"You are right," I admitted, after a minute's consideration. "I see it now, though I should never have thought of it."

"That is the use of being a woman," she answered.

I waited a second once more, and mused. "Still, that is only one doubtful case," I objected.

"There was another, you must remember: his uncle Alfred."

"Alfred Le Geyt?"

"No; HE died in his bed, quietly. Alfred Faskally."

"What a memory you have!" I cried, astonished. "Why, that was before our time, in the days of the Chartist riots!"

She smiled a certain curious sibylline smile of hers. Her earnest face looked prettier than ever. "I told you I could remember many things that happened before I was born," she answered. "THIS is one of them."

"You remember it directly?"

"How impossible! Have I not often explained to you that I am no diviner? I read no book of fate; I call no spirits from the vasty deep. I simply remember with exceptional clearness what I read and hear. And I have many times heard the story about Alfred Faskally."

"So have I, but I forget it."

"Unfortunately, I CAN'T forget. That is a sort of disease with me.... He was a special constable in the Chartist riots; and being a very strong and powerful man, like his nephew Hugo, he used his truncheon, his special constable's baton, or whatever you call it, with excessive force upon a starveling London tailor in the mob near Charing Cross. The man was hit on the forehead, badly hit, so that he died almost immediately of concussion of the brain. A woman rushed out of the crowd at once, seized the dying man, laid his head on her lap, and shrieked out in a wildly despairing voice that he was her husband, and the father of thirteen children. Alfred Faskally, who never meant to kill the man, or even to hurt him, but who was laying about him roundly, without realising the terrific force of his blows, was so horrified at what he had done when he heard the woman's cry, that he rushed off straight to Waterloo Bridge in an agony of remorse and—flung himself over. He was drowned instantly."

"I recall the story now," I answered; "but, do you know, as it was told me, I think they said the mob THREW Faskally over in their desire for vengeance."

"That is the official account, as told by the Le Geyts and the Faskallys; they like to have it believed their kinsman was murdered, not that he committed suicide. But my grandfather"—I started; during the twelve months that I had been brought into daily relations with Hilda Wade, that was the first time I had heard her mention any member of her own family, except once her mother—"my grandfather, who knew him well, and who was present in the crowd at the time, assured me many times that Alfred Faskally really jumped over of his own accord, NOT pursued by the mob, and that his last horrified words as he leaped were, 'I never meant it! I never meant it!' However, the family have always had luck in their suicides. The jury believed the throwing-over story, and found a verdict of 'wilful murder' against some person or persons unknown."

"Luck in their suicides! What a curious phrase! And you say, ALWAYS. Were there other cases, then?"

"Constructively, yes; one of the Le Geyts, you must recollect, went down with his ship (just like his uncle, the General, in India) when he might have quitted her. It is believed he had given a mistaken order. You remember, of course, he was navigating lieutenant. Another, Marcus, was SAID to have shot himself by accident while cleaning his gun—after a quarrel with his wife. But you have heard all about it. 'The wrong was on my side,' he moaned, you know, when they picked him up, dying, in the gun-room. And one of the Faskally girls, his cousin, of whom his wife was jealous, that beautiful Linda, became a Catholic, and went into a convent at once on Marcus's death; which, after all, in such cases, is merely a religious and moral way of committing suicide, I mean, for a woman who takes the veil just to cut herself off from the world, and who has no vocation, as I hear she had not."

She filled me with amazement. "That is true," I exclaimed, "when one comes to think of it. It shows the same temperament in fibre.... But I should never have thought of it."

"No? Well, I believe it is true, for all that. In every case, one sees they choose much the same way of meeting a reverse, a blunder, an unpremeditated crime. The brave way is to go through with it, and face the music, letting what will come; the cowardly way is to hide one's head incontinently in a river, a noose, or a convent cell."

"Le Geyt is not a coward," I interposed, with warmth.

"No, not, a coward, a manly spirited, great-hearted gentleman, but still, not quite of the bravest type. He lacks one element. The Le Geyts have physical courage, enough and to spare, but their moral courage fails them at a pinch. They rush into suicide or its equivalent at critical moments, out of pure boyish impulsiveness."

A few minutes later, Mrs. Mallet came in. She was not broken down, on the contrary, she was calm, stoically, tragically, pitiably calm; with that ghastly calmness which is more terrible by far than the most demonstrative grief. Her face, though deadly white, did not move a muscle. Not a tear was in her eyes. Even her bloodless hands hardly twitched at the folds of her hastily assumed black gown. She clenched them after a minute when she had grasped mine silently; I could see that the nails dug deep into the palms in her painful resolve to keep herself from collapsing.

Hilda Wade, with infinite sisterly tenderness, led her over to a chair by the window in the summer twilight, and took one quivering hand in hers. "I have been telling Dr. Cumberledge, Lina, about what I most fear for your dear brother, darling; and... I think... he agrees with me."

Mrs. Mallet turned to me, with hollow eyes, still preserving her tragic calm. "I am afraid of it, too," she said, her drawn lips tremulous. "Dr. Cumberledge, we must get him back! We must induce him to face it!"

"And yet," I answered, slowly, turning it over in my own mind; "he has run away at first. Why should he do that if he means, to commit suicide?" I hated to utter the words before that broken soul; but there was no way out of it.

Hilda interrupted me with a quiet suggestion. "How do you know he has run away?" she asked. "Are you not taking it for granted that, if he meant suicide, he would blow his brains out in his own house? But surely that would not be the Le Geyt way. They are gentle-natured folk; they would never blow their brains out or cut their throats. For all we know, he may have made straight for Waterloo Bridge,"—she framed her lips to the unspoken words, unseen by Mrs. Mallet, "like his uncle Alfred."

"That is true," I answered, lip-reading. "I never thought of that either."

"Still, I do not attach importance to this idea," she went on. "I have some reason for thinking he has run away... elsewhere; and if so, our first task must be to entice him back again."

"What are your reasons?" I asked, humbly. Whatever they might be, I knew enough of Hilda Wade by this time to know that she had probably good grounds for accepting them.

"Oh, they may wait for the present," she answered. "Other things are more pressing. First, let Lina tell us what she thinks of most moment."

Mrs. Mallet braced herself up visibly to a distressing effort. "You have seen the body, Dr. Cumberledge?" she faltered.

"No, dear Mrs. Mallet, I have not. I came straight from Nathaniel's. I have had no time to see it."

"Dr. Sebastian has viewed it by my wish, he has been so kind, and he will be present as representing the family at the post-mortem. He notes that the wound was inflicted with a dagger, a small ornamental Norwegian dagger, which always lay, as I know, on the little what-not by the blue sofa."

I nodded assent. "Exactly; I have seen it there."

"It was blunt and rusty, a mere toy knife, not at all the sort of weapon a man would make use of who designed to commit a deliberate murder. The crime, if there WAS a crime (which we do not admit), must therefore have been wholly unpremeditated."

I bowed my head. "For us who knew Hugo that goes without saying."

She leaned forward eagerly. "Dr. Sebastian has pointed out to me a line of defence which would probably succeed, if we could only induce poor Hugo to adopt it. He has examined the blade and scabbard, and finds that the dagger fits its sheath very tight, so that it can only be withdrawn with considerable violence. The blade sticks." (I nodded again.) "It needs a hard pull to wrench it out.... He has also inspected the wound, and assures me its character is such that it MIGHT have been self-inflicted." She paused now and again, and brought out her words with difficulty. "Self-inflicted, he suggests; therefore, that THIS may have happened. It is admitted, WILL be admitted, the servants overheard it, we can make no reservation there, a difference of opinion, an altercation, even, took place between Hugo and Clara that evening"—she started suddenly—"why, it was only last night—it seems like ages—an altercation about the children's schooling. Clara held strong views on the subject of the children"—her eyes blinked hard—"which Hugo did not share. We throw out the hint, then, that Clara, during the course of the dispute, we must call it a dispute, accidentally took up this dagger and toyed with it. You know her habit of toying, when she had no knitting or needlework. In the course of playing with it (we suggest) she tried to pull the knife out of its sheath; failed; held it up, so, point upward; pulled again; pulled harder, with a jerk, at last the sheath came off; the dagger sprang up; it wounded Clara fatally. Hugo, knowing that they had disagreed, knowing that the servants had heard, and seeing her fall suddenly dead before him, was seized with horror, the Le Geyt impulsiveness!—lost his head; rushed out; fancied the accident would be mistaken for murder. But why? A Q.C., don't you know! Recently married! Most attached to his wife. It is plausible, isn't it?"

"So plausible," I answered, looking it straight in the face, "that... it has but one weak point. We might make a coroner's jury or even a common jury accept it, on Sebastian's expert evidence. Sebastian can work wonders; but we could never make—"

Hilda Wade finished the sentence for me as I paused: "Hugo Le Geyt consent to advance it."

I lowered my head. "You have said it," I answered.

"Not for the children's sake?" Mrs. Mallet cried, with clasped hands.

"Not for the children's sake, even," I answered. "Consider for a moment, Mrs. Mallet: IS it true? Do you yourself BELIEVE it?"

She threw herself back in her chair with a dejected face. "Oh, as for that," she cried, wearily, crossing her hands, "before you and Hilda, who know all, what need to prevaricate? How CAN I believe it? We understand how it came about. That woman! That woman!"

"The real wonder is," Hilda murmured, soothing her white hand, "that he contained himself so long!"

"Well, we all know Hugo," I went on, as quietly as I was able; "and, knowing Hugo, we know that he might be urged to commit this wild act in a fierce moment of indignation, righteous indignation on behalf of his motherless girls, under tremendous provocation. But we also know that, having once committed it, he would never stoop to disown it by a subterfuge."

The heart-broken sister let her head drop faintly. "So Hilda told me," she murmured; "and what Hilda says in these matters is almost always final."

We debated the question for some minutes more. Then Mrs. Mallet cried at last: "At any rate, he has fled for the moment, and his flight alone brings the worst suspicion upon him. That is our chief point. We must find out where he is; and if he has gone right away, we must bring him back to London."

"Where do you think he has taken refuge?"

"The police, Dr. Sebastian has ascertained, are watching the railway stations, and the ports for the Continent."

"Very like the police!" Hilda exclaimed, with more than a touch of contempt in her voice. "As if a clever man-of-the-world like Hugo Le Geyt would run away by rail, or start off to the Continent! Every Englishman is noticeable on the Continent. It would be sheer madness!"

"You think he has not gone there, then?" I cried, deeply interested.

"Of course not. That is the point I hinted at just now. He has defended many persons accused of murder, and he often spoke to me of their incredible folly, when trying to escape, in going by rail, or in setting out from England for Paris. An Englishman, he used to say, is least observed in his own country. In this case, I think I KNOW where he has gone, how he went there."

"Where, then?"

"WHERE comes last; HOW first. It is a question of inference."

"Explain. We know your powers."

"Well, I take it for granted that he killed her, we must not mince matters, about twelve o'clock; for after that hour, the servants told Lina, there was quiet in the drawing-room. Next, I conjecture, he went upstairs to change his clothes: he could not go forth on the world in an evening suit; and the housemaid says his black coat and trousers were lying as usual on a chair in his dressing-room, which shows at least that he was not unduly flurried. After that, he put on another suit, no doubt, WHAT suit I hope the police will not discover too soon; for I suppose you must just accept the situation that we are conspiring to defeat the ends of justice."

"No, no!" Mrs. Mallet cried. "To bring him back voluntarily, that he may face his trial like a man!"

"Yes, dear. That is quite right. However, the next thing, of course, would be that he would shave in whole or in part. His big black beard was so very conspicuous; he would certainly get rid of that before attempting to escape. The servants being in bed, he was not pressed for time; he had the whole night before him. So, of course, he shaved. On the other hand, the police, you may be sure, will circulate his photograph, we must not shirk these points"—for Mrs. Mallet winced again—"will circulate his photograph, BEARD AND ALL; and that will really be one of our great safeguards; for the bushy beard so masks the face that, without it, Hugo would be scarcely recognisable. I conclude, therefore, that he must have shorn himself BEFORE leaving home; though naturally I did not make the police a present of the hint by getting Lina to ask any questions in that direction of the housemaid."

"You are probably right," I answered. "But would he have a razor?"

"I was coming to that. No; certainly he would not. He had not shaved for years. And they kept no men-servants; which makes it difficult for him to borrow one from a sleeping man. So what he would do would doubtless be to cut off his beard, or part of it, quite close, with a pair of scissors, and then get himself properly shaved next morning in the first country town he came to."

"The first country town?"

"Certainly. That leads up to the next point. We must try to be cool and collected." She was quivering with suppressed emotion herself, as she said it, but her soothing hand still lay on Mrs. Mallet's. "The next thing is—he would leave London."

"But not by rail, you say?"

"He is an intelligent man, and in the course of defending others has thought about this matter. Why expose himself to the needless risk and observation of a railway station? No; I saw at once what he would do. Beyond doubt, he would cycle. He always wondered it was not done oftener, under similar circumstances."

"But has his bicycle gone?"

"Lina looked. It has not. I should have expected as much. I told her to note that point very unobtrusively, so as to avoid giving the police the clue. She saw the machine in the outer hall as usual."

"He is too good a criminal lawyer to have dreamt of taking his own," Mrs. Mallet interposed, with another effort.

"But where could he have hired or bought one at that time of night?" I exclaimed.

"Nowhere, without exciting the gravest suspicion. Therefore, I conclude, he stopped in London for the night, sleeping at an hotel, without luggage, and paying for his room in advance. It is frequently done, and if he arrived late, very little notice would be taken of him. Big hotels about the Strand, I am told, have always a dozen such casual bachelor guests every evening."

"And then?"

"And then, this morning, he would buy a new bicycle, a different make from his own, at the nearest shop; would rig himself out, at some ready-made tailor's, with a fresh tourist suit, probably an ostentatiously tweedy bicycling suit; and, with that in his luggage-carrier, would make straight on his machine for the country. He could change in some copse, and bury his own clothes, avoiding the blunders he has seen in others. Perhaps he might ride for the first twenty or thirty miles out of London to some minor side-station, and then go on by train towards his destination, quitting the rail again at some unimportant point where the main west road crosses the Great Western or the South-Western line."

"Great Western or South-Western? Why those two in particular? Then, you have settled in your own mind which direction he has taken?"

"Pretty well. I judge by analogy. Lina, your brother was brought up in the West Country, was he not?"

Mrs. Mallet gave a weary nod. "In North Devon," she answered; "on the wild stretch of moor about Hartland and Clovelly."

Hilda Wade seemed to collect herself. "Now, Mr. Le Geyt is essentially a Celt, a Celt in temperament," she went on; "he comes by origin and ancestry from a rough, heather-clad country; he belongs to the moorland. In other words, his type is the mountaineer's. But a mountaineer's instinct in similar circumstances is—what? Why, to fly straight to his native mountains. In an agony of terror, in an access of despair, when all else fails, he strikes a bee-line for the hills he loves; rationally or irrationally, he seems to think he can hide there. Hugo Le Geyt, with his frank boyish nature, his great Devonian frame, is sure to have done so. I know his mood. He has made for the West Country!"

"You are, right, Hilda," Mrs. Mallet exclaimed, with conviction. "I'm quite sure, from what I know of Hugo, that to go to the West would be his first impulse."

"And the Le Geyts are always governed by first impulses," my character-reader added.

She was quite correct. From the time we two were at Oxford together, I as an undergraduate, he as a don, I had always noticed that marked trait in my dear old friend's temperament.

After a short pause, Hilda broke the silence again. "The sea again; the sea! The Le Geyts love the water. Was there any place on the sea where he went much as a boy, any lonely place, I mean, in that North Devon district?"

Mrs. Mallet reflected a moment. "Yes, there was a little bay, a mere gap in high cliffs, with some fishermen's huts and a few yards of beach, where he used to spend much of his holidays. It was a weird-looking break in a grim sea-wall of dark-red rocks, where the tide rose high, rolling in from the Atlantic."

"The very thing! Has he visited it since he grew up?"

"To my knowledge, never."

Hilda's voice had a ring of certainty. "Then THAT is where we shall find him, dear! We must look there first. He is sure to revisit just such a solitary spot by the sea when trouble overtakes him."

Later in the evening, as we were walking home towards Nathaniel's together, I asked Hilda why she had spoken throughout with such unwavering confidence. "Oh, it was simple enough," she answered. "There were two things that helped me through, which I didn't like to mention in detail before Lina. One was this: the Le Geyts have all of them an instinctive horror of the sight of blood; therefore, they almost never commit suicide by shooting themselves or cutting their throats. Marcus, who shot himself in the gun-room, was an exception to both rules; he never minded blood;

he could cut up a deer. But Hugo refused to be a doctor, because he could not stand the sight of an operation; and even as a sportsman he never liked to pick up or handle the game he had shot himself; he said it sickened him. He rushed from that room last night, I feel sure, in a physical horror at the deed he had done; and by now he is as far as he can get from London. The sight of his act drove him away; not craven fear of an arrest. If the Le Geyts kill themselves, a seafaring race on the whole, their impulse is to trust to water."

"And the other thing?"

"Well, that was about the mountaineer's homing instinct. I have often noticed it. I could give you fifty instances, only I didn't like to speak of them before Lina. There was Williams, for example, the Dolgelly man who killed a game-keeper at Petworth in a poaching affray; he was taken on Cader Idris, skulking among rocks, a week later. Then there was that unhappy young fellow, Mackinnon, who shot his sweetheart at Leicester; he made, straight as the crow flies, for his home in the Isle of Skye, and there drowned himself in familiar waters. Lindner, the Tyrolese, again, who stabbed the American swindler at Monte Carlo, was tracked after a few days to his native place, St. Valentin, in the Zillerthal. It is always so. Mountaineers in distress fly to their mountains. It is a part of their nostalgia. I know it from within, too: if I were in poor Hugo LeGeyt's place, what do you think I would do? Why, hide myself at once in the greenest recesses of our Carnarvonshire mountains."

"What an extraordinary insight into character you have!" I cried. "You seem to divine what everybody's action will be under given circumstances."

She paused, and held her parasol half poised in her hand. "Character determines action," she said, slowly, at last. "That is the secret of the great novelists. They put themselves behind and within their characters, and so make us feel that every act of their personages is not only natural but even, given the conditions, inevitable. We recognise that their story is the sole logical outcome of the interaction of their dramatis personae. Now, I am not a great novelist; I cannot create and imagine characters and situations. But I have something of the novelist's gift; I apply the same method to the real life of the people around me. I try to throw myself into the person of others, and to feel how their character will compel them to act in each set of circumstances to which they may expose themselves."

"In one word," I said, "you are a psychologist."

"A psychologist," she assented; "I suppose so; and the police, well, the police are not; they are at best but bungling materialists. They require a CLUE. What need of a CLUE if you can interpret character?"

So certain was Hilda Wade of her conclusions, indeed, that Mrs. Mallet begged me next day to take my holiday at once, which I could easily do, and go down to the little bay in the Hartland district of which she had spoken, in search of Hugo. I consented. She herself proposed to set out quietly for Bideford, where she could be within easy reach of me, in order to hear of my success or failure; while Hilda Wade, whose summer vacation was to have begun in two days' time, offered to ask for an extra day's leave so as to accompany her. The broken-hearted sister accepted the offer; and, secrecy being above all things necessary, we set off by different routes: the two women by Waterloo, myself by Paddington.

We stopped that night at different hotels in Bideford; but next morning, Hilda rode out on her bicycle, and accompanied me on mine for a mile or two along the tortuous way towards Hartland. "Take nothing for granted," she said, as we parted; "and be prepared to find poor Hugo Le Geyt's appearance greatly changed. He has eluded the police and their 'clues' so far; therefore, I imagine he must have largely altered his dress and exterior."

"I will find him," I answered, "if he is anywhere within twenty miles of Hartland."

She waved her hand to me in farewell. I rode on after she left me towards the high promontory in front, the wildest and least-visited part of North Devon. Torrents of rain had fallen during the night; the slimy cart-ruts and cattle-tracks on the moor were brimming with water. It was a lowering day. The clouds drifted low. Black peat-bogs filled the hollows; grey stone homesteads, lonely and forbidding, stood out here and there against the curved sky-line. Even the high road was uneven and in places flooded. For an hour I passed hardly a soul. At last, near a crossroad with a defaced finger-post, I descended from my machine, and consulted my ordnance map, on which Mrs. Mallet had marked ominously, with a cross of red rink, the exact position of the little fishing hamlet where Hugo used to spend his holidays. I took the turning which seemed to me most likely to lead to it; but the tracks were so confused, and the run of the lanes so uncertain, let alone the map being some years out of date, that I soon felt I had lost my bearings. By a little wayside inn, half hidden in a deep combe, with bog on every side, I descended and asked for a bottle of ginger-beer; for the day was hot and close, in spite of the packed clouds. As they were opening the bottle, I inquired casually the way to the Red Gap bathing-place.

The landlord gave me directions which confused me worse than ever, ending at last with the concise remark: "An' then, zur, two or dree more turns to the right an' to the left 'ull bring 'ee right up alongzide o' ut."

I despaired of finding the way by these unintelligible sailing-orders; but just at that moment, as luck would have it, another cyclist flew past, the first soul I had seen on the road that morning. He was a man with the loose-knit air of a shop assistant, badly got up in a rather loud and obtrusive tourist suit of brown homespun, with baggy knickerbockers and thin thread stockings. I judged him a gentleman on the cheap at sight. "Very Stylish; this Suit Complete, only thirty-seven and sixpence!" The landlady glanced out at him with a friendly nod. He turned and smiled at her, but did not see me; for I stood in the shade behind the half-open door. He had a short black moustache and a not unpleasing, careless face. His features, I thought, were better than his garments.

However, the stranger did not interest me just then I was far too full of more important matters. "Why don't 'ee taake an' vollow thik ther gen'leman, zur?" the landlady said, pointing one large red hand after him. "Ur do go down to Urd Gap to zwim every mornin'. Mr. Jan Smith, o' Oxford, they do call un. 'Ee can't go wrong if 'ee do vollow un to the Gap. Ur's lodgin' up to wold Varmer Moore's, an' ur's that vond o' the zay, the vishermen do tell me, as wasn't never any gen'leman like un."

I tossed off my ginger-beer, jumped on to my machine, and followed the retreating brown back of Mr. John Smith, of Oxford, surely a most non-committing name, round sharp corners and over rutty lanes, tire-deep in mud, across the rusty-red moor, till, all at once, at a turn, a gap of stormy sea appeared wedge-shape between two shelving rock-walls.

It was a lonely spot. Rocks hemmed it in; big breakers walled it. The sou'-wester roared through the gap. I rode down among loose stones and water-worn channels in the solid grit very carefully. But the man in brown had torn over the wild path with reckless haste, zigzagging madly, and was now on the little three-cornered patch of beach, undressing himself with a sort of careless glee, and flinging his clothes down anyhow on the shingle beside him. Something about the action caught my eye. That movement of the arm! It was not, it could not be, no, no, not Hugo!

A very ordinary person; and Le Geyt bore the stamp of a born gentleman.

He stood up bare at last. He flung out his arms, as if to welcome the boisterous wind to his naked bosom. Then, with a sudden burst of recognition, the man stood revealed. We had bathed together a hundred times in London and elsewhere. The face, the clad figure, the dress, all were different. But the body, the actual frame and make of the man, the well-knit limbs, the splendid trunk, no disguise could alter. It was Le Geyt himself, big, powerful, vigorous.

That ill-made suit, those baggy knickerbockers, the slouched cap, the thin thread stockings, had only distorted and hidden his figure. Now that I saw him as he was, he came out the same bold and manly form as ever.

He did not notice me. He rushed down with a certain wild joy into the turbulent water, and, plunging in with a loud cry, buffeted the huge waves with those strong curving arms of his. The sou'-wester was rising. Each breaker as it reared caught him on its crest and tumbled him over like a cork, but like a cork he rose again. He was swimming now, arm over arm, straight out seaward. I saw the lifted hands between the crest and the trough. For a moment I hesitated whether I ought to strip and follow him. Was he doing as so many others of his house had done, courting death from the water?

But some strange hand restrained me. Who was I that I should stand between Hugo Le Geyt and the ways of Providence?

The Le Geyts loved ever the ordeal by water.

Presently, he turned again. Before he turned, I had taken the opportunity to look hastily at his clothes. Hilda Wade had surmised aright once more. The outer suit was a cheap affair from a big ready-made tailor's in St. Martin's Lane, turned out by the thousand; the underclothing, on the other hand, was new and unmarked, but fine in quality, bought, no doubt, at Bideford. An eerie sense of doom stole over me. I felt the end was near. I withdrew behind a big rock, and waited there unseen till Hugo had landed. He began to dress again, without troubling to dry himself. I drew a deep breath of relief. Then this was not suicide!

By the time he had pulled on his vest and drawers, I came out suddenly from my ambush and faced him. A fresh shock awaited me. I could hardly believe my eyes. It was NOT Le Geyt, no, nor anything like him!

Nevertheless, the man rose with a little cry and advanced, half crouching, towards me. "YOU are not hunting me down, with the police?" he exclaimed, his neck held low and his forehead wrinkling.

The voice, the voice was Le Geyt's. It was an unspeakable mystery. "Hugo," I cried, "dear Hugo—hunting you down?—COULD you imagine it?"

He raised his head, strode forward, and grasped my hand. "Forgive me, Cumberledge," he cried. "But a proscribed and hounded man! If you knew what a relief it is to me to get out on the water!"

"You forget all there?"

"I forget IT—the red horror!"

"You meant just now to drown yourself?"

"No! If I had meant it I would have done it.... Hubert, for my children's sake, I WILL not commit suicide!"

"Then listen!" I cried. I told him in a few words of his sister's scheme, Sebastian's defence, the plausibility of the explanation, the whole long story. He gazed at me moodily. Yet it was not Hugo!

"No, no," he said, shortly; and as he spoke it was HE. "I have done it; I have killed her; I will not owe my life to a falsehood."

"Not for the children's sake?"

He dashed his hand down impatiently. "I have a better way for the children. I will save them still.... Hubert, you are not afraid to speak to a murderer?"

"Dear Hugo, I know all; and to know all is to forgive all."

He grasped my hand once more. "Know ALL!" he cried, with a despairing gesture. "Oh, no; no one knows ALL but myself; not even the children. But the children know much; THEY will forgive me. Lina knows something; SHE will forgive me. You know a little; YOU forgive me. The world can never know. It will brand my darlings as a murderer's children."

"It was the act of a minute," I interposed. "And, though she is dead, poor lady, and one must speak no ill of her, we can at least gather dimly, for your children's sake, how deep was the provocation."

He gazed at me fixedly. His voice was like lead. "For the children's sake—yes," he answered, as in a dream. "It was all for the children! I have killed her, murdered her, she has paid her penalty; and, poor dead soul, I will utter no word against her, the woman I have murdered! But one thing I will say: If omniscient justice sends me for this to eternal punishment, I can endure it gladly, like a man, knowing that so I have redeemed my Marian's motherless girls from a deadly tyranny."

It was the only sentence in which he ever alluded to her.

I sat down by his side and watched him closely. Mechanically, methodically, he went on with his dressing. The more he dressed, the less could I believe it was Hugo. I had expected to find him close-shaven; so did the police, by their printed notices. Instead of that, he had shaved his beard and whiskers, but only trimmed his moustache; trimmed it quite short, so as to reveal the boyish corners of the mouth, a trick which entirely altered his rugged expression. But that was not all; what puzzled me most was the eyes, they were not Hugo's. At first I could not imagine why. By degrees the truth dawned upon me. His eyebrows were naturally thick and shaggy, great overhanging growth, interspersed with many of those stiff long hairs to which Darwin called attention in certain men as surviving traits from a monkey-like ancestor. In order to disguise himself, Hugo had pulled out all these coarser hairs, leaving nothing on his brows but the soft and closely pressed coat of down which underlies the longer bristles in all such cases. This had wholly altered the expression of the eyes, which no longer looked out keenly from their cavernous penthouse; but being deprived of their relief, had acquired a much more ordinary and less individual aspect. From a good-natured but shaggy giant, my old friend was transformed by his shaving and his costume into a well-fed and well-grown, but not very colossal, commercial gentleman. Hugo was scarcely six feet high, indeed, though by his broad shoulders and bushy beard he had always impressed one with such a sense of size; and now that the hirsuteness had been got rid of, and the dress altered, he hardly struck one as taller or bigger than the average of his fellows.

We sat for some minutes and talked. Le Geyt would not speak of Clara; and when I asked him his intentions, he shook his head moodily. "I shall act for the best," he said—"what of best is left—to guard the dear children. It was a terrible price to pay for their redemption; but it was the only one possible, and, in a moment of wrath, I paid it. Now, I have to pay, in turn, myself. I do not shirk it."

"You will come back to London, then, and stand your trial?" I asked, eagerly.

"Come back TO LONDON?" he cried, with a face of white panic. Hitherto he had seemed to me rather relieved in expression than otherwise; his countenance had lost its worn and anxious look; he was no longer watching each moment over his children's safety. "Come back... TO LONDON... and face my trial! Why, did you think, Hubert, 'twas the court or the hanging I was shirking? No, no; not that; but IT—the red horror! I must get away from IT to the sea, to the water, to wash away the stain, as far from IT, that red pool, as possible!"

I answered nothing. I left him to face his own remorse in silence.

At last he rose to go, and held one foot undecided on his bicycle.

"I leave myself in Heaven's hands," he said, as he lingered. "IT will requite.... The ordeal is by water."

"So I judged," I answered.

"Tell Lina this from me," he went on, still loitering: "that if she will trust me, I will strive to do the best that remains for my darlings. I will do it, Heaven helping. She will know WHAT, to-morrow."

He mounted his machine and sailed off. My eyes followed him up the path with sad forebodings.

All day long I loitered about the Gap. It consisted of two bays, the one I had already seen, and another, divided from it by a saw-edge of rock. In the further cove crouched a few low stone cottages. A broad-bottomed sailing boat lay there, pulled up high on the beach. About three o'clock, as I sat and watched, two men began to launch it. The sea ran high; tide coming in; the sou'-wester still increasing in force to a gale; at the signal-staff on the cliff, the danger-cone was hoisted. White spray danced in air. Big black clouds rolled up seething from windward; low thunder rumbling; a storm threatened.

One of the men was Le Geyt, the other a fisherman.

He jumped in, and put off through the surf with an air of triumph. He was a splendid sailor. His boat leapt through the breakers and flew before the wind with a mere rag of canvas. "Dangerous weather to be out!" I exclaimed to the fisherman, who stood with hands buried in his pockets, watching him.

"Ay that ur be, zur!" the man answered. "Doan't like the look o' ut. But thik there gen'leman, 'ee's one o' Oxford, 'ee do tell me; and they'm a main venturesome lot, they college volk. 'Ee's off by 'isself droo the starm, all so var as Lundy!"

"Will he reach it?" I asked, anxiously, having my own idea on the subject.

"Doan't seem like ut, zur, do ut? Ur must, an' ur mustn't, an' yit again ur must. Powerful 'ard place ur be to maake in a starm, to be zure, Lundy. Zaid the Lord 'ould dezide. But ur 'ouldn't be warned, ur 'ouldn't; an' voolhardy volk, as the zayin' is, must go their own voolhardy waay to perdition!"

It was the last I saw of Le Geyt alive. Next morning the lifeless body of "the man who was wanted for the Campden Hill mystery" was cast up by the waves on the shore of Lundy. The Lord had decided.

Hugo had not miscalculated. "Luck in their suicides," Hilda Wade said; and, strange to say, the luck of the Le Geyts stood him in good stead still. By a miracle of fate, his children were not branded as a murderer's daughters. Sebastian gave evidence at the inquest on the wife's body: "Self-inflicted, a recoil, accidental, I am SURE of it." His specialist knowledge, his assertive certainty, combined with that arrogant, masterful manner of his, and his keen, eagle eye, overbore the jury. Awed by the great man's look, they brought in a submissive verdict of "Death by misadventure." The coroner thought it a most proper finding. Mrs. Mallet had made the most of the innate Le Geyt horror of blood. The newspapers charitably surmised that the unhappy husband, crazed by the instantaneous unexpectedness of his loss, had wandered away like a madman to the scenes of his childhood, and had there been drowned by accident while trying to cross a stormy sea to Lundy, under some wild impression that he would find his dead wife alive on the island. Nobody whispered MURDER. Everybody dwelt on the utter absence of motive, a model husband!—such a charming young wife, and such a devoted stepmother. We three alone knew—we three, and the children.

On the day when the jury brought in their verdict at the adjourned inquest on Mrs. Le Geyt, Hilda Wade stood in the room, trembling and white-faced, awaiting their decision. When the foreman uttered the words, "Death by misadventure," she burst into tears of relief. "He did well!" she cried to me, passionately. "He did well, that poor father! He placed his life in the hands of his Maker, asking only for mercy to his innocent children. And mercy has been shown to him and to them. He was taken gently in the way he wished. It would have broken my heart for those two poor girls if the verdict had gone otherwise. He knew how terrible a lot it is to be called a murderer's daughter."

I did not realise at the time with what profound depth of personal feeling she said it.

CHAPTER V

THE EPISODE OF THE NEEDLE THAT DID NOT MATCH

"Sebastian is a great man," I said to Hilda Wade, as I sat one afternoon over a cup of tea she had brewed for me in her own little sitting-room. It is one of the alleviations of an hospital doctor's lot that he may drink tea now and again with the Sister of his ward. "Whatever else you choose to think of him, you must admit he is a very great man."

I admired our famous Professor, and I admired Hilda Wade: 'twas a matter of regret to me that my two admirations did not seem in return sufficiently to admire one another. "Oh, yes," Hilda answered, pouring out my second cup; "he is a very great man. I never denied that. The greatest man, on the whole, I think, that I have ever come across."

"And he has done splendid work for humanity," I went on, growing enthusiastic.

"Splendid work! Yes, splendid! (Two lumps, I believe?) He has done more, I admit, for medical science than any other man I ever met."

I gazed at her with a curious glance. "Then why, dear lady, do you keep telling me he is cruel?" I inquired, toasting my feet on the fender. "It seems contradictory."

She passed me the muffins, and smiled her restrained smile.

"Does the desire to do good to humanity in itself imply a benevolent disposition?" she answered, obliquely.

"Now you are talking in paradox. Surely, if a man works all his life long for the good of mankind, that shows he is devoured by sympathy for his species."

"And when your friend Mr. Bates works all his life long at observing, and classifying lady-birds, I suppose that shows he is devoured by sympathy for the race of beetles!"

I laughed at her comical face, she looked at me so quizzically. "But then," I objected, "the cases are not parallel. Bates kills and collects his lady-birds; Sebastian cures and benefits humanity."

Hilda smiled her wise smile once more, and fingered her apron. "Are the cases so different as you suppose?" she went on, with her quick glance. "Is it not partly accident? A man of science, you see, early in life, takes up, half by chance, this, that, or the other particular form of study. But what the study is in itself, I fancy, does not greatly matter; do not mere circumstances as often as not determine it? Surely it is the temperament, on the whole, that tells: the temperament that is or is not scientific."

"How do you mean? You ARE so enigmatic!"

"Well, in a family of the scientific temperament, it seems to me, one brother may happen to go in for butterflies—may he not?—and another for geology, or for submarine telegraphs. Now, the man who happens to take up butterflies does not make a fortune out of his hobby, there is no money in butterflies; so we say, accordingly, he is an unpractical person, who cares nothing for business, and who is only happy when he is out in the fields with a net, chasing emperors and tortoise-shells. But the man who happens to fancy submarine telegraphy most likely invents a lot of new improvements, takes out dozens of patents, finds money flow in upon him as he sits in his study, and becomes at last a peer and a millionaire; so then we say, What a splendid business head he has got, to be sure, and how immensely he differs from his poor wool-gathering brother, the entomologist, who can only invent new ways of hatching out wire-worms! Yet all may really depend on the first chance direction which led one brother as a boy to buy a butterfly net, and sent the other into the school laboratory to dabble with an electric wheel and a cheap battery."

"Then you mean to say it is chance that has made Sebastian?"

Hilda shook her pretty head. "By no means. Don't be so stupid. We both know Sebastian has a wonderful brain. Whatever was the work he undertook with that brain in science, he would carry it out consummately. He is a born thinker. It is like this, don't you know." She tried to arrange her thoughts. "The particular branch of science to which Mr. Hiram Maxim's mind happens to have been directed was the making of machine-guns, and he slays his thousands. The particular branch to which Sebastian's mind happens to have been directed was medicine, and he cures as many as Mr. Maxim kills. It is a turn of the hand that makes all the difference."

"I see," I said. "The aim of medicine happens to be a benevolent one."

"Quite so; that's just what I mean. The aim is benevolent; and Sebastian pursues that aim with the single-minded energy of a lofty, gifted, and devoted nature, but not a good one!'

"Not good?"

"Oh, no. To be quite frank, he seems to me to pursue it ruthlessly, cruelly, unscrupulously. He is a man of high ideals, but without principle. In that respect he reminds one of the great spirits of the Italian Renaissance, Benvenuto Cellini and so forth, men who could pore for hours with conscientious artistic care over the detail of a hem in a sculptured robe, yet could steal out in the midst of their disinterested toil to plunge a knife in the back of a rival."

"Sebastian would not do that," I cried. "He is wholly free from the mean spirit of jealousy."

"No, Sebastian would not do that. You are quite right there; there is no tinge of meanness in the man's nature. He likes to be first in the field; but he would acclaim with delight another man's scientific triumph, if another anticipated him; for would it not mean a triumph for universal science?—and is not the advancement of science Sebastian's religion? But... he would do almost as much, or more. He would stab a man without remorse, if he thought that by stabbing him he could advance knowledge."

I recognised at once the truth of her diagnosis. "Nurse Wade," I cried, "you are a wonderful woman! I believe you are right; but—how did you come to think of it?"

A cloud passed over her brow. "I have reason to know it," she answered, slowly. Then her voice changed. "Take another muffin."

I helped myself and paused. I laid down my cup, and gazed at her. What a beautiful, tender, sympathetic face! And yet, how able! She stirred the fire uneasily. I looked and hesitated. I had often wondered why I never dared ask Hilda Wade one question that was nearest my heart. I think it must have been because I respected her so profoundly. The deeper your admiration and respect for a woman, the harder you find it in the end to ask her. At last I ALMOST made up my mind. "I cannot think," I began, "what can have induced a girl like you, with means and friends, with brains and"—I drew back, then I plumped it out—"beauty, to take to such a life as this, a life which seems, in many ways, so unworthy of you!"

She stirred the fire more pensively than ever, and rearranged the muffin-dish on the little wrought-iron stand in font of the grate. "And yet," she murmured, looking down, "what life can be better than the service of one's kind? You think it a great life for Sebastian!"

"Sebastian! He is a man. That is different; quite different. But a woman! Especially YOU, dear lady, for whom one feels that nothing is quite high enough, quite pure enough, quite good enough. I cannot imagine how—"

She checked me with one wave of her gracious hand. Her movements were always slow and dignified. "I have a Plan in my life," she answered earnestly, her eyes meeting mine with a sincere, frank gaze; "a Plan to which I have resolved to sacrifice everything. It absorbs my being. Till that Plan is fulfilled—" I saw the tears were gathering fast on her lashes. She suppressed them with an effort. "Say no more," she added, faltering. "Infirm of purpose! I WILL not listen."

I leant forward eagerly, pressing my advantage. The air was electric. Waves of emotion passed to and fro. "But surely," I cried, "you do not mean to say—"

She waved me aside once more. "I will not put my hand to the plough, and then look back," she answered, firmly. "Dr. Cumberledge, spare me. I came to Nathaniel's for a purpose. I told you at the time what that purpose was—in part: to be near Sebastian. I want to be near him... for an object I have at heart. Do not ask me to reveal it; do not ask me to forego it. I am a woman, therefore weak. But I need your aid. Help me, instead of hindering me."

"Hilda," I cried, leaning forward, with quiverings of my heart, "I will help you in whatever way you will allow me. But let me at any rate help you with the feeling that I am helping one who means in time—"

At that moment, as unkindly fate would have it, the door opened, and Sebastian entered.

"Nurse Wade," he began, in his iron voice, glancing about him with stern eyes, "where are those needles I ordered for that operation? We must be ready in time before Nielsen comes.... Cumberledge, I shall want you."

The golden opportunity had come and gone. It was long before I found a similar occasion for speaking to Hilda.

Every day after that the feeling deepened upon me that Hilda was there to watch Sebastian. WHY, I did not know; but it was growing certain that a life-long duel was in progress between these two, a duel of some strange and mysterious import.

The first approach to a solution of the problem which I obtained came a week or two later. Sebastian was engaged in observing a case where certain unusual symptoms had suddenly supervened. It was a case of some obscure affection of the heart. I will not trouble you here with the particular details. We all suspected a tendency to aneurism. Hilda Wade was in attendance, as she always was on Sebastian's observation cases. We crowded round, watching. The Professor himself leaned over the cot with some medicine for external application in a basin. He gave it to Hilda to hold. I noticed that as she held it her fingers trembled, and that her eyes were fixed harder than ever upon Sebastian. He turned round to his students. "Now this," he began, in a very unconcerned voice, as if the patient were a toad, "is a most unwonted turn for the disease to take. It occurs very seldom. In point of fact, I have only observed the symptom once before; and then it was fatal. The patient in that instance"—he paused dramatically—"was the notorious poisoner, Dr. Yorke-Bannerman."

As he uttered the words, Hilda Wade's hands trembled more than ever, and with a little scream she let the basin fall, breaking it into fragments.

Sebastian's keen eyes had transfixed her in a second. "How did you manage to do that?" he asked, with quiet sarcasm, but in a tone full of meaning.

"The basin was heavy," Hilda faltered. "My hands were trembling, and it somehow slipped through them. I am not... quite myself... not quite well this afternoon. I ought not to have attempted it."

The Professor's deep-set eyes peered out like gleaming lights from beneath their overhanging brows. "No; you ought not to have attempted it," he answered, withering her with a glance. "You might have let the thing fall on the patient and killed him. As it is, can't you see you have agitated him with the flurry? Don't stand there holding your breath, woman: repair your mischief. Get a cloth and wipe it up, and give ME the bottle."

With skilful haste he administered a little sal volatile and nux vomica to the swooning patient; while Hilda set about remedying the damage. "That's better," Sebastian said, in a mollified tone, when she had brought another basin. There was a singular note of cloaked triumph in his voice. "Now, we'll begin again.... I was just saying, gentlemen, before this accident, that I had seen only ONE case of this peculiar form of the tendency before; and that case was the notorious"—he kept his glittering eyes fixed harder on Hilda than ever—"the notorious Dr. Yorke-Bannerman."

I was watching Hilda, too. At the words, she trembled violently all over once more, but with an effort restrained herself. Their looks met in a searching glance. Hilda's air was proud and fearless: in Sebastian's, I fancied I detected, after a second, just a tinge of wavering.

"You remember Yorke-Bannerman's case," he went on. "He committed a murder—"

"Let ME take the basin!" I cried, for I saw Hilda's hands giving way a second time, and I was anxious to spare her.

"No, thank you," she answered low, but in a voice that was full of suppressed defiance. "I will wait and hear this out. I PREFER to stop here."

As for Sebastian, he seemed now not to notice her, though I was aware all the time of a sidelong glance of his eye, parrot-wise, in her direction. "He committed a murder," he went on, "by means of aconitine, then an almost unknown poison; and, after committing it, his heart being already weak, he was taken himself with symptoms of aneurism in a curious form, essentially similar to these; so that he died before the trial, a lucky escape for him."

He paused rhetorically once more; then he added in the same tone: "Mental agitation and the terror of detection no doubt accelerated the fatal result in that instance. He died at once from the shock of the arrest. It was a natural conclusion. Here we may hope for a more successful issue."

He spoke to the students, of course, but I could see for all that that he was keeping his falcon eye fixed hard on Hilda's face. I glanced aside at her. She never flinched for a second. Neither said anything directly to the other; still, by their eyes and mouths, I knew some strange passage of arms had taken place between them. Sebastian's tone was one of provocation, of defiance, I might almost say of challenge. Hilda's air I took rather for the air of calm and resolute, but assured, resistance. He expected her to answer; she said nothing. Instead of that, she went on holding the basin now with fingers that WOULD not tremble. Every muscle was strained. Every tendon was strung. I could see she held herself in with a will of iron.

The rest of the episode passed off quietly. Sebastian, having delivered his bolt, began to think less of Hilda and more of the patient. He went on with his demonstration. As for Hilda, she gradually relaxed her muscles, and, with a deep-drawn breath, resumed her natural attitude. The tension was over. They had had their little skirmish, whatever it might mean, and had it out; now, they called a truce over the patient's body.

When the case had been disposed of, and the students dismissed, I went straight into the laboratory to get a few surgical instruments I had chanced to leave there. For a minute or two, I mislaid my clinical thermometer, and began hunting for it behind a wooden partition in the corner of the room by the place for washing test-tubes. As I stooped down, turning over the various objects about the tap in my search, Sebastian's voice came to me. He had paused outside the door, and was speaking in his calm, clear tone, very low, to Hilda. "So NOW we understand one another, Nurse Wade," he said, with a significant sneer. "I know whom I have to deal with!"

"And I know, too," Hilda answered, in a voice of placid confidence.

"Yet you are not afraid?"

"It is not I who have cause for fear. The accused may tremble, not the prosecutor."

"What! You threaten?"

"No; I do not threaten. Not in words, I mean. My presence here is in itself a threat, but I make no other. You know now, unfortunately, WHY I have come. That makes my task harder. But I will NOT give it up. I will wait and conquer."

Sebastian answered nothing. He strode into the laboratory alone, tall, grim, unbending, and let himself sink into his easy chair, looking up with a singular and somewhat sinister smile at his bottles of microbes. After a minute he stirred the fire, and bent his head forward, brooding. He held it between his hands, with his elbows on his knees, and gazed moodily straight before him into the glowing caves of white-hot coal in the fireplace. That sinister smile still played lambent around the corners of his grizzled moustaches.

I moved noiselessly towards the door, trying to pass behind him unnoticed. But, alert as ever, his quick ears detected me. With a sudden start, he raised his head and glanced round. "What! you here?" he cried, taken aback. For a second he appeared almost to lose his self-possession.

"I came for my clinical," I answered, with an unconcerned air. "I have somehow managed to mislay it in the laboratory."

My carefully casual tone seemed to reassure him. He peered about him with knit brows. "Cumberledge," he asked at last, in a suspicious voice, "did you hear that woman?"

"The woman in 93? Delirious?"

"No, no. Nurse Wade?"

"Hear her?" I echoed, I must candidly admit with intent to deceive. "When she broke the basin?"

His forehead relaxed. "Oh! it is nothing," he muttered, hastily. "A mere point of discipline. She spoke to me just now, and I thought her tone unbecoming in a subordinate.... Like Korah and his crew, she takes too much upon her.... We must get rid of her, Cumberledge; we must get rid of her. She is a dangerous woman!"

"She is the most intelligent nurse we have ever had in the place, sir," I objected, stoutly.

He nodded his head twice. "Intelligent, je vous l'accorde; but dangerous, dangerous!"

Then he turned to his papers, sorting them out one by one with a preoccupied face and twitching fingers. I recognised that he desired to be left alone, so I quitted the laboratory.

I cannot quite say WHY, but ever since Hilda Wade first came to Nathaniel's my enthusiasm for Sebastian had been cooling continuously. Admiring his greatness still, I had doubts as to his goodness. That day I felt I positively mistrusted him. I wondered what his passage of arms with Hilda might mean. Yet, somehow, I was shy of alluding to it before her.

One thing, however, was clear to me now, this great campaign that was being waged between the nurse and the Professor had reference to the case of Dr. Yorke-Bannerman.

For a time, nothing came of it; the routine of the hospital went on as usual. The patient with the suspected predisposition to aneurism kept fairly well for a week or two, and then took a sudden turn for the worse, presenting at times most unwonted symptoms. He died unexpectedly. Sebastian, who had watched him every hour, regarded the matter as of prime importance. "I'm glad it happened here," he said, rubbing his hands. "A grand opportunity. I wanted to catch an instance like this before that fellow in Paris had time to anticipate me. They're all on the lookout. Von Strahlendorff, of Vienna, has been waiting for just such a patient for years. So have I. Now fortune has favoured me. Lucky for us he died! We shall find out everything."

We held a post-mortem, of course, the condition of the blood being what we most wished to observe; and the autopsy revealed some unexpected details. One remarkable feature consisted in a certain undescribed and impoverished state of the contained bodies which Sebastian, with his eager zeal for science, desired his students to see and identify. He said it was likely to throw much light on other ill-understood conditions of the brain and nervous system, as well as on the peculiar faint odour of the insane, now so well recognised in all large asylums. In order to compare this abnormal state with the aspect of the healthy circulating medium, he proposed to examine a little good living blood side by side with the morbid specimen under the microscope. Nurse Wade was in attendance in the laboratory, as usual. The Professor, standing by the instrument, with one hand on the brass screw, had got the diseased drop ready arranged for our inspection beforehand, and was gloating over it himself with scientific enthusiasm. "Grey corpuscles, you will observe," he said, "almost entirely deficient. Red, poor in number, and irregular in outline. Plasma, thin. Nuclei, feeble. A state of body which tells severely against the due rebuilding of the wasted tissues. Now compare with typical normal specimen." He removed his eye from the microscope, and wiped a glass slide with a clean cloth as he spoke. "Nurse Wade, we know of old the purity and vigour of your circulating fluid. You shall have the honour of advancing science once more. Hold up your finger."

Hilda held up her forefinger unhesitatingly. She was used to such requests; and, indeed, Sebastian had acquired by long experience the faculty of pinching the finger-tip so hard, and pressing the point of a needle so dexterously into a minor vessel, that he could draw at once a small drop of blood without the subject even feeling it.

The Professor nipped the last joint between his finger and thumb for a moment till it was black at the end; then he turned to the saucer at his side, which Hilda herself had placed there, and chose from it, cat-like, with great deliberation and selective care, a particular needle. Hilda's eyes followed his every movement as closely and as fearlessly as ever. Sebastian's hand was raised, and he was just about to pierce the delicate white skin, when, with a sudden, quick scream of terror, she snatched her hand away hastily.

The Professor let the needle drop in his astonishment. "What did you do that for?" he cried, with an angry dart of the keen eyes. "This is not the first time I have drawn your blood. You KNEW I would not hurt you."

Hilda's face had grown strangely pale. But that was not all. I believe I was the only person present who noticed one unobtrusive piece of sleight-of-hand which she hurriedly and skilfully executed. When the needle slipped from Sebastian's hand, she leant forward even as she screamed, and caught it, unobserved, in the folds of her apron. Then her nimble fingers closed over it as if by magic, and conveyed it with a rapid movement at once to her pocket. I do not think even Sebastian himself noticed the quick forward jerk of her eager hands, which would have done honour to a conjurer. He was too much taken aback by her unexpected behaviour to observe the needle.

Just as she caught it, Hilda answered his question in a somewhat flurried voice. "I—I was afraid," she broke out, gasping. "One gets these little accesses of terror now and again. I—I feel rather weak. I don't think I will volunteer to supply any more normal blood this morning."

Sebastian's acute eyes read her through, as so often. With a trenchant dart he glanced from her to me. I could see he began to suspect a confederacy. "That will do," he went on, with slow deliberateness. "Better so. Nurse Wade, I don't know what's beginning to come over you. You are losing your nerve—which is fatal in a nurse. Only the other day you let fall and broke a basin at a most critical moment; and now, you scream aloud on a trifling apprehension." He paused and glanced around him. "Mr. Callaghan," he said, turning to our tall, red-haired Irish student, "YOUR blood is good normal, and YOU are not hysterical." He selected another needle with studious care. "Give me your finger."

As he picked out the needle, I saw Hilda lean forward again, alert and watchful, eyeing him with a piercing glance; but, after a second's consideration, she seemed to satisfy herself, and fell back without a word. I gathered that she was ready to interfere, had occasion demanded. But occasion did not demand; and she held her peace quietly.

The rest of the examination proceeded without a hitch. For a minute or two, it is true, I fancied that Sebastian betrayed a certain suppressed agitation, a trifling lack of his accustomed perspicuity and his luminous exposition. But, after meandering for a while through a few vague sentences, he soon recovered his wonted calm; and as he went on with his demonstration, throwing himself eagerly into the case, his usual scientific enthusiasm came back to him undiminished. He waxed eloquent (after his fashion) over the "beautiful" contrast between Callaghan's wholesome blood, "rich in the vivifying architectonic grey corpuscles which rebuild worn tissues," and the effete, impoverished, unvitalised fluid which stagnated in the sluggish veins of the dead patient. The carriers of oxygen had neglected their proper task; the granules whose duty it was to bring elaborated food-stuffs to supply the waste of brain and nerve and muscle had forgotten their cunning. The bricklayers of the bodily fabric had gone out on strike; the weary scavengers had declined to remove the useless by-products. His vivid tongue, his picturesque fancy, ran away with him. I had never heard him talk better or more incisively before; one could feel sure, as he spoke, that the arteries of his own acute and teeming brain at that moment of exaltation were by no means deficient in those energetic and highly vital globules on whose reparative worth he so eloquently descanted. "Sure, the Professor makes annywan see right inside wan's own vascular system," Callaghan whispered aside to me, in unfeigned admiration.

The demonstration ended in impressive silence. As we streamed out of the laboratory, aglow with his electric fire, Sebastian held me back with a bent motion of his shrivelled forefinger. I stayed behind unwillingly. "Yes, sir?" I said, in an interrogative voice.

The Professor's eyes were fixed intently on the ceiling. His look was one of rapt inspiration. I stood and waited. "Cumberledge," he said at last, coming back to earth with a start, "I see it more plainly each day that goes. We must get rid of that woman."

"Of Nurse Wade?" I asked, catching my breath.

He roped the grizzled moustache, and blinked the sunken eyes. "She has lost nerve," he went on, "lost nerve entirely. I shall suggest that she be dismissed. Her sudden failures of stamina are most embarrassing at critical junctures."

"Very well, sir," I answered, swallowing a lump in my throat. To say the truth, I was beginning to be afraid on Hilda's account. That morning's events had thoroughly disquieted me.

He seemed relieved at my unquestioning acquiescence. "She is a dangerous edged-tool; that's the truth of it," he went on, still twirling his moustache with a preoccupied air, and turning over his stock of needles. "When she's clothed and in her right mind, she is a valuable accessory, sharp and trenchant like a clean, bright lancet; but when she allows one of these causeless hysterical fits to override her tone, she plays one false at once, like a lancet that slips, or grows dull and rusty." He polished one of the needles on a soft square of new chamois-leather while he spoke, as if to give point and illustration to his simile.

I went out from him, much perturbed. The Sebastian I had once admired and worshipped was beginning to pass from me; in his place I found a very complex and inferior creation. My idol had feet of clay. I was loth to acknowledge it.

I stalked along the corridor moodily towards my own room. As I passed Hilda Wade's door, I saw it half ajar. She stood a little within, and beckoned me to enter.

I passed in and closed the door behind me. Hilda looked at me with trustful eyes. Resolute still, her face was yet that of a hunted creature. "Thank Heaven, I have ONE friend here, at least!" she said, slowly seating herself. "You saw me catch and conceal the needle?"

"Yes, I saw you."

She drew it forth from her purse, carefully but loosely wrapped up in a small tag of tissue-paper. "Here it is!" she said, displaying it. "Now, I want you to test it."

"In a culture?" I asked; for I guessed her meaning.

She nodded. "Yes, to see what that man has done to it."

"What do you suspect?"

She shrugged her graceful shoulders half imperceptibly.

"How should I know? Anything!"

I gazed at the needle closely. "What made you distrust it?" I inquired at last, still eyeing it.

She opened a drawer, and took out several others. "See here," she said, handing me one; "THESE are the needles I keep in antiseptic wool, the needles with which I always supply the Professor. You observe their shape, the common surgical patterns. Now, look at THIS needle, with which the Professor was just going to prick my finger! You can see for yourself at once it is of bluer steel and of a different manufacture."

"That is quite true," I answered, examining it with my pocket lens, which I always carry. "I see the difference. But how did you detect it?"

"From his face, partly; but partly, too, from the needle itself. I had my suspicions, and I was watching him closely. Just as he raised the thing in his hand, half concealing it, so, and showing only the point, I caught the blue gleam of the steel as the light glanced off it. It was not the kind I knew. Then I withdrew my hand at once, feeling sure he meant mischief."

"That was wonderfully quick of you!"

"Quick? Well, yes. Thank Heaven, my mind works fast; my perceptions are rapid. Otherwise—" she looked grave. "One second more, and it would have been too late. The man might have killed me."

"You think it is poisoned, then?"

Hilda shook her head with confident dissent. "Poisoned? Oh, no. He is wiser now. Fifteen years ago, he used poison. But science has made gigantic strides since then. He would not needlessly expose himself to-day to the risks of the poisoner."

"Fifteen years ago he used poison?"

She nodded, with the air of one who knows. "I am not speaking at random," she answered. "I say what I know. Some day I will explain. For the present, it is enough to tell you I know it."

"And what do you suspect now?" I asked, the weird sense of her strange power deepening on me every second.

She held up the incriminated needle again.

"Do you see this groove?" she asked, pointing to it with the tip of another.

I examined it once more at the light with the lens. A longitudinal groove, apparently ground into one side of the needle, lengthwise, by means of a small grinding-stone and emery powder, ran for a quarter of an inch above the point. This groove seemed to me to have been produced by an amateur, though he must have been one accustomed to delicate microscopic manipulation; for the edges under the lens showed slightly rough, like the surface of a file on a small scale: not smooth and polished, as a needle-maker would have left them. I said so to Hilda.

"You are quite right," she answered. "That is just what it shows. I feel sure Sebastian made that groove himself. He could have bought grooved needles, it is true, such as they sometimes use for retaining small quantities of lymphs and medicines; but we had none in stock, and to buy them would be to manufacture evidence against himself, in case of detection. Besides, the rough, jagged edge would hold the material he wished to inject all the better, while its saw-like points would tear the flesh, imperceptibly, but minutely, and so serve his purpose."

"Which was?"

"Try the needle, and judge for yourself. I prefer you should find out. You can tell me to-morrow."

"It was quick of you to detect it!" I cried, still turning the suspicious object over. "The difference is so slight."

"Yes; but you tell me my eyes are as sharp as the needle. Besides, I had reason to doubt; and Sebastian himself gave me the clue by selecting his instrument with too great deliberation. He had put it there with the rest, but it lay a little apart; and as he picked it up gingerly, I began to doubt. When I saw the blue gleam, my doubt was at once converted into certainty. Then his eyes, too, had the look which I know means victory. Benign or baleful, it goes with his triumphs. I have seen that look before, and when once it lurks scintillating in the luminous depths of his gleaming eyeballs, I recognise at once that, whatever his aim, he has succeeded in it."

"Still, Hilda, I am loth—"

She waved her hand impatiently. "Waste no time," she cried, in an authoritative voice. "If you happen to let that needle rub carelessly against the sleeve of your coat you may destroy the evidence. Take it at once to your room, plunge it into a culture, and lock it up safe at a proper temperature, where Sebastian cannot get at it, till the consequences develop."

I did as she bid me. By this time, I was not wholly unprepared for the result she anticipated. My belief in Sebastian had sunk to zero, and was rapidly reaching a negative quantity.

At nine the next morning, I tested one drop of the culture under the microscope. Clear and limpid to the naked eye, it was alive with small objects of a most suspicious nature, when properly magnified. I knew those hungry forms. Still, I would not decide offhand on my own authority in a matter of such moment. Sebastian's character was at stake, the character of the man who led the profession. I called in Callaghan, who happened to be in the ward, and asked him to put his eye to the instrument for a moment. He was a splendid fellow for the use of high powers, and I had magnified the culture 300 diameters. "What do you call those?" I asked, breathless.

He scanned them carefully with his experienced eye. "Is it the microbes ye mean?" he answered. "An' what 'ud they be, then, if it wasn't the bacillus of pyaemia?"

"Blood-poisoning!" I ejaculated, horror-struck.

"Aye; blood-poisoning: that's the English of it."

I assumed an air of indifference. "I made them that myself," I rejoined, as if they were mere ordinary experimental germs; "but I wanted confirmation of my own opinion. You're sure of the bacillus?"

"An' haven't I been keeping swarms of those very same bacteria under close observation for Sebastian for seven weeks past? Why, I know them as well as I know me own mother."

"Thank you," I said. "That will do." And I carried off the microscope, bacilli and all, into Hilda Wade's sitting-room. "Look yourself!" I cried to her.

She stared at them through the instrument with an unmoved face. "I thought so," she answered shortly. "The bacillus of pyaemia. A most virulent type. Exactly what I expected."

"You anticipated that result?"

"Absolutely. You see, blood-poisoning matures quickly, and kills almost to a certainty. Delirium supervenes so soon that the patient has no chance of explaining suspicions. Besides, it would all seem so very natural! Everybody would say: 'She got some slight wound, which microbes from some case she was attending contaminated.' You may be sure Sebastian thought out all that. He plans with consummate skill. He had designed everything."

I gazed at her, uncertain. "And what will you DO?" I asked. "Expose him?"

She opened both her palms with a blank gesture of helplessness. "It is useless!" she answered. "Nobody would believe me. Consider the situation. YOU know the needle I gave you was the one Sebastian meant to use, the one he dropped and I caught, BECAUSE you are a friend of mine, and because you have learned to trust me. But who else would credit it? I have only my word against his, an unknown nurse's against the great Professor's. Everybody would say I was malicious or hysterical. Hysteria is always an easy stone to fling at an injured woman who asks for justice. They would declare I had trumped up the case to forestall my dismissal. They would set it down to spite. We can do nothing against him. Remember, on his part, the utter absence of overt motive."

"And you mean to stop on here, in close attendance on a man who has attempted your life?" I cried, really alarmed for her safety.

"I am not sure about that," she answered. "I must take time to think. My presence at Nathaniel's was necessary to my Plan. The Plan fails for the present. I have now to look round and reconsider my position."

"But you are not safe here now," I urged, growing warm. "If Sebastian really wishes to get rid of you, and is as unscrupulous as you suppose, with his gigantic brain he can soon compass his end. What he plans he executes. You ought not to remain within the Professor's reach one hour longer."

"I have thought of that, too," she replied, with an almost unearthly calm. "But there are difficulties either way. At any rate, I am glad he did not succeed this time. For, to have killed me now, would have frustrated my Plan", she clasped her hands, "my Plan is ten thousand times dearer than life to me!"

"Dear lady!" I cried, drawing a deep breath, "I implore you in this strait, listen to what I urge. Why fight your battle alone? Why refuse assistance? I have admired you so long, I am so eager to help you. If only you will allow me to call you—"

Her eyes brightened and softened. Her whole bosom heaved. I felt in a flash she was not wholly indifferent to me. Strange tremors in the air seemed to play about us. But she waved me aside once more. "Don't press me," she said, in a very low voice. "Let me go my own way. It is hard enough already, this task I have undertaken, without YOUR making it harder.... Dear friend, dear friend, you don't quite understand. There are TWO men at Nathaniel's whom I desire to escape, because they both alike stand in the way of my Purpose." She took my hands in hers. "Each in a different way," she murmured once more. "But each I must avoid. One is Sebastian. The other—" she let my hand drop again, and broke off suddenly. "Dear Hubert," she cried, with a catch, "I cannot help it: forgive me!"

It was the first time she had ever called me by my Christian name. The mere sound of the word made me unspeakably happy.

Yet she waved me away. "Must I go?" I asked, quivering.

"Yes, yes: you must go. I cannot stand it. I must think this thing out, undisturbed. It is a very great crisis."

That afternoon and evening, by some unhappy chance, I was fully engaged in work at the hospital. Late at night a letter arrived for me. I glanced at it in dismay. It bore the Basingstoke postmark. But, to my alarm and surprise, it was in Hilda's hand. What could this change portend? I opened it, all tremulous.

"DEAR HUBERT, " I gave a sigh of relief. It was no longer "Dear Dr. Cumberledge" now, but "Hubert." That was something gained, at any rate. I read on with a beating heart. What had Hilda to say to me?

"DEAR HUBERT, By the time this reaches you, I shall be far away, irrevocably far, from London. With deep regret, with fierce searchings of spirit, I have come to the conclusion that, for the Purpose I have in view, it would be better for me at once to leave Nathaniel's. Where I go, or what I mean to do, I do not wish to tell you. Of your charity, I pray, refrain from asking me. I am aware that your kindness and generosity deserve better recognition. But, like Sebastian himself, I am the slave of my Purpose. I have lived for it all these years, and it is still very dear to me. To tell you my plans would interfere with that end. Do not, therefore, suppose I am insensible to your goodness.... Dear Hubert, spare me, I dare not say more, lest I say too much. I dare not trust myself. But one thing I MUST say. I am flying from YOU quite as much as from Sebastian. Flying from my own heart, quite as much as from my enemy. Some day, perhaps, if I accomplish my object, I may tell you all. Meanwhile, I can only beg of you of your kindness to trust me. We shall not meet again, I fear, for years. But I shall never forget you, you, the kind counsellor, who have half turned me aside from my life's Purpose. One word more, and I should falter. In very great haste, and amid much disturbance, yours ever affectionately and gratefully,

"HILDA."

It was a hurried scrawl in pencil, as if written in a train. I felt utterly dejected. Was Hilda, then, leaving England?

Rousing myself after some minutes, I went straight to Sebastian's rooms, and told him in brief terms that Nurse Wade had disappeared at a moment's notice, and had sent a note to tell me so.

He looked up from his work, and scanned me hard, as was his wont. "That is well," he said at last, his eyes glowing deep; "she was getting too great a hold on you, that young woman!"

"She retains that hold upon me, sir," I answered curtly.

"You are making a grave mistake in life, my dear Cumberledge," he went on, in his old genial tone, which I had almost forgotten. "Before you go further, and entangle yourself more deeply, I think it is only right that I should undeceive you as to this girl's true position. She is passing under a false name, and she comes of a tainted stock.... Nurse Wade, as she chooses to call herself, is a daughter of the notorious murderer, Yorke-Bannerman."

My mind leapt back to the incident of the broken basin. Yorke-Bannerman's name had profoundly moved her. Then I thought of Hilda's face. Murderers, I said to myself, do not beget such daughters as that. Not even accidental murderers, like my poor friend Le Geyt. I saw at once the prima facie evidence was strongly against her. But I had faith in her still. I drew myself up firmly, and stared him back full in the face. "I do not believe it," I answered, shortly.

"You do not believe it? I tell you it is so. The girl herself as good as acknowledged it to me."

I spoke slowly and distinctly. "Dr. Sebastian," I said, confronting him, "let us be quite clear with one another. I have found you out. I know how you tried to poison that lady. To poison her with bacilli which I detected. I cannot trust your word; I cannot trust your inferences. Either she is not Yorke-Bannerman's daughter at all, or else... Yorke-Bannerman was NOT a murderer...." I watched his face closely. Conviction leaped upon me. "And someone else was," I went on. "I might put a name to him."

With a stern white face, he rose and opened the door. He pointed to it slowly. "This hospital is not big enough for you and me abreast," he said, with cold politeness. "One or other of us must go. Which, I leave to your good sense to determine."

Even at that moment of detection and disgrace, in one man's eyes, at least, Sebastian retained his full measure of dignity.

CHAPTER VI

THE EPISODE OF THE LETTER WITH THE BASINGSTOKE POSTMARK

I have a vast respect for my grandfather. He was a man of forethought. He left me a modest little income of seven hundred a-year, well invested. Now, seven hundred a-year is not exactly wealth; but it is an unobtrusive competence; it permits a bachelor to move about the world and choose at will his own profession. I chose medicine; but I was not wholly dependent upon it. So I honoured my grandfather's wise disposition of his worldly goods; though, oddly enough, my cousin Tom (to whom he left his watch and five hundred pounds) speaks MOST disrespectfully of his character and intellect.

Thanks to my grandfather's silken-sailed barque, therefore, when I found myself practically dismissed from Nathaniel's I was not thrown on my beam-ends, as most young men in my position would have been; I had time and opportunity for the favourite pastime of looking about me. Of course, had I chosen, I might have fought the case to the bitter end against Sebastian; he could not dismiss me, that lay with the committee. But I hardly cared to fight. In the first place, though I had found him out as a man, I still respected him as a great teacher; and in the second place (which is always more important), I wanted to find and follow Hilda.

To be sure, Hilda, in that enigmatic letter of hers, had implored me not to seek her out; but I think you will admit there is one request which no man can grant to the girl he loves, and that is the request to keep away from her. If Hilda did not want ME, I wanted Hilda; and, being a man, I meant to find her.

My chances of discovering her whereabouts, however, I had to confess to myself (when it came to the point) were extremely slender. She had vanished from my horizon, melted into space. My sole hint of a clue consisted in the fact that the letter she sent me had been posted at Basingstoke. Here, then, was my problem: given an envelope with the Basingstoke postmark, to find in what part of Europe, Asia, Africa, or America the writer of it might be discovered. It opened up a fine field for speculation.

When I set out to face this broad puzzle, my first idea was: "I must ask Hilda." In all circumstances of difficulty, I had grown accustomed to submitting my doubts and surmises to her acute intelligence; and her instinct almost always supplied the right solution. But now Hilda was gone; it was Hilda herself I wished to track through the labyrinth of the world. I could expect no assistance in tracking her from Hilda.

"Let me think," I said to myself, over a reflective pipe, with feet poised on the fender. "How would Hilda herself have approached this problem? Imagine I'm Hilda. I must try to strike a trail by applying her own methods to her own character. She would have attacked the question, no doubt,"—here I eyed my pipe wisely, "from the psychological side. She would have asked herself"—I stroked my chin—"what such a temperament as hers was likely to do under such-and-such circumstances. And she would have answered it aright. But then"—I puffed away once or twice—"SHE is Hilda."

When I came to reconnoitre the matter in this light, I became at once aware how great a gulf separated the clumsy male intelligence from the immediate and almost unerring intuitions of a clever woman. I am considered no fool; in my own profession, I may venture to say, I was Sebastian's favourite pupil. Yet, though I asked myself over and over again where Hilda would be likely to go, Canada, China, Australia, as the outcome of her character, in these given conditions, I got no answer. I stared at the fire and reflected. I smoked two successive pipes, and shook out the ashes. "Let me consider how Hilda's temperament would work," I said, looking sagacious. I said it several times, but there I stuck. I went no further. The solution would not come. I felt that in order to play Hilda's part, it was necessary first to have Hilda's head-piece. Not every man can bend the bow of Ulysses.

As I turned the problem over in my mind, however, one phrase at last came back to me, a phrase which Hilda herself had let fall when we were debating a very similar point about poor Hugo Le Geyt: "If I were in his place, what do you think I would do?—why, hide myself at once in the greenest recesses of our Carnarvonshire mountains."

She must have gone to Wales, then. I had her own authority for saying so.... And yet—Wales? Wales? I pulled myself up with a jerk. In that case, how did she come to be passing by Basingstoke?

Was the postmark a blind? Had she hired someone to take the letter somewhere for her, on purpose to put me off on a false track? I could hardly think so. Besides, the time was against it. I saw Hilda at Nathaniel's in the morning; the very same evening I received the envelope with the Basingstoke postmark.

"If I were in his place." Yes, true; but, now I come to think on it, WERE the positions really parallel? Hilda was not flying for her life from justice; she was only endeavouring to escape Sebastian—and myself. The instances she had quoted of the mountaineer's curious homing instinct, the wild yearning he feels at moments of great straits to bury himself among the nooks of his native hills, were they not all instances of murderers pursued by the police? It was abject terror that drove these men to their burrows. But Hilda was not a murderer; she was not dogged by remorse, despair, or the myrmidons of the law; it was murder she was avoiding, not the punishment of murder. That made, of course, an obvious difference. "Irrevocably far from London," she said. Wales is a suburb. I gave up the idea that it was likely to prove her place of refuge from the two men she was bent on escaping. Hong-Kong, after all, seemed more probable than Llanberis.

That first failure gave me a clue, however, as to the best way of applying Hilda's own methods. "What would such a person do under the circumstances?" that was her way of putting the question. Clearly, then, I must first decide what WERE the circumstances. Was Sebastian speaking the truth? Was Hilda Wade, or was she not, the daughter of the supposed murderer, Dr. Yorke-Bannerman?

I looked up as much of the case as I could, in unobtrusive ways, among the old law-reports, and found that the barrister who had had charge of the defence was my father's old friend, Mr. Horace Mayfield, a man of elegant tastes, and the means to gratify them.

I went to call on him on Sunday evening at his artistically luxurious house in Onslow Gardens. A sedate footman answered the bell. Fortunately, Mr. Mayfield was at home, and, what is rarer, disengaged. You do not always find a successful Q.C. at his ease among his books, beneath the electric light, ready to give up a vacant hour to friendly colloquy.

"Remember Yorke-Bannerman's case?" he said, a huge smile breaking slowly like a wave over his genial fat face, Horace Mayfield resembles a great good-humoured toad, with bland manners and a capacious double chin—"I should just say I DID! Bless my soul—why, yes," he beamed, "I was Yorke-Bannerman's counsel. Excellent fellow, Yorke-Bannerman, most unfortunate end, though, precious clever chap, too! Had an astounding memory. Recollected every symptom of every patient he ever attended. And SUCH an eye! Diagnosis? It was clairvoyance! A gift, no less. Knew what was the matter with you the moment he looked at you."

That sounded like Hilda. The same surprising power of recalling facts; the same keen faculty for interpreting character or the signs of feeling. "He poisoned somebody, I believe," I murmured, casually. "An uncle of his, or something."

Mayfield's great squat face wrinkled; the double chin, folding down on the neck, became more ostentatiously double than ever. "Well, I can't admit that," he said, in his suave voice, twirling the string of his eye-glass. "I was Yorke-Bannerman's advocate, you see; and therefore I was paid not to admit it. Besides, he was a friend of mine, and I always liked him. But I WILL allow that the case DID look a trifle black against him."

"Ha? Looked black, did it?" I faltered.

The judicious barrister shrugged his shoulders. A genial smile spread oilily once more over his smooth face. "None of my business to say so," he answered, puckering the corners of his eyes. "Still, it was a long time ago; and the circumstances certainly WERE suspicious. Perhaps, on the whole, Hubert, it was just as well the poor fellow died before the trial came off; otherwise"—he pouted his lips—"I might have had my work cut out to save him." And he eyed the blue china gods on the mantelpiece affectionately.

"I believe the Crown urged money as the motive?" I suggested.

Mayfield glanced inquiry at me. "Now, why do you want to know all this?" he asked, in a suspicious voice, coming back from his dragons. "It is irregular, very, to worm information out of an innocent barrister in his hours of ease about a former client. We are a guileless race, we lawyers; don't abuse our confidence."

He seemed an honest man, I thought, in spite of his mocking tone. I trusted him, and made a clean breast of it. "I believe," I answered, with an impressive little pause, "I want to marry Yorke-Bannerman's daughter."

He gave a quick start. "What, Maisie?" he exclaimed.

I shook my head. "No, no; that is not the name," I replied.

He hesitated a moment. "But there IS no other," he hazarded cautiously at last. "I knew the family."

"I am not sure of it," I went on. "I have merely my suspicions. I am in love with a girl, and something about her makes me think she is probably a Yorke-Bannerman."

"But, my dear Hubert, if that is so," the great lawyer went on, waving me off with one fat hand, "it must be at once apparent to you that I am the last person on earth to whom you ought to apply for information. Remember my oath. The practice of our clan: the seal of secrecy!"

I was frank once more. "I do not know whether the lady I mean is or is not Yorke-Bannerman's daughter," I persisted. "She may be, and she may not. She gives another name, that's certain. But whether she is or isn't, one thing I know, I mean to marry her. I believe in her; I trust her. I only seek to gain this information now because I don't know where she is, and I want to track her."

He crossed his big hands with an air of Christian resignation, and looked up at the panels of the coffered ceiling. "In that," he answered, "I may honestly say, I can't help you. Humbug apart, I have not known Mrs. Yorke-Bannerman's address, or Maisie's either, ever since my poor friend's death. Prudent woman, Mrs. Yorke-Bannerman! She went away, I believe, to somewhere in North Wales, and afterwards to Brittany. But she probably changed her name; and—she did not confide in me."

I went on to ask him a few questions about the case, premising that I did so in the most friendly spirit. "Oh, I can only tell you what is publicly known," he answered, beaming, with the usual professional pretence of the most sphinx-like reticence. "But the plain facts, as universally admitted, were these. I break no confidence. Yorke-Bannerman had a rich uncle from whom he had expectations—a certain Admiral Scott Prideaux. This uncle had lately made a will in Yorke-Bannerman's favour; but he was a cantankerous old chap, naval, you know autocratic, crusty, given to changing his mind with each change of the wind, and easily offended by his relations, the sort of cheerful old party who makes a new will once every month, disinheriting the nephew he last dined with. Well, one day the Admiral was taken ill, at his own house, and Yorke-Bannerman attended him. OUR contention was, I speak now as my old friend's counsel, that Scott Prideaux, getting as tired of life as we were all tired of him, and weary of this recurrent worry of will-making, determined at last to clear out for good from a world where he was so little appreciated, and, therefore, tried to poison himself."

"With aconitine?" I suggested, eagerly.

"Unfortunately, yes; he made use of aconitine for that otherwise laudable purpose. Now, as ill luck would have it"—Mayfield's wrinkles deepened—"Yorke-Bannerman and Sebastian, then two rising doctors engaged in physiological researches together, had just been occupied in experimenting upon this very drug—testing the use of aconitine. Indeed, you will no doubt remember"—he crossed his fat hands again comfortably—"it was these precise researches on a then little-known poison that first brought Sebastian prominently before the public. What was the consequence?" His smooth, persuasive voice flowed on as if I were a concentrated jury. "The Admiral grew rapidly worse, and insisted upon calling in a second opinion. No doubt he didn't like the aconitine when it came to the pinch, for it DOES pinch, I can tell you, and repented him of his evil. Yorke-Bannerman suggested Sebastian as the second opinion; the uncle acquiesced; Sebastian was called in, and, of course, being fresh from his researches, immediately recognised the symptoms of aconitine poisoning."

"What! Sebastian found it out?" I cried, starting.

"Oh, yes! Sebastian. He watched the case from that point to the end; and the oddest part of it all was this, that though he communicated with the police, and himself prepared every morsel of food that the poor old Admiral took from that moment forth, the symptoms continually increased in severity. The police contention was that Yorke-Bannerman somehow managed to put the stuff into the milk beforehand; my own theory was, as counsel for the accused", he blinked his fat eyes, "that old Prideaux had concealed a large quantity of aconitine in the bed, before his illness, and went on taking it from time to time, just to spite his nephew."

"And you BELIEVE that, Mr. Mayfield?"

The broad smile broke concentrically in ripples over the great lawyer's face. His smile was Mayfield's main feature. He shrugged his shoulders and expanded his big hands wide open before him. "My dear Hubert," he said, with a most humorous expression of countenance, "you are a professional man yourself; therefore you know that every profession has its own little courtesies, its own small fictions. I was Yorke-Bannerman's counsel, as well as his friend. 'Tis a point of honour with us that no barrister will ever admit a doubt as to a client's innocence, is he not paid to maintain it?—and to my dying day I will constantly maintain that old Prideaux poisoned himself. Maintain it with that dogged and meaningless obstinacy with which we always cling to whatever is least provable.... Oh, yes! He poisoned himself; and Yorke-Bannerman was innocent.... But still, you know, it WAS the sort of case where an acute lawyer, with a reputation to make, would prefer to be for the Crown rather than for the prisoner."

"But it was never tried," I ejaculated.

"No, happily for us, it was never tried. Fortune favoured us. Yorke-Bannerman had a weak heart, a conveniently weak heart, which the inquest sorely affected; and besides, he was deeply angry at what he persisted in calling Sebastian's defection. He evidently thought Sebastian ought to have stood by him. His colleague preferred the claims of public duty, as he understood them, I mean, to those of private friendship. It was a very sad case, for Yorke-Bannerman was really a charming fellow. But I confess I WAS relieved when he died unexpectedly on the morning of his arrest. It took off my shoulders a most serious burden."

"You think, then, the case would have gone against him?"

"My dear Hubert," his whole face puckered with an indulgent smile, "of course the case must have gone against us. Juries are fools; but they are not such fools as to swallow everything, like ostriches: to let me throw dust in their eyes about so plain an issue. Consider the facts, consider them impartially. Yorke-Bannerman had easy access to aconitine; had whole ounces of it in his possession; he treated the uncle from whom he was to inherit; he was in temporary embarrassments, that came out at the inquest; it was known that the Admiral had just made a twenty-third will in his favour, and that the Admiral's wills were liable to alteration every time a nephew ventured upon an opinion in politics, religion, science, navigation, or the right card at whist, differing by a shade from that of the uncle. The Admiral died of aconitine poisoning; and Sebastian observed and detailed the symptoms. Could anything be plainer, I mean, could any combination of fortuitous circumstances"—he blinked pleasantly again—"be more adverse to an advocate sincerely convinced of his client's innocence—as a professional duty?" And he gazed at me comically.

The more he piled up the case against the man who I now felt sure was Hilda's father, the less did I believe him. A dark conspiracy seemed to loom up in the background. "Has it ever occurred to you," I asked, at last, in a very tentative tone, "that perhaps—I throw out the hint as the merest suggestion—perhaps it may have been Sebastian who—"

He smiled this time till I thought his smile would swallow him.

"If Yorke-Bannerman had NOT been my client," he mused aloud, "I might have been inclined to suspect rather that Sebastian aided him to avoid justice by giving him something violent to take, if he wished it: something which might accelerate the inevitable action of the heart-disease from which he was suffering. Isn'T THAT more likely?"

I saw there was nothing further to be got out of Mayfield. His opinion was fixed; he was a placid ruminant. But he had given me already much food for thought. I thanked him for his assistance, and returned on foot to my rooms at the hospital.

I was now, however, in a somewhat different position for tracking Hilda from that which I occupied before my interview with the famous counsel. I felt certain by this time that Hilda Wade and Maisie Yorke-Bannerman were one and the same person. To be sure, it gave me a twinge to think that Hilda should be masquerading under an assumed name; but I waived that question for the moment, and awaited her explanations. The great point now was to find Hilda. She was flying from Sebastian to mature a new plan. But whither? I proceeded to argue it out on her own principles; oh, how lamely! The world is still so big! Mauritius, the Argentine, British Columbia, New Zealand!

The letter I had received bore the Basingstoke postmark. Now a person may be passing Basingstoke on his way either to Southampton or Plymouth, both of which are ports of embarcation for various foreign countries. I attached importance to that clue. Something about the tone of Hilda's letter made me realise that she intended to put the sea between us. In concluding so much, I felt sure I was not mistaken. Hilda had too big and too cosmopolitan a mind to speak of being "irrevocably far from London," if she were only going to some town in England, or even to Normandy, or the Channel Islands. "Irrevocably far" pointed rather to a destination outside Europe altogether, to India, Africa, America: not to Jersey, Dieppe, or Saint-Malo.

Was it Southampton or Plymouth to which she was first bound?—that was the next question. I inclined to Southampton. For the sprawling lines (so different from her usual neat hand) were written hurriedly in a train, I could see; and, on consulting Bradshaw, I found that the Plymouth expresses stop longest at Salisbury, where Hilda would, therefore, have been likely to post her note if she were going to the far west; while some of the Southampton trains stop at Basingstoke, which is, indeed, the most convenient point on that route for sending off a letter. This was mere blind guesswork, to be sure, compared with Hilda's immediate and unerring intuition; but it had some probability in its favour, at any rate. Try both: of the two, she was likelier to be going to Southampton.

My next move was to consult the list of outgoing steamers. Hilda had left London on a Saturday morning. Now, on alternate Saturdays, the steamers of the Castle line sail from Southampton, where they call to take up passengers and mails. Was this one of those alternate Saturdays? I looked at the list of dates: it was. That told further in favour of Southampton. But did any steamer of any passenger line sail from Plymouth on the same day? None, that I could find. Or from Southampton elsewhere? I looked them all up. The Royal Mail Company's boats start on Wednesdays; the North German Lloyd's on Wednesdays and Sundays. Those were the only likely vessels I could discover. Either, then, I concluded, Hilda meant to sail on Saturday by the Castle line for South Africa, or else on Sunday by North German Lloyd for some part of America.

How I longed for one hour of Hilda to help me out with her almost infallible instinct. I realised how feeble and fallacious was my own groping in the dark. Her knowledge of temperament would have revealed to her at once what I was trying to discover, like the police she despised, by the clumsy "clues" which so roused her sarcasm.

However, I went to bed and slept on it. Next morning I determined to set out for Southampton on a tour of inquiry to all the steamboat agencies. If that failed, I could go on to Plymouth.

But, as chance would have it, the morning post brought me an unexpected letter, which helped me not a little in unravelling the problem. It was a crumpled letter, written on rather soiled paper, in an uneducated hand, and it bore, like Hilda's, the Basingstoke postmark.

"Charlotte Churtwood sends her duty to Dr. Cumberledge," it said, with somewhat uncertain spelling, "and I am very sorry that I was not able to Post the letter to you in London, as the lady ast me, but after her train ad left has I was stepping into mine the Ingine started and I was knocked down and badly hurt and the lady gave me a half-sovering to Post it in London has soon as I got there but bein unable to do so I now return it dear sir not knowing the lady's name and adress she having trusted me through seeing me on the platform, and perhaps you can send it back to her, and was very sorry I could not Post it were she ast me, but time bein an objeck put it in the box in Basingstoke station and now inclose post office order for ten Shillings whitch dear sir kindly let the young lady have from your obedient servant,

"CHARLOTTE CHURTWOOD."

In the corner was the address: "11, Chubb's Cottages, Basingstoke."

The happy accident of this letter advanced things for me greatly, though it also made me feel how dependent I was upon happy accidents, where Hilda would have guessed right at once by mere knowledge of character. Still, the letter explained many things which had hitherto puzzled me. I had felt not a little surprise that Hilda, wishing to withdraw from me and leave no traces, should have sent off her farewell letter from Basingstoke, so as to let me see at once in what direction she was travelling. Nay, I even wondered at times whether she had really posted it herself at Basingstoke, or given it to somebody who chanced to be going there to post for her as a blind. But I did not think she would deliberately deceive me; and, in my opinion, to get a letter posted at Basingstoke would be deliberate deception, while to get it posted in London was mere vague precaution. I understood now that she had written it in the train, and then picked out a likely person as she passed to take it to Waterloo for her.

Of course, I went straight down to Basingstoke, and called at once at Chubb's Cottages. It was a squalid little row on the outskirts of the town. I found Charlotte Churtwood herself exactly such a girl as Hilda, with her quick judgment of character, might have hit upon for such a purpose. She was a conspicuously honest and transparent country servant, of the lumpy type, on her way to London to take a place as housemaid. Her injuries were severe, but not dangerous. "The lady saw me on the platform," she said, "and beckoned to me to come to her. She ast me where I was going, and I says, 'To London, miss.' Says she, smiling kind-like, 'Could you post a letter for me, certain sure?' Says I, 'You can depend upon me.' An' then she give me the arf-sovering, an' says, says she, 'Mind, it's VERY par-tickler; if the gentleman don't get it, 'e'll fret 'is 'eart out.' An' through 'aving a young man o' my own, as is a groom at Andover, o' course I understood 'er, sir. An' then, feeling all full of it, as yu may say, what with the arf-sovering, and what with one thing and what with another, an' all of a fluster with not being used to travelling, I run up, when the train for London come in, an' tried to scramble into it, afore it 'ad quite stopped moving. An' a guard, 'e rushes up, an' 'Stand back!' says 'e; 'wait till the train stops,' says 'e, an' waves his red flag at me. But afore I could stand back, with one foot on the step, the train sort of jumped away from me, and knocked me down like this; and they say it'll be a week now afore I'm well enough to go on to London. But I posted the letter all the same, at Basingstoke station, as they was carrying me off; an' I took down the address, so as to return the arf-sovering." Hilda was right, as always. She had chosen instinctively the trustworthy person, chosen her at first sight, and hit the bull's-eye.

"Do you know what train the lady was in?" I asked, as she paused. "Where was it going, did you notice?"

"It was the Southampton train, sir. I saw the board on the carriage."

That settled the question. "You are a good and an honest girl," I said, pulling out my purse; "and you came to this misfortune through trying, too eagerly, to help the young lady. A ten-pound note is not overmuch as compensation for your accident. Take it, and get well. I should be sorry to think you lost a good place through your anxiety to help us."

The rest of my way was plain sailing now. I hurried on straight to Southampton. There my first visit was to the office of the Castle line. I went to the point at once. Was there a Miss Wade among the passengers by the Dunottar Castle?

No; nobody of that name on the list.

Had any lady taken a passage at the last moment?

The clerk perpended. Yes; a lady had come by the mail train from London, with no heavy baggage, and had gone on board direct, taking what cabin she could get. A young lady in grey. Quite unprepared. Gave no name. Called away in a hurry.

What sort of lady?

Youngish; good-looking; brown hair and eyes, the clerk thought; a sort of creamy skin; and a—well, a mesmeric kind of glance that seemed to go right through you.

"That will do," I answered, sure now of my quarry. "To which port did she book?"

"To Cape Town."

"Very well," I said, promptly. "You may reserve me a good berth in the next outgoing steamer."

It was just like Hilda's impulsive character to rush off in this way at a moment's notice; and just like mine to follow her. But it piqued me a little to think that, but for the accident of an accident, I might never have tracked her down. If the letter had been posted in London as she intended, and not at Basingstoke, I might have sought in vain for her from then till Doomsday.

Ten days later, I was afloat on the Channel, bound for South Africa.

I always admired Hilda's astonishing insight into character and motive; but I never admired it quite so profoundly as on the glorious day when we arrived at Cape Town. I was standing on deck, looking out for the first time in my life on that tremendous view, the steep and massive bulk of Table Mountain, a mere lump of rock, dropped loose from the sky, with the long white town spread gleaming at its base, and the silver-tree plantations that cling to its lower slopes and merge by degrees into gardens and vineyards, when a messenger from the shore came up to me tentatively.

"Dr. Cumberledge?" he said, in an inquiring tone.

I nodded. "That is my name."

"I have a letter for you, sir."

I took it, in great surprise. Who on earth in Cape Town could have known I was coming? I had not a friend to my knowledge in the colony. I glanced at the envelope. My wonder deepened. That prescient brain! It was Hilda's handwriting.

I tore it open and read:

"MY DEAR HUBERT, I KNOW you will come; I KNOW you will follow me. So I am leaving this letter at Donald Currie & Co.'s office, giving their agent instructions to hand it to you as soon as you reach Cape Town. I am quite sure you will track me so far at least; I understand your temperament. But I beg you, I implore you, to go no further. You will ruin my plan if you do. And I still adhere to it. It is good of you to come so far; I cannot blame you for that. I know your motives. But do not try to find me out. I warn you, beforehand, it will be quite useless. I have made up my mind. I have an object in life, and, dear as you are to me, THAT I will not pretend to deny, I can never allow even YOU to interfere with it. So be warned in time. Go back quietly by the next steamer.

"Your ever attached and grateful,

"HILDA."

I read it twice through with a little thrill of joy. Did any man ever court so strange a love? Her very strangeness drew me. But go back by the next steamer! I felt sure of one thing: Hilda was far too good a judge of character to believe that I was likely to obey that mandate.

I will not trouble you with the remaining stages of my quest. Except for the slowness of South African mail coaches, they were comparatively easy. It is not so hard to track strangers in Cape Town as strangers in London. I followed Hilda to her hotel, and from her hotel up country, stage after stage, jolted by rail, worse jolted by mule-waggon, inquiring, inquiring, inquiring, till I learned at last she was somewhere in Rhodesia.

That is a big address; but it does not cover as many names as it covers square miles. In time I found her. Still, it took time; and before we met, Hilda had had leisure to settle down quietly to her new existence. People in Rhodesia had noted her coming, as a new portent, because of one strange peculiarity. She was the only woman of means who had ever gone up of her own free will to Rhodesia. Other women had gone there to accompany their husbands, or to earn their livings; but that a lady should freely select that half-baked land as a place of residence, a lady of position, with all the world before her where to choose, that puzzled the Rhodesians. So she was a marked person. Most people solved the vexed problem, indeed, by suggesting that she had designs against the stern celibacy of a leading South African politician. "Depend upon it," they said, "it's Rhodes she's after." The moment I arrived at Salisbury, and stated my object in coming, all the world in the new town was ready to assist me. The lady was to be found (vaguely speaking) on a young farm to the north, a budding farm, whose general direction was expansively indicated to me by a wave of the arm, with South African uncertainty.

I bought a pony at Salisbury, a pretty little seasoned sorrel mare, and set out to find Hilda. My way lay over a brand-new road, or what passes for a road in South Africa, very soft and lumpy, like an English cart-track. I am a fair cross-country rider in our own Midlands, but I never rode a more tedious journey than that one. I had crawled several miles under a blazing sun along the shadeless new track, on my African pony, when, to my surprise I saw, of all sights in the world, a bicycle coming towards me.

I could hardly believe my eyes. Civilisation indeed! A bicycle in these remotest wilds of Africa!

I had been picking my way for some hours through a desolate plateau, the high veldt, about five thousand feet above the sea level, and entirely treeless. In places, to be sure, a few low bushes of prickly aspect rose in tangled clumps; but for the most part the arid table-land was covered by a thick growth of short brown grass, about nine inches high, burnt up in the sun, and most wearisome to look at. The distressing nakedness of a new country confronted me. Here and there a bald farm or two had been literally pegged out, the pegs were almost all one saw of them as yet; the fields were in the future. Here and there, again, a scattered range of low granite hills, known locally as kopjes, red, rocky prominences, flaunting in the sunshine, diversified the distance. But the road itself, such as it was, lay all on the high plain, looking down now and again into gorges or kloofs, wooded on their slopes with scrubby trees, and comparatively well-watered. In the midst of all this crude, unfinished land, the mere sight of a bicycle, bumping over the rubbly road, was a sufficient surprise; but my astonishment reached a climax when I saw, as it drew near, that it was ridden by a woman!

One moment later I had burst into a wild cry, and rode forward to her hurriedly. "Hilda!" I shouted aloud, in my excitement: "Hilda!"

She stepped lightly from her pedals, as if it had been in the park: head erect and proud; eyes liquid, lustrous. I dismounted, trembling, and stood beside her. In the wild joy of the moment, for the first time in my life, I kissed her fervently. Hilda took the kiss, unreproving. She did not attempt to refuse me.

"So you have come at last!" she murmured, with a glow on her face, half nestling towards me, half withdrawing, as if two wills tore her in different directions. "I have been expecting you for some days; and, somehow, to-day, I was almost certain you were coming!"

"Then you are not angry with me?" I cried. "You remember, you forbade me!"

"Angry with you? Dear Hubert, could I ever be angry with you, especially for thus showing me your devotion and your trust? I am never angry with you. When one knows, one understands. I have thought of you so often; sometimes, alone here in this raw new land, I have longed for you to come. It is inconsistent of me, of course; but I am so solitary, so lonely!"

"And yet you begged me not to follow you!"

She looked up at me shyly, I was not accustomed to see Hilda shy. Her eyes gazed deep into mine beneath the long, soft lashes. "I begged you not to follow me," she repeated, a strange gladness in her tone. "Yes, dear Hubert, I begged you, and I meant it. Cannot you understand that sometimes one hopes a thing may never happen, and is supremely happy because it happens, in spite of one? I have a purpose in life for which I live: I live for it still. For its sake I told you you must not come to me. Yet you HAVE come, against my orders; and—" she paused, and drew a deep sigh—"oh, Hubert, I thank you for daring to disobey me!"

I clasped her to my bosom. She allowed me, half resisting. "I am too weak," she murmured. "Only this morning, I made up my mind that when I saw you I would implore you to return at once. And now that you are here—" she laid her little hand confidingly in mine—"see how foolish I am!—I cannot dismiss you."

"Which means to say, Hilda, that, after all, you are still a woman!"

"A woman; oh, yes; very much a woman! Hubert, I love you; I half wish I did not."

"Why, darling?" I drew her to me.

"Because, if I did not, I could send you away, so easily! As it is, I cannot let you stop, and... I cannot dismiss you."

"Then divide it," I cried gaily; "do neither; come away with me!"

"No, no; nor that, either. I will not stultify my whole past life. I will not dishonour my dear father's memory."

I looked around for something to which to tether my horse. A bridle is in one's way, when one has to discuss important business. There was really nothing about that seemed fit for the purpose. Hilda saw what I sought, and pointed mutely to a stunted bush beside a big granite boulder which rose abruptly from the dead level of the grass, affording a little shade from that sweltering sunlight. I tied my mare to the gnarled root, it was the only part big enough, and sat down by Hilda's side, under the shadow of a great rock in a thirsty land. I realised at that moment the force and appropriateness of the Psalmist's simile. The sun beat fiercely on the seeding grasses. Away on the southern horizon we could faintly perceive the floating yellow haze of the prairie fires lit by the Mashonas.

"Then you knew I would come?" I began, as she seated herself on the burnt-up herbage, while my hand stole into hers, to nestle there naturally.

She pressed it in return. "Oh, yes; I knew you would come," she answered, with that strange ring of confidence in her voice. "Of course you got my letter at Cape Town?"

"I did, Hilda, and I wondered at you more than ever as I read it. But if you KNEW I would come, why write to prevent me?"

Her eyes had their mysterious far-away air. She looked out upon infinity. "Well, I wanted to do my best to turn you aside," she said, slowly. "One must always do one's best, even when one feels and believes it is useless. That surely is the first clause in a doctor's or a nurse's rubric."

"But WHY didn't you want me to come?" I persisted. "Why fight against your own heart? Hilda, I am sure, I KNOW you love me."

Her bosom rose and fell. Her eyes dilated. "Love you?" she cried, looking away over the bushy ridges, as if afraid to trust herself. "Oh, yes, Hubert, I love you! It is not for that that I wish to avoid you. Or, rather, it is just because of that. I cannot endure to spoil your life, by a fruitless affection."

"Why fruitless?" I asked, leaning forward.

She crossed her hands resignedly. "You know all by this time," she answered. "Sebastian would tell you, of course, when you went to announce that you were leaving Nathaniel's. He could not do otherwise; it is the outcome of his temperament, an integral part of his nature."

"Hilda," I cried, "you are a witch! How COULD you know that? I can't imagine."

She smiled her restrained, Chaldean smile. "Because I KNOW Sebastian," she answered, quietly. "I can read that man to the core. He is simple as a book. His composition is plain, straightforward, quite natural, uniform. There are no twists and turns in him. Once learn the key, and it discloses everything, like an open sesame. He has a gigantic intellect, a burning thirst for knowledge; one love, one hobby, science; and no moral instincts. He goes straight for his ends; and whatever comes in his way," she dug her little heel in the brown soil, "he tramples on it as ruthlessly as a child will trample on a worm or a beetle."

"And yet," I said, "he is so great."

"Yes, great, I grant you; but the easiest character to unravel that I have ever met. It is calm, austere, unbending, yet not in the least degree complex. He has the impassioned temperament, pushed to its highest pitch; the temperament that runs deep, with irresistible force; but the passion that inspires him, that carries him away headlong, as love carries some men, is a rare and abstract one, the passion of science."

I gazed at her as she spoke, with a feeling akin to awe. "It must destroy the plot-interest of life for you, Hilda," I cried, out there in the vast void of that wild African plateau, "to foresee so well what each person will do, how each will act under such given circumstances."

She pulled a bent of grass and plucked off its dry spikelets one by one. "Perhaps so," she answered, after a meditative pause; "though, of course, all natures are not equally simple. Only with great souls can you be sure beforehand like that, for good or for evil. It is essential to anything worth calling character that one should be able to predict in what way it will act under given circumstances, to feel certain, 'This man will do nothing small or mean,' 'That one could never act dishonestly, or speak deceitfully.' But smaller natures are more complex. They defy analysis, because their motives are not consistent."

"Most people think to be complex is to be great," I objected.

She shook her head. "That is quite a mistake," she answered. "Great natures are simple, and relatively predictable, since their motives balance one another justly. Small natures are complex, and hard to predict, because small passions, small jealousies, small discords and perturbations come in at all moments, and override for a time the permanent underlying factors of character. Great natures, good or bad, are equably poised; small natures let petty motives intervene to upset their balance."

"Then you knew I would come," I exclaimed, half pleased to find I belonged inferentially to her higher category.

Her eyes beamed on me with a beautiful light. "Knew you would come? Oh, yes. I begged you not to come; but I felt sure you were too deeply in earnest to obey me. I asked a friend in Cape Town to telegraph your arrival; and almost ever since the telegram reached me I have been expecting you and awaiting you."

"So you believed in me?"

"Implicitly—as you in me. That is the worst of it, Hubert. If you did NOT believe in me, I could have told you all—and then, you would have left me. But, as it is, you KNOW all, and yet, you want to cling to me."

"You know I know all—because Sebastian told me?"

"Yes; and I think I even know how you answered him."

"How?"

She paused. The calm smile lighted up her face once more. Then she drew out a pencil. "You think life must lack plot-interest for me," she began, slowly, "because, with certain natures, I can partially guess beforehand what is coming. But have you not observed that, in reading a novel, part of the pleasure you feel arises from your conscious anticipation of the end, and your satisfaction in seeing that you anticipated correctly? Or part, sometimes, from the occasional unexpectedness of the real denouement? Well, life is like that. I enjoy observing my successes, and, in a way, my failures. Let me show you what I mean. I think I know what you said to Sebastian, not the words, of course, but the purport; and I will write it down now for you. Set down YOUR version, too. And then we will compare them."

It was a crucial test. We both wrote for a minute or two. Somehow, in Hilda's presence, I forgot at once the strangeness of the scene, the weird oddity of the moment. That sombre plain disappeared for me. I was only aware that I was with Hilda once more, and therefore in Paradise. Pison and Gihon watered the desolate land. Whatever she did seemed to me supremely right. If she had proposed to me to begin a ponderous work on Medical Jurisprudence, under the shadow of the big rock, I should have begun it incontinently.

She handed me her slip of paper; I took it and read: "Sebastian told you I was Dr. Yorke-Bannerman's daughter. And you answered, 'If so, Yorke-Bannerman was innocent, and YOU are the poisoner.' Is not that correct?"

I handed her in answer my own paper. She read it with a faint flush. When she came to the words: "Either she is not Yorke-Bannerman's daughter; or else, Yorke-Bannerman was not a poisoner, and someone else was, I might put a name to him," she rose to her feet with a great rush of long-suppressed feeling, and clasped me passionately. "My Hubert!" she cried, "I read you aright. I knew it! I was sure of you!"

I folded her in my arms, there, on the rusty-red South African desert. "Then, Hilda dear," I murmured, "you will consent to marry me?"

The words brought her back to herself. She unfolded my arms with slow reluctance. "No, dearest," she said, earnestly, with a face where pride fought hard against love. "That is WHY, above all things, I did not want you to follow me. I love you; I trust you: you love me; you trust me. But I never will marry anyone till I have succeeded in clearing my father's memory. I KNOW he did not do it; I KNOW Sebastian did. But that is not enough. I must prove it, I must prove it!"

"I believe it already," I answered. "What need, then, to prove it?"

"To you, Hubert? Oh, no; not to you. There I am safe. But to the world that condemned him, condemned him untried. I must vindicate him; I must clear him!"

I bent my face close to hers. "But may I not marry you first?" I asked—"and after that, I can help you to clear him."

She gazed at me fearlessly. "No, no!" she cried, clasping her hands; "much as I love you, dear Hubert, I cannot consent to it. I am too proud!—too proud! I will not allow the world to say, not even to say falsely", her face flushed crimson; her voice dropped low—"I will not allow them to say those hateful words, 'He married a murderer's daughter.'"

I bowed my head. "As you will, my darling," I answered. "I am content to wait. I trust you in this, too. Some day, we will prove it."

And all this time, preoccupied as I was with these deeper concerns, I had not even asked where Hilda lived, or what she was doing!

CHAPTER VII

THE EPISODE OF THE STONE THAT LOOKED ABOUT IT

Hilda took me back with her to the embryo farm where she had pitched her tent for the moment; a rough, wild place. It lay close to the main road from Salisbury to Chimoio.

Setting aside the inevitable rawness and newness of all things Rhodesian, however, the situation itself was not wholly unpicturesque. A ramping rock or tor of granite, which I should judge at a rough guess to extend to an acre in size, sprang abruptly from the brown grass of the upland plain. It rose like a huge boulder. Its summit was crowned by the covered grave of some old Kaffir chief, a rude cairn of big stones under a thatched awning. At the foot of this jagged and cleft rock the farmhouse nestled, four square walls of wattle-and-daub, sheltered by its mass from the sweeping winds of the South African plateau. A stream brought water from a spring close by: in front of the house, rare sight in that thirsty land, spread a garden of flowers. It was an oasis in the desert. But the desert itself stretched grimly all round. I could never quite decide how far the oasis was caused by the water from the spring, and how far by Hilda's presence.

"Then you live here?" I cried, gazing round, my voice, I suppose, betraying my latent sense of the unworthiness of the position.

"For the present," Hilda answered, smiling. "You know, Hubert, I have no abiding city anywhere, till my Purpose is fulfilled. I came here because Rhodesia seemed the farthest spot on earth where a white woman just now could safely penetrate, in order to get away from you and Sebastian."

"That is an unkind conjunction!" I exclaimed, reddening.

"But I mean it," she answered, with a wayward little nod. "I wanted breathing-space to form fresh plans. I wanted to get clear away for a time from all who knew me. And this promised best.... But nowadays, really, one is never safe from intrusion anywhere."

"You are cruel, Hilda!"

"Oh, no. You deserve it. I asked you not to come, and you came in spite of me. I have treated you very nicely under the circumstances, I think. I have behaved like an angel. The question is now, what ought I to do next? You have upset my plans so."

"Upset your plans? How?"

"Dear Hubert,"—she turned to me with an indulgent smile, "for a clever man, you are really TOO foolish! Can't you see that you have betrayed my whereabouts to Sebastian? I crept away secretly, like a thief in the night, giving no name or place; and, having the world to ransack, he might have found it hard to track me; for HE had not YOUR clue of the Basingstoke letter, nor your reason for seeking me. But now that YOU have followed me openly, with your name blazoned forth in the company's passenger-lists, and your traces left plain in hotels and stages across the map of South Africa, why, the spoor is easy. If Sebastian cares to find us, he can follow the scent all through without trouble."

"I never thought of that!" I cried, aghast.

She was forbearance itself. "No, I knew you would never think of it. You are a man, you see. I counted that in. I was afraid from the first you would wreck all by following me."

I was mutely penitent. "And yet, you forgive me, Hilda?"

Her eyes beamed tenderness. "To know all, is to forgive all," she answered. "I have to remind you of that so often! How can I help forgiving, when I know WHY you came, what spur it was that drove you? But it is the future we have to think of now, not the past. And I must wait and reflect. I have NO plan just at present."

"What are you doing at this farm?" I gazed round at it, dissatisfied.

"I board here," Hilda answered, amused at my crestfallen face. "But, of course, I cannot be idle; so I have found work to do. I ride out on my bicycle to two or three isolated houses about, and give lessons to children in this desolate place, who would otherwise grow up ignorant. It fills my time, and supplies me with something besides myself to think about."

"And what am I to do?" I cried, oppressed with a sudden sense of helplessness.

She laughed at me outright. "And is this the first moment that that difficulty has occurred to you?" she asked, gaily. "You have hurried all the way from London to Rhodesia without the slightest idea of what you mean to do now you have got here?"

I laughed at myself in turn. "Upon my word, Hilda," I cried, "I set out to find you. Beyond the desire to find you, I had no plan in my head. That was an end in itself. My thoughts went no farther."

She gazed at me half saucily. "Then don't you think, sir, the best thing you can do, now you HAVE found me, is—to turn back and go home again?"

"I am a man," I said, promptly, taking a firm stand. "And you are a judge of character. If you really mean to tell me you think THAT likely, well, I shall have a lower opinion of your insight into men than I have been accustomed to harbour."

Her smile was not wholly without a touch of triumph.

"In that case," she went on, "I suppose the only alternative is for you to remain here."

"That would appear to be logic," I replied. "But what can I do? Set up in practice?"

"I don't see much opening," she answered. "If you ask my advice, I should say there is only one thing to be done in Rhodesia just now—turn farmer."

"It IS done," I answered, with my usual impetuosity. "Since YOU say the word, I am a farmer already. I feel an interest in oats that is simply absorbing. What steps ought I to take first in my present condition?"

She looked at me, all brown with the dust of my long ride. "I would suggest," she said slowly, "a good wash, and some dinner."

"Hilda," I cried, surveying my boots, or what was visible of them, "that is REALLY clever of you. A wash and some dinner! So practical, so timely! The very thing! I will see to it."

Before night fell, I had arranged everything. I was to buy the next farm from the owner of the one where Hilda lodged; I was also to learn the rudiments of South African agriculture from him for a valuable consideration; and I was to lodge in his house while my own was building. He gave me his views on the cultivation of oats. He gave them at some length—more length than perspicuity. I knew nothing about oats, save that they were employed in the manufacture of porridge—which I detest; but I was to be near Hilda once more, and I was prepared to undertake the superintendence of the oat from its birth to its reaping if only I might be allowed to live so close to Hilda.

The farmer and his wife were Boers, but they spoke English. Mr. Jan Willem Klaas himself was a fine specimen of the breed, tall, erect, broad-shouldered, and genial. Mrs. Klaas, his wife, was mainly suggestive, in mind and person, of suet-pudding. There was one prattling little girl of three years old, by name Sannie, a most engaging child; and also a chubby baby.

"You are betrothed, of course?" Mrs. Klaas said to Hilda before me, with the curious tactlessness of her race, when we made our first arrangement.

Hilda's face flushed. "No; we are nothing to one another," she answered, which was only true formally. "Dr. Cumberledge had a post at the same hospital in London where I was a nurse; and he thought he would like to try Rhodesia. That is all."

Mrs. Klaas gazed from one to other of us suspiciously. "You English are strange!" she answered, with a complacent little shrug. "But there—from Europe! Your ways, we know, are different."

Hilda did not attempt to explain. It would have been impossible to make the good soul understand. Her horizon was so simple. She was a harmless housewife, given mostly to dyspepsia and the care of her little ones. Hilda had won her heart by unfeigned admiration for the chubby baby. To a mother, that covers a multitude of eccentricities, such as one expects to find in incomprehensible English. Mrs. Klaas put up with me because she liked Hilda.

We spent some months together on Klaas's farm. It was a dreary place, save for Hilda. The bare daub-and-wattle walls; the clumps of misshapen and dusty prickly-pears that girt round the thatched huts of the Kaffir workpeople; the stone-penned sheep-kraals, and the corrugated iron roof of the bald stable for the waggon oxen, all was as crude and ugly as a new country can make things. It seemed to me a desecration that Hilda should live in such an unfinished land, Hilda, whom I imagined as moving by nature through broad English parks, with Elizabethan cottages and immemorial oaks, Hilda, whose proper atmosphere seemed to be one of coffee-coloured laces, ivy-clad abbeys, lichen-incrusted walls, all that is beautiful and gracious in time-honoured civilisations.

Nevertheless, we lived on there in a meaningless sort of way, I hardly knew why. To me it was a puzzle. When I asked Hilda, she shook her head with her sibylline air and answered, confidently: "You do not understand Sebastian as well as I do. We have to wait for HIM. The next move is his. Till he plays his piece, I cannot tell how I may have to checkmate him."

So we waited for Sebastian to advance a pawn. Meanwhile, I toyed with South African farming, not very successfully, I must admit. Nature did not design me for growing oats. I am no judge of oxen, and my views on the feeding of Kaffir sheep raised broad smiles on the black faces of my Mashona labourers.

I still lodged at Tant Mettie's, as everybody called Mrs. Klaas; she was courtesy aunt to the community at large, while Oom Jan Willem was its courtesy uncle. They were simple, homely folk, who lived up to their religious principles on an unvaried diet of stewed ox-beef and bread; they suffered much from chronic dyspepsia, due in part, at least, no doubt, to the monotony of their food, their life, their interests. One could hardly believe one was still in the nineteenth century; these people had the calm, the local seclusion of the prehistoric epoch. For them, Europe did not exist; they knew it merely as a place where settlers came from. What the Czar intended, what the Kaiser designed, never disturbed their rest. A sick ox, a rattling tile on the roof, meant more to their lives than war in Europe. The one break in the sameness of their daily routine was family prayers; the one weekly event, going to church at Salisbury. Still, they had a single enthusiasm. Like everybody else for fifty miles around, they believed profoundly in the "future of Rhodesia." When I gazed about me at the raw new land, the weary flat of red soil and brown grasses, I felt at least that, with a present like that, it had need of a future.

I am not by disposition a pioneer; I belong instinctively to the old civilisations. In the midst of rudimentary towns and incipient fields, I yearn for grey houses, a Norman church, an English thatched cottage.

However, for Hilda's sake, I braved it out, and continued to learn the A B C of agriculture on an unmade farm with great assiduity from Oom Jan Willem.

We had been stopping some months at Klaas's together when business compelled me one day to ride in to Salisbury. I had ordered some goods for my farm from England which had at last arrived. I had now to arrange for their conveyance from the town to my plot of land, a portentous matter. Just as I was on the point of leaving Klaas's, and was tightening the saddle-girth on my sturdy little pony, Oom Jan Willem himself sidled up to me with a mysterious air, his broad face all wrinkled with anticipatory pleasure. He placed a sixpence in my palm, glancing about him on every side as he did so, like a conspirator.

"What am I to buy with it?" I asked, much puzzled, and suspecting tobacco. Tant Mettie declared he smoked too much for a church elder.

He put his finger to his lips, nodded, and peered round. "Lollipops for Sannie," he whispered low, at last, with a guilty smile. "But"—he glanced about him again—"give them to me, please, when Tant Mettie isn't looking." His nod was all mystery.

"You may rely on my discretion," I replied, throwing the time-honoured prejudices of the profession to the winds, and well pleased to aid and abet the simple-minded soul in his nefarious designs against little Sannie's digestive apparatus. He patted me on the back. "PEPPERMINT lollipops, mind!" he went on, in the same solemn undertone. "Sannie likes them best—peppermint."

I put my foot in the stirrup, and vaulted into my saddle. "They shall not be forgotten," I answered, with a quiet smile at this pretty little evidence of fatherly feeling. I rode off. It was early morning, before the heat of the day began. Hilda accompanied me part of the way on her bicycle. She was going to the other young farm, some eight miles off, across the red-brown plateau, where she gave lessons daily to the ten-year old daughter of an English settler. It was a labour of love; for settlers in Rhodesia cannot afford to pay for what are beautifully described as "finishing governesses"; but Hilda was of the sort who cannot eat the bread of idleness. She had to justify herself to her kind by finding some work to do which should vindicate her existence.

I parted from her at a point on the monotonous plain where one rubbly road branched off from another. Then I jogged on in the full morning sun over that scorching plain of loose red sand all the way to Salisbury. Not a green leaf or a fresh flower anywhere. The eye ached at the hot glare of the reflected sunlight from the sandy level.

My business detained me several hours in the half-built town, with its flaunting stores and its rough new offices; it was not till towards afternoon that I could get away again on my sorrel, across the blazing plain once more to Klaas's.

I moved on over the plateau at an easy trot, full of thoughts of Hilda. What could be the step she expected Sebastian to take next? She did not know, herself, she had told me; there, her faculty failed her. But SOME step he WOULD take; and till he took it she must rest and be watchful.

I passed the great tree that stands up like an obelisk in the midst of the plain beyond the deserted Matabele village. I passed the low clumps of dry karroo-bushes by the rocky kopje. I passed the fork of the rubbly roads where I had parted from Hilda. At last, I reached the long, rolling ridge which looks down upon Klaas's, and could see in the slant sunlight the mud farmhouse and the corrugated iron roof where the oxen were stabled.

The place looked more deserted, more dead-alive than ever. Not a black boy moved in it. Even the cattle and Kaffir sheep were nowhere to be seen.... But then it was always quiet; and perhaps I noticed the obtrusive air of solitude and sleepiness even more than usual, because I had just returned from Salisbury. All things are comparative. After the lost loneliness of Klaas's farm, even brand-new Salisbury seemed busy and bustling.

I hurried on, ill at ease. But Tant Mettie would, doubtless, have a cup of tea ready for me as soon as I arrived, and Hilda would be waiting at the gate to welcome me.

I reached the stone enclosure, and passed up through the flower-garden. To my great surprise, Hilda was not there. As a rule, she came to meet me, with her sunny smile. But perhaps she was tired, or the sun on the road might have given her a headache. I dismounted from my mare, and called one of the Kaffir boys to take her to the stable. Nobody answered.... I called again. Still silence.... I tied her up to the post, and strode over to the door, astonished at the solitude. I began to feel there was something weird and uncanny about this home-coming. Never before had I known Klaas's so entirely deserted.

I lifted the latch and opened the door. It gave access at once to the single plain living-room. There, all was huddled. For a moment my eyes hardly took in the truth. There are sights so sickening that the brain at the first shock wholly fails to realise them.

On the stone slab floor of the low living-room Tant Mettie lay dead. Her body was pierced through by innumerable thrusts, which I somehow instinctively recognised as assegai wounds. By her side lay Sannie, the little prattling girl of three, my constant playmate, whom I had instructed in cat's-cradle, and taught the tales of Cinderella and Red Riding Hood. My hand grasped the lollipops in my pocket convulsively. She would never need them. Nobody else was about. What had become of Oom Jan Willem—and the baby?

I wandered out into the yard, sick with the sight I had already seen. There Oom Jan Willem himself lay stretched at full length; a bullet had pierced his left temple; his body was also riddled through with assegai thrusts.

I saw at once what this meant. A rising of the Matabele!

I had come back from Salisbury, unknowing it, into the midst of a revolt of bloodthirsty savages.

Yet, even if I had known, I must still have hurried home with all speed to Klaas's, to protect Hilda.

Hilda? Where was Hilda? A breathless sinking crept over me.

I staggered out into the open. It was impossible to say what horror might not have happened. The Matabele might even now be lurking about the kraal, for the bodies were hardly cold. But Hilda? Hilda? Whatever came, I must find Hilda.

Fortunately, I had my loaded revolver in my belt. Though we had not in the least anticipated this sudden revolt, it broke like a thunder-clap from a clear sky, the unsettled state of the country made even women go armed about their daily avocations.

I strode on, half maddened. Beside the great block of granite which sheltered the farm there rose one of those rocky little hillocks of loose boulders which are locally known in South Africa by the Dutch name of kopjes. I looked out upon it drearily. Its round brown ironstones lay piled irregularly together, almost as if placed there in some earlier age by the mighty hands of prehistoric giants. My gaze on it was blank. I was thinking, not of it, but of Hilda, Hilda.

I called the name aloud: "Hilda! Hilda! Hilda!"

As I called, to my immense surprise, one of the smooth round boulders on the hillside seemed slowly to uncurl, and to peer about it cautiously. Then it raised itself in the slant sunlight, put a hand to its eyes, and gazed out upon me with a human face for a moment. After that it descended, step by step, among the other stones, with a white object in its arms. As the boulder uncurled and came to life, I was aware, by degrees... yes, yes, it was Hilda, with Tant Mettie's baby!

In the fierce joy of that discovery I rushed forward to her, trembling, and clasped her in my arms. I could find no words but "Hilda! Hilda!"

"Are they gone?" she asked, staring about her with a terrified air, though still strangely preserving her wonted composure of manner.

"Who gone? The Matabele?"

"Yes, yes!"

"Did you see them, Hilda?"

"For a moment, with black shields and assegais, all shouting madly. You have been to the house, Hubert? You know what has happened?"

"Yes, yes, I know—a rising. They have massacred the Klaases."

She nodded. "I came back on my bicycle, and, when I opened the door, found Tant Mettie and little Sannie dead. Poor, sweet little Sannie! Oom Jan was lying shot in the yard outside. I saw the cradle overturned, and looked under it for the baby. They did not kill her, perhaps did not notice her. I caught her up in my arms, and rushed out to my machine, thinking to make for Salisbury, and give the alarm to the men there. One must try to save others, and YOU were coming, Hubert! Then I heard horses' hoofs, the Matabele returning. They dashed back, mounted, stolen horses from other farms, they have taken poor Oom Jan's, and they have gone on, shouting, to murder elsewhere! I flung down my machine among the bushes as they came, I hope they have not seen it, and I crouched here between the boulders, with the baby in my arms, trusting for protection to the colour of my dress, which is just like the ironstone."

"It is a perfect deception," I answered, admiring her instinctive cleverness even then. "I never so much as noticed you."

"No, nor the Matabele either, for all their sharp eyes. They passed by without stopping. I clasped the baby hard, and tried to keep it from crying, if it had cried, all would have been lost; but they passed just below, and swept on toward Rozenboom's. I lay still for a while, not daring to look out. Then I raised myself warily, and tried to listen. Just at that moment, I heard a horse's hoofs ring out once more. I couldn't tell, of course, whether it was YOU returning, or one of the Matabele, left behind by the others. So I crouched again.... Thank God, you are safe, Hubert!"

All this took a moment to say, or was less said than hinted. "Now, what must we do?" I cried. "Bolt back again to Salisbury?"

"It is the only thing possible, if my machine is unhurt. They may have taken it... or ridden over and broken it."

We went down to the spot, and picked it up where it lay, half-concealed among the brittle, dry scrub of milk-bushes. I examined the bearings carefully; though there were hoof-marks close by, it had received no hurt. I blew up the tire, which was somewhat flabby, and went on to untie my sturdy pony. The moment I looked at her I saw the poor little brute was wearied out with her two long rides in the sweltering sun. Her flanks quivered. "It is no use," I cried, patting her, as she turned to me with appealing eyes that asked for water. "She CAN'T go back as far as Salisbury; at least, till she has had a feed of corn and a drink. Even then, it will be rough on her."

"Give her bread," Hilda suggested. "That will hearten her more than corn. There is plenty in the house; Tant Mettie baked this morning."

I crept in reluctantly to fetch it. I also brought out from the dresser a few raw eggs, to break into a tumbler and swallow whole; for Hilda and I needed food almost as sorely as the poor beast herself.

There was something gruesome in thus rummaging about for bread and meat in the dead woman's cupboard, while she herself lay there on the floor; but one never realises how one will act in these great emergencies until they come upon one. Hilda, still calm with unearthly calmness, took a couple of loaves from my hand, and began feeding the pony with them. "Go and draw water for her," she said, simply, "while I give her the bread; that will save time. Every minute is precious."

I did as I was bid, not knowing each moment but that the insurgents would return. When I came back from the spring with the bucket, the mare had demolished the whole two loaves, and was going on upon some grass which Hilda had plucked for her.

"She hasn't had enough, poor dear," Hilda said, patting her neck. "A couple of loaves are penny buns to her appetite. Let her drink the water, while I go in and fetch out the rest of the baking."

I hesitated. "You CAN'T go in there again, Hilda!" I cried. "Wait, and let me do it."

Her white face was resolute. "Yes, I CAN," she answered. "It is a work of necessity; and in works of necessity a woman, I think, should flinch at nothing. Have I not seen already every varied aspect of death at Nathaniel's?" And in she went, undaunted, to that chamber of horrors, still clasping the baby.

The pony made short work of the remaining loaves, which she devoured with great zest. As Hilda had predicted, they seemed to hearten her. The food and drink, with a bucket of water dashed on her hoofs, gave her new vigour like wine. We gulped down our eggs in silence. Then I held Hilda's bicycle. She vaulted lightly on to the seat, white and tired as she was, with the baby in her left arm, and her right hand on the handle-bar.

"I must take the baby," I said.

She shook her head.

"Oh, no. I will not trust her to you."

"Hilda, I insist."

"And I insist, too. It is my place to take her."

"But can you ride so?" I asked, anxiously.

She began to pedal. "Oh, dear, yes. It is quite, quite easy. I shall get there all right, if the Matabele don't burst upon us."

Tired as I was with my long day's work, I jumped into my saddle. I saw I should only lose time if I disputed about the baby. My little horse seemed to understand that something grave had occurred; for, weary as she must have been, she set out with a will once more over that great red level. Hilda pedalled bravely by my side. The road was bumpy, but she was well accustomed to it. I could have ridden faster than she went, for the baby weighted her. Still, we rode for dear life. It was a grim experience.

All round, by this time, the horizon was dim with clouds of black smoke which went up from burning farms and plundered homesteads. The smoke did not rise high; it hung sullenly over the hot plain in long smouldering masses, like the smoke of steamers on foggy days in England. The sun was nearing the horizon; his slant red rays lighted up the red plain, the red sand, the brown-red grasses, with a murky, spectral glow of crimson. After those red pools of blood, this universal burst of redness appalled one. It seemed as though all nature had conspired in one unholy league with the Matabele. We rode on without a word. The red sky grew redder.

"They may have sacked Salisbury!" I exclaimed at last, looking out towards the brand-new town.

"I doubt it," Hilda answered. Her very doubt reassured me.

We began to mount a long slope. Hilda pedalled with difficulty. Not a sound was heard save the light fall of my pony's feet on the soft new road, and the shrill cry of the cicalas. Then, suddenly, we started. What was that noise in our rear? Once, twice, it rang out. The loud ping of a rifle!

Looking behind us, we saw eight or ten mounted Matabele! Stalwart warriors they were, half naked, and riding stolen horses. They were coming our way! They had seen us! They were pursuing us!

"Put on all speed!" I cried, in my agony. "Hilda, can you manage it?" She pedalled with a will. But, as we mounted the slope, I saw they were gaining upon us. A few hundred yards were all our start. They had the descent of the opposite hill as yet in their favour.

One man, astride on a better horse than the rest, galloped on in front and came within range of us. He had a rifle in his hand, he pointed it twice, and covered us. But he did not shoot. Hilda gave a cry of relief. "Don't you see?" she exclaimed. "It is Oom Jan Willem's rifle! That was their last cartridge. They have no more ammunition."

I saw she was probably right; for Klaas was out of cartridges, and was waiting for my new stock to arrive from England. If that were correct, they must get near enough to attack us with assegais. They are more dangerous so. I remembered what an old Boer had said to me at Buluwayo: "The Zulu with his assegai is an enemy to be feared; with a gun, he is a bungler."

We pounded on up the hill. It was deadly work, with those brutes at our heels. The child on Hilda's arm was visibly wearying her. It kept on whining. "Hilda," I cried, "that baby will lose your life! You CANNOT go on carrying it."

She turned to me with a flash of her eyes. "What! You are a man," she broke out, "and you ask a woman to save her life by abandoning a baby! Hubert, you shame me!"

I felt she was right. If she had been capable of giving it up, she would not have been Hilda. There was but one other way left.

"Then YOU must take the pony," I called out, "and let me have the bicycle!"

"You couldn't ride it," she called back. "It is a woman's machine, remember."

"Yes, I could," I replied, without slowing. "It is not much too short; and I can bend my knees a bit. Quick, quick! No words! Do as I tell you!"

She hesitated a second. The child's weight distressed her. "We should lose time in changing," she answered, at last, doubtful but still pedalling, though my hand was on the rein, ready to pull up the pony.

"Not if we manage it right. Obey orders! The moment I say 'Halt,' I shall slacken my mare's pace. When you see me leave the saddle, jump off instantly, you, and mount her! I will catch the machine before it falls. Are you ready? Halt, then!"

She obeyed the word without one second's delay. I slipped off, held the bridle, caught the bicycle, and led it instantaneously. Then I ran beside the pony, bridle in one hand, machine in the other, till Hilda had sprung with a light bound into the stirrup. At that, a little leap, and I mounted the bicycle. It was all done nimbly, in less time than the telling takes, for we are both of us naturally quick in our movements. Hilda rode like a man, astride, her short, bicycling skirt, unobtrusively divided in front and at the back, made this easily possible. Looking behind me with a hasty glance, I could see that the savages, taken aback, had reined in to deliberate at our unwonted evolution. I feel sure that the novelty of the iron horse, with a woman riding it, played not a little on their superstitious fears; they suspected, no doubt, this was some ingenious new engine of war devised against them by the unaccountable white man; it might go off unexpectedly in their faces at any moment. Most of them, I observed, as they halted, carried on their backs black ox-hide shields, interlaced with white thongs; they were armed with two or three assegais apiece and a knobkerry.

Instead of losing time by the change, as it turned out, we had actually gained it. Hilda was able to put on my sorrel to her full pace, which I had not dared to do, for fear of outrunning my companion; the wise little beast, for her part, seemed to rise to the occasion, and to understand that we were pursued; for she stepped out bravely. On the other hand, in spite of the low seat and the short crank of a woman's machine, I could pedal up the slope with more force than Hilda, for I am a practised hill-climber; so that in both ways we gained, besides having momentarily disconcerted and checked the enemy. Their ponies were tired, and they rode them full tilt with savage recklessness, making them canter up-hill, and so needlessly fatiguing them. The Matabele, indeed, are unused to horses, and manage them but ill. It is as foot soldiers, creeping stealthily through bush or long grass, that they are really formidable. Only one of their mounts was tolerably fresh, the one which had once already almost overtaken us. As we neared the top of the slope, Hilda, glancing behind her, exclaimed, with a sudden thrill, "He is spurting again, Hubert!"

I drew my revolver and held it in my right hand, using my left for steering. I did not look back; time was far too precious. I set my teeth hard. "Tell me when he draws near enough for a shot," I said, quietly.

Hilda only nodded. Being mounted on the mare, she could see behind her more steadily now than I could from the machine; and her eye was trustworthy. As for the baby, rocked by the heave and fall of the pony's withers, it had fallen asleep placidly in the very midst of this terror!

After a second, I asked once more, with bated breath, "Is he gaining?"

She looked back. "Yes; gaining."

A pause. "And now?"

"Still gaining. He is poising an assegai."

Ten seconds more passed in breathless suspense. The thud of their horses' hoofs alone told me their nearness. My finger was on the trigger. I awaited the word. "Fire!" she said at last, in a calm, unflinching voice. "He is well within distance."

I turned half round and levelled as true as I could at the advancing black man. He rode, nearly naked, showing all his teeth and brandishing his assegai; the long white feathers stuck upright in his hair gave him a wild and terrifying barbaric aspect. It was difficult to preserve one's balance, keep the way on, and shoot, all at the same time; but, spurred by necessity, I somehow did it. I fired three shots in quick succession. My first bullet missed; my second knocked the man over; my third grazed the horse. With a ringing shriek, the Matabele fell in the road, a black writhing mass; his horse, terrified, dashed back with maddened snorts into the midst of the others. Its plunging disconcerted the whole party for a minute.

We did not wait to see the rest. Taking advantage of this momentary diversion in our favour, we rode on at full speed to the top of the slope, I never knew before how hard I could pedal, and began to descend at a dash into the opposite hollow.

The sun had set by this time. There is no twilight in those latitudes. It grew dark at once. We could see now, in the plain all round, where black clouds of smoke had rolled before, one lurid red glare of burning houses, mixed with a sullen haze of tawny light from the columns of prairie fire kindled by the insurgents.

We made our way still onward across the open plain without one word towards Salisbury. The mare was giving out. She strode with a will; but her flanks were white with froth; her breath came short; foam flew from her nostrils.

As we mounted the next ridge, still distancing our pursuers, I saw suddenly, on its crest, defined against the livid red sky like a silhouette, two more mounted black men!

"It's all up, Hilda!" I cried, losing heart at last. "They are on both sides of us now! The mare is spent; we are surrounded!"

She drew rein and gazed at them. For a moment suspense spoke in all her attitude. Then she burst into a sudden deep sigh of relief. "No, no," she cried; "these are friendlies!"

"How do you know?" I gasped. But I believed her.

"They are looking out this way, with hands shading their eyes against the red glare. They are looking away from Salisbury, in the direction of the attack. They are expecting the enemy. They MUST be friendlies! See, see! they have caught sight of us!"

As she spoke, one of the men lifted his rifle and half pointed it. "Don't shoot! don't shoot!" I shrieked aloud. "We are English! English!"

The men let their rifles drop, and rode down towards us. "Who are you?" I cried.

They saluted us, military fashion. "Matabele police, sah," the leader answered, recognising me. "You are flying from Klaas's?"

"Yes," I answered. "They have murdered Klaas, with his wife and child. Some of them are now following us."

The spokesman was a well-educated Cape Town negro. "All right sah," he answered. "I have forty men here right behind de kopje. Let dem come! We can give a good account of dem. Ride on straight wit de lady to Salisbury!"

"The Salisbury people know of this rising, then?" I asked.

"Yes, sah. Dem know since five o'clock. Kaffir boys from Klaas's brought in de news; and a white man escaped from Rozenboom's confirm it. We have pickets all round. You is safe now; you can ride on into Salisbury witout fear of de Matabele."

I rode on, relieved. Mechanically, my feet worked to and fro on the pedals. It was a gentle down-gradient now towards the town. I had no further need for special exertion.

Suddenly, Hilda's voice came wafted to me, as through a mist. "What are you doing, Hubert? You'll be off in a minute!"

I started and recovered my balance with difficulty. Then I was aware at once that one second before I had all but dropped asleep, dog tired, on the bicycle. Worn out with my long day and with the nervous strain, I began to doze off, with my feet still moving round and round automatically, the moment the anxiety of the chase was relieved, and an easy down-grade gave me a little respite.

I kept myself awake even then with difficulty. Riding on through the lurid gloom, we reached Salisbury at last, and found the town already crowded with refugees from the plateau. However, we succeeded in securing two rooms at a house in the long street, and were soon sitting down to a much-needed supper.

As we rested, an hour or two later, in the ill-furnished back room, discussing this sudden turn of affairs with our host and some neighbours, for, of course, all Salisbury was eager for news from the scene of the massacres, I happened to raise my head, and saw, to my great surprise... a haggard white face peering in at us through the window.

It peered round a corner, stealthily. It was an ascetic face, very sharp and clear-cut. It had a stately profile. The long and wiry grizzled moustache, the deep-set, hawk-like eyes, the acute, intense, intellectual features, all were very familiar. So was the outer setting of long, white hair, straight and silvery as it fell, and just curled in one wave-like inward sweep where it turned and rested on the stooping shoulders. But the expression on the face was even stranger than the sudden apparition. It was an expression of keen and poignant disappointment, as of a man whom fate has baulked of some well-planned end, his due by right, which mere chance has evaded.

"They say there's a white man at the bottom of all this trouble," our host had been remarking, one second earlier. "The niggers know too much; and where did they get their rifles? People at Rozenboom's believe some black-livered traitor has been stirring up the Matabele for weeks and weeks. An enemy of Rhodes's, of course, jealous of our advance; a French agent, perhaps; but more likely one of these confounded Transvaal Dutchmen. Depend upon it, it's Kruger's doing."

As the words fell from his lips, I saw the face. I gave a quick little start, then recovered my composure.

But Hilda noted it. She looked up at me hastily. She was sitting with her back to the window, and therefore, of course, could not see the face itself, which indeed was withdrawn with a hurried movement, yet with a certain strange dignity, almost before I could feel sure of having seen it. Still, she caught my startled expression, and the gleam of surprise and recognition in my eye. She laid one hand upon my arm. "You have seen him?" she asked quietly, almost below her breath.

"Seen whom?"

"Sebastian."

It was useless denying it to HER. "Yes, I have seen him," I answered, in a confidential aside.

"Just now, this moment, at the back of the house, looking in at the window upon us?"

"You are right, as always."

She drew a deep breath. "He has played his game," she said low to me, in an awed undertone. "I felt sure it was he. I expected him to play; though what piece, I knew not; and when I saw those poor dead souls, I was certain he had done it, indirectly done it. The Matabele are his pawns. He wanted to aim a blow at ME; and THIS was the way he chose to aim it."

"Do you think he is capable of that?" I cried. For, in spite of all, I had still a sort of lingering respect for Sebastian. "It seems so reckless, like the worst of anarchists, when he strikes at one head, to involve so many irrelevant lives in one common destruction."

Hilda's face was like a drowned man's.

"To Sebastian," she answered, shuddering, "the End is all; the Means are unessential. Who wills the End, wills the Means; that is the sum and substance of his philosophy of life. From first to last, he has always acted up to it. Did I not tell you once he was a snow-clad volcano?"

"Still, I am loth to believe—" I cried.

She interrupted me calmly. "I knew it," she said. "I expected it. Beneath that cold exterior, the fires of his life burn fiercely still. I told you we must wait for Sebastian's next move; though I confess, even from HIM, I hardly dreamt of this one. But, from the moment when I opened the door on poor Tant Mettie's body, lying there in its red horror, I felt it must be he. And when you started just now, I said to myself in a flash of intuition—'Sebastian has come! He has come to see how his devil's work has prospered.' He sees it has gone wrong. So now he will try to devise some other."

I thought of the malign expression on that cruel white face as it stared in at the window from the outer gloom, and I felt convinced she was right. She had read her man once more. For it was the desperate, contorted face of one appalled to discover that a great crime attempted and successfully carried out has failed, by mere accident, of its central intention.

CHAPTER VIII

THE EPISODE OF THE EUROPEAN WITH THE KAFFIR HEART

Unfashionable as it is to say so, I am a man of peace. I belong to a profession whose province is to heal, not to destroy. Still there ARE times which turn even the most peaceful of us perforce into fighters—times when those we love, those we are bound to protect, stand in danger of their lives; and at moments like that, no man can doubt what is his plain duty. The Matabele revolt was one such moment. In a conflict of race we MUST back our own colour. I do not know whether the natives were justified in rising or not; most likely, yes; for we had stolen their country; but when once they rose, when the security of white women depended upon repelling them, I felt I had no alternative. For Hilda's sake, for the sake of every woman and child in Salisbury, and in all Rhodesia, I was bound to bear my part in restoring order.

For the immediate future, it is true, we were safe enough in the little town; but we did not know how far the revolt might have spread; we could not tell what had happened at Charter, at Buluwayo, at the outlying stations. The Matabele, perhaps, had risen in force over the whole vast area which was once Lo-Bengula's country; if so, their first object would certainly be to cut us off from communication with the main body of English settlers at Buluwayo.

"I trust to you, Hilda," I said, on the day after the massacre at Klaas's, "to divine for us where these savages are next likely to attack us."

She cooed at the motherless baby, raising one bent finger, and then turned to me with a white smile. "Then you ask too much of me," she answered. "Just think what a correct answer would imply! First, a knowledge of these savages' character; next, a knowledge of their mode of fighting. Can't you see that only a person who possessed my trick of intuition, and who had also spent years in warfare among the Matabele, would be really able to answer your question?"

"And yet such questions have been answered before now by people far less intuitive than you," I went on. "Why, I've read somewhere how, when the war between Napoleon the First and the Prussians broke out, in 1806, Jomini predicted that the decisive battle of the campaign would be fought near Jena; and near Jena it was fought. Are not YOU better than many Jominis?"

Hilda tickled the baby's cheek. "Smile, then, baby, smile!" she said, pouncing one soft finger on a gathering dimple. "And who WAS your friend Jomini?"

"The greatest military critic and tactician of his age," I answered. "One of Napoleon's generals. I fancy he wrote a book, don't you know, a book on war, Des Grandes Operations Militaires, or something of that sort."

"Well, there you are, then! That's just it! Your Jomini, or Hominy, or whatever you call him, not only understood Napoleon's temperament, but understood war and understood tactics. It was all a question of the lie of the land, and strategy, and so forth. If I had been asked, I could never have answered a quarter as well as Jomini Piccolomini—could I, baby? Jomini would have been worth a good many me's. There, there, a dear, motherless darling! Why, she crows just as if she hadn't lost all her family!"

"But, Hilda, we must be serious. I count upon you to help us in this matter. We are still in danger. Even now these Matabele may attack and destroy us."

She laid the child on her lap, and looked grave. "I know it, Hubert; but I must leave it now to you men. I am no tactician. Don't take ME for one of Napoleon's generals."

"Still," I said, "we have not only the Matabele to reckon with, recollect. There is Sebastian as well. And, whether you know your Matabele or not, you at least know your Sebastian."

She shuddered. "I know him; yes, I know him.... But this case is so difficult. We have Sebastian, complicated by a rabble of savages, whose habits and manners I do not understand. It is THAT that makes the difficulty."

"But Sebastian himself?" I urged. "Take him first, in isolation."

She paused for a full minute, with her chin on her hand and her elbow on the table. Her brow gathered. "Sebastian?" she repeated. "Sebastian?—ah, there I might guess something. Well, of course, having once begun this attempt, and being definitely committed, as it were, to a policy of killing us, he will go through to the bitter end, no matter how many other lives it may cost. That is Sebastian's method."

"You don't think, having once found out that I saw and recognised him, he would consider the game lost, and slink away to the coast again?"

"Sebastian? Oh, no; that is the absolute antipodes of his type and temperament."

"He will never give up because of a temporary check, you think?"

"No, never. The man has a will of sheer steel, it may break, but it will not bend. Besides, consider: he is too deeply involved. You have seen him; you know; and he knows you know. You may bring this thing home to him. Then what is his plain policy? Why, to egg on the natives whose confidence he has somehow gained into making a further attack, and cutting off all Salisbury. If he had succeeded in getting you and me massacred at Klaas's, as he hoped, he would no doubt have slunk off to the coast at once, leaving his black dupes to be shot down at leisure by Rhodes's soldiers."

"I see; but having failed in that?"

"Then he is bound to go through with it, and kill us if he can, even if he has to kill all Salisbury with us. That, I feel sure, is Sebastian's plan. Whether he can get the Matabele to back him up in it or not is a different matter."

"But taking Sebastian himself; alone?"

"Oh, Sebastian himself alone would naturally say: 'Never mind Buluwayo! Concentrate round Salisbury, and kill off all there first; when that is done, then you can move on at your ease and cut them to pieces in Charter and Buluwayo.' You see, he would have no interest in the movement, himself, once he had fairly got rid of us here. The Matabele are only the pieces in his game. It is ME he wants, not Salisbury. He would clear out of Rhodesia as soon as he had carried his point. But he would have to give some reasonable ground to the Matabele for his first advice; and it seems a reasonable ground to say, 'Don't leave Salisbury in your rear, so as to put yourselves between two fires. Capture the outpost first; that down, march on undistracted to the principal stronghold.'"

"Who is no tactician?" I murmured, half aloud.

She laughed. "That's not tactics, Hubert; that's plain common sense, and knowledge of Sebastian. Still, it comes to nothing. The question is not, 'What would Sebastian wish?' it is, 'Could Sebastian persuade these angry black men to accept his guidance?'"

"Sebastian!" I cried; "Sebastian could persuade the very devil! I know the man's fiery enthusiasm, his contagious eloquence. He thrilled me through, myself, with his electric personality, so that it took me six years, and your aid, to find him out at last. His very abstractness tells. Why, even in this war, you may be sure, he will be making notes all the time on the healing of wounds in tropical climates, contrasting the African with the European constitution."

"Oh, yes; of course. Whatever he does, he will never forget the interests of science. He is true to his lady-love, to whomever else he plays false. That is his saving virtue."

"And he will talk down the Matabele," I went on, "even if he doesn't know their language. But I suspect he does; for, you must remember, he was three years in South Africa as a young man, on a scientific expedition, collecting specimens. He can ride like a trooper; and he knows the country. His masterful ways, his austere face, will cow the natives. Then, again, he has the air of a prophet; and prophets always stir the negro. I can imagine with what air he will bid them drive out the intrusive white men who have usurped their land, and draw them flattering pictures of a new Matabele empire about to arise under a new chief, too strong for these gold-grubbing, diamond-hunting mobs from over sea to meddle with."

She reflected once more. "Do you mean to say anything of our suspicions in Salisbury, Hubert?" she asked at last.

"It is useless," I answered. "The Salisbury folk believe there is a white man at the bottom of this trouble already. They will try to catch him; that's all that is necessary. If we said it was Sebastian, people would only laugh at us. They must understand Sebastian, as you and I understand him, before they would think such a move credible. As a rule in life, if you know anything which other people do not know, better keep it to yourself; you will only get laughed at as a fool for telling it."

"I think so, too. That is why I never say what I suspect or infer from my knowledge of types, except to a few who can understand and appreciate. Hubert, if they all arm for the defence of the town, you will stop here, I suppose, to tend the wounded?"

Her lips trembled as she spoke, and she gazed at me with a strange wistfulness. "No, dearest," I answered at once, taking her face in my hands. "I shall fight with the rest. Salisbury has more need to-day of fighters than of healers."

"I thought you would," she answered, slowly. "And I think you do right." Her face was set white; she played nervously with the baby. "I would not urge you; but I am glad you say so. I want you to stop; yet I could not love you so much if I did not see you ready to play the man at such a crisis."

"I shall give in my name with the rest," I answered.

"Hubert, it is hard to spare you, hard to send you to such danger. But for one other thing, I am glad you are going.... They must take Sebastian alive; they must NOT kill him."

"They will shoot him red-handed if they catch him," I answered confidently. "A white man who sides with the blacks in an insurrection!"

"Then YOU must see that they do not do it. They must bring him in alive, and try him legally. For me, and therefore for you, that is of the first importance."

"Why so, Hilda?"

"Hubert, you want to marry me." I nodded vehemently. "Well, you know I can only marry you on one condition, that I have succeeded first in clearing my father's memory. Now, the only man living who can clear it is Sebastian. If Sebastian were to be shot, it could NEVER be cleared, and then, law of Medes and Persians, I could never marry you."

"But how can you expect Sebastian, of all men, to clear it, Hilda?" I cried. "He is ready to kill us both, merely to prevent your attempting a revision; is it likely you can force him to confess his crime, still less induce him to admit it voluntarily?"

She placed her hands over her eyes and pressed them hard with a strange, prophetic air she often had about her when she gazed into the future. "I know my man," she answered, slowly, without uncovering her eyes. "I know how I can do it, if the chance ever comes to me. But the chance must come first. It is hard to find. I lost it once at Nathaniel's. I must not lose it again. If Sebastian is killed skulking here in Rhodesia, my life's purpose will have failed; I shall not have vindicated my father's good name; and then, we can never marry."

"So I understand, Hilda, my orders are these: I am to go out and fight for the women and children, if possible; that Sebastian shall be made prisoner alive, and on no account to let him be killed in the open!"

"I give you no orders, Hubert. I tell you how it seems best to me. But if Sebastian is shot dead, then you understand it must be all over between us. I NEVER can marry you until, or unless, I have cleared my father."

"Sebastian shall not be shot dead," I cried, with my youthful impetuosity. "He shall be brought in alive, though all Salisbury as one man try its best to lynch him."

I went out to report myself as a volunteer for service. Within the next few hours the whole town had been put in a state of siege, and all available men armed to oppose the insurgent Matabele. Hasty preparations were made for defence. The ox-waggons of settlers were drawn up outside in little circles here and there, so as to form laagers, which acted practically as temporary forts for the protection of the outskirts. In one of these I was posted. With our company were two American scouts, named Colebrook and Doolittle, irregular fighters whose value in South African campaigns had already been tested in the old Matabele war against Lo-Bengula. Colebrook, in particular, was an odd-looking creature, a tall, spare man, bodied like a weasel. He was red-haired, ferret-eyed, and an excellent scout, but scrappier and more inarticulate in his manner of speech than any human being I had ever encountered. His conversation was a series of rapid interjections, jerked out at intervals, and made comprehensible by a running play of gesture and attitude.

"Well, yes," he said, when I tried to draw him out on the Matabele mode of fighting. "Not on the open. Never! Grass, if you like. Or bushes. The eyes of them! The eyes!..." He leaned eagerly forward, as if looking for something. "See here, Doctor; I'm telling you. Spots. Gleaming. Among the grass. Long grass. And armed, too. A pair of 'em each. One to throw"—he raised his hand as if lancing something—"the other for close fighting. Assegais, you know. That's the name of it. Only the eyes. Creeping, creeping, creeping. No noise. One raised. Waggons drawn up in laager. Oxen out-spanned in the middle. Trekking all day. Tired out; dog tired. Crawl, crawl, crawl! Hands and knees. Might be snakes. A wriggle. Men sitting about the camp fire. Smoking. Gleam of their eyes! Under the waggons. Nearer, nearer, nearer! Then, the throwing ones in your midst. Shower of 'em. Right and left. 'Halloa! stand by, boys!' Look up; see 'em swarming, black like ants, over the waggons. Inside the laager. Snatch up rifles! All up! Oxen stampeding, men running, blacks sticking 'em like pigs in the back with their assegais. Bad job, the whole thing. Don't care for it, myself. Very tough 'uns to fight. If they once break laager."

"Then you should never let them get to close quarters," I suggested, catching the general drift of his inarticulate swift pictures.

"You're a square man, you are, Doctor! There you touch the spot. Never let 'em get at close quarters. Sentries?—creep past 'em. Outposts?—crawl between. Had Forbes and Wilson like that. Cut 'em off. Perdition!... But Maxims will do it! Maxims! Never let em get near. Sweep the ground all round. Durned hard, though, to know just WHEN they're coming. A night; two nights; all clear; only waste ammunition. Third, they swarm like bees; break laager; all over!"

This was not exactly an agreeable picture of what we had to expect, the more so as our particular laager happened to have no Maxims. However, we kept a sharp lookout for those gleaming eyes in the long grass of which Colebrook warned us; their flashing light was the one thing to be seen, at night above all, when the black bodies could crawl unperceived through the tall dry herbage. On our first night out we had no adventures. We watched by turns outside, relieving sentry from time to time, while those of us who slept within the laager slept on the bare ground with our arms beside us. Nobody spoke much. The tension was too great. Every moment we expected an attack of the enemy.

Next day news reached us by scouts from all the other laagers. None of them had been attacked; but in all there was a deep, half-instinctive belief that the Matabele in force were drawing step by step closer and closer around us. Lo-Bengula's old impis, or native regiments, had gathered together once more under their own indunas, men trained and drilled in all the arts and ruses of savage warfare. On their own ground, and among their native scrub, those rude strategists are formidable. They know the country, and how to fight in it. We had nothing to oppose to them but a handful of the new Matabeleland police, an old regular soldier or two, and a raw crowd of volunteers, most of whom, like myself, had never before really handled a rifle.

That afternoon, the Major in command decided to send out the two American scouts to scour the grass and discover, if possible, how near our lines the Matabele had penetrated. I begged hard to be permitted to accompany them. I wanted, if I could, to get evidence against Sebastian; or, at least, to learn whether he was still directing and assisting the enemy. At first, the scouts laughed at my request; but when I told them privately that I believed I had a clue against the white traitor who had caused the revolt, and that I wished to identify him, they changed their tone, and began to think there might be something in it.

"Experience?" Colebrook asked in his brief shorthand of speech, running his ferret eyes over me.

"None," I answered; "but a noiseless tread and a capacity for crawling through holes in hedges which may perhaps be useful."

He glanced inquiry at Doolittle, who was a shorter and stouter man, with a knack of getting over obstacles by sheer forcefulness.

"Hands and knees!" he said, abruptly, in the imperative mood, pointing to a clump of dry grass with thorny bushes ringed about it.

I went down on my hands and knees, and threaded my way through the long grasses and matted boughs as noiselessly as I could. The two old hands watched me. When I emerged several yards off, much to their surprise, Colebrook turned to Doolittle. "Might answer," he said curtly. "Major says, 'Choose your own men.' Anyhow, if they catch him, nobody's fault but his. Wants to go. Will do it."

We set out through the long grass together, walking erect at first, till we had got some distance from the laager, and then, creeping as the Matabele themselves creep, without displacing the grass-flowers, for a mere wave on top would have betrayed us at once to the quick eyes of those observant savages. We crept on for a mile or so. At last, Colebrook turned to me, one finger on his lips. His ferret eyes gleamed. We were approaching a wooded hill, all interspersed with boulders. "Kaffirs here!" he whispered low, as if he knew by instinct. HOW he knew, I cannot tell; he seemed almost to scent them.

We stole on farther, going more furtively than ever now. I could notice by this time that there were waggons in front, and could hear men speaking in them. I wanted to proceed, but Colebrook held up one warning hand. "Won't do," he said, shortly, in a low tone. "Only myself. Danger ahead! Stop here and wait for me."

Doolittle and myself waited. Colebrook kept on cautiously, squirming his long body in sinuous waves like a lizard's through the grass, and was soon lost to us. No snake could have been lither. We waited, with ears intent. One minute, two minutes, many minutes passed. We could catch the voices of the Kaffirs in the bush all round. They were speaking freely, but what they said I did not know, as I had picked up only a very few words of the Matabele language.

It seemed hours while we waited, still as mice in our ambush, and alert. I began to think Colebrook must have been lost or killed, so long was he gone, and that we must return without him. At last, we leaned forward, a muffled movement in the grass ahead! A slight wave at the base! Then it divided below, bit by bit, while the tops remained stationary. A weasel-like body slank noiselessly through. Finger on lips once more, Colebrook glided beside us. We turned and crawled back, stifling our very pulses. For many minutes none of us spoke. But we heard in our rear a loud cry and a shaking of assegais; the Kaffirs behind us were yelling frightfully. They must have suspected something, seen some movement in the tufted heads of grass, for they spread abroad, shouting. We halted, holding our breath. After a time, however; the noise died down. They were moving another way. We crept on again, stealthily.

When, at last, after many minutes, we found ourselves beyond a sheltering belt of brushwood, we ventured to rise and speak. "Well?" I asked of Colebrook. "Did you discover anything?"

He nodded assent. "Couldn't see him," he said shortly. "But he's there, right enough. White man. Heard 'em talk of him."

"What did they say?" I asked, eagerly.

"Said he had a white skin, but his heart was a Kaffir's. Great induna; leader of many impis. Prophet, wise weather doctor! Friend of old Moselekatse's. Destroy the white men from over the big water; restore the land to the Matabele. Kill all in Salisbury, especially the white women. Witches, all witches. They give charms to the men; cook lions' hearts for them; make them brave with love-drinks."

"They said that?" I exclaimed, taken aback. "Kill all the white women!"

"Yes. Kill all. White witches, every one. The young ones worst. Word of the great induna."

"And you could not see him?"

"Crept near waggons, close. Fellow himself inside. Heard his voice; spoke English, with a little Matabele. Kaffir boy who was servant at the mission interpreted."

"What sort of voice? Like this?" And I imitated Sebastian's cold, clear-cut tone as well as I was able.

"The man! That's him, Doctor. You've got him down to the ground. The very voice. Heard him giving orders."

That settled the question. I was certain of it now. Sebastian was with the insurgents.

We made our way back to our laager, flung ourselves down, and slept a little on the ground before taking our turn in the fatigues of the night watch. Our horses were loosely tied, ready for any sudden alarm. About midnight, we three were sitting with others about the fire, talking low to one another. All at once Doolittle sprang up, alert and eager. "Look out, boys!" he cried, pointing his hands under the waggons. "What's wriggling in the grass there?"

I looked, and saw nothing. Our sentries were posted outside, about a hundred yards apart, walking up and down till they met, and exchanging "All's well" aloud at each meeting.

"They should have been stationary!" one of our scouts exclaimed, looking out at them. "It's easier for the Matabele to see them so, when they walk up and down, moving against the sky. The Major ought to have posted them where it wouldn't have been so simple for a Kaffir to see them and creep in between them!"

"Too late now, boys!" Colebrook burst out, with a rare effort of articulateness. "Call back the sentries, Major! The blacks have broken line! Hold there! They're in upon us!"

Even as he spoke, I followed his eager pointing hand with my eyes, and just descried among the grass two gleaming objects, seen under the hollow of one of the waggons. Two: then two; then two again; and behind, whole pairs of them. They looked like twin stars; but they were eyes, black eyes, reflecting the starlight and the red glare of the camp-fire. They crept on tortuously in serpentine curves through the long, dry grasses. I could feel, rather than see, that they were Matabele, crawling prone on their bellies, and trailing their snake-like way between the dark jungle. Quick as thought, I raised my rifle and blazed away at the foremost. So did several others. But the Major shouted, angrily: "Who fired? Don't shoot, boys, till you hear the word of command! Back, sentries, to laager! Not a shot till they're safe inside! You'll hit your own people!"

Almost before he said it, the sentries darted back. The Matabele, crouching on hands and knees in the long grass, had passed between them unseen. A wild moment followed. I can hardly describe it; the whole thing was so new to me, and took place so quickly. Hordes of black human ants seemed to surge up all at once over and under the waggons. Assegais whizzed through the air, or gleamed brandished around one. Our men fell back to the centre of the laager, and formed themselves hastily under the Major's orders. Then a pause; a deadly fire. Once, twice, thrice we volleyed. The Matabele fell by dozens, but they came on by hundreds. As fast as we fired and mowed down one swarm, fresh swarms seemed to spring from the earth and stream over the waggons. Others appeared to grow up almost beneath our feet as they wormed their way on their faces along the ground between the wheels, squirmed into the circle, and then rose suddenly, erect and naked, in front of us. Meanwhile, they yelled and shouted, clashing their spears and shields. The oxen bellowed. The rifles volleyed. It was a pandemonium of sound in an orgy of gloom. Darkness, lurid flame, blood, wounds, death, horror!

Yet, in the midst of all this hubbub, I could not help admiring the cool military calm and self-control of our Major. His voice rose clear above the confused tumult. "Steady, boys, steady! Don't fire at random. Pick each your likeliest man, and aim at him deliberately. That's right; easy, easy! Shoot at leisure, and don't waste ammunition!"

He stood as if he were on parade, in the midst of this palpitating turmoil of savages. Some of us, encouraged by his example, mounted the waggons, and shot from the tops at our approaching assailants.

How long the hurly-burly went on, I cannot say. We fired, fired, fired, and Kaffirs fell like sheep; yet more Kaffirs rose fresh from the long grass to replace them. They swarmed with greater ease now over the covered waggons, across the mangled and writhing bodies of their fellows; for the dead outside made an inclined plane for the living to mount by. But the enemy were getting less numerous, I thought, and less anxious to fight. The steady fire told on them. By-and-by, with a little halt, for the first time they wavered. All our men now mounted the waggons, and began to fire on them in regular volleys as they came up. The evil effects of the surprise were gone by this time; we were acting with coolness and obeying orders. But several of our people dropped close beside me, pierced through with assegais.

All at once, as if a panic had burst over them, the Matabele, with one mind, stopped dead short in their advance and ceased fighting. Till that moment, no number of deaths seemed to make any difference to them. Men fell, disabled; others sprang up from the ground by magic. But now, of a sudden, their courage flagged, they faltered, gave way, broke, and shambled in a body. At last, as one man, they turned and fled. Many of them leapt up with a loud cry from the long grass where they were skulking, flung away their big shields with the white thongs interlaced, and ran for dear life, black, crouching figures, through the dense, dry jungle. They held their assegais still, but did not dare to use them. It was a flight, pell-mell, and the devil take the hindmost.

Not until then had I leisure to THINK, and to realise my position. This was the first and only time I had ever seen a battle. I am a bit of a coward, I believe, like most other men, though I have courage enough to confess it; and I expected to find myself terribly afraid when it came to fighting. Instead of that, to my immense surprise, once the Matabele had swarmed over the laager, and were upon us in their thousands, I had no time to be frightened. The absolute necessity for keeping cool, for loading and reloading, for aiming and firing, for beating them off at close quarters, all this so occupied one's mind, and still more one's hands, that one couldn't find room for any personal terrors. "They are breaking over there!" "They will overpower us yonder!" "They are faltering now!" Those thoughts were so uppermost in one's head, and one's arms were so alert, that only after the enemy gave way, and began to run at full pelt, could a man find breathing-space to think of his own safety. Then the thought occurred to me, "I have been through my first fight, and come out of it alive; after all, I was a deal less afraid than I expected!"

That took but a second, however. Next instant, awaking to the altered circumstances, we were after them at full speed; accompanying them on their way back to their kraals in the uplands with a running fire as a farewell attention.

As we broke laager in pursuit of them, by the uncertain starlight we saw a sight which made us boil with indignation. A mounted man turned and fled before them. He seemed their leader, unseen till then. He was dressed like a European, tall, thin, unbending, in a greyish-white suit. He rode a good horse, and sat it well; his air was commanding, even as he turned and fled in the general rout from that lost battle.

I seized Colebrook's arm, almost speechless with anger. "The white man!" I cried. "The traitor!"

He did not answer a word, but with a set face of white rage loosed his horse from where it was tethered among the waggons. At the same moment, I loosed mine. So did Doolittle. Quick as thought, but silently, we led them out all three where the laager was broken. I clutched my mare's mane, and sprang to the stirrup to pursue our enemy. My sorrel bounded off like a bird. The fugitive had a good two minutes start of us; but our horses were fresh, while his had probably been ridden all day. I patted my pony's neck; she responded with a ringing neigh of joy. We tore after the outlaw, all three of us abreast. I felt a sort of fierce delight in the reaction after the fighting. Our ponies galloped wildly over the plain; we burst out into the night, never heeding the Matabele whom we passed on the open in panic-stricken retreat. I noticed that many of them in their terror had even flung away their shields and their assegais.

It was a mad chase across the dark veldt, we three, neck to neck, against that one desperate runaway. We rode all we knew. I dug my heels into my sorrel's flanks, and she responded bravely. The tables were turned now on our traitor since the afternoon of the massacre. HE was the pursued, and WE were the pursuers. We felt we must run him down, and punish him for his treachery.

At a breakneck pace, we stumbled over low bushes; we grazed big boulders; we rolled down the sides of steep ravines; but we kept him in sight all the time, dim and black against the starry sky; slowly, slowly, yes, yes!—we gained upon him. My pony led now. The mysterious white man rode and rode, head bent, neck forward, but never looked behind him. Bit by bit we lessened the distance between us. As we drew near him at last, Doolittle called out to me, in a warning voice: "Take care, Doctor! Have your revolvers ready! He's driven to bay now! As we approach, he'll fire at us!"

Then it came home to me in a flash. I felt the truth of it. "He DARE not fire!" I cried. "He dare not turn towards us. He cannot show his face! If he did, we might recognise him!"

On we rode, still gaining. "Now, now," I cried, "we shall catch him!"

Even as I leaned forward to seize his rein, the fugitive, without checking his horse, without turning his head, drew his revolver from his belt, and, raising his hand, fired behind him at random. He fired towards us, on the chance. The bullet whizzed past my ear, not hitting anyone. We scattered, right and left, still galloping free and strong. We did not return his fire, as I had told the others of my desire to take him alive. We might have shot his horse; but the risk of hitting the rider, coupled with the confidence we felt of eventually hunting him to earth, restrained us. It was the great mistake we made.

He had gained a little by his shots, but we soon caught it up. Once more I said, "We are on him!"

A minute later, we were pulled up short before an impenetrable thicket of prickly shrubs, through which I saw at once it would have been quite impossible to urge our staggering horses.

The other man, of course, reached it before us, with his mare's last breath. He must have been making for it, indeed, of set purpose; for the second he arrived at the edge of the thicket he slipped off his tired pony, and seemed to dive into the bush as a swimmer dives off a rock into the water.

"We have him now!" I cried, in a voice of triumph. And Colebrook echoed, "We have him!"

We sprang down quickly. "Take him alive, if you can!" I exclaimed, remembering Hilda's advice. "Let us find out who he is, and have him properly tried and hanged at Buluwayo! Don't give him a soldier's death! All he deserves is a murderer's!"

"You stop here," Colebrook said, briefly, flinging his bridle to Doolittle to hold. "Doctor and I follow him. Thick bush. Knows the ways of it. Revolvers ready!"

I handed my sorrel to Doolittle. He stopped behind, holding the three foam-bespattered and panting horses, while Colebrook and I dived after our fugitive into the matted bushes.

The thicket, as I have said, was impenetrable above; but it was burrowed at its base by over-ground runs of some wild animal, not, I think, a very large one; they were just like the runs which rabbits make among gorse and heather, only on a bigger scale, bigger, even, than a fox's or badger's. By crouching and bending our backs, we could crawl through them with difficulty into the scrubby tangle. It was hard work creeping. The runs divided soon. Colebrook felt with his hands on the ground: "I can make out the spoor!" he muttered, after a minute. "He has gone on this way!"

We tracked him a little distance in, crawling at times, and rising now and again where the runs opened out on to the air for a moment. The spoor was doubtful and the tunnels tortuous. I felt the ground from time to time, but could not be sure of the tracks with my fingers; I was not a trained scout, like Colebrook or Doolittle. We wriggled deeper into the tangle. Something stirred once or twice. It was not far from me. I was uncertain whether it was HIM, Sebastian, or a Kaffir earth-hog, the animal which seemed likeliest to have made the burrows. Was he going to elude us, even now? Would he turn upon us with a knife? If so, could we hold him?

At last, when we had pushed our way some distance in, we heard a wild cry from outside. It was Doolittle's voice. "Quick! quick! out again! The man will escape! He has come back on his tracks, and rounded!"

I saw our mistake at once. We had left our companion out there alone, rendered helpless by the care of all three horses.

Colebrook said never a word. He was a man of action. He turned with instinctive haste, and followed our own spoor back again with his hands and knees to the opening in the thicket by which we had first entered.

Before we could reach it, however, two shots rang out clear in the direction where we had left poor Doolittle and the horses. Then a sharp cry broke the stillness, the cry of a wounded man. We redoubled our pace. We knew we were outwitted.

When we reached the open, we saw at once by the uncertain light what had happened. The fugitive was riding away on my own little sorrel, riding for dear life; not back the way we came from Salisbury, but sideways across the veldt towards Chimoio and the Portuguese seaports. The other two horses, riderless and terrified, were scampering with loose heels over the dark plain. Doolittle was not to be seen; he lay, a black lump, among the black bushes about him.

We looked around for him, and found him. He was severely, I may even say dangerously, wounded. The bullet had lodged in his right side. We had to catch our two horses, and ride them back with our wounded man, leading the fugitive's mare in tow, all blown and breathless. I stuck to the fugitive's mare; it was the one clue we had now against him. But Sebastian, if it WAS Sebastian, had ridden off scot-free. I understood his game at a glance. He had got the better of us once more. He would make for the coast by the nearest road, give himself out as a settler escaped from the massacre, and catch the next ship for England or the Cape, now this coup had failed him.

Doolittle had not seen the traitor's face. The man rose from the bush, he said, shot him, seized the pony, and rode off in a second with ruthless haste. He was tall and thin, but erect, that was all the wounded scout could tell us about his assailant. And THAT was not enough to identify Sebastian.

All danger was over. We rode back to Salisbury. The first words Hilda said when she saw me were: "Well, he has got away from you!"

"Yes; how did you know?"

"I read it in your step. But I guessed as much before. He is so very keen; and you started too confident."

CHAPTER IX

THE EPISODE OF THE LADY WHO WAS VERY EXCLUSIVE

The Matabele revolt gave Hilda a prejudice against Rhodesia. I will confess that I shared it. I may be hard to please; but it somehow sets one against a country when one comes home from a ride to find all the other occupants of the house one lives in massacred. So Hilda decided to leave South Africa. By an odd coincidence, I also decided on the same day to change my residence. Hilda's movements and mine, indeed, coincided curiously. The moment I learned she was going anywhere, I discovered in a flash that I happened to be going there too. I commend this strange case of parallel thought and action to the consideration of the Society for Psychical Research.

So I sold my farm, and had done with Rhodesia. A country with a future is very well in its way; but I am quite Ibsenish in my preference for a country with a past. Oddly enough, I had no difficulty in getting rid of my white elephant of a farm. People seemed to believe in Rhodesia none the less firmly because of this slight disturbance. They treated massacres as necessary incidents in the early history of a colony with a future. And I do not deny that native risings add picturesqueness. But I prefer to take them in a literary form.

"You will go home, of course?" I said to Hilda, when we came to talk it all over.

She shook her head. "To England? Oh, no. I must pursue my Plan. Sebastian will have gone home; he expects me to follow."

"And why don't you?"

"Because—he expects it. You see, he is a good judge of character; he will naturally infer, from what he knows of my temperament, that after this experience I shall want to get back to England and safety. So I should—if it were not that I know he will expect it. As it is, I must go elsewhere; I must draw him after me."

"Where?"

"Why do you ask, Hubert?"

"Because—I want to know where I am going myself. Wherever you go, I have reason to believe, I shall find that I happen to be going also."

She rested her little chin on her hand and reflected a minute. "Does it occur to you," she asked at last, "that people have tongues? If you go on following me like this, they will really begin to talk about us."

"Now, upon my word, Hilda," I cried, "that is the very first time I have ever known you show a woman's want of logic! I do not propose to follow you; I propose to happen to be travelling by the same steamer. I ask you to marry me; you won't; you admit you are fond of me; yet you tell me not to come with you. It is I who suggest a course which would prevent people from chattering—by the simple device of a wedding. It is YOU who refuse. And then you turn upon me like this! Admit that you are unreasonable."

"My dear Hubert, have I ever denied that I was a woman?"

"Besides," I went on, ignoring her delicious smile, "I don't intend to FOLLOW you. I expect, on the contrary, to find myself beside you. When I know where you are going, I shall accidentally turn up on the same steamer. Accidents WILL happen. Nobody can prevent coincidences from occurring. You may marry me, or you may not; but if you don't marry me, you can't expect to curtail my liberty of action, can you? You had better know the worst at once; if you won't take me, you must count upon finding me at your elbow all the world over, till the moment comes when you choose to accept me."

"Dear Hubert, I am ruining your life!"

"An excellent reason, then, for taking my advice, and marrying me instantly! But you wander from the question. Where are you going? That is the issue now before the house. You persist in evading it."

She smiled, and came back to earth. "Oh, if you MUST know, to India, by the east coast, changing steamers at Aden."

"Extraordinary!" I cried. "Do you know, Hilda, as luck will have it, I also shall be on my way to Bombay by the very same steamer!"

"But you don't know what steamer it is?"

"No matter. That only makes the coincidence all the odder. Whatever the name of the ship may be, when you get on board, I have a presentiment that you will be surprised to find me there."

She looked up at me with a gathering film in her eyes. "Hubert, you are irrepressible!"

"I am, my dear child; so you may as well spare yourself the needless trouble of trying to repress me."

If you rub a piece of iron on a loadstone, it becomes magnetic. So, I think, I must have begun to acquire some part of Hilda's own prophetic strain; for, sure enough, a few weeks later, we both of us found ourselves on the German East African steamer Kaiser Wilhelm, on our way to Aden, exactly as I had predicted. Which goes to prove that there is really something after all in presentiments!

"Since you persist in accompanying me," Hilda said to me, as we sat in our chairs on deck the first evening out, "I see what I must do. I must invent some plausible and ostensible reason for our travelling together."

"We are not travelling together," I answered. "We are travelling by the same steamer; that is all, exactly like the rest of our fellow-passengers. I decline to be dragged into this imaginary partnership."

"Now do be serious, Hubert! I am going to invent an object in life for us."

"What object?"

"How can I tell yet? I must wait and see what turns up. When we tranship at Aden, and find out what people are going on to Bombay with us, I shall probably discover some nice married lady to whom I can attach myself."

"And am I to attach myself to her, too?"

"My dear boy, I never asked you to come. You came unbidden. You must manage for yourself as best you may. But I leave much to the chapter of accidents. We never know what will turn up, till it turns up in the end. Everything comes at last, you know, to him that waits."

"And yet," I put in, with a meditative air, "I have never observed that waiters are so much better off than the rest of the community. They seem to me—"

"Don't talk nonsense. It is YOU who are wandering from the question now. Please return to it."

I returned at once. "So I am to depend on what turns up?"

"Yes. Leave that to me. When we see our fellow-passengers on the Bombay steamer, I shall soon discover some ostensible reason why we two should be travelling through India with one of them."

"Well, you are a witch, Hilda," I answered. "I found that out long ago; but if you succeed between here and Bombay in inventing a Mission, I shall begin to believe you are even more of a witch than I ever thought you."

At Aden we changed into a P. and O. steamer. Our first evening out on our second cruise was a beautiful one; the bland Indian Ocean wore its sweetest smile for us. We sat on deck after dinner. A lady with a husband came up from the cabin while we sat and gazed at the placid sea. I was smoking a quiet digestive cigar. Hilda was seated in her deck chair next to me.

The lady with the husband looked about her for a vacant space on which to place the chair a steward was carrying for her. There was plenty of room on the quarter-deck. I could not imagine why she gazed about her with such obtrusive caution. She inspected the occupants of the various chairs around with deliberate scrutiny through a long-handled tortoise-shell optical abomination. None of them seemed to satisfy her. After a minute's effort, during which she also muttered a few words very low to her husband, she selected an empty spot midway between our group and the most distant group on the other side of us. In other words, she sat as far away from everybody present as the necessarily restricted area of the quarter-deck permitted.

Hilda glanced at me and smiled. I snatched a quick look at the lady again. She was dressed with an amount of care and a smartness of detail that seemed somewhat uncalled for on the Indian Ocean. A cruise on a P. and O. steamer is not a garden party. Her chair was most luxurious, and had her name painted on it, back and front, in very large letters, with undue obtrusiveness. I read it from where I sat, "Lady Meadowcroft."

The owner of the chair was tolerably young, not bad looking, and most expensively attired. Her face had a certain vacant, languid, half ennuyee air which I have learned to associate with women of the nouveau-riche type, women with small brains and restless minds, habitually plunged in a vortex of gaiety, and miserable when left for a passing moment to their own resources.

Hilda rose from her chair, and walked quietly forward towards the bow of the steamer. I rose, too, and accompanied her. "Well?" she said, with a faint touch of triumph in her voice when we had got out of earshot.

"Well, what?" I answered, unsuspecting.

"I told you everything turned up at the end!" she said, confidently. "Look at the lady's nose!"

"It does turn up at the end—certainly," I answered, glancing back at her. "But I hardly see—"

"Hubert, you are growing dull! You were not so at Nathaniel's.... It is the lady herself who has turned up, not her nose, though I grant you THAT turns up too, the lady I require for our tour in India; the not impossible chaperon."

"Her nose tells you that?"

"Her nose, in part; but her face as a whole, too, her dress, her chair, her mental attitude to things in general."

"My dear Hilda, you can't mean to tell me you have divined her whole nature at a glance, by magic!"

"Not wholly at a glance. I saw her come on board, you know, she transhipped from some other line at Aden as we did, and I have been watching her ever since. Yes, I think I have unravelled her."

"You have been astonishingly quick!" I cried.

"Perhaps, but then, you see, there is so little to unravel! Some books, we all know, you must 'chew and digest'; they can only be read slowly; but some you can glance at, skim, and skip; the mere turning of the pages tells you what little worth knowing there is in them."

"She doesn't LOOK profound," I admitted, casting an eye at her meaningless small features as we paced up and down. "I incline to agree you might easily skim her."

"Skim her, and learn all. The table of contents is SO short.... You see, in the first place, she is extremely 'exclusive'; she prides herself on her 'exclusiveness': it, and her shoddy title, are probably all she has to pride herself upon, and she works them both hard. She is a sham great lady."

As Hilda spoke, Lady Meadowcroft raised a feebly querulous voice. "Steward! this won't do! I can smell the engine here. Move my chair. I must go on further."

"If you go on further that way, my lady," the steward answered, good-humouredly, but with a man-servant's deference for any sort of title, "you'll smell the galley, where they're cooking the dinner. I don't know which your ladyship would like best, the engine or the galley."

The languid figure leaned back in the chair with an air of resignation. "I'm sure I don't know why they cook the dinners up so high," she murmured, pettishly, to her husband. "Why can't they stick the kitchens underground, in the hold, I mean, instead of bothering us up here on deck with them?"

The husband was a big, burly, rough-and-ready Yorkshireman, stout, somewhat pompous, about forty, with hair wearing bald on the forehead: the personification of the successful business man. "My dear Emmie," he said, in a loud voice, with a North Country accent, "the cooks have got to live. They've got to live like the rest of us. I can never persuade you that the hands must always be humoured. If you don't humour 'em, they won't work for you. It's a poor tale when the hands won't work. Even with galleys on deck, the life of a sea-cook is not generally thowt an enviable position. Is not a happy one, not a happy one, as the fellah says in the opera. You must humour your cooks. If you stuck 'em in the hold, you'd get no dinner at all, that's the long and the short of it."

The languid lady turned away with a sickly, disappointed air. "Then they ought to have a conscription, or something," she said, pouting her lips. "The Government ought to take it in hand and manage it somehow. It's bad enough having to go by these beastly steamers to India at all, without having one's breath poisoned by—" the rest of the sentence died away inaudibly in a general murmur of ineffective grumbling.

"Why do you think she is EXCLUSIVE?" I asked Hilda as we strolled on towards the stern, out of the spoilt child's hearing.

"Why, didn't you notice?—she looked about her when she came on deck to see whether there was anybody who WAS anybody sitting there, whom she might put her chair near. But the Governor of Madras hadn't come up from his cabin yet; and the wife of the chief Commissioner of Oude had three civilians hanging about her seat; and the daughters of the Commander-in-Chief drew their skirts away as she passed. So she did the next best thing, sat as far apart as she could from the common herd: meaning all the rest of us. If you can't mingle at once with the Best People, you can at least assert your exclusiveness negatively, by declining to associate with the mere multitude."

"Now, Hilda, that is the first time I have ever known you to show any feminine ill-nature!"

"Ill-nature! Not at all. I am merely trying to arrive at the lady's character for my own guidance. I rather like her, poor little thing. Don't I tell you she will do? So far from objecting to her, I mean to go the round of India with her."

"You have decided quickly."

"Well, you see, if you insist upon accompanying me, I MUST have a chaperon; and Lady Meadowcroft will do as well as anybody else. In fact, being be-ladied, she will do a little better, from the point of view of Society, though THAT is a detail. The great matter is to fix upon a possible chaperon at once, and get her well in hand before we arrive at Bombay."

"But she seems so complaining!" I interposed. "I'm afraid, if you take her on, you'll get terribly bored with her."

"If SHE takes ME on, you mean. She's not a lady's-maid, though I intend to go with her; and she may as well give in first as last, for I'm going. Now see how nice I am to you, sir! I've provided you, too, with a post in her suite, as you WILL come with me. No, never mind asking me what it is just yet; all things come to him who waits; and if you will only accept the post of waiter, I mean all things to come to you."

"All things, Hilda?" I asked, meaningly, with a little tremor of delight.

She looked at me with a sudden passing tenderness in her eyes. "Yes, all things, Hubert. All things. But we mustn't talk of that, though I begin to see my way clearer now. You shall be rewarded for your constancy at last, dear knight-errant. As to my chaperon, I'm not afraid of her boring me; she bores herself, poor lady; one can see that, just to look at her; but she will be much less bored if she has us two to travel with. What she needs is constant companionship, bright talk, excitement. She has come away from London, where she swims with the crowd; she has no resources of her own, no work, no head, no interests. Accustomed to a whirl of foolish gaieties, she wearies her small brain; thrown back upon herself, she bores herself at once, because she has nothing interesting to tell herself. She absolutely requires somebody else to interest her. She can't even amuse herself with a book for three minutes together. See, she has a yellow-backed French novel now, and she is only able to read five lines at a time; then she gets tired and glances about her listlessly. What she wants is someone gay, laid on, to divert her all the time from her own inanity."

"Hilda, how wonderfully quick you are at reading these things! I see you are right; but I could never have guessed so much myself from such small premises."

"Well, what can you expect, my dear boy? A girl like this, brought up in a country rectory, a girl of no intellect, busy at home with the fowls, and the pastry, and the mothers' meetings, suddenly married offhand to a wealthy man, and deprived of the occupations which were her salvation in life, to be plunged into the whirl of a London season, and stranded at its end for want of the diversions which, by dint of use, have become necessaries of life to her!"

"Now, Hilda, you are practising upon my credulity. You can't possibly tell from her look that she was brought up in a country rectory."

"Of course not. You forget. There my memory comes in. I simply remember it."

"You remember it? How?"

"Why, just in the same way as I remembered your name and your mother's when I was first introduced to you. I saw a notice once in the births, deaths, and marriages—'At St. Alphege's, Millington, by the Rev. Hugh Clitheroe, M.A., father of the bride, Peter Gubbins, Esq., of The Laurels, Middleston, to Emilia Frances, third daughter of the Rev. Hugh Clitheroe, rector of Millington.'"

"Clitheroe—Gubbins; what on earth has that to do with it? That would be Mrs. Gubbins: this is Lady Meadowcroft."

"The same article, as the shopmen say—only under a different name. A year or two later I read a notice in the Times that 'I, Ivor de Courcy Meadowcroft, of The Laurels, Middleston, Mayor-elect of the Borough of Middleston, hereby give notice, that I have this day discontinued the use of the name Peter Gubbins, by which I was formerly known, and have assumed in lieu thereof the style and title of Ivor de Courcy Meadowcroft, by which I desire in future to be known.'

"A month or two later, again I happened to light upon a notice in the Telegraph that the Prince of Wales had opened a new hospital for incurables at Middleston, and that the Mayor, Mr. Ivor Meadowcroft, had received an intimation of Her Majesty's intention of conferring upon him the honour of knighthood. Now what do you make of it?"

"Putting two and two together," I answered, with my eye on our subject, "and taking into consideration the lady's face and manner, I should incline to suspect that she was the daughter of a poor parson, with the usual large family in inverse proportion to his means. That she unexpectedly made a good match with a very wealthy manufacturer who had raised himself; and that she was puffed up accordingly with a sense of self-importance."

"Exactly. He is a millionaire, or something very like it; and, being an ambitious girl, as she understands ambition, she got him to stand for the mayoralty, I don't doubt, in the year when the Prince of Wales was going to open the Royal Incurables, on purpose to secure him the chance of a knighthood. Then she said, very reasonably, 'I WON'T be Lady Gubbins—Sir Peter Gubbins!' There's an aristocratic name for you!—and, by a stroke of his pen, he straightway dis-Gubbinised himself, and emerged as Sir Ivor de Courcy Meadowcroft."

"Really, Hilda, you know everything about everybody! And what do you suppose they're going to India for?"

"Now, you've asked me a hard one. I haven't the faintest notion.... And yet... let me think. How is this for a conjecture? Sir Ivor is interested in steel rails, I believe, and in railway plant generally. I'm almost sure I've seen his name in connection with steel rails in reports of public meetings. There's a new Government railway now being built on the Nepaul frontier, one of these strategic railways, I think they call them, it's mentioned in the papers we got at Aden. He MIGHT be going out for that. We can watch his conversation, and see what part of India he talks about."

"They don't seem inclined to give us much chance of talking," I objected.

"No; they are VERY exclusive. But I'm very exclusive, too. And I mean to give them a touch of my exclusiveness. I venture to predict that, before we reach Bombay, they'll be going down on their knees and imploring us to travel with them."

At table, as it happened, from next morning's breakfast the Meadowcrofts sat next to us. Hilda was on one side of me; Lady Meadowcroft on the other; and beyond her again, bluff Yorkshire Sir Ivor, with his cold, hard, honest blue North Country eyes, and his dignified, pompous English, breaking down at times into a North Country colloquialism. They talked chiefly to each other. Acting on Hilda's instructions, I took care not to engage in conversation with our "exclusive" neighbour, except so far as the absolute necessities of the table compelled me. I "troubled her for the salt" in the most frigid voice. "May I pass you the potato salad?" became on my lips a barrier of separation. Lady Meadowcroft marked and wondered. People of her sort are so anxious to ingratiate themselves with "all the Best People" that if they find you are wholly unconcerned about the privilege of conversation with a "titled person," they instantly judge you to be a distinguished character. As the days rolled on, Lady Meadowcroft's voice began to melt by degrees. Once, she asked me, quite civilly, to send round the ice; she even saluted me on the third day out with a polite "Good-morning, doctor."

Still, I maintained (by Hilda's advice) my dignified reserve, and took my seat severely with a cold "Good-morning." I behaved like a high-class consultant, who expects to be made Physician in Ordinary to Her Majesty.

At lunch that day, Hilda played her first card with delicious unconsciousness, apparent unconsciousness; for, when she chose, she was a consummate actress. She played it at a moment when Lady Meadowcroft, who by this time was burning with curiosity on our account, had paused from her talk with her husband to listen to us. I happened to say something about some Oriental curios belonging to an aunt of mine in London. Hilda seized the opportunity. "What did you say was her name?" she asked, blandly.

"Why, Lady Tepping," I answered, in perfect innocence. "She has a fancy for these things, you know. She brought a lot of them home with her from Burma."

As a matter of fact, as I have already explained, my poor dear aunt is an extremely commonplace old Army widow, whose husband happened to get knighted among the New Year's honours for some brush with the natives on the Shan frontier. But Lady Meadowcroft was at the stage where a title is a title; and the discovery that I was the nephew of a "titled person" evidently interested her. I could feel rather than see that she glanced significantly aside at Sir Ivor, and that Sir Ivor in return made a little movement of his shoulders equivalent to "I told you so."

Now Hilda knew perfectly well that the aunt of whom I spoke WAS Lady Tepping; so I felt sure that she had played this card of malice prepense, to pique Lady Meadowcroft.

But Lady Meadowcroft herself seized the occasion with inartistic avidity. She had hardly addressed us as yet. At the sound of the magic passport, she pricked up her ears, and turned to me suddenly. "Burma?" she said, as if to conceal the true reason for her change of front. "Burma? I had a cousin there once. He was in the Gloucestershire Regiment."

"Indeed?" I answered. My tone was one of utter unconcern in her cousin's history. "Miss Wade, will you take Bombay ducks with your curry?" In public, I thought it wise under the circumstances to abstain from calling her Hilda. It might lead to misconceptions; people might suppose we were more than fellow-travellers.

"You have had relations in Burma?" Lady Meadowcroft persisted.

I manifested a desire to discontinue the conversation. "Yes," I answered, coldly, "my uncle commanded there."

"Commanded there! Really! Ivor, do you hear? Dr. Cumberledge's uncle commanded in Burma." A faint intonation on the word commanded drew unobtrusive attention to its social importance. "May I ask what was his name?—my cousin was there, you see." An insipid smile. "We may have friends in common."

"He was a certain Sir Malcolm Tepping," I blurted out, staring hard at my plate.

"Tepping! I think I have heard Dick speak of him, Ivor."

"Your cousin," Sir Ivor answered, with emphatic dignity, "is certain to have mixed with nobbut the highest officials in Burma."

"Yes, I'm sure Dick used to speak of a certain Sir Malcolm. My cousin's name, Dr. Cumberledge, was Maltby—Captain Richard Maltby."

"Indeed," I answered, with an icy stare. "I cannot pretend to the pleasure of having met him."

Be exclusive to the exclusive, and they burn to know you. From that moment forth Lady Meadowcroft pestered us with her endeavours to scrape acquaintance. Instead of trying how far she could place her chair from us, she set it down as near us as politeness permitted. She entered into conversation whenever an opening afforded itself, and we two stood off haughtily. She even ventured to question me about our relation to one another: "Miss Wade is your cousin, I suppose?" she suggested.

"Oh, dear, no," I answered, with a glassy smile. "We are not connected in any way."

"But you are travelling together!"

"Merely as you and I are travelling together, fellow-passengers on the same steamer."

"Still, you have met before."

"Yes, certainly. Miss Wade was a nurse at St. Nathaniel's, in London, where I was one of the house doctors. When I came on board at Cape Town, after some months in South Africa, I found she was going by the same steamer to India." Which was literally true. To have explained the rest would have been impossible, at least to anyone who did not know the whole of Hilda's history.

"And what are you both going to do when you get to India?"

"Really, Lady Meadowcroft," I said, severely, "I have not asked Miss Wade what she is going to do. If you inquire of her point-blank, as you have inquired of me, I dare say she will tell you. For myself, I am just a globe-trotter, amusing myself. I only want to have a look round at India."

"Then you are not going out to take an appointment?"

"By George, Emmie," the burly Yorkshireman put in, with an air of annoyance, "you are cross-questioning Dr. Cumberledge; nowt less than cross-questioning him!"

I waited a second. "No," I answered, slowly. "I have not been practising of late. I am looking about me. I travel for enjoyment."

That made her think better of me. She was of the kind, indeed, who think better of a man if they believe him to be idle.

She dawdled about all day on deck chairs, herself, seldom even reading; and she was eager now to drag Hilda into conversation. Hilda resisted; she had found a volume in the library which immensely interested her.

"What ARE you reading, Miss Wade?" Lady Meadowcroft cried at last, quite savagely. It made her angry to see anybody else pleased and occupied when she herself was listless.

"A delightful book!" Hilda answered. "The Buddhist Praying Wheel, by William Simpson."

Lady Meadowcroft took it from her and turned the pages over with a languid air. "Looks awfully dull!" she observed, with a faint smile, at last, returning it.

"It's charming," Hilda retorted, glancing at one of the illustrations. "It explains so much. It shows one why one turns round one's chair at cards for luck; and why, when a church is consecrated, the bishop walks three times about it sunwise."

"Our Bishop is a dreadfully prosy old gentleman," Lady Meadowcroft answered, gliding off at a tangent on a personality, as is the wont of her kind; "he had, oh, such a dreadful quarrel with my father over the rules of the St. Alphege Schools at Millington."

"Indeed," Hilda answered, turning once more to her book. Lady Meadowcroft looked annoyed. It would never have occurred to her that within a few weeks she was to owe her life to that very abstruse work, and what Hilda had read in it.

That afternoon, as we watched the flying fish from the ship's side, Hilda said to me abruptly, "My chaperon is an extremely nervous woman."

"Nervous about what?"

"About disease, chiefly. She has the temperament that dreads infection, and therefore catches it."

"Why do you think so?"

"Haven't you noticed that she often doubles her thumb under her fingers, folds her fist across it, so—especially when anybody talks about anything alarming? If the conversation happens to turn on jungle fever, or any subject like that, down goes her thumb instantly, and she clasps her fist over it with a convulsive squeeze. At the same time, too, her face twitches. I know what that trick means. She's horribly afraid of tropical diseases, though she never says so."

"And you attach importance to her fear?"

"Of course. I count upon it as probably our chief means of catching and fixing her."

"As how?"

She shook her head and quizzed me. "Wait and see. You are a doctor; I, a trained nurse. Before twenty-four hours, I foresee she will ask us. She is sure to ask us, now she has learned that you are Lady Tepping's nephew, and that I am acquainted with several of the Best People."

That evening, about ten o'clock, Sir Ivor strolled up to me in the smoking-room with affected unconcern. He laid his hand on my arm and drew me aside mysteriously. The ship's doctor was there, playing a quiet game of poker with a few of the passengers. "I beg your pardon, Dr. Cumberledge," he began, in an undertone, "could you come outside with me a minute? Lady Meadowcroft has sent me up to you with a message."

I followed him on to the open deck. "It is quite impossible, my dear sir," I said, shaking my head austerely, for I divined his errand. "I can't go and see Lady Meadowcroft. Medical etiquette, you know; the constant and salutary rule of the profession!"

"Why not?" he asked, astonished.

"The ship carries a surgeon," I replied, in my most precise tone. "He is a duly qualified gentleman, very able in his profession, and he ought to inspire your wife with confidence. I regard this vessel as Dr. Boyell's practice, and all on board it as virtually his patients."

Sir Ivor's face fell. "But Lady Meadowcroft is not at all well," he answered, looking piteous; "and—she can't endure the ship's doctor. Such a common man, you know! His loud voice disturbs her. You MUST have noticed that my wife is a lady of exceptionally delicate nervous organisation." He hesitated, beamed on me, and played his trump card. "She dislikes being attended by owt but a GENTLEMAN."

"If a gentleman is also a medical man," I answered, "his sense of duty towards his brother practitioners would, of course, prevent him from interfering in their proper sphere, or putting upon them the unmerited slight of letting them see him preferred before them."

"Then you positively refuse?" he asked, wistfully, drawing back. I could see he stood in a certain dread of that imperious little woman.

I conceded a point. "I will go down in twenty minutes," I admitted, looking grave, "not just now, lest I annoy my colleague, and I will glance at Lady Meadowcroft in an unprofessional way. If I think her case demands treatment, I will tell Dr. Boyell." And I returned to the smoking-room and took up a novel.

Twenty minutes later I knocked at the door of the lady's private cabin, with my best bedside manner in full play. As I suspected, she was nervous, nothing more, my mere smile reassured her. I observed that she held her thumb fast, doubled under in her fist, all the time I was questioning her, as Hilda had said; and I also noticed that the fingers closed about it convulsively at first, but gradually relaxed as my voice restored confidence. She thanked me profusely, and was really grateful.

On deck next day she was very communicative. They were going to make the regular tour first, she said, but were to go on to the Tibetan frontier at the end, where Sir Ivor had a contract to construct a railway, in a very wild region. Tigers? Natives? Oh, she didn't mind either of THEM; but she was told that that district, what did they call it? the Terai, or something, was terribly unwholesome. Fever was what-you-may-call-it there—yes, "endemic"—that was the word; "oh, thank you, Dr. Cumberledge." She hated the very name of fever. "Now you, Miss Wade, I suppose," with an awestruck smile, "are not in the least afraid of it?"

Hilda looked up at her calmly. "Not in the least," she answered. "I have nursed hundreds of cases."

"Oh, my, how dreadful! And never caught it?"

"Never. I am not afraid, you see."

"I wish I wasn't! Hundreds of cases! It makes one ill to think of it!... And all successfully?"

"Almost all of them."

"You don't tell your patients stories when they're ill about your other cases who died, do you?" Lady Meadowcroft went on, with a quick little shudder.

Hilda's face by this time was genuinely sympathetic. "Oh, never!" she answered, with truth. "That would be very bad nursing! One's object in treating a case is to make one's patient well; so one naturally avoids any sort of subject that might be distressing or alarming."

"You really mean it?" Her face was pleading.

"Why, of course. I try to make my patients my friends; I talk to them cheerfully; I amuse them and distract them; I get them away, as far as I can, from themselves and their symptoms."

"Oh, what a lovely person to have about one when one's ill!" the languid lady exclaimed, ecstatically. "I SHOULD like to send for you if I wanted nursing! But there, it's always so, of course, with a real lady; common nurses frighten one so. I wish I could always have a lady to nurse me!"

"A person who sympathises, that is the really important thing," Hilda answered, in her quiet voice. "One must find out first one's patient's temperament. YOU are nervous, I can see." She laid one hand on her new friend's arm. "You need to be kept amused and engaged when you are ill; what YOU require most is—insight—and sympathy."

The little fist doubled up again; the vacant face grew positively sweet. "That's just it! You have hit it! How clever you are! I want all that. I suppose, Miss Wade, YOU never go out for private nursing?"

"Never," Hilda answered. "You see, Lady Meadowcroft, I don't nurse for a livelihood. I have means of my own; I took up this work as an occupation and a sphere in life. I haven't done anything yet but hospital nursing."

Lady Meadowcroft drew a slight sigh. "What a pity!" she murmured, slowly. "It does seem hard that your sympathies should all be thrown away, so to speak, on a horrid lot of wretched poor people, instead of being spent on your own equals, who would so greatly appreciate them."

"I think I can venture to say the poor appreciate them, too," Hilda answered, bridling up a little, for there was nothing she hated so much as class-prejudices. "Besides, they need sympathy more; they have fewer comforts. I should not care to give up attending my poor people for the sake of the idle rich."

The set phraseology of the country rectory recurred to Lady Meadowcroft, "our poorer brethren," and so forth. "Oh, of course," she answered, with the mechanical acquiescence such women always give to moral platitudes. "One must do one's best for the poor, I know, for conscience' sake and all that; it's our duty, and we all try hard to do it. But they're so terribly ungrateful! Don't you think so? Do you know, Miss Wade, in my father's parish—"

Hilda cut her short with a sunny smile, half contemptuous toleration, half genuine pity. "We are all ungrateful," she said; "but the poor, I think, the least so. I'm sure the gratitude I've often had from my poor women at St. Nathaniel's has made me sometimes feel really ashamed of myself. I had done so little, and they thanked me so much for it."

"Which only shows," Lady Meadowcroft broke in, "that one ought always to have a LADY to nurse one."

"Ca marche!" Hilda said to me, with a quiet smile, a few minutes after, when her ladyship had disappeared in her fluffy robe down the companion-ladder.

"Yes, ca marche," I answered. "In an hour or two you will have succeeded in landing your chaperon. And what is most amusing, landed her, too, Hilda, just by being yourself, letting her see frankly the actual truth of what you think and feel about her and about everyone!"

"I could not do otherwise," Hilda answered, growing grave. "I must be myself, or die for it. My method of angling consists in showing myself just as I am. You call me an actress, but I am not really one; I am only a woman who can use her personality for her own purposes. If I go with Lady

Meadowcroft, it will be a mutual advantage. I shall really sympathise with her for I can see the poor thing is devoured with nervousness."

"But do you think you will be able to stand her?" I asked.

"Oh, dear, yes. She's not a bad little thing, au fond, when you get to know her. It is society that has spoilt her. She would have made a nice, helpful, motherly body if she'd married the curate."

As we neared Bombay, conversation grew gradually more and more Indian; it always does under similar circumstances. A sea voyage is half retrospect, half prospect; it has no personal identity. You leave Liverpool for New York at the English standpoint, and are full of what you did in London or Manchester; half-way over, you begin to discuss American custom-houses and New York hotels; by the time you reach Sandy Hook, the talk is all of quick trains west and the shortest route from Philadelphia to New Orleans. You grow by slow stages into the new attitude; at Malta you are still regretting Europe; after Aden, your mind dwells most on the hire of punkah-wallahs and the proverbial toughness of the dak-bungalow chicken.

"How's the plague at Bombay now?" an inquisitive passenger inquired of the Captain at dinner our last night out. "Getting any better?"

Lady Meadowcroft's thumb dived between her fingers again. "What! is there plague in Bombay?" she asked, innocently, in her nervous fashion.

"Plague in Bombay!" the Captain burst out, his burly voice resounding down the saloon. "Why, bless your soul, ma'am, where else would you expect it? Plague in Bombay! It's been there these five years. Better? Not quite. Going ahead like mad. They're dying by thousands."

"A microbe, I believe, Dr. Boyell," the inquisitive passenger observed deferentially, with due respect for medical science.

"Yes," the ship's doctor answered, helping himself to an olive. "Forty million microbes to each square inch of the Bombay atmosphere."

"And we are going to Bombay!" Lady Meadowcroft exclaimed, aghast.

"You must have known there was plague there, my dear," Sir Ivor put in, soothingly, with a deprecating glance. "It's been in all the papers. But only the natives get it."

The thumb uncovered itself a little. "Oh, only the natives!" Lady Meadowcroft echoed, relieved; as if a few thousand Hindus more or less would hardly be missed among the blessings of British rule in India. "You know, Ivor, I never read those DREADFUL things in the papers. I read the Society news, and Our Social Diary, and columns that are headed 'Mainly About People.' I don't care for anything but the Morning Post and the World and Truth. I hate horrors.... But it's a blessing to think it's only the natives."

"Plenty of Europeans, too, bless your heart," the Captain thundered out unfeelingly. "Why, last time I was in port, a nurse died at the hospital."

"Oh, only a nurse—" Lady Meadowcroft began, and then coloured up deeply, with a side glance at Hilda.

"And lots besides nurses," the Captain continued, positively delighted at the terror he was inspiring. "Pucka Englishmen and Englishwomen. Bad business this plague, Dr. Cumberledge! Catches particularly those who are most afraid of it."

"But it's only in Bombay?" Lady Meadowcroft cried, clutching at the last straw. I could see she was registering a mental determination to go straight up-country the moment she landed.

"Not a bit of it!" the Captain answered, with provoking cheerfulness. "Rampaging about like a roaring lion all over India!"

Lady Meadowcroft's thumb must have suffered severely. The nails dug into it as if it were someone else's.

Half an hour later, as we were on deck in the cool of the evening, the thing was settled. "My wife," Sir Ivor said, coming up to us with a serious face, "has delivered her ultimatum. Positively her ultimatum. I've had a mort o' trouble with her, and now she's settled. EITHER, she goes back from Bombay by the return steamer; OR ELSE, you and Miss Wade must name your own terms to accompany us on our tour, in case of emergencies." He glanced wistfully at Hilda. "DO you think you can help us?"

Hilda made no hypocritical pretence of hanging back. Her nature was transparent. "If you wish it, yes," she answered, shaking hands upon the bargain. "I only want to go about and see India; I can see it quite as well with Lady Meadowcroft as without her, and even better. It is unpleasant for a woman to travel unattached. I require a chaperon, and am glad to find one. I will join your party, paying my own hotel and travelling expenses, and considering myself as engaged in case your wife should need my services. For that, you can pay me, if you like, some nominal retaining fee, five pounds or anything. The money is immaterial to me. I like to be useful, and I sympathise with nerves; but it may make your wife feel she is really keeping a hold over me if we put the arrangement on a business basis. As a matter of fact, whatever sum she chooses to pay, I shall hand it over at once to the Bombay Plague Hospital."

Sir Ivor looked relieved. "Thank you ever so much!" he said, wringing her hand warmly. "I thowt you were a brick, and now I know it. My wife says your face inspires confidence, and your voice sympathy. She MUST have you with her. And you, Dr. Cumberledge?"

"I follow Miss Wade's lead," I answered, in my most solemn tone, with an impressive bow. "I, too, am travelling for instruction and amusement only; and if it would give Lady Meadowcroft a greater sense of security to have a duly qualified practitioner in her suite, I shall be glad on the same terms to swell your party. I will pay my own way; and I will allow you to name any nominal sum you please for your claim on my medical attendance, if necessary. I hope and believe, however, that our presence will so far reassure our prospective patient as to make our post in both cases a sinecure."

Three minutes later Lady Meadowcroft rushed on deck and flung her arms impulsively round Hilda. "You dear, good girl!" she cried; "how sweet and kind of you! I really COULDN'T have landed if you hadn't promised to come with us. And Dr. Cumberledge, too! So nice and friendly of you both. But there, it IS so much pleasanter to deal with ladies and gentlemen!"

So Hilda won her point; and what was best, won it fairly.

CHAPTER X

THE EPISODE OF THE GUIDE WHO KNEW THE COUNTRY

We toured all round India with the Meadowcrofts; and really the lady who was "so very exclusive" turned out not a bad little thing, when once one had succeeded in breaking through the ring-fence with which she surrounded herself. She had an endless, quenchless restlessness, it is true; her eyes wandered aimlessly; she never was happy for two minutes together, unless she was surrounded by friends, and was seeing something. What she saw did not interest her much; certainly her tastes were on the level with those of a very young child. An odd-looking house, a queerly dressed man, a tree cut into shape to look like a peacock, delighted her far more than the most glorious view of the quaintest old temple. Still, she must be seeing. She could no more sit still than a fidgety child or a monkey at the Zoo. To be up and doing was her nature, doing nothing, to be sure; but still, doing it strenuously.

So we went the regulation round of Delhi and Agra, the Taj Mahal, and the Ghats at Benares, at railroad speed, fulfilling the whole duty of the modern globe-trotter. Lady Meadowcroft looked at everything, for ten minutes at a stretch; then she wanted to be off, to visit the next thing set down for her in her guide-book. As we left each town she murmured mechanically: "Well, we've seen THAT, thank Heaven!" and straightway went on, with equal eagerness, and equal boredom, to see the one after it.

The only thing that did NOT bore her, indeed, was Hilda's bright talk.

"Oh, Miss Wade," she would say, clasping her hands, and looking up into Hilda's eyes with her own empty blue ones, "you ARE so funny! So original, don't you know! You never talk or think of anything like other people. I can't imagine how such ideas come up in your mind. If I were to try all day, I'm sure I should never hit upon them!" Which was so perfectly true as to be a trifle obvious.

Sir Ivor, not being interested in temples, but in steel rails, had gone on at once to his concession, or contract, or whatever else it was, on the north-east frontier, leaving his wife to follow and rejoin him in the Himalayas as soon as she had exhausted the sights of India. So, after a few dusty weeks of wear and tear on the Indian railways, we met him once more in the recesses of Nepaul, where he was busy constructing a light local line for the reigning Maharajah.

If Lady Meadowcroft had been bored at Allahabad and Ajmere, she was immensely more bored in a rough bungalow among the trackless depths of the Himalayan valleys. To anybody with eyes in his head, indeed, Toloo, where Sir Ivor had pitched his headquarters, was lovely enough to keep one interested for a twelvemonth. Snow-clad needles of rock hemmed it in on either side; great deodars rose like huge tapers on the hillsides; the plants and flowers were a joy to look at. But Lady Meadowcroft did not care for flowers which one could not wear in one's hair; and what was the good of dressing here, with no one but Ivor and Dr. Cumberledge to see one? She yawned till she was tired; then she began to grow peevish.

"Why Ivor should want to build a railway at all in this stupid, silly place," she said, as we sat in the veranda in the cool of evening, "I'm sure I can't imagine. We MUST go somewhere. This is maddening, maddening! Miss Wade, Dr. Cumberledge, I count upon you to discover SOMETHING for me to do. If I vegetate like this, seeing nothing all day long but those eternal hills"—she clenched her little fist—"I shall go MAD with ennui."

Hilda had a happy thought. "I have a fancy to see some of these Buddhist monasteries," she said, smiling as one smiles at a tiresome child whom one likes in spite of everything. "You remember, I was reading that book of Mr. Simpson's on the steamer, coming out, a curious book about the Buddhist Praying Wheels; and it made me want to see one of their temples immensely. What do you say to camping out? A few weeks in the hills? It would be an adventure, at any rate."

"Camping out?" Lady Meadowcroft exclaimed, half roused from her languor by the idea of a change. "Oh, do you think that would be fun? Should we sleep on the ground? But, wouldn't it be dreadfully, horribly uncomfortable?"

"Not half so uncomfortable as you'll find yourself here at Toloo in a few days, Emmie," her husband put in, grimly. "The rains will soon be on, lass; and when the rains are on, by all accounts, they're precious heavy hereabouts, rare fine rains, so that a man's half-flooded out of his bed o' nights, which won't suit YOU, my lady."

The poor little woman clasped her twitching hands in feeble agony. "Oh, Ivor, how dreadful! Is it what they call the mongoose, or monsoon, or something? But if they're so bad here, surely they'll be worse in the hills, and camping out, too, won't they?"

"Not if you go the right way to work. Ah'm told it never rains t'other side o' the hills. The mountains stop the clouds, and once you're over, you're safe enough. Only, you must take care to keep well in the Maharajah's territory. Cross the frontier t'other side into Tibet, an' they'll skin thee alive as soon as look at thee. They don't like strangers in Tibet; prejudiced against them, somehow; they pretty well skinned that young chap Landor who tried to go there a year ago."

"But, Ivor, I don't want to be skinned alive! I'm not an eel, please!"

"That's all right, lass. Leave that to me. I can get thee a guide, a man that's very well acquainted with the mountains. I was talking to a scientific explorer here t'other day, and he knows of a good guide who can take you anywhere. He'll get you the chance of seeing the inside of a Buddhist monastery, if you like, Miss Wade. He's hand in glove with all the religion they've got in this part o' the country. They've got noan much, but at what there is, he's a rare devout one."

We discussed the matter fully for two or three days before we made up our minds. Lady Meadowcroft was undecided between her hatred of dulness and her haunting fear that scorpions and snakes would intrude upon our tents and beds while we were camping. In the end, however, the desire for change carried the day. She decided to dodge the rainy season by getting behind the Himalayan-passes, in the dry region to the north of the great range, where rain seldom falls, the country being watered only by the melting of the snows on the high summits.

This decision delighted Hilda, who, since she came to India, had fallen a prey to the fashionable vice of amateur photography. She took to it enthusiastically. She had bought herself a first-rate camera of the latest scientific pattern at Bombay, and ever since had spent all her time and spoiled her pretty hands in "developing." She was also seized with a craze for Buddhism. The objects that everywhere particularly attracted her were the old Buddhist temples and tombs and sculptures with which India is studded. Of these she had taken some hundreds of views, all printed by herself with the greatest care and precision. But in India, after all, Buddhism is a dead creed. Its monuments alone remain; she was anxious to see the Buddhist religion in its living state; and that she could only do in these remote outlying Himalayan valleys.

Our outfit, therefore, included a dark tent for Hilda's photographic apparatus; a couple of roomy tents to live and sleep in; a small cooking-stove; a cook to look after it; half-a-dozen bearers; and the highly recommended guide who knew his way about the country. In three days we were ready, to Sir Ivor's great delight. He was fond of his pretty wife, and proud of her, I believe; but when once she was away from the whirl and bustle of the London that she loved, it was a relief to him, I fancy, to pursue his work alone, unhampered by her restless and querulous childishness.

On the morning when we were to make our start, the guide who was "well acquainted with the mountains" turned up, as villainous-looking a person as I have ever set eyes on. He was sullen and furtive. I judged him at sight to be half Hindu, half Tibetan. He had a dark complexion, between brown and tawny; narrow slant eyes, very small and beady-black, with a cunning leer in their oblique corners; a flat nose much broadened at the wings; a cruel, thick, sensuous mouth, and high cheek-bones; the whole surmounted by a comprehensive scowl and an abundant crop of lank black hair, tied up in a knot at the nape of the neck with a yellow ribbon. His face was shifty; his short, stout form looked well adapted to mountain climbing, and also to wriggling. A deep scar on his left cheek did not help to inspire confidence. But he was polite and civil-spoken. Altogether a clever, unscrupulous, wide-awake soul, who would serve you well if he thought he could make by it, and would betray you at a pinch to the highest bidder.

We set out, in merry mood, prepared to solve all the abstruse problems of the Buddhist religion. Our spoilt child stood the camping out better than I expected. She was fretful, of course, and worried about trifles; she missed her maid and her accustomed comforts; but she minded the roughing it less, on the whole, than she had minded the boredom of inaction in the bungalow; and, being cast on Hilda and myself for resources, she suddenly evolved an unexpected taste for producing, developing, and printing photographs. We took dozens, as we went along, of little villages on our route, wood-built villages with quaint houses and turrets; and as Hilda had brought her collection of prints with her, for comparison of the Indian and Nepaulese monuments, we spent the evenings after our short day's march each day in arranging and collating them. We had planned to be away six weeks, at least. In that time the monsoon would have burst and passed. Our guide thought we might see all that was worth seeing of the Buddhist monasteries, and Sir Ivor thought we should have fairly escaped the dreaded wet season.

"What do you make of our guide?" I asked of Hilda on our fourth day out. I began somehow to distrust him.

"Oh, he seems all right," Hilda answered, carelessly, and her voice reassured me. "He's a rogue, of course; all guides and interpreters, and dragomans and the like, in out-of-the-way places, always ARE rogues. If they were honest men, they would share the ordinary prejudices of their countrymen, and would have nothing to do with the hated stranger. But in this case our friend, Ram Das, has no end to gain by getting us into mischief. If he had, he wouldn't scruple for a second to cut our throats; but then, there are too many of us. He will probably try to cheat us by making preposterous charges when he gets us back to Toloo; but that's Lady Meadowcroft's business. I don't doubt Sir Ivor will be more than a match for him there. I'll back one shrewd Yorkshireman against any three Tibetan half-castes, any day."

"You're right that he would cut our throats if it served his purpose," I answered. "He's servile, and servility goes hand in hand with treachery. The more I watch him, the more I see 'scoundrel' written in large type on every bend of the fellow's oily shoulders."

"Oh, yes, he's a bad lot, I know. The cook, who can speak a little English and a little Tibetan, as well as Hindustani, tells me Ram Das has the worst reputation of any man in the mountains. But he says he's a very good guide to the passes, for all that, and if he's well paid will do what he's paid for."

Next day but one we approached at last, after several short marches, the neighbourhood of what our guide assured us was a Buddhist monastery. I was glad when he told us of it, giving the place the name of a well-known Nepaulese village; for, to say the truth, I was beginning to get frightened. Judging by the sun, for I had brought no compass, it struck me that we seemed to have been marching almost due north ever since we left Toloo; and I fancied such a line of march must have brought us by this time suspiciously near the Tibetan frontier. Now, I had no desire to be "skinned alive," as Sir Ivor put it. I did not wish to emulate St. Bartholomew and others of the early Christian martyrs; so I was pleased to learn that we were really drawing near to Kulak, the first of the Nepaulese Buddhist monasteries to which our well-informed guide, himself a Buddhist, had promised to introduce us.

We were tramping up a beautiful high mountain valley, closed round on every side by snowy peaks. A brawling river ran over a rocky bed in cataracts down its midst. Crags rose abruptly a little in front of us. Half-way up the slope to the left, on a ledge of rock, rose a long, low building with curious, pyramid-like roofs, crowned at either end by a sort of minaret, which resembled more than anything else a huge earthenware oil-jar. This was the monastery or lamasery we had come so far to see. Honestly, at first sight, I did not feel sure it was worth the trouble.

Our guide called a halt, and turned to us with a sudden peremptory air. His servility had vanished. "You stoppee here," he said, slowly, in broken English, "while me-a go on to see whether Lama-sahibs ready to take you. Must ask leave from Lama-sahibs to visit village; if no ask leave"—he drew his hand across his throat with a significant gesture—"Lama-sahibs cuttee head off Eulopean."

"Goodness gracious!" Lady Meadowcroft cried, clinging tight to Hilda. "Miss Wade, this is dreadful! Where on earth have you brought us to?"

"Oh, that's all right," Hilda answered, trying to soothe her, though she herself began to look a trifle anxious. "That's only Ram Das's graphic way of putting things."

We sat down on a bank of trailing club-moss by the side of the rough track, for it was nothing more, and let our guide go on to negotiate with the Lamas. "Well, to-night, anyhow," I exclaimed, looking up, "we shall sleep on our own mattresses with a roof over our heads. These monks will find us quarters. That's always something."

We got out our basket and made tea. In all moments of doubt, your Englishwoman makes tea. As Hilda said, she will boil her Etna on Vesuvius. We waited and drank our tea; we drank our tea and waited. A full hour passed away. Ram Das never came back. I began to get frightened.

At last something stirred. A group of excited men in yellow robes issued forth from the monastery, wound their way down the hill, and approached us, shouting. They gesticulated as they came. I could see they looked angry. All at once Hilda clutched my arm: "Hubert," she cried, in an undertone, "we are betrayed! I see it all now. These are Tibetans, not Nepaulese." She paused a second, then went on: "I see it all—all, all. Our guide, Ram Das, he HAD a reason, after all, for getting us into mischief. Sebastian must have tracked us; he was bribed by Sebastian! It was HE who recommended Ram Das to Sir Ivor!"

"Why do you think so?" I asked, low.

"Because—look for yourself; these men who come are dressed in yellow. That means Tibetans. Red is the colour of the Lamas in Nepaul; yellow in Tibet and all other Buddhist countries. I read it in the book—The Buddhist Praying Wheel, you know. These are Tibetan fanatics, and, as Ram Das said, they will probably cut our throats for us."

I was thankful that Hilda's marvellous memory gave us even that moment for preparation and facing the difficulty. I saw in a flash that she was quite right: we had been inveigled across the frontier. These moutis were Tibetans, Buddhist inquisitors, enemies. Tibet is the most jealous country on earth; it allows no stranger to intrude upon its borders. I had to meet the worst. I stood there, a single white man, armed only with one revolver, answerable for the lives of two English ladies, and accompanied by a cringing out-caste Ghoorka cook and half-a-dozen doubtful Nepaulese bearers. To fly was impossible. We were fairly trapped. There was nothing for it but to wait and put a bold face on our utter helplessness.

I turned to our spoilt child. "Lady Meadowcroft," I said, very seriously, "this is danger; real danger. Now, listen to me. You must do as you are bid. No crying; no cowardice. Your life and ours depend upon it. We must none of us give way. We must pretend to be brave. Show one sign of fear, and these people will probably cut our throats on the spot here."

To my immense surprise, Lady Meadowcroft rose to the height of the situation. "Oh, as long as it isn't disease," she answered, resignedly; "I'm not much afraid of anything. I should mind the plague a great deal more than I mind a set of howling savages."

By that time the men in yellow robes had almost come up to us. It was clear they were boiling over with indignation; but they still did everything decently and in order. One, who was dressed in finer vestments than the rest, a portly person, with the fat, greasy cheeks and drooping flesh of a celibate church dignitary, whom I therefore judged to be the abbot, or chief Lama of the monastery, gave orders to his subordinates in a language which we did not understand. His men obeyed him. In a second they had closed us round, as in a ring or cordon.

Then the chief Lama stepped forward, with an authoritative air, like Pooh-Bah in the play, and said something in the same tongue to the cook, who spoke a little Tibetan. It was obvious from his manner that Ram Das had told them all about us; for the Lama selected the cook as interpreter at once, without taking any notice of myself, the ostensible head of the petty expedition.

"What does he, say?" I asked, as soon as he had finished speaking.

The cook, who had been salaaming all the time, at the risk of a broken back, in his most utterly abject and grovelling attitude, made answer tremulously in his broken English: "This is priest-sahib of the temple. He very angry, because why? Eulopean-sahib and mem-sahibs come into Tibet-land. No Eulopean, no Hindu, must come into Tibet-land. Priest-sahib say, cut all Eulopean throats. Let Nepaul man go back like him come, to him own country."

I looked as if the message were purely indifferent to me. "Tell him," I said, smiling—though at some little effort—"we were not trying to enter Tibet. Our rascally guide misled us. We were going to Kulak, in the Maharajah's territory. We will turn back quietly to the Maharajah's land if the priest-sahib will allow us to camp out for the night here."

I glanced at Hilda and Lady Meadowcroft. I must say their bearing under these trying circumstances was thoroughly worthy of two English ladies. They stood erect, looking as though all Tibet might come, and they would smile at it scornfully.

The cook interpreted my remarks as well as he was able, his Tibetan being probably about equal in quality to his English. But the chief Lama made a reply which I could see for myself was by no means friendly.

"What is his answer?" I asked the cook, in my haughtiest voice. I am haughty with difficulty.

Our interpreter salaamed once more, shaking in his shoes, if he wore any. "Priest-sahib say, that all lies. That all dam-lies. You is Eulopean missionary, very bad man; you want to go to Lhasa. But no white sahib must go to Lhasa. Holy city, Lhasa; for Buddhists only. This is not the way to Kulak; this not Maharajah's land. This place belong-a Dalai-Lama, head of all Lamas; have house at Lhasa. But priest-sahib know you Eulopean missionary, want to go Lhasa, convert Buddhists, because... Ram Das tell him so."

"Ram Das!" I exclaimed, thoroughly angry by this time. "The rogue! The scoundrel! He has not only deserted us, but betrayed us as well. He has told this lie on purpose to set the Tibetans against us. We must face the worst now. Our one chance is, to cajole these people."

The fat priest spoke again. "What does he say this time?" I asked.

"He say, Ram Das tell him all this because Ram Das good man, very good man: Ram Das converted Buddhist. You pay Ram Das to guidee you to Lhasa. But Ram Das good man, not want to let Eulopean see holy city; bring you here instead; then tell priest-sahib about it." And he chuckled inwardly.

"What will they do to us?" Lady Meadowcroft asked, her face very white, though her manner was more courageous than I could easily have believed of her.

"I don't know," I answered, biting my lip. "But we must not give way. We must put a bold face upon it. Their bark, after all, may be worse than their bite. We may still persuade them to let us go back again."

The men in yellow robes motioned us to move on towards the village and monastery. We were their prisoners, and it was useless to resist. So I ordered the bearers to take up the tents and baggage. Lady Meadowcroft resigned herself to the inevitable. We mounted the path in a long line, the Lamas in yellow closely guarding our draggled little procession. I tried my best to preserve my composure, and above all else not to look dejected.

As we approached the village, with its squalid and fetid huts, we caught the sound of bells, innumerable bells, tinkling at regular intervals. Many people trooped out from their houses to look at us, all flat-faced, all with oblique eyes, all stolidly, sullenly, stupidly passive. They seemed curious as to our dress and appearance, but not apparently hostile. We walked on to the low line of the monastery with its pyramidal roof and its queer, flower-vase minarets. After a moment's discussion they ushered us into the temple or chapel, which was evidently also their communal council-room and place of deliberation. We entered, trembling. We had no great certainty that we would ever get out of it alive again.

The temple was a large, oblong hall, with a great figure of Buddha, cross-legged, imperturbable, enthroned in a niche at its further end, like the apse or recess in a church in Italy. Before it stood an altar. The Buddha sat and smiled on us with his eternal smile. A complacent deity, carved out of white stone, and gaudily painted; a yellow robe, like the Lamas', dangled across his shoulders. The air seemed close with incense and also with bad ventilation. The centre of the nave, if I may so call it, was occupied by a huge wooden cylinder, a sort of overgrown drum, painted in bright colours, with ornamental designs and Tibetan letters. It was much taller than a man, some nine feet high, I should say, and it revolved above and below on an iron spindle. Looking closer, I saw it had a crank attached to it, with a string tied to the crank. A solitary monk, absorbed in his devotions, was pulling this string as we entered, and making the cylinder revolve with a jerk as he pulled it. At each revolution, a bell above rang once. The monk seemed as if his whole soul was bound up in the huge revolving drum and the bell worked by it.

We took this all in at a glance, somewhat vaguely at first, for our lives were at stake, and we were scarcely in a mood for ethnological observations. But the moment Hilda saw the cylinder her eye lighted up. I could see at once an idea had struck her. "This is a praying-wheel!" she cried, in quite a delighted voice. "I know where I am now, Hubert, Lady Meadowcroft, I see a way out of this! Do exactly as you see me do, and all may yet go well. Don't show surprise at anything. I think we can work upon these people's religious feelings."

Without a moment's hesitation she prostrated herself thrice on the ground before the figure of Buddha, knocking her head ostentatiously in the dust as she did so. We followed suit instantly. Then Hilda rose and began walking slowly round the big drum in the nave, saying aloud at each step, in a sort of monotonous chant, like a priest intoning, the four mystic words, "Aum, mani, padme, hum," "Aum, mani, padme, hum," many times over. We repeated the sacred formula after her, as if we had always been brought up to it. I noticed that Hilda walked the way of the sun. It is an important point in all these mysterious, half-magical ceremonies.

At last, after about ten or twelve such rounds, she paused, with an absorbed air of devotion, and knocked her head three times on the ground once more, doing poojah, before the ever-smiling Buddha.

By this time, however, the lessons of St. Alphege's rectory began to recur to Lady Meadowcroft's mind. "Oh, Miss Wade," she murmured in an awestruck voice, "OUGHT we to do like this? Isn't it clear idolatry?"

Hilda's common sense waved her aside at once. "Idolatry or not, it is the only way to save our lives," she answered, in her firmest voice.

"But, OUGHT we to save our lives? Oughtn't we to be... well, Christian martyrs?"

Hilda was patience itself. "I think not, dear," she replied, gently but decisively. "You are not called upon to be a martyr. The danger of idolatry is scarcely so great among Europeans of our time that we need feel it a duty to protest with our lives against it. I have better uses to which to put my life myself. I don't mind being a martyr, where a sufficient cause demands it. But I don't think such a sacrifice is required of us now in a Tibetan monastery. Life was not given us to waste on gratuitous martyrdoms."

"But... really... I'm afraid..."

"Don't be afraid of anything, dear, or you will risk all. Follow my lead; I will answer for your conduct. Surely, if Naaman, in the midst of idolaters, was permitted to bow down in the house of Rimmon, to save his place at court, you may blamelessly bow down to save your life in a Buddhist temple. Now, no more casuistry, but do as I tell you! 'Aum, mani, padme, hum,' again! Once more round the drum there!"

We followed her a second time, Lady Meadowcroft giving in after a feeble protest. The priests in yellow looked on, profoundly impressed by our circumnavigation. It was clear they began to reconsider the question of our nefarious designs on their holy city.

After we had finished our second tour round the drum, with the utmost solemnity, one of the monks approached Hilda, whom he seemed to take now for an important priestess. He said something to her in Tibetan, which, of course, we did not understand; but, as he pointed at the same time to the brother on the floor who was turning the wheel, Hilda nodded acquiescence. "If you wish it," she said in English, and he appeared to comprehend. "He wants to know whether I would like to take a turn at the cylinder."

She knelt down in front of it, before the little stool where the brother in yellow had been kneeling till that moment, and took the string in her hand, as if she were well accustomed to it. I could see that the abbot gave the cylinder a surreptitious push with his left hand, before she began, so as to make it revolve in the opposite direction from that in which the monk had just been moving it. This was obviously to try her. But Hilda let the string drop, with a little cry of horror. That was the wrong way round, the unlucky, uncanonical direction; the evil way, widdershins, the opposite of sunwise. With an awed air she stopped short, repeated once more the four mystic words, or mantra, and bowed thrice with well-assumed reverence to the Buddha. Then she set the cylinder turning of her own accord, with her right hand, in the propitious direction, and sent it round seven times with the utmost gravity.

At this point, encouraged by Hilda's example, I too became possessed of a brilliant inspiration. I opened my purse and took out of it four brand-new silver rupees of the Indian coinage. They were very handsome and shiny coins, each impressed with an excellent design of the head of the Queen as Empress of India. Holding them up before me, I approached the Buddha, and laid the four in a row submissively at his feet, uttering at the same time an appropriate formula. But as I did not know the proper mantra for use upon such an occasion, I supplied one from memory, saying, in a hushed voice, "Hokey—pokey—winky—wum," as I laid each one before the benignly-smiling statue. I have no doubt from their faces the priests imagined I was uttering a most powerful spell or prayer in my own language.

As soon as I retreated, with my face towards the image, the chief Lama glided up and examined the coins carefully. It was clear he had never seen anything of the sort before, for he gazed at them for some minutes, and then showed them round to his monks with an air of deep reverence. I do not doubt he took the image of her gracious Majesty for a very mighty and potent goddess. As soon as all had inspected them, with many cries of admiration, he opened a little secret drawer or relic-holder in the pedestal of the statue, and deposited them in it with a muttered prayer, as precious offerings from a European Buddhist.

By this time, we could easily see we were beginning to produce a most favourable impression. Hilda's study of Buddhism had stood us in good stead. The chief Lama or abbot motioned to us to be seated, in a much politer mood; after which he and his principal monks held a long and animated conversation together. I gathered from their looks and gestures that the head Lama inclined to regard us as orthodox Buddhists, but that some of his followers had grave doubts of their own as to the depth and reality of our religious convictions.

While they debated and hesitated, Hilda had another splendid idea. She undid her portfolio, and took out of it the photographs of ancient Buddhist topes and temples which she had taken in India. These she produced triumphantly. At once the priests and monks crowded round us to look at them. In a moment, when they recognised the meaning of the pictures, their excitement grew quite intense. The photographs were passed round from hand to hand, amid loud exclamations of joy and surprise. One brother would point out with astonishment to another some familiar symbol or some ancient text; two or three of them, in their devout enthusiasm, fell down on their knees and kissed the pictures.

We had played a trump card! The monks could see for themselves by this time that we were deeply interested in Buddhism. Now, minds of that calibre never understand a disinterested interest; the moment they saw we were collectors of Buddhist pictures, they jumped at once to the conclusion that we must also, of course, be devout believers. So far did they carry their sense of fraternity, indeed, that they insisted upon embracing us. That was a hard trial to Lady Meadowcroft, for the brethren were not conspicuous for personal cleanliness. She suspected germs, and she dreaded typhoid far more than she dreaded the Tibetan cutthroat.

The brethren asked, through the medium of our interpreter, the cook, where these pictures had been made. We explained as well as we could by means of the same mouthpiece, a very earthen vessel, that they came from ancient Buddhist buildings in India. This delighted them still more, though I know not in what form our Ghoorka retainer may have conveyed the information. At any rate, they insisted on embracing us again; after which the chief Lama said something very solemnly to our amateur interpreter.

The cook interpreted. "Priest-sahib say, he too got very sacred thing, come from India. Sacred Buddhist poojah-thing. Go to show it to you."

We waited, breathless. The chief Lama approached the altar before the recess, in front of the great cross-legged, vapidly smiling Buddha. He bowed himself to the ground three times over, as well as his portly frame would permit him, knocking his forehead against the floor, just as Hilda had done; then he proceeded, almost awestruck, to take from the altar an object wrapped round with gold brocade, and very carefully guarded. Two acolytes accompanied him. In the most reverent way, he slowly unwound the folds of gold cloth, and released from its hiding-place the highly sacred deposit. He held it up before our eyes with an air of triumph. It was an English bottle!

The label on it shone with gold and bright colours. I could see it was figured. The figure represented a cat, squatting on its haunches. The sacred inscription ran, in our own tongue, "Old Tom Gin, Unsweetened."

The monks bowed their heads in profound silence as the sacred thing was produced. I caught Hilda's eye. "For Heaven's sake," I murmured low, "don't either of you laugh! If you do, it's all up with us."

They kept their countenances with admirable decorum.

Another idea struck me. "Tell them," I said to the cook, "that we, too, have a similar and very powerful god, but much more lively." He interpreted my words to them.

Then I opened our stores, and drew out with a flourish, our last remaining bottle of Simla soda-water.

Very solemnly and seriously I unwired the cork, as if performing an almost sacrosanct ceremony. The monks crowded round, with the deepest curiosity. I held the cork down for a second with my thumb, while I uttered once more, in my most awesome tone, the mystic words:
"Hokey—pokey—winky—wum!" then I let it fly suddenly. The soda-water was well up. The cork bounded to the ceiling; the contents of the bottle spurted out over the place in the most impressive fashion.

For a minute the Lamas drew back alarmed. The thing seemed almost devilish. Then slowly, reassured by our composure, they crept back and looked. With a glance of inquiry at the abbot, I took out my pocket corkscrew, and drew the cork of the gin-bottle, which had never been opened. I signed for a cup. They brought me one, reverently. I poured out a little gin, to which I added some soda-water, and drank first of it myself, to show them it was not poison. After that, I handed it to the chief Lama, who sipped at it, sipped again, and emptied the cup at the third trial. Evidently the sacred drink was very much to his taste, for he smacked his lips after it, and turned with exclamations of surprised delight to his inquisitive companions.

The rest of the soda-water, duly mixed with gin, soon went the round of the expectant monks. It was greatly approved of. Unhappily, there was not quite enough soda water to supply a drink for all of them; but those who tasted it were deeply impressed. I could see that they took the bite of carbonic-acid gas for evidence of a most powerful and present deity.

That settled our position. We were instantly regarded, not only as Buddhists, but as mighty magicians from a far country. The monks made haste to show us rooms destined for our use in the monastery. They were not unbearably filthy, and we had our own bedding. We had to spend the night there, that was certain. We had, at least, escaped the worst and most pressing danger. I may add that I believe our cook to have been a most arrant liar, which was a lucky circumstance. Once the wretched creature saw the tide turn, I have reason to infer that he supported our cause by telling the chief Lama the most incredible stories about our holiness and power. At any rate, it is certain that we were regarded with the utmost respect, and treated thenceforth with the affectionate deference due to acknowledged and certified sainthood.

It began to strike us now, however, that we had almost overshot the mark in this matter of sanctity. We had made ourselves quite too holy. The monks, who were eager at first to cut our throats, thought so much of us now that we grew a little anxious as to whether they would not wish to keep such devout souls in their midst forever. As a matter of fact, we spent a whole week against our wills in the monastery, being very well fed and treated meanwhile, yet virtually captives. It was the camera that did it. The Lamas had never seen any photographs before. They asked how these miraculous pictures were produced; and Hilda, to keep up the good impression, showed them how she operated. When a full-length portrait of the chief Lama, in his sacrificial robes, was actually printed off and exhibited before their eyes, their delight knew no bounds. The picture was handed about among the astonished brethren, and received with loud shouts of joy and wonder. Nothing would satisfy them then but that we must photograph every individual monk in the place. Even the Buddha himself, cross-legged and imperturbable, had to sit for his portrait. As he was used to sitting, never, indeed, having done anything else, he came out admirably.

Day after day passed; suns rose and suns set; and it was clear that the monks did not mean to let us leave their precincts in a hurry. Lady Meadowcroft, having recovered by this time from her first fright, began to grow bored. The Buddhists' ritual ceased to interest her. To vary the monotony, I hit upon an expedient for killing time till our too pressing hosts saw fit to let us depart. They were fond of religious processions of the most protracted sort, dances before the altar, with animal masks or heads, and other weird ceremonial orgies. Hilda, who had read herself up in Buddhist ideas, assured me that all these things were done in order to heap up Karma.

"What is Karma?" I asked, listlessly.

"Karma is good works, or merit. The more praying-wheels you turn, the more bells you ring, the greater the merit. One of the monks is always at work turning the big wheel that moves the bell, so as to heap up merit night and day for the monastery."

This set me thinking. I soon discovered that, no matter how the wheel is turned, the Karma or merit is equal. It is the turning it that counts, not the personal exertion. There were wheels and bells in convenient situations all over the village, and whoever passed one gave it a twist as he went by, thus piling up Karma for all the inhabitants. Reflecting upon these facts, I was seized with an idea. I got Hilda to take instantaneous photographs of all the monks during a sacred procession, at rapid intervals. In that sunny climate we had no difficulty at all in printing off from the plates as soon as developed. Then I took a small wheel, about the size of an oyster-barrel, the monks had dozens of them, and pasted the photographs inside in successive order, like what is called a zoetrope, or wheel of life. By cutting holes in the side, and arranging a mirror from Lady Meadowcroft's dressing-bag, I completed my machine, so that, when it was turned round rapidly, one saw the procession actually taking place as if the figures were moving. The thing, in short, made a living picture like a cinematograph. A mountain stream ran past the monastery, and supplied it with water. I had a second inspiration. I was always mechanical. I fixed a water-wheel in the stream, where it made a petty cataract, and connected it by means of a small crank with the barrel of photographs. My zoetrope thus worked off itself, and piled up Karma for all the village whether anyone happened to be looking at it or not.

The monks, who were really excellent fellows when not engaged in cutting throats in the interest of the faith, regarded this device as a great and glorious religious invention. They went down on their knees to it, and were profoundly respectful. They also bowed to me so deeply, when I first exhibited it, that I began to be puffed up with spiritual pride. Lady Meadowcroft recalled me to my better self by murmuring, with a sigh: "I suppose we really can't draw a line now; but it DOES seem to me like encouraging idolatry!"

"Purely mechanical encouragement," I answered, gazing at my handicraft with an inventor's pardonable pride. "You see, it is the turning itself that does good, not any prayers attached to it. I divert the idolatry from human worshippers to an unconscious stream, which must surely be meritorious." Then I thought of the mystic sentence, "Aum, mani, padme, hum." "What a pity it is," I cried, "I couldn't make them a phonograph to repeat their mantra! If I could, they might fulfil all their religious duties together by machinery!"

Hilda reflected a second. "There is a great future," she said at last, "for the man who first introduces smoke-jacks into Tibet! Every household will buy one, as an automatic means of acquiring Karma."

"Don't publish that idea in England!" I exclaimed, hastily—"if ever we get there. As sure as you do, somebody will see in it an opening for British trade; and we shall spend twenty millions on conquering Tibet, in the interests of civilisation and a smoke-jack syndicate."

How long we might have stopped at the monastery I cannot say, had it not been for the intervention of an unexpected episode which occurred just a week after our first arrival. We were comfortable enough in a rough way, with our Ghoorka cook to prepare our food for us, and our bearers to wait; but to the end I never felt quite sure of our hosts, who, after all, were entertaining us under false pretences. We had told them, truly enough, that Buddhist missionaries had now penetrated to England; and though they had not the slightest conception where England might be, and knew not the name of Madame Blavatsky, this news interested them. Regarding us as promising neophytes, they were anxious now that we should go on to Lhasa, in order to receive full instruction in the faith from the chief fountainhead, the Grand Lama in person. To this we demurred. Mr. Landor's experiences did not encourage us to follow his lead. The monks, for their part, could not understand our reluctance. They thought that every well-intentioned convert must wish to make the pilgrimage to Lhasa, the Mecca of their creed. Our hesitation threw some doubt on the reality of our conversion. A proselyte, above all men, should never be lukewarm. They expected us to embrace the opportunity with fervour. We might be massacred on the way, to be sure; but what did that matter? We should be dying for the faith, and ought to be charmed at so splendid a prospect.

On the day-week after our arrival time chief Lama came to me at nightfall. His face was serious. He spoke to me through our accredited interpreter, the cook. "Priest-sahib say, very important; the sahib and mem-sahibs must go away from here before sun get up to-morrow morning."

"Why so?" I asked, as astonished as I was pleased.

"Priest-sahib say, he like you very much; oh, very, very much; no want to see village people kill you."

"Kill us! But I thought they believed we were saints!"

"Priest say, that just it; too much saint altogether. People hereabout all telling that the sahib and the mem-sahibs very great saints; much holy, like Buddha. Make picture; work miracles. People think, if them kill you, and have your tomb here, very holy place; very great Karma; very good for trade; plenty Tibetan man hear you holy men, come here on pilgrimage. Pilgrimage make fair, make market, very good for village. So people want to kill you, build shrine over your body."

This was a view of the advantages of sanctity which had never before struck me. Now, I had not been eager even for the distinction of being a Christian martyr; as to being a Buddhist martyr, that was quite out of the question. "Then what does the Lama advise us to do?" I asked.

"Priest-sahib say he love you; no want to see village people kill you. He give you guide, very good guide, know mountains well; take you back straight to Maharajah's country."

"Not Ram Das?" I asked, suspiciously.

"No, not Ram Das. Very good man—Tibetan."

I saw at once this was a genuine crisis. All was hastily arranged. I went in and told Hilda and Lady Meadowcroft. Our spoilt child cried a little, of course, at the idea of being enshrined; but on the whole behaved admirably. At early dawn next morning, before the village was awake, we crept with stealthy steps out of the monastery, whose inmates were friendly. Our new guide accompanied us. We avoided the village, on whose outskirts the lamasery lay, and made straight for the valley. By six o'clock, we were well out of sight of the clustered houses and the pyramidal spires. But I did not breathe freely till late in the afternoon, when we found ourselves once more under British protection in the first hamlet of the Maharajah's territory.

As for that scoundrel, Ram Das, we heard nothing more of him. He disappeared into space from the moment he deserted us at the door of the trap into which he had led us. The chief Lama told me he had gone back at once by another route to his own country.

CHAPTER XI

After our fortunate escape from the clutches of our too-admiring Tibetan hosts, we wound our way slowly back through the Maharajah's territory towards Sir Ivor's headquarters. On the third day out from the lamasery we camped in a romantic Himalayan valley, a narrow, green glen, with a brawling stream running in white cataracts and rapids down its midst. We were able to breathe freely now; we could enjoy the great tapering deodars that rose in ranks on the hillsides, the snow-clad needles of ramping rock that bounded the view to north and south, the feathery bamboo-jungle that fringed and half-obscured the mountain torrent, whose cool music, alas, fallaciously cool, was borne to us through the dense screen of waving foliage. Lady Meadowcroft was so delighted at having got clear away from those murderous and saintly Tibetans that for a while she almost forgot to grumble. She even condescended to admire the deep-cleft ravine in which we bivouacked for the night, and to admit that the orchids which hung from the tall trees were as fine as any at her florist's in Piccadilly. "Though how they can have got them out here already, in this outlandish place, the most fashionable kinds, when we in England have to grow them with such care in expensive hot-houses," she said, "really passes my comprehension."

She seemed to think that orchids originated in Covent Garden.

Early next morning I was engaged with one of my native men in lighting the fire to boil our kettle, for in spite of all misfortunes we still made tea with creditable punctuality, when a tall and good-looking Nepaulese approached us from the hills, with cat-like tread, and stood before me in an attitude of profound supplication. He was a well-dressed young man, like a superior native servant; his face was broad and flat, but kindly and good-humoured. He salaamed many times, but still said nothing.

"Ask him what he wants," I cried, turning to our fair-weather friend, the cook.

The deferential Nepaulese did not wait to be asked. "Salaam, sahib," he said, bowing again very low till his forehead almost touched the ground. "You are Eulopean doctor, sahib?"

"I am," I answered, taken aback at being thus recognised in the forests of Nepaul. "But how in wonder did you come to know it?"

"You camp near here when you pass dis way before, and you doctor little native girl, who got sore eyes. All de country here tell you is very great physician. So I come and to see if you will turn aside to my village to help us."

"Where did you learn English?" I exclaimed, more and more astonished.

"I is servant one time at British Lesident's at de Maharajah's city. Pick up English dere. Also pick up plenty lupee. Velly good business at British Lesident's. Now gone back home to my own village, letired gentleman." And he drew himself up with conscious dignity.

I surveyed the retired gentleman from head to foot. He had an air of distinction, which not even his bare toes could altogether mar. He was evidently a person of local importance. "And what did you want me to visit your village for?" I inquired, dubiously.

"White traveller sahib ill dere, sir. Vely ill; got plague. Great first-class sahib, all same like Governor. Ill, fit to die; send me out all times to try find Eulopean doctor."

"Plague?" I repeated, startled. He nodded.

"Yes, plague; all same like dem hab him so bad down Bombay way."

"Do you know his name?" I asked; for though one does not like to desert a fellow-creature in distress, I did not care to turn aside from my road on such an errand, with Hilda and Lady Meadowcroft, unless for some amply sufficient reason.

The retired gentleman shook his head in the most emphatic fashion. "How me know?" he answered, opening the palms of his hands as if to show he had nothing concealed in them. "Forget Eulopean name all times so easily. And traveller sahib name very hard to lemember. Not got English name. Him Eulopean foleigner."

"A European foreigner!" I repeated. "And you say he is seriously ill? Plague is no trifle. Well, wait a minute; I'll see what the ladies say about it. How far off is your village?"

He pointed with his hand, somewhat vaguely, to the hillside. "Two hours' walk," he answered, with the mountaineer's habit of reckoning distance by time, which extends, under the like circumstances, the whole world over.

I went back to the tents, and consulted Hilda and Lady Meadowcroft. Our spoilt child pouted, and was utterly averse to any detour of any sort. "Let's get back straight to Ivor," she said, petulantly. "I've had enough of camping out. It's all very well in its way for a week but when they begin to talk about cutting your throat and all that, it ceases to be a joke and becomes a wee bit uncomfortable. I want my feather bed. I object to their villages."

"But consider, dear," Hilda said, gently. "This traveller is ill, all alone in a strange land. How can Hubert desert him? It is a doctor's duty to do what he can to alleviate pain and to cure the sick. What would we have thought ourselves, when we were at the lamasery, if a body of European travellers had known we were there, imprisoned and in danger of our lives, and had passed by on the other side without attempting to rescue us?"

Lady Meadowcroft knit her forehead. "That was us," she said, with an impatient nod, after a pause—"and this is another person. You can't turn aside for everybody who's ill in all Nepaul. And plague, too!—so horrid! Besides, how do we know this isn't another plan of these hateful people to lead us into danger?"

"Lady Meadowcroft is quite right," I said, hastily. "I never thought about that. There may be no plague, no patient at all. I will go up with this man alone, Hilda, and find out the truth. It will only take me five hours at most. By noon I shall be back with you."

"What? And leave us here unprotected among the wild beasts and the savages?" Lady Meadowcroft cried, horrified. "In the midst of the forest! Dr. Cumberledge, how can you?"

"You are NOT unprotected," I answered, soothing her. "You have Hilda with you. She is worth ten men. And besides, our Nepaulese are fairly trustworthy."

Hilda bore me out in my resolve. She was too much of a nurse, and had imbibed too much of the true medical sentiment, to let me desert a man in peril of his life in a tropical jungle. So, in spite of Lady Meadowcroft, I was soon winding my way up a steep mountain track, overgrown with creeping Indian weeds, on my road to the still problematical village graced by the residence of the retired gentleman.

After two hours' hard climbing we reached it at last. The retired gentleman led the way to a house in a street of the little wooden hamlet. The door was low; I had to stoop to enter it. I saw in a moment this was indeed no trick. On a native bed, in a corner of the one room, a man lay desperately ill; a European, with white hair and with a skin well bronzed by exposure to the tropics. Ominous dark spots beneath the epidermis showed the nature of the disease. He tossed restlessly as he lay, but did not raise his fevered head or look at my conductor. "Well, any news of Ram Das?" he asked at last, in a parched and feeble voice. Parched and feeble as it was, I recognised it instantly. The man on the bed was Sebastian—no other!

"No news of Lam Das," the retired gentleman replied, with an unexpected display of womanly tenderness. "Lam Das clean gone; not come any more. But I bling you back Eulopean doctor, sahib."

Sebastian did not look up from his bed even then. I could see he was more anxious about a message from his scout than about his own condition. "The rascal!" he moaned, with his eyes closed tight. "The rascal! he has betrayed me." And he tossed uneasily.

I looked at him and said nothing. Then I seated myself on a low stool by the bedside and took his hand in mine to feel his pulse. The wrist was thin and wasted. The face, too, I noticed, had fallen away greatly. It was clear that the malignant fever which accompanies the disease had wreaked its worst on him. So weak and ill was he, indeed, that he let me hold his hand, with my fingers on his pulse, for half a minute or more without ever opening his eyes or displaying the slightest curiosity at my presence. One might have thought that European doctors abounded in Nepaul, and that I had been attending him for a week, with "the mixture as before" at every visit.

"Your pulse is weak and very rapid," I said slowly, in a professional tone. "You seem to me to have fallen into a perilous condition."

At the sound of my voice, he gave a sudden start. Yet even so, for a second, he did not open his eyes. The revelation of my presence seemed to come upon him as in a dream. "Like Cumberledge's," he muttered to himself, gasping. "Exactly like Cumberledge's.... But Cumberledge is dead... I must be delirious.... If I didn't KNOW to the contrary, I could have sworn it was Cumberledge's!"

I spoke again, bending over him. "How long have the glandular swellings been present, Professor?" I asked, with quiet deliberativeness.

This time he opened his eyes sharply, and looked up in my face. He swallowed a great gulp of surprise. His breath came and went. He raised himself on his elbows and stared at me with a fixed stare. "Cumberledge!" he cried; "Cumberledge! Come back to life, then! They told me you were dead! And here you are, Cumberledge!"

"WHO told you I was dead?" I asked, sternly.

He stared at me, still in a dazed way. He was more than half comatose. "Your guide, Ram Das," he answered at last, half incoherently. "He came back by himself. Came back without you. He swore to me he had seen all your throats cut in Tibet. He alone had escaped. The Buddhists had massacred you."

"He told you a lie," I said, shortly.

"I thought so. I thought so. And I sent him back for confirmatory evidence. But the rogue has never brought it." He let his head drop on his rude pillow heavily. "Never, never brought it!"

I gazed at him, full of horror. The man was too ill to hear me, too ill to reason, too ill to recognise the meaning of his own words, almost. Otherwise, perhaps, he would hardly have expressed himself quite so frankly. Though to be sure he had said nothing to criminate himself in any way; his action might have been due to anxiety for our safety.

I fixed my glance on him long and dubiously. What ought I to do next? As for Sebastian, he lay with his eyes closed, half oblivious of my presence. The fever had gripped him hard. He shivered, and looked helpless as a child. In such circumstances, the instincts of my profession rose imperative within me. I could not nurse a case properly in this wretched hut. The one thing to be done was to carry the patient down to our camp in the valley. There, at least, we had air and pure running water.

I asked a few questions from the retired gentleman as to the possibility of obtaining sufficient bearers in the village. As I supposed, any number were forthcoming immediately. Your Nepaulese is by nature a beast of burden; he can carry anything up and down the mountains, and spends his life in the act of carrying.

I pulled out my pencil, tore a leaf from my note-book, and scribbled a hasty note to Hilda: "The invalid is—whom do you think?—Sebastian! He is dangerously ill with some malignant fever. I am bringing him down into camp to nurse. Get everything ready for him." Then I handed it over to a messenger, found for me by the retired gentleman, to carry to Hilda. My host himself I could not spare, as he was my only interpreter.

In a couple of hours we had improvised a rough, woven-grass hammock as an ambulance couch, had engaged our bearers, and had got Sebastian under way for the camp by the river.

When I arrived at our tents, I found Hilda had prepared everything for our patient with her usual cleverness. Not only had she got a bed ready for Sebastian, who was now almost insensible, but she had even cooked some arrowroot from our stores beforehand, so that he might have a little food, with a dash of brandy in it, to recover him after the fatigue of the journey down the mountain. By the time we had laid him out on a mattress in a cool tent, with the fresh air blowing about him, and had made him eat the meal prepared for him, he really began to look comparatively comfortable.

Lady Meadowcroft was now our chief trouble. We did not dare to tell her it was really plague; but she had got near enough back to civilisation to have recovered her faculty for profuse grumbling; and the idea of the delay that Sebastian would cause us drove her wild with annoyance. "Only two days off from Ivor," she cried, "and that comfortable bungalow! And now to think we must stop here in the woods a week or ten days for this horrid old Professor! Why can't he get worse at once and die like a gentleman? But, there! with YOU to nurse him, Hilda, he'll never get worse. He couldn't die if he tried. He'll linger on and on for weeks and weeks through a beastly convalescence!"

"Hubert," Hilda said to me, when we were alone once more; "we mustn't keep her here. She will be a hindrance, not a help. One way or another we must manage to get rid of her."

"How can we?" I asked. "We can't turn her loose upon the mountain roads with a Nepaulese escort. She isn't fit for it. She would be frantic with terror."

"I've thought of that, and I see only one thing possible. I must go on with her myself as fast as we can push to Sir Ivor's place, and then return to help you nurse the Professor."

I saw she was right. It was the sole plan open to us. And I had no fear of letting Hilda go off alone with Lady Meadowcroft and the bearers. She was a host in herself, and could manage a party of native servants at least as well as I could.

So Hilda went, and came back again. Meanwhile, I took charge of the nursing of Sebastian. Fortunately, I had brought with me a good stock of jungle-medicines in my little travelling-case, including plenty of quinine; and under my careful treatment the Professor passed the crisis and began to mend slowly. The first question he asked me when he felt himself able to talk once more was, "Nurse Wade, what has become of her?"—for he had not yet seen her. I feared the shock for him.

"She is here with me," I answered, in a very measured voice. "She is waiting to be allowed to come and help me in taking care of you."

He shuddered and turned away. His face buried itself in the pillow. I could see some twinge of remorse had seized upon him. At last he spoke. "Cumberledge," he said, in a very low and almost frightened tone, "don't let her come near me! I can't bear it. I can't bear it."

Ill as he was, I did not mean to let him think I was ignorant of his motive. "You can't bear a woman whose life you have attempted," I said, in my coldest and most deliberate way, "to have a hand in nursing you! You can't bear to let her heap coals of fire on your head! In that you are right. But, remember, you have attempted MY life too; you have twice done your best to get me murdered."

He did not pretend to deny it. He was too weak for subterfuges. He only writhed as he lay. "You are a man," he said, shortly, "and she is a woman. That is all the difference." Then he paused for a minute or two. "Don't let her come near me," he moaned once more, in a piteous voice. "Don't let her come near me!"

"I will not," I answered. "She shall not come near you. I spare you that. But you will have to eat the food she prepares; and you know SHE will not poison you. You will have to be tended by the servants she chooses; and you know THEY will not murder you. She can heap coals of fire on your head without coming into your tent. Consider that you sought to take her life, and she seeks to save yours! She is as anxious to keep you alive as you are anxious to kill her."

He lay as in a reverie. His long white hair made his clear-cut, thin face look more unearthly than ever, with the hectic flush of fever upon it. At last he turned to me. "We each work for our own ends," he said, in a weary way. "We pursue our own objects. It suits ME to get rid of HER: it suits HER to keep ME alive. I am no good to her dead; living, she expects to wring a confession out of me. But she shall not have it. Tenacity of purpose is the one thing I admire in life. She has the tenacity of purpose, and so have I. Cumberledge, don't you see it is a mere duel of endurance between us?"

"And may the just side win," I answered, solemnly.

It was several days later before he spoke to me of it again. Hilda had brought some food to the door of the tent and passed it in to me for our patient. "How is he now?" she whispered.

Sebastian overheard her voice, and, cowering within himself, still managed to answer: "Better, getting better. I shall soon be well now. You have carried your point. You have cured your enemy."

"Thank God for that!" Hilda said, and glided away silently.

Sebastian ate his cup of arrowroot in silence; then he looked at me with wistful, musing eyes. "Cumberledge," he murmured at last; "after all, I can't help admiring that woman. She is the only person who has ever checkmated me. She checkmates me every time. Steadfastness is what I love. Her steadfastness of purpose and her determination move me."

"I wish they would move you to tell the truth," I answered.

He mused again. "To tell the truth!" he muttered, moving his head up and down. "I have lived for science. Shall I wreck all now? There are truths which it is better to hide than to proclaim. Uncomfortable truths, truths that never should have been, truths which help to make greater truths incredible. But, all the same, I cannot help admiring that woman. She has Yorke-Bannerman's intellect, with a great deal more than Yorke-Bannerman's force of will. Such firmness! such energy! such resolute patience! She is a wonderful creature. I can't help admiring her!"

I said no more to him just then. I thought it better to let nascent remorse and nascent admiration work out their own natural effects unimpeded. For I could see our enemy was beginning to feel some sting of remorse. Some men are below it. Sebastian thought himself above it. I felt sure he was mistaken.

Yet even in the midst of these personal preoccupations, I saw that our great teacher was still, as ever, the pure man of science. He noted every symptom and every change of the disease with professional accuracy. He observed his own case, whenever his mind was clear enough, as impartially as he would have observed any outside patient's. "This is a rare chance, Cumberledge," he whispered to me once, in an interval of delirium. "So few Europeans have ever had the complaint, and probably none who were competent to describe the specific subjective and psychological symptoms. The delusions one gets as one sinks into the coma, for example, are of quite a peculiar type, delusions of wealth and of absolute power, most exhilarating and magnificent. I think myself a millionaire or a Prime Minister. Be sure you make a note of that, in case I die. If I recover, of course I can write an exhaustive monograph on the whole history of the disease in the British Medical Journal. But if I die, the task of chronicling these interesting observations will devolve upon you. A most exceptional chance! You are much to be congratulated."

"You MUST not die, Professor," I cried, thinking more, I will confess, of Hilda Wade than of himself. "You must live... to report this case for science." I used what I thought the strongest lever I knew for him.

He closed his eyes dreamily. "For science! Yes, for science! There you strike the right chord! What have I not dared and done for science? But, in case I die, Cumberledge, be sure you collect the notes I took as I was sickening, they are most important for the history and etiology of the disease. I made them hourly. And don't forget the main points to be observed as I am dying. You know what they are. This is a rare, rare chance! I congratulate you on being the man who has the first opportunity ever afforded us of questioning an intelligent European case, a case where the patient is fully capable of describing with accuracy his symptoms and his sensations in medical phraseology."

He did not die, however. In about another week he was well enough to move. We carried him down to Mozufferpoor, the first large town in the plains thereabouts, and handed him over for the stage of convalescence to the care of the able and efficient station doctor, to whom my thanks are due for much courteous assistance.

"And now, what do you mean to do?" I asked Hilda, when our patient was placed in other hands, and all was over.

She answered me without one second's hesitation: "Go straight to Bombay, and wait there till Sebastian takes passage for England."

"He will go home, you think, as soon as he is well enough?"

"Undoubtedly. He has now nothing more to stop in India for."

"Why not as much as ever?"

She looked at me curiously. "It is so hard to explain," she replied, after a moment's pause, during which she had been drumming her little forefinger on the table. "I feel it rather than reason it. But don't you see that a certain change has lately come over Sebastian's attitude? He no longer desires to follow me; he wants to avoid me. That is why I wish more than ever to dog his steps. I feel the beginning of the end has come. I am gaining my point. Sebastian is wavering."

"Then when he engages a berth, you propose to go by the same steamer?"

"Yes. It makes all the difference. When he tries to follow me, he is dangerous; when he tries to avoid me, it becomes my work in life to follow him. I must keep him in sight every minute now. I must quicken his conscience. I must make him FEEL his own desperate wickedness. He is afraid to face me: that means remorse. The more I compel him to face me, the more the remorse is sure to deepen."

I saw she was right. We took the train to Bombay. I found rooms at the hospitable club, by a member's invitation, while Hilda went to stop with some friends of Lady Meadowcroft's on the Malabar Hill. We waited for Sebastian to come down from the interior and take his passage. Hilda, with her intuitive certainty, felt sure he would come.

A steamer, two steamers, three steamers, sailed, and still no Sebastian. I began to think he must have made up his mind to go back some other way. But Hilda was confident, so I waited patiently. At last one morning I dropped in, as I had often done before, at the office of one of the chief steamship companies. It was the very morning when a packet was to sail. "Can I see the list of passengers on the Vindhya?" I asked of the clerk, a sandy-haired Englishman, tall, thin, and sallow.

The clerk produced it.

I scanned it in haste. To my surprise and delight, a pencilled entry half-way down the list gave the name, "Professor Sebastian."

"Oh, Sebastian is going by this steamer?" I murmured, looking up.

The sandy-haired clerk hummed and hesitated. "Well, I believe he's going, sir," he answered at last; "but it's a bit uncertain. He's a fidgety man, the Professor. He came down here this morning and asked to see the list, the same as you have done. Then he engaged a berth provisionally—'mind, provisionally,' he said—that's why his name is only put in on the list in pencil. I take it he's waiting to know whether a party of friends he wishes to meet are going also."

"Or wishes to avoid," I thought to myself, inwardly; but I did not say so. I asked instead, "Is he coming again?"

"Yes, I think so: at 5.30."

"And she sails at seven?"

"At seven, punctually. Passengers must be aboard by half-past six at latest."

"Very good," I answered, making up my mind promptly. "I only called to know the Professor's movements. Don't mention to him that I came. I may look in again myself an hour or two later."

"You don't want a passage, sir? You may be the friend he's expecting."

"No, I don't want a passage, not at present certainly." Then I ventured on a bold stroke. "Look here," I said, leaning across towards him, and assuming a confidential tone: "I am a private detective", which was perfectly true in essence, "and I'm dogging the Professor, who, for all his eminence, is gravely suspected of a great crime. If you will help me, I will make it worth your while. Let us understand one another. I offer you a five-pound note to say nothing of all this to him."

The sallow clerk's fishy eye glistened. "You can depend upon me," he answered, with an acquiescent nod. I judged that he did not often get the chance of earning some eighty rupees so easily.

I scribbled a hasty note and sent it round to Hilda: "Pack your boxes at once, and hold yourself in readiness to embark on the Vindhya at six o'clock precisely." Then I put my own things straight; and waited at the club till a quarter to six. At that time I strolled on unconcernedly into the office. A cab outside held Hilda and our luggage. I had arranged it all meanwhile by letter.

"Professor Sebastian been here again?" I asked.

"Yes, sir; he's been here; and he looked over the list again; and he's taken his passage. But he muttered something about eavesdroppers, and said that if he wasn't satisfied when he got on board, he would return at once and ask for a cabin in exchange by the next steamer."

"That will do," I answered, slipping the promised five-pound note into the clerk's open palm, which closed over it convulsively. "Talked about eavesdroppers, did he? Then he knows he's been shadowed. It may console you to learn that you are instrumental in furthering the aims of justice and unmasking a cruel and wicked conspiracy. Now, the next thing is this: I want two berths at once by this very steamer, one for myself, name of Cumberledge; one for a lady, name of Wade; and look sharp about it."

The sandy-haired man did look sharp; and within three minutes we were driving off with our tickets to Prince's Dock landing-stage.

We slipped on board unobtrusively, and instantly took refuge in our respective staterooms till the steamer was well under way, and fairly out of sight of Kolaba Island. Only after all chance of Sebastian's avoiding us was gone forever did we venture up on deck, on purpose to confront him.

It was one of those delicious balmy evenings which one gets only at sea and in the warmer latitudes. The sky was alive with myriads of twinkling and palpitating stars, which seemed to come and go, like sparks on a fire-back, as one gazed upward into the vast depths and tried to place them. They played hide-and-seek with one another and with the innumerable meteors which shot recklessly every now and again across the field of the firmament, leaving momentary furrows of light behind them. Beneath, the sea sparkled almost like the sky, for every turn of the screw churned up the scintillating phosphorescence in the water, so that countless little jets of living fire seemed to flash and die away at the summit of every wavelet. A tall, spare man in a picturesque cloak, and with long, lank, white hair, leant over the taffrail, gazing at the numberless flashing lights of the surface. As he gazed, he talked on in his clear, rapt voice to a stranger by his side. The voice and the ring of enthusiasm were unmistakable. "Oh, no," he was saying, as we stole up behind him, "that hypothesis, I venture to assert, is no longer tenable by the light of recent researches. Death and decay have nothing to do directly with the phosphorescence of the sea, though they have a little indirectly. The light is due in the main to numerous minute living organisms, most of them bacilli, on which I once made several close observations and crucial experiments. They possess organs which may be regarded as miniature bull's-eye lanterns. And these organs—"

"What a lovely evening, Hubert!" Hilda said to me, in an apparently unconcerned voice, as the Professor reached this point in his exposition.

Sebastian's voice quavered and stammered for a moment. He tried just at first to continue and complete his sentence: "And these organs," he went on, aimlessly, "these bull's-eyes that I spoke about, are so arranged, so arranged, I was speaking on the subject of crustaceans, I think, crustaceans so arranged, " then he broke down utterly and turned sharply round to me. He did not look at Hilda, I think he did not dare; but he faced me with his head down and his long, thin neck protruded, eyeing me from under those overhanging, penthouse brows of his. "You sneak!" he cried, passionately. "You sneak! You have dogged me by false pretences. You have lied to bring this about! You have come aboard under a false name, you and your accomplice!"

I faced him in turn, erect and unflinching. "Professor Sebastian," I answered, in my coldest and calmest tone, "you say what is not true. If you consult the list of passengers by the Vindhya, now posted near the companion-ladder, you will find the names of Hilda Wade and Hubert Cumberledge duly entered. We took our passage AFTER you inspected the list at the office to see whether our names were there, in order to avoid us. But you cannot avoid us. We do not mean that you shall avoid us. We will dog you now through life, not by lies or subterfuges, as you say, but openly and honestly. It is YOU who need to slink and cower, not we. The prosecutor need not descend to the sordid shifts of the criminal."

The other passenger had sidled away quietly the moment he saw our conversation was likely to be private; and I spoke in a low voice, though clearly and impressively, because I did not wish for a scene. I was only endeavouring to keep alive the slow, smouldering fire of remorse in the man's bosom. And I saw I had touched him on a spot that hurt. Sebastian drew himself up and answered nothing. For a minute or two he stood erect, with folded arms, gazing moodily before him. Then he said, as if to himself: "I owe the man my life. He nursed me through the plague. If it had not been for that, if he had not tended me so carefully in that valley in Nepaul, I would throw him overboard now, catch him in my arms and throw him overboard! I would—and be hanged for it!"

He walked past us as if he saw us not, silent, erect, moody. Hilda stepped aside and let him pass. He never even looked at her. I knew why; he dared not. Every day now, remorse for the evil part he had played in her life, respect for the woman who had unmasked and outwitted him, made it more and more impossible for Sebastian to face her. During the whole of that voyage, though he dined in the same saloon and paced the same deck, he never spoke to her, he never so much as looked at her. Once or twice their eyes met by accident, and Hilda stared him down; Sebastian's eyelids dropped, and he stole away uneasily. In public, we gave no overt sign of our differences; but it was understood on board that relations were strained: that Professor Sebastian and Dr. Cumberledge had been working at the same hospital in London together; and that owing to some disagreement between them Dr. Cumberledge had resigned, which made it most awkward for them to be travelling together by the same steamer.

We passed through the Suez Canal and down the Mediterranean. All the time, Sebastian never again spoke to us. The passengers, indeed, held aloof from the solitary, gloomy old man, who strode along the quarter-deck with his long, slow stride, absorbed in his own thoughts, and intent only on avoiding Hilda and myself. His mood was unsociable. As for Hilda, her helpful, winning ways made her a favourite with all the women, as her pretty face did with all the men. For the first time in his life, Sebastian seemed to be aware that he was shunned. He retired more and more within himself for company; his keen eye began to lose in some degree its extraordinary fire, his expression to forget its magnetic attractiveness. Indeed, it was only young men of scientific tastes that Sebastian could ever attract. Among them, his eager zeal, his single-minded devotion to the cause of science, awoke always a responsive chord which vibrated powerfully.

Day after day passed, and we steamed through the Straits and neared the Channel. Our thoughts began to assume a home complexion. Everybody was full of schemes as to what he would do when he reached England. Old Bradshaws were overhauled and trains looked out, on the supposition that we would get in by such an hour on Tuesday. We were steaming along the French coast, off the western promontory of Brittany. The evening was fine, and though, of course, less warm than we had experienced of late, yet pleasant and summer-like. We watched the distant cliffs of the Finistere mainland and the numerous little islands that lie off the shore, all basking in the unreal glow of a deep red sunset. The first officer was in charge, a very cock-sure and careless young man, handsome and dark-haired; the sort of young man who thought more of creating an impression upon the minds of the lady passengers than of the duties of his position.

"Aren't you going down to your berth?" I asked of Hilda, about half-past ten that night; "the air is so much colder here than you have been feeling it of late, that I'm afraid of your chilling yourself."

She looked up at me with a smile, and drew her little fluffy, white woollen wrap closer about her shoulders. "Am I so very valuable to you, then?" she asked, for I suppose my glance had been a trifle too tender for a mere acquaintance's. "No, thank you, Hubert; I don't think I'll go down, and, if you're wise, you won't go down either. I distrust this first officer. He's a careless navigator, and to-night his head's too full of that pretty Mrs. Ogilvy. He has been flirting with her desperately ever since we left Bombay, and to-morrow he knows he will lose her forever. His mind isn't occupied with the navigation at all; what HE is thinking of is how soon his watch will be over, so that he may come down off the bridge on to the quarter-deck to talk to her. Don't you see she's lurking over yonder, looking up at the stars and waiting for him by the compass? Poor child! she has a bad husband, and now she has let herself get too much entangled with this empty young fellow. I shall be glad for her sake to see her safely landed and out of the man's clutches."

As she spoke, the first officer glanced down towards Mrs. Ogilvy, and held out his chronometer with an encouraging smile which seemed to say, "Only an hour and a half more now! At twelve, I shall be with you!"

"Perhaps you're right, Hilda," I answered, taking a seat beside her and throwing away my cigar. "This is one of the worst bits on the French coast that we're approaching. We're not far off Ushant. I wish the captain were on the bridge instead of this helter-skelter, self-conceited young fellow. He's too cock-sure. He knows so much about seamanship that he could take a ship through any rocks on his course, blindfold, in his own opinion. I always doubt a man who is so much at home in his subject that he never has to think about it. Most things in this world are done by thinking."

"We can't see the Ushant light," Hilda remarked, looking ahead.

"No; there's a little haze about on the horizon, I fancy. See, the stars are fading away. It begins to feel damp. Sea mist in the Channel."

Hilda sat uneasily in her deck-chair. "That's bad," she answered; "for the first officer is taking no more heed of Ushant than of his latter end. He has forgotten the existence of the Breton coast. His head is just stuffed with Mrs. Ogilvy's eyelashes. Very pretty, long eyelashes, too; I don't deny it; but they won't help him to get through the narrow channel. They say it's dangerous."

"Dangerous!" I answered. "Not a bit of it, with reasonable care. Nothing at sea is dangerous, except the inexplicable recklessness of navigators. There's always plenty of sea-room, if they care to take it. Collisions and icebergs, to be sure, are dangers that can't be avoided at times, especially if there's fog about. But I've been enough at sea in my time to know this much at least, that no coast in the world is dangerous except by dint of reckless corner-cutting. Captains of great ships behave exactly like two hansom-drivers in the streets of London; they think they can just shave past without grazing; and they DO shave past nine times out of ten. The tenth time they run on the rocks through sheer recklessness, and lose their vessel; and then, the newspapers always ask the same solemn question, in childish good faith, how did so experienced and able a navigator come to make such a mistake in his reckoning? He made NO mistake; he simply tried to cut it fine, and cut it too fine for once, with the result that he usually loses his own life and his passengers. That's all. We who have been at sea understand that perfectly."

Just at that moment another passenger strolled up and joined us, a Bengal Civil servant. He drew his chair over by Hilda's, and began discussing Mrs. Ogilvy's eyes and the first officer's flirtations. Hilda hated gossip, and took refuge in generalities. In three minutes the talk had wandered off to Ibsen's influence on the English drama, and we had forgotten the very existence of the Isle of Ushant.

"The English public will never understand Ibsen," the newcomer said, reflectively, with the omniscient air of the Indian civilian. "He is too purely Scandinavian. He represents that part of the Continental mind which is farthest removed from the English temperament. To him, respectability, our god, is not only no fetish, it is the unspeakable thing, the Moabitish abomination. He will not bow down to the golden image which our British Nebuchadnezzar, King Demos, has made, and which he asks us to worship. And the British Nebuchadnezzar will never get beyond the worship of his Vishnu, respectability, the deity of the pure and blameless ratepayer. So Ibsen must always remain a sealed book to the vast majority of the English people."

"That is true," Hilda answered, "as to his direct influence; but don't you think, indirectly, he is leavening England? A man so wholly out of tune with the prevailing note of English life could only affect it, of course, by means of disciples and popularisers, often even popularisers who but dimly and distantly apprehend his meaning. He must be interpreted to the English by English intermediaries, half Philistine themselves, who speak his language ill, and who miss the greater part of his message. Yet only by such half-hints—Why, what was that? I think I saw something!"

Even as she uttered the words, a terrible jar ran fiercely through the ship from stem to stern, a jar that made one clench one's teeth and hold one's jaws tight, the jar of a prow that shattered against a rock. I took it all in at a glance. We had forgotten Ushant, but Ushant had not forgotten us. It had revenged itself upon us by revealing its existence.

In a moment all was turmoil and confusion on deck. I cannot describe the scene that followed. Sailors rushed to and fro, unfastening ropes and lowering boats, with admirable discipline. Women shrieked and cried aloud in helpless terror. The voice of the first officer could be heard above the din, endeavouring to atone by courage and coolness in the actual disaster for his recklessness in causing it. Passengers rushed on deck half clad, and waited for their turn to take places in the boats. It was a time of terror, turmoil, and hubbub. But, in the midst of it all, Hilda turned to me with infinite calm in her voice. "Where is Sebastian?" she asked, in a perfectly collected tone. "Whatever happens, we must not lose sight of him."

"I am here," another voice, equally calm, responded beside her. "You are a brave woman. Whether I sink or swim, I admire your courage, your steadfastness of purpose." It was the only time he had addressed a word to her during the entire voyage.

They put the women and children into the first boats lowered. Mothers and little ones went first; single women and widows after. "Now, Miss Wade," the first officer said, taking her gently by the shoulders when her turn arrived. "Make haste; don't keep us waiting!"

But Hilda held back. "No, no," she said, firmly. "I won't go yet. I am waiting for the men's boat. I must not leave Professor Sebastian."

The first officer shrugged his shoulders. There was no time for protest. "Next, then," he said, quickly. "Miss Martin—Miss Weatherly!"

Sebastian took her hand and tried to force her in. "You MUST go," he said, in a low, persuasive tone. "You must not wait for me!"

He hated to see her, I knew. But I imagined in his voice, for I noted it even then, there rang some undertone of genuine desire to save her.

Hilda loosened his grasp resolutely. "No, no," she answered, "I cannot fly. I shall never leave you."

"Not even if I promise—"

She shook her head and closed her lips hard. "Certainly not," she said again, after a pause. "I cannot trust you. Besides, I must stop by your side and do my best to save you. Your life is all in all to me. I dare not risk it."

His gaze was now pure admiration. "As you will," he answered. "For he that loseth his life shall gain it."

"If ever we land alive," Hilda answered, glowing red in spite of the danger, "I shall remind you of that word. I shall call upon you to fulfil it."

The boat was lowered, and still Hilda stood by my side. One second later, another shock shook us. The Vindhya parted amidships, and we found ourselves struggling and choking in the cold sea water.

It was a miracle that every soul of us was not drowned that moment, as many of us were. The swirling eddy which followed as the Vindhya sank swamped two of the boats, and carried down not a few of those who were standing on the deck with us. The last I saw of the first officer was a writhing form whirled about in the water; before he sank, he shouted aloud, with a seaman's frank courage, "Say it was all my fault; I accept the responsibility. I ran her too close. I am the only one to blame for it." Then he disappeared in the whirlpool caused by the sinking ship, and we were left still struggling.

One of the life-rafts, hastily rigged by the sailors, floated our way. Hilda struck out a stroke or two and caught it. She dragged herself on to it, and beckoned me to follow. I could see she was holding on to something tightly. I struck out in turn and reached the raft, which was composed of two seats, fastened together in haste at the first note of danger. I hauled myself up by Hilda's side. "Help me to pull him aboard!" she cried, in an agonised voice. "I am afraid he has lost consciousness!" Then I looked at the object she was clutching in her hands. It was Sebastian's white head, apparently quite lifeless.

I pulled him up with her and laid him out on the raft. A very faint breeze from the south-west had sprung up; that and a strong seaward current that sets round the rocks were carrying us straight out from the Breton coast and all chance of rescue, towards the open channel.

But Hilda thought nothing of such physical danger. "We have saved him, Hubert!" she cried, clasping her hands. "We have saved him! But do you think he is alive? For unless he is, MY chance, OUR chance, is gone forever!"

I bent over and felt his pulse. As far as I could make out, it still beat feebly.

CHAPTER XII

THE EPISODE OF THE DEAD MAN WHO SPOKE

I will not trouble you with details of those three terrible days and nights when we drifted helplessly about at the mercy of the currents on our improvised life-raft up and down the English Channel. The first night was the worst. Slowly after that we grew used to the danger, the cold, the hunger, and the thirst. Our senses were numbed; we passed whole hours together in a sort of torpor, just vaguely wondering whether a ship would come in sight to save us, obeying the merciful law that those who are utterly exhausted are incapable of acute fear, and acquiescing in the probability of our own extinction. But however slender the chance, and as the hours stole on it seemed slender enough, Hilda still kept her hopes fixed mainly on Sebastian. No daughter could have watched the father she loved more eagerly and closely than Hilda watched her life-long enemy, the man who had wrought such evil upon her and hers. To save our own lives without him would be useless. At all hazards, she must keep him alive, on the bare chance of a rescue. If he died, there died with him the last hope of justice and redress.

As for Sebastian, after the first half-hour, during which he lay white and unconscious, he opened his eyes faintly, as we could see by the moonlight, and gazed around him with a strange, puzzled state of inquiry. Then his senses returned to him by degrees. "What! you, Cumberledge?" he murmured, measuring me with his eye; "and you, Nurse Wade? Well, I thought you would manage it." There was a tone almost of amusement in his voice, a half-ironical tone which had been familiar to us in the old hospital days. He raised himself on one arm and gazed at the water all round. Then he was silent for some minutes. At last he spoke again. "Do you know what I ought to do if I were consistent?" he asked, with a tinge of pathos in his words. "Jump off this raft, and deprive you of your last chance of triumph, the triumph which you have worked for so hard. You want to save my life for your own ends, not for mine. Why should I help you to my own undoing?"

Hilda's voice was tenderer and softer than usual as she answered: "No, not for my own ends alone, and not for your undoing, but to give you one last chance of unburdening your conscience. Some men are too small to be capable of remorse; their little souls have no room for such a feeling. You are great enough to feel it and to try to crush it down. But you CANNOT crush it down; it crops up in spite of you. You have tried to bury it in your soul, and you have failed. It is your remorse that has driven you to make so many attempts against the only living souls who knew and understood. If ever we get safely to land once more, and God knows it is not likely, I give you still the chance of repairing the mischief you have done, and of clearing my father's memory from the cruel stain which you and only you can wipe away."

Sebastian lay long, silent once more, gazing up at her fixedly, with the foggy, white moonlight shining upon his bright, inscrutable eyes. "You are a brave woman, Maisie Yorke-Bannerman," he said, at last, slowly; "a very brave woman. I will try to live, I too, for a purpose of my own. I say it again: he that loseth his life shall gain it."

Incredible as it may sound, in half an hour more he was lying fast asleep on that wave-tossed raft, and Hilda and I were watching him tenderly. And it seemed to us as we watched him that a change had come over those stern and impassive features. They had softened and melted until his face was that of a gentler and better type. It was as if some inward change of soul was moulding the fierce old Professor into a nobler and more venerable man.

Day after day we drifted on, without food or water. The agony was terrible; I will not attempt to describe it, for to do so is to bring it back too clearly to my memory. Hilda and I, being younger and stronger, bore up against it well; but Sebastian, old and worn, and still weak from the plague, grew daily weaker. His pulse just beat, and sometimes I could hardly feel it thrill under my finger. He became delirious, and murmured much about Yorke-Bannerman's daughter. Sometimes he forgot all, and spoke to me in the friendly terms of our old acquaintance at Nathaniel's, giving me directions and advice about imaginary operations. Hour after hour we watched for a sail, and no sail appeared. One could hardly believe we could toss about so long in the main highway of traffic without seeing a ship or spying more than the smoke-trail of some passing steamer.

As far as I could judge, during those days and nights, the wind veered from south-west to south-east, and carried us steadily and surely towards the open Atlantic. On the third evening out, about five o'clock, I saw a dark object on the horizon. Was it moving towards us? We strained our eyes in breathless suspense. A minute passed, and then another. Yes, there could be no doubt. It grew larger and larger. It was a ship, a steamer. We made all the signs of distress we could manage. I stood up and waved Hilda's white shawl frantically in the air. There was half an hour of suspense, and our hearts sank as we thought that they were about to pass us. Then the steamer hove to a little and seemed to notice us. Next instant we dropped upon our knees, for we saw they were lowering a boat. They were coming to our aid. They would be in time to save us.

Hilda watched our rescuers with parted lips and agonised eyes. Then she felt Sebastian's pulse. "Thank Heaven," she cried, "he still lives! They will be here before he is quite past confession."

Sebastian opened his eyes dreamily. "A boat?" he asked.

"Yes, a boat!"

"Then you have gained your point, child. I am able to collect myself. Give me a few hours' more life, and what I can do to make amends to you shall be done."

I don't know why, but it seemed longer between the time when the boat was lowered and the moment when it reached us than it had seemed during the three days and nights we lay tossing about helplessly on the open Atlantic. There were times when we could hardly believe it was really moving. At last, however, it reached us, and we saw the kindly faces and outstretched hands of our rescuers. Hilda clung to Sebastian with a wild clasp as the men reached out for her.

"No, take HIM first!" she cried, when the sailors, after the custom of men, tried to help her into the gig before attempting to save us; "his life is worth more to me than my own. Take him, and for God's sake lift him gently, for he is nearly gone!"

They took him aboard and laid him down in the stern. Then, and then only, Hilda stepped into the boat, and I staggered after her. The officer in charge, a kind young Irishman, had had the foresight to bring brandy and a little beef essence. We ate and drank what we dared as they rowed us back to the steamer. Sebastian lay back, with his white eyelashes closed over the lids, and the livid hue of death upon his emaciated cheeks; but he drank a teaspoonful or two of brandy, and swallowed the beef essence with which Hilda fed him.

"Your father is the most exhausted of the party," the officer said, in a low undertone. "Poor fellow, he is too old for such adventures. He seems to have hardly a spark of life left in him."

Hilda shuddered with evident horror. "He is not my father, thank Heaven!" she cried, leaning over him and supporting his drooping head, in spite of her own fatigue and the cold that chilled our very bones. "But I think he will live. I mean him to live. He is my best friend now, and my bitterest enemy!"

The officer looked at her in surprise, and then touched his forehead, inquiringly, with a quick glance at me. He evidently thought cold and hunger had affected her reason. I shook my head. "It is a peculiar case," I whispered. "What the lady says is right. Everything depends for us upon our keeping him alive till we reach England."

They rowed us to the boat, and we were handed tenderly up the side. There, the ship's surgeon and everybody else on board did their best to restore us after our terrible experience. The ship was the Don, of the Royal Mail Steamship Company's West Indian line; and nothing could exceed the kindness with which we were treated by every soul on board, from the captain to the stewardess and the junior cabin-boy. Sebastian's great name carried weight even here. As soon as it was generally understood on board that we had brought with us the famous physiologist and pathologist, the man whose name was famous throughout Europe, we might have asked for anything that the ship contained without fear of a refusal. But, indeed, Hilda's sweet face was enough in itself to win the interest and sympathy of all who saw it.

By eleven next morning we were off Plymouth Sound; and by midday we had landed at the Mill Bay Docks, and were on our way to a comfortable hotel in the neighbourhood.

Hilda was too good a nurse to bother Sebastian at once about his implied promise. She had him put to bed, and kept him there carefully.

"What do you think of his condition?" she asked me, after the second day was over. I could see by her own grave face that she had already formed her own conclusions.

"He cannot recover," I answered. "His constitution, shattered by the plague and by his incessant exertions, has received too severe a shock in this shipwreck. He is doomed."

"So I think. The change is but temporary. He will not last out three days more, I fancy."

"He has rallied wonderfully to-day," I said; "but 'tis a passing rally; a flicker, no more. If you wish to do anything, now is the moment. If you delay, you will be too late."

"I will go in and see him," Hilda answered. "I have said nothing more to him, but I think he is moved. I think he means to keep his promise. He has shown a strange tenderness to me these last few days. I almost believe he is at last remorseful, and ready to undo the evil which he has done."

She stole softly into the sick room. I followed her on tip-toe, and stood near the door behind the screen which shut off the draught from the patient. Sebastian stretched his arms out to her. "Ah, Maisie, my child," he cried, addressing her by the name she had borne in her childhood, both were her own, "don't leave me anymore! Stay with me always, Maisie! I can't get on without you."

"But you hated once to see me!"

"Because I have so wronged you."

"And now? Will you do nothing to repair the wrong?"

"My child, I can never undo that wrong. It is irreparable, for the past can never be recalled; but I will try my best to minimise it. Call Cumberledge in. I am quite sensible now, quite conscious. You will be my witness, Cumberledge, that my pulse is normal and that my brain is clear. I will confess it all. Maisie, your constancy and your firmness have conquered me. And your devotion to your father. If only I had had a daughter like you, my girl, one whom I could have loved and trusted, I might have been a better man. I might even have done better work for science, though on that side, at least, I have little with which to reproach myself."

Hilda bent over him. "Hubert and I are here," she said, slowly, in a strangely calm voice; "but that is not enough. I want a public, an attested, confession. It must be given before witnesses, and signed and sworn to. Somebody might throw doubt upon my word and Hubert's."

Sebastian shrank back. "Given before witnesses, and signed and sworn to! Maisie, is this humiliation necessary; do you exact it?"

Hilda was inexorable. "You know yourself how you are situated. You have only a day or two to live," she said, in an impressive voice. "You must do it at once, or never. You have postponed it all your life. Now, at this last moment, you must make up for it. Will you die with an act of injustice unconfessed on your conscience?"

He paused and struggled. "I could, if it were not for you," he answered.

"Then do it for me," Hilda cried. "Do it for me! I ask it of you not as a favour, but as a right. I DEMAND it!" She stood, white, stern, inexorable, by his couch, and laid her hand upon his shoulder.

He paused once more. Then he murmured feebly, in a querulous tone, "What witnesses? Whom do you wish to be present?"

Hilda spoke clearly and distinctly. She had thought it all out with herself beforehand. "Such witnesses as will carry absolute conviction to the mind of all the world; irreproachable, disinterested witnesses; official witnesses. In the first place, a commissioner of oaths. Then a Plymouth doctor, to show that you are in a fit state of mind to make a confession. Next, Mr. Horace Mayfield, who defended my father. Lastly, Dr. Blake Crawford, who watched the case on your behalf at the trial."

"But, Hilda," I interposed, "we may possibly find that they cannot come away from London just now. They are busy men, and likely to be engaged."

"They will come if I pay their fees. I do not mind how much this costs me. What is money compared to this one great object of my life?"

"And then—the delay! Suppose that we are too late?"

"He will live some days yet. I can telegraph up at once. I want no hole-and-corner confession, which may afterwards be useless, but an open avowal before the most approved witnesses. If he will make it, well and good; if not, my life-work will have failed. But I had rather it failed than draw back one inch from the course which I have laid down for myself."

I looked at the worn face of Sebastian. He nodded his head slowly. "She has conquered," he answered, turning upon the pillow. "Let her have her own way. I hid it for years, for science' sake. That was my motive, Cumberledge, and I am too near death to lie. Science has now nothing more to gain or lose by me. I have served her well, but I am worn out in her service. Maisie may do as she will. I accept her ultimatum."

We telegraphed up, at once. Fortunately, both men were disengaged, and both keenly interested in the case. By that evening, Horace Mayfield was talking it all over with me in the hotel at Southampton. "Well, Hubert, my boy," he said, "a woman, we know, can do a great deal"; he smiled his familiar smile, like a genial fat toad; "but if your Yorke-Bannerman succeeds in getting a confession out of Sebastian, she'll extort my admiration." He paused a moment, then he added, in an afterthought: "I say that she'll extort my admiration; but, mind you, I don't know that I shall feel inclined to believe it. The facts have always appeared to me, strictly between ourselves, you know, to admit of only one explanation."

"Wait and see," I answered. "You think it more likely that Miss Wade will have persuaded Sebastian to confess to things that never happened than that he will convince you of Yorke-Bannerman's innocence?"

The great Q.C. fingered his cigarette-holder affectionately.

"You hit it first time," he answered. "That is precisely my attitude. The evidence against our poor friend was so peculiarly black. It would take a great deal to make me disbelieve it."

"But surely a confession—"

"Ah, well, let me hear the confession, and then I shall be better able to judge."

Even as he spoke Hilda had entered the room.

"There will be no difficulty about that, Mr. Mayfield. You shall hear it, and I trust that it will make you repent for taking so black a view of the case of your own client."

"Without prejudice, Miss Bannerman, without prejudice," said the lawyer, with some confusion. "Our conversation is entirely between ourselves, and to the world I have always upheld that your father was an innocent man."

But such distinctions are too subtle for a loving woman.

"He WAS an innocent man," said she, angrily. "It was your business not only to believe it, but to prove it. You have neither believed it nor proved it; but if you will come upstairs with me, I will show you that I have done both."

Mayfield glanced at me and shrugged his fat shoulders. Hilda had led the way, and we both followed her. In the room of the sick man our other witnesses were waiting: a tall, dark, austere man who was introduced to me as Dr. Blake Crawford, whose name I had heard as having watched the case for Sebastian at the time of the investigation. There were present also a commissioner of oaths, and Dr. Mayby, a small local practitioner, whose attitude towards the great scientist was almost absurdly reverential. The three men were grouped at the foot of the bed, and Mayfield and I joined them. Hilda stood beside the dying man, and rearranged the pillow against which he was propped. Then she held some brandy to his lips. "Now!" said she.

The stimulant brought a shade of colour into his ghastly cheeks, and the old quick, intelligent gleam came back into his deep sunk eyes.

"A remarkable woman, gentlemen," said he, "a very noteworthy woman. I had prided myself that my willpower was the most powerful in the country, I had never met any to match it, but I do not mind admitting that, for firmness and tenacity, this lady is my equal. She was anxious that I should adopt one course of action. I was determined to adopt another. Your presence here is a proof that she has prevailed."

He paused for breath, and she gave him another small sip of the brandy.

"I execute her will ungrudgingly and with the conviction that it is the right and proper course for me to take," he continued. "You will forgive me some of the ill which I have done you, Maisie, when I tell you that I really died this morning, all unknown to Cumberledge and you, and that nothing but my will force has sufficed to keep spirit and body together until I should carry out your will in the manner which you suggested. I shall be glad when I have finished, for the effort is a painful one, and I long for the peace of dissolution. It is now a quarter to seven. I have every hope that I may be able to leave before eight."

It was strange to hear the perfect coolness with which he discussed his own approaching dissolution. Calm, pale, and impassive, his manner was that of a professor addressing his class. I had seen him speak so to a ring of dressers in the old days at Nathaniel's.

"The circumstances which led up to the death of Admiral Scott Prideaux, and the suspicions which caused the arrest of Doctor Yorke-Bannerman, have never yet been fully explained, although they were by no means so profound that they might not have been unravelled at the time had a man of intellect concentrated his attention upon them. The police, however, were incompetent and the legal advisers of Dr. Bannerman hardly less so, and a woman only has had the wit to see that a gross injustice has been done. The true facts I will now lay before you."

Mayfield's broad face had reddened with indignation; but now his curiosity drove out every other emotion, and he leaned forward with the rest of us to hear the old man's story.

"In the first place, I must tell you that both Dr. Bannerman and myself were engaged at the time in an investigation upon the nature and properties of the vegetable alkaloids, and especially of aconitine. We hoped for the very greatest results from this drug, and we were both equally enthusiastic in our research. Especially, we had reason to believe that it might have a most successful action in the case of a certain rare but deadly disease, into the nature of which I need not enter. Reasoning by analogy, we were convinced that we had a certain cure for this particular ailment.

"Our investigation, however, was somewhat hampered by the fact that the condition in question is rare out of tropical countries, and that in our hospital wards we had not, at that time, any example of it. So serious was this obstacle, that it seemed that we must leave other men more favourably situated to reap the benefit of our work and enjoy the credit of our discovery, but a curious chance gave us exactly what we were in search of, at the instant when we were about to despair. It was Yorke-Bannerman who came to me in my laboratory one day to tell me that he had in his private practice the very condition of which we were in search.

"'The patient,' said he, 'is my uncle, Admiral Scott Prideaux.'

"'Your uncle!' I cried, in amazement. 'But how came he to develop such a condition?'

"'His last commission in the Navy was spent upon the Malabar Coast, where the disease is endemic. There can be do doubt that it has been latent in his system ever since, and that the irritability of temper and indecision of character, of which his family have so often had to complain, were really among the symptoms of his complaint.'

"I examined the Admiral in consultation with my colleague, and I confirmed his diagnosis. But, to my surprise, Yorke-Bannerman showed the most invincible and reprehensible objection to experiment upon his relative. In vain I assured him that he must place his duty to science high above all other considerations. It was only after great pressure that I could persuade him to add an infinitesimal portion of aconitine to his prescriptions. The drug was a deadly one, he said, and the toxic dose was still to be determined. He could not push it in the case of a relative who trusted himself to his care. I tried to shake him in what I regarded as his absurd squeamishness, but in vain.

"But I had another resource. Bannerman's prescriptions were made up by a fellow named Barclay, who had been dispenser at Nathaniel's and afterwards set up as a chemist in Sackville Street. This man was absolutely in my power. I had discovered him at Nathaniel's in dishonest practices, and I held evidence which would have sent him to gaol. I held this over him now, and I made him, unknown to Bannerman, increase the doses of aconitine in the medicine until they were sufficient for my experimental purposes. I will not enter into figures, but suffice it that Bannerman was giving more than ten times what he imagined.

"You know the sequel. I was called in, and suddenly found that I had Bannerman in my power. There had been a very keen rivalry between us in science. He was the only man in England whose career might impinge upon mine. I had this supreme chance of putting him out of my way. He could not deny that he had been giving his uncle aconitine. I could prove that his uncle had died of aconitine.

He could not himself account for the facts, he was absolutely in my power. I did not wish him to be condemned, Maisie. I only hoped that he would leave the court discredited and ruined. I give you my word that my evidence would have saved him from the scaffold."

Hilda was listening, with a set, white face.

"Proceed!" said she, and held out the brandy once more.

"I did not give the Admiral any more aconitine after I had taken over the case. But what was already in his system was enough. It was evident that we had seriously under-estimated the lethal dose. As to your father, Maisie, you have done me an injustice. You have always thought that I killed him."

"Proceed!" said she.

"I speak now from the brink of the grave, and I tell you that I did not. His heart was always weak, and it broke down under the strain. Indirectly I was the cause, I do not seek to excuse anything; but it was the sorrow and the shame that killed him. As to Barclay, the chemist, that is another matter. I will not deny that I was concerned in that mysterious disappearance, which was a seven days' wonder in the Press. I could not permit my scientific calm to be interrupted by the blackmailing visits of so insignificant a person. And then after many years you came, Maisie. You also got between me and that work which was life to me. You also showed that you would rake up this old matter and bring dishonour upon a name which has stood for something in science. You also, but you will forgive me. I have held on to life for your sake as an atonement for my sins. Now, I go! Cumberledge, your notebook. Subjective sensations, swimming in the head, light flashes before the eyes, soothing torpor, some touch of coldness, constriction of the temples, humming in the ears, a sense of sinking—sinking—sinking!"

It was an hour later, and Hilda and I were alone in the chamber of death. As Sebastian lay there, a marble figure, with his keen eyes closed and his pinched, thin face whiter and serener than ever, I could not help gazing at him with some pangs of recollection. I could not avoid recalling the time when his very name was to me a word of power, and when the thought of him roused on my cheek a red flush of enthusiasm. As I looked I murmured two lines from Browning's Grammarian's Funeral:

This is our Master, famous, calm, and dead,
Borne on our shoulders.

Hilda Wade, standing beside me, with an awestruck air, added a stanza from the same great poem:

Lofty designs must close in like effects:
Loftily lying,
Leave him, still loftier than the world suspects,
Living and dying.

I gazed at her with admiration. "And it is YOU, Hilda, who pay him this generous tribute!" I cried, "YOU, of all women!"

"Yes, it is I," she answered. "He was a great man, after all, Hubert. Not good, but great. And greatness by itself extorts our unwilling homage."

"Hilda," I cried, "you are a great woman; and a good woman, too. It makes me proud to think you will soon be my wife. For there is now no longer any just cause or impediment."

Beside the dead master, she laid her hand solemnly and calmly in mine. "No impediment," she answered. "I have vindicated and cleared my father's memory. And now, I can live. 'Actual life comes next.' We have much to do, Hubert."

Grant Allen – A Short Biography

Charles Grant Blairfindie Allen was born on February 24th, 1848 at Alwington, near Kingston, Canada West (now part of Ontario). He was the second son of the Rev. Joseph Antisell Allen, a Protestant minister from Dublin, Ireland and Catharine Ann Grant, the daughter of the fifth Baron of Longueuil.

Grant was educated at home until he was thirteen at which time the family moved, initially to the United States, then France and finally settling in the United Kingdom.

Whilst growing up the family background was obviously religious but Grant developed his own views on life and the world and turned to agnosticism and socialism.

He was educated at King Edward's School in Birmingham and Merton College in Oxford. After graduating, Grant studied in France and also taught at Brighton College. By 1870, still only in his mid-twenties, he became a professor at Queen's College, a black college in Jamaica.

Whilst in Jamaica Grant met and married his first wife Ellen Jerrard in 1873 and they produced a son five years later; Jerrard Grant Allen, who grew up to become a theatrical agent/manager.

In 1876 Grant and his family left Jamaica to return to England with both the talent and ambition to become a writer.

He quickly turned to writing essays, gaining a reputation for his work on science and literary works. An early article, 'Note-Deafness' a description of what is now called amusia, was published in 1878 in the learned journal Mind and was cited approvingly by Oliver Sacks very recently.

From essays in magazines and journals he now turned to books, initially on scientific subjects. These include Physiological Æsthetics 1877 and Flowers and Their Pedigrees 1886.

His first major influence was associationist psychology, as then expounded by Alexander Bain and Herbert Spencer, the latter is often considered the most important individual in the transition from associationist psychology to Darwinian functionalism. In Grant's many articles on flowers and perception in insects, Darwinian arguments now replaced the old Spencerian terms.

On a personal level, a long friendship that started when Grant met Herbert Spencer on his return from Jamaica, turned eventually to one of unease over its long course. Grant was to write a critical and revealing biographical article on Spencer that was published after Spencer was dead.

In the early 1880's Grant began to assist Sir W. W. Hunter in his Gazeteer of India. It is at this time that Grant now turned his full attention away from the factual and towards the world of imagination and fiction.

Between this shift to fiction in 1884 and his death fifteen years later Grant was to write about 30 novels.

Many were adventure novels which were very common in the late Victorian period as writers turned their literary talents to the voracious appetites of the weekly or monthly serial magazines.

Some however were to cause quite a stir. For instance in 1895 Grant took the subject of children born out of wedlock as his subject matter. The result was The Woman Who Did, that suggested, indeed pushed, for its time, certain quite startling views on marriage and related areas. In keeping with his then glowing reputation it became a bestseller despite it being seemingly at odds with society's unease at its provocative subject matter.

Interestingly Grant wrote novels under female pseudonyms. One of these was the short novel The Type-writer Girl, which he wrote under the name Olive Pratt Rayner.

Another work, The Evolution of the Idea of God 1897, propounding a theory of religion on heterodox lines, has the disadvantage of endeavoring to explain everything by one theory. This "ghost theory" was often seen as a derivative of Herbert Spencer's theory. However, at the time, it was well known and brief references to it can be found in a review by Marcel Mauss, Durkheim's nephew, in the articles of William James and in the works of Sigmund Freud. The young G. K. Chesterton wrote on what he considered the flawed premise of the idea, arguing that the idea of God preceded human mythologies, rather than developing from them. Chesterton said of Grant Allen's book on the evolution of the idea of God "it would be much more interesting if God wrote a book on the evolution of the idea of Grant Allen".

From this and other instances, it can be seen that his work was in debate and whether agreed with or not could always ensure a lively discussion.

Grant also helped to pioneer science fiction, with the 1895 novel The British Barbarians. This book, was published at about the same time as H. G. Wells was to publish The Time Machine. The plots are quite different but both describe time travel. A few years later his short story The Thames Valley Catastrophe (published 1901 in The Strand magazine) describes the destruction of London by a massive volcanic eruption. Whilst the premise now may seem outlandish, at the time genuine panic and concern set in as, like his contemporary, Jules Verne, much of great science fiction writing is rooted in a plausibility that is set out very convincingly.

In detective fiction too his works include female detectives, very much an innovation in the young genre and his gentleman rogue, Colonel Clay, is seen as a forerunner to other, perhaps more famous characters, by other later writers.

In 1881 he had settled at Dorking, where he took great delight in botanical walks in the woods and sandy heaths. He never enjoyed particularly good health and so almost every winter he would depart for milder climes, to winter in the south of Europe, usually at Antibes, though occasionally as far as Algiers and Egypt.

In 1892 he bought land almost on the summit of Hind Head, and built himself a charming cottage which he called the Croft. Here he found that it was possible to endure the vagaries of the English winter and in landscape more beautiful and wilder than at Dorking and that his long scientific training could better appreciate.

His growing re-discovery and interest in art in the later part of his life allowed him to blend together literature, art and history in a series of guide books on Paris, Florence, Venice, and the cities of Belgium.

On October 25th 1899 Grant Allen died at his home in Hindhead, Haslemere, Surrey, England. He died just before finishing Hilda Wade. The novel's final episode, which he dictated to his friend, doctor and neighbour Sir Arthur Conan Doyle from his bed appeared under the appropriate title, The Episode of the Dead Man Who Spoke in the Strand Magazine in 1900.

Grant Allen is rarely heard of today, although an occasional short story can be heard on the radio or reprinted among magazine enthusiasts but in his time he did much to entertain the masses and push several genres along a richer journey they are still proceeding on today.

Grant Allen – A Concise Bibliography

Physiological Æsthetics. 1877
The Colour-Sense: Its Origin and Development. 1879
Evolutionist at Large. 1881
Vignettes from Nature. 1881
The Colours of Flowers. 1882
Colin Clout's Calendar. 1883
Flowers and Their Pedigrees. 1883
Philistia. 1884
Strange Stories. Short Stories. 1884
Babylon. A novel in 3 volumes. 1885
For Mamie's Sake. 1886
In All Shades. 1886
The Beckoning Hand & Other Stories. 1887
This Mortal Coil: A Novel. 1888
Force and Energy. 1888
The Devil's Die. 1888
The White Man's Foot. 1888
Falling in Love. 1889
The Tents of Shem. 1889
Wednesday the Tenth. 1890
The Great Taboo. 1890
Dumaresq's Daughter. 1891
What's Bred in the Bone. 1891
The Duchess of Powysland. 1892
The Scallywag. 1893
Michael's Crag. 1893
The Lower Slopes. 1894
Post-Prandial Philosophy. 1894
The British Barbarians. 1895
At Market Value. 1895
The Story of the Plants. 1895
The Desire of the Eyes. 1895
The Woman Who Did. 1895
The Jaws of Death. 1896
A Bride from the Desert. 1896
Under Sealed Orders. 1896
Moorland Idylls. 1896

An African Millionaire. Colonel Clay's novel. 1897
The Evolution of the Idea of God. 1897
Paris. 1897
The Type-writer Girl. (as Olive Pratt Rayner) 1897
Tom, Unlimited. (as Martin Leach Warborough) 1897
Flashlights on Nature. 1898
The Incidental Bishop. 1898
Venice. 1898
The European Tour. 1899
A Splendid Sin. 1899
Miss Cayley's Adventures. 1899
Twelve Tales: With a Headpiece, a Tailpiece, and an Intermezzo. 1899
Hilda Wade (finished by Arthur Conan Doyle). 1900
Linnet. 1900
The Backslider. 1901
Sir Theodore's Guest & Other Stories. 1902
Evolution in Italian Art. 1908
The Hand of God. 1909
The Plants. 1909

Short Stories
The Empress of Andorra. 1878
My New Year Among the Mummies. 1878
Lucretia. 1879
My Circular Tour. 1880
A Ballade of Evolution. 1880
Ram Das of Cawnpore. 1880
The Chinese Play at the Haymarket. 1880
The Senior Proctor's Wooing. 1881
Pausodyne. 1881
Caribbean Twelve Per Cents. 1882
An Episode in High Life. 1882
Mr Chung. 1882
Isadine and I. 1883
The Backsider. 1883
The Reverend John Creedy. 1883
The Foundering of the Fortuna. 1883
The Third Time
The Gold Wulfric
My Uncle's Will. 1884
Carvalho. 1884
The Mysterious Occurence in Piccadilly. 1884
Dr Greatex's Engagement. 1884
Hugh Portledown's Return from Normandy. 1884
The Child of Phalanstery. 1884
The Curate of Churnside. 1884
John Cann's Treasure. 1884
Olga Davidoff's Husband. 1884
The Search Party's Find. 1885
The Two Carnegie's. 1885

Professor Milliter's Dilemma. 1885
In Strict Confidence. 1885
The Beckoning Hand. 1885
The Third Time. 1886
Harry's Inheritance. 1886
The Gold Wulfric. 1886
Mr Pierpoint's Repentance. 1886
Claude Tyack's Ordeal. 1887
Leonard's Recovery. 1887
A Social Difficulty. 1887
Dr Palliser's Patient. 1888
My Christmas Eve at Marzin. 1888
The Sultan's Sister. 1888
His First Crime. 1889
The Mayfield Mystery. 1889
Andre Canivet's Curse. 1890
Old Margaret. 1890
My One Gorilla. 1890
Dick Prothero's Luck. 1890
A Deadly Dilemna. 1891
Jerry Stokes. 1891
Selwyn Utterton's Nemesis. 1891
General Passavant's Will. 1891
The Briefless Barrister. 1891
Melissa's Tour. 1891
Karen – A Canadian Romance. 1891
The Prisoner of Assiout. 1891
The Abbe's Repentance. 1891
Masie Bowman's Fate. 1891
Naomi's Christmas Eves. 1891
That Friend of Sylvia's. 1892
The Conscientious Burglar. 1892
The Minor Poet. 1892
The Governor's Story. 1892
The Pot Boiler. 1892
The Great Ruby. 1892
Ewen Murray's Swim. 1892
Ivan Greet's Masterpiece. 1892
Pallinghurst Barrow. 1892
Langalula. 1893
The Assasin's Knife. 1893
The Artist and the Penny-a-Liner. 1893
A Casual Conversation. 1893
How To Succeed in Literature. 1893
Torrigiano. 1893
A Modern Sibyl: A Florentine Sketch. 1893
Nemesis Wins. 1894
Cecca's Lover. 1894
A Self Respecting Servant. 1894
Passiflora Sanguinea. 1894
An Excellent Match. 1894

Major Kinfaun's Marriage. 1894
Grateful Joe. 1894
An Idyll of the Ice. 1894
Criss Cross Love. 1894
Poor Little Soul. 1894
Amour de Voyage. 1894
The Dynamiter's Sweetheart. 1894
A Triumph of Civilisation. 1894
Dr Wardroper's Lie. 1894
The Miraclous Explorer. 1894
Leon and Leonie. 1895
A Comic Emotion. 1895
Joe's Rascality. 1895
Evelyn Moore's Poet. 1895
Frasine's First Communion. 1895
TheDead Man Speaks. 1895
A Study From the Nude. 1895
Cecca's Choice. 1895
The Desire of the Eyes. 1895
The Making of a Poet. 1895
The Man From Cumbrae. 1895
Fogo Skerries. 1895
The Great Californian Heiress. 1895
Cap'n Tom Woolley. 1895
The Girl at the Fair. 1895
Love's Old Dream. 1895
A Modern Pygmalion. 1895
A Bride From the Desert. 1895
The Practical Test. 1896
A Confidential Communication. 1896
The Great Temperance Preacher. 1896
A Day on the River. 1896
The Episode of the Mexican Seer. 1896
A Midsummer Episode. 1896
The Episode of the Diamond Links. 1896
Omar at Marlow. 1896
A Mere Matter of Standpoint. 1896
Fair Exchange. 1896
The Cowardly Dynamiter. 1896
The Episode of the Old Master. 1896
The Episode of the Tyrolean Castle. 1896
Janet's Nemesis. 1896
Entirely Accidential. 1896
The Episode of the Drawn Game. 1896
Wolverden Tower. 1896
The Episode of the German Professor. 1896
The Episode of the Arrest of the Colonel. 1896
The Episode of the Seldom Gold Mine. 1897
The Camisard's Bride. 1897
The Episode of the Japanned Dispatch Box. 1897
Llanfihangel Skerries. 1897

The Episode of the Game of Poker. 1897
The Episode of the Bertillon Method. 1897
A Lady of Florence. 1897
The Episode of the Old Bailey. 1897
A British Verdict. 1897
A Domestic Tragedy. 1897
A College Charm. 1897
A Freak of Memory. 1897
The Judge's Cross. 1897
The Thames Valley Catastrophe. 1897
The Great Oriental Seer. 1897
The Adventures of the Cantankerous Old Lady. 1898
The Adventure of the Supercilious Attache. 1898
The Pirate of Cliveden Reach. 1898
The Adventure of the Amateur Commission. 1898.
The Adventure of the Impromptu Mountaineer. 1898
Joe's Wife. 1898
The Adventure of the Urbane Old Gentleman. 1898
The Adventure of the Unobtrusive Oasis. 1898
The Adventure of the Pea Green Patrician. 1898
Isenberg's Regiment. 1898
The Adventure of the Magnificent Maharajah. 1898
A Woman's Hand: A Story. 1898
The Adventure of the Cross Eyed QC. 1898
The Christmas Eve Concert. 1898
The Adventure of the Oriental Attendant. 1899
Joseph's Dream. 1899
The Adventure of the Unprofessional Detective. 1899
Hobbling Mary. 1899
The Episode of the Patient Who Disappointed Her Doctor. 1899
The Episode of the Gentleman Who Had Failed For Everything. 1899
The Episode of the Wife Who Did Her Duty. 1899
The Episode of the Man Who Would Not Commit Suicide. 1899
A Regrettable Error. 1899
Peace-At-Any-Price Bill. 1899
The Episode of the Letter with a Basingstoke Post-Mark. 1899
The Episode of the Stone That Looked About It. 1899
His Ways Inscrutable. 1899
The Episode of the European With A Kaffir Heart. 1899
The Episode of the Lady Who Was Very Exclusive. 1899
The Episode of the Guide Who Knew the Country. 1899
Luigi and the Salvationist. 1899.
A Christmas Adventure. 1899.
The Episode of the Officer Who Understood Perfectly. 1900
Meriel Stanley, Poacher. 1900
The Episode of the Dead Man Who Spoke. 1900
A Question of Colour. 1900
Fra Benedett's Medal: A Story. 1900
The Temple of Fate: A Fable. 1900
The Way to Keronan. 1902
Lucy Lockett. 1902

Spencerian. 1904

Articles

1878. Hellas and Civilization, Gentleman's Magazine, Vol. CCXLIII
1878. Nation-making: A Theory of National Characters, Gentleman's Magazine, Vol. CCXLIII
1878. The Origin of Fruits, in Popular Science Monthly Volume 13
1879. Why Do We Eat our Dinner? in Popular Science Monthly Volume 14
1879. A Problem in Human Evolution, in Popular Science Monthly Volume
1879. Pleased with a Feather, in Popular Science Monthly Volume 15
1880. Why Keep India? The Contemporary Review, Vol. XXXVIII
1880. The Growth of Sculpture, The Cornhill Magazine, Vol. XLII
1880. The English Chronicle, Gentleman's Magazine, Vol. CCXLV
1880. The Venerable Bede, Gentleman's Magazine, Vol. CCXLIX
1880. The Dog's Universe, Gentleman's Magazine, Vol. CCXLIX
1880. Evolution and Geological Time, Gentleman's Magazine, Vol. CCXLIX
1880. Geology and History, in Popular Science Monthly Volume 17
1880. Aesthetic Feeling in Birds, in Popular Science Monthly Volume 17
1880. Aesthetic Evolution in Man, in Popular Science Monthly Volume 18
1881. The Story of Wulfgeat, Gentleman's Magazine, Vol. CCLI
1882. An English Shire, Gentleman's Magazine, Vol. CCLII
1882. The Welsh in the West Country, Gentleman's Magazine, Vol. CCLIII
1882. The Colours of Flowers, The Cornhill Magazine, Vol. XLV
1882. An English Weed, The Cornhill Magazine, Vol. XLV
1882. Sir Charles Lyell, in Popular Science Monthly Volume 20
1882. Hyacinth-Bulbs, in Popular Science Monthly Volume 20
1882. Who was Primitive Man? in Popular Science Monthly Volume 22
1883. The Pedigree of Wheat, in Popular Science Monthly Volume 22
1883. From Buttercups to Monk's-Hood, in Popular Science Monthly Volume 23
1883. Honeysuckle, Gentleman's Magazine, Vol. CCLV
1884. The Garden Snail, Gentleman's Magazine, Vol. CCLVI
1884. Our Debt to Insects, Gentleman's Magazine, Vol. CCLVI
1884. Idiosyncrasy, in Popular Science Monthly Volume 24
1884. The Ancestry of Birds, in Popular Science Monthly Volume 24
1884. The Milk in the Cocoa-Nut, in Popular Science Monthly Volume 25
1884. Our Debt to Insects, in Popular Science Monthly Volume 25
1884. Hickory-Nuts and Butternuts, in Popular Science Monthly Volume 25
1884. Queer Flowers, in Popular Science Monthly Volume 26
1885. Food and Feeding, in Popular Science Monthly Volume 26
1885. Concerning Clover, in Popular Science Monthly Volume 28
1886. A Thinking Machine, Gentleman's Magazine, Vol. CCLX
1886. Fish Out of Water, in Popular Science Monthly Volume 28
1886. A Thinking Machine, in Popular Science Monthly Volume 28
1886. Thistles, in Popular Science Monthly Volume 30, November 1886
1887. A Mount Washington Sandwort, in Popular Science Monthly Volume 30
1887. Among the Thousand Islands, in Popular Science Monthly Volume 31
1887. The Progress of Science from 1836 to 1886, in Popular Science Monthly Volume 31
1887. American Cinque-Foils, in Popular Science Monthly Volume 32
1888. Gourds and Bottles, in Popular Science Monthly Volume 33
1888. A Living Mystery, in Popular Science Monthly Volume 33
1888. Evolving the Camel, in Popular Science Monthly Volume 34

1889. From Africa, Gentleman's Magazine, Vol. CCLXVII
1889. Genius and Talent, in Popular Science Monthly Volume 34
1889. Plain Words on the Woman Question, in Popular Science Monthly Volume 36
1890. The Girl of the Future, Universal Review, Vol. VII.
1891. Democracy and Diamonds, The Contemporary Review, Vol. LIX
1892. A Desert Fruit, in Popular Science Monthly Volume 41
1893. Ghost Worship and Tree Worship I, in Popular Science Monthly Volume 42
1893. Ghost Worship and Tree Worship II, in Popular Science Monthly Volume 42
1897. Spencer and Darwin, in Popular Science Monthly Volume 50
1898. The Romance of Race, in Popular Science Monthly Volume 53
1898. The Season of the Year, in Popular Science Monthly Volume 54

Poetry

Grant Allen wrote various poems published in many magazines etc. We have not listed them here but hope to record some of them in the future.

Printed in Great Britain
by Amazon

80837374R10092